ISLANDS

"Resolve me of all ambiguities."

— Christopher Marlowe, *Doctor Faustus*

ISLANDS

SARA STAMEY

Tarragon
Books

Copyright © 2001 by Sara Stamey, LLC.
All rights reserved. Printed in the United States of America.
No part of this publication may be reproduced, stored in a retrieval system, or transmitted, in any form or by any means, electronic, mechanical, photocopying, recording, or otherwise, without written permission except in the case of brief quotations embodied in critical articles and reviews. For information, contact Tarragon Books.

REVISED EDITION, 2003

This is a work of fiction. Names, characters, places and incidents either are the product of the author's imagination or are used fictitiously, and any resemblance to any actual persons, living or dead, events, or locales, is entirely coincidental.

Lyrics quoted by Bob Marley, "Revolution." Copyright© 1975 Fifty-Six Hope Road Music Ltd./Blue Mountain Music Ltd. (PRS). All rights for the United States controlled and administered by Rykomusic, Inc. (ASCAP). International Copyright Secured. All rights reserved. Used by permission.

ISBN
0-9724986-1-3

Library of Congress Control Number:
2002094857

10 9 8 7 6 5 4 3 2 1

Tarragon Books
1424 E. Maplewood Ave.
Bellingham, WA 98225
360-738-7875
www.TarragonBooks.com

Also by Sara Stamey, from Berkley/Putnam Publishing:

Wild Card Run
Win, Lose, Draw
Double Blind

ADVANCE PRAISE FOR
ISLANDS

"A memorable heroine, a poignant quest, a vivid setting, an engaging story, a Sara Stamey novel. Of course."

— Laura Kalpakian, NEA award-winning author of *Graced Land*

"Using elements of Christopher Marlowe's *'Doctor Faustus'* and John Donne's observation that 'no man is an island,' Stamey steers her intrepid heroine toward enlightenment. On the way to self-realization, what fabulous adventures she has.... A passionate writer, Stamey has concocted a mystery here that is a page turner from intriguing beginning to end."

— Book review, *The Bellingham Herald*

First, to Kim, for his patience and keen eye.

Thanks to Mary Alice Kier and Anna Cottle for invaluable editorial assistance and enthusiastic support.

More thanks to Laura Kalpakian, Meredith Cary, and R.D. Brown, for reading and moral support.

And to my writers group for essential feedback: Kate Trueblood, Gary McKinney, and Margi Fox.

Finally, to Captain Hawkins: "And the adventure goes on...."

ISLAND ARCHIVES:

The Parker Manuscript

On this Day of Our Lord 24 November, 1768, I, Bartholomew Parker, Second Pilot of the trading vessel Phoenix, following the horrendous murther of Captain Hawkins and casting-away of the other officers whereupon the Christian souls remaining aboard are entrusted to my authority, do hereby in travail of spirit and body record these words of her dire straits.

Even as we poor few gather below decks to pray God mercy on our souls, whiles the sea rages unabated and the timbers scarce hold, the black fiends on deck howl and dance to their accursed pagan deities 'round the sprung mainmast. They bedevil still the mortal remains of Captain Hawkins, whom they did most cruelly and fiendishly mutilate and secure with his own bowels to the mast, may God have mercy on his soul. Tormented man, no more may he suffer this accursed and ill-timed voyage!

The slaves erst did rise from their chains in the hold and take the ship through treachery, causing myself and the crew remain to see them to a landing. Defying the laws of God and man, raising themselves above their Christian masters, they make wild talk of bearing a great token to free their king from exiled bondage. Withal they now wear bracelets and ornaments of gold and jewels which they had secreted aboard through trickery. They practise all manner of vile magicks with unholy effigies, and the foul sacrilege of a blood sacrament imbibed from the veins of Lucifer Himself! Yet now by God's hand are they cast down from their savage arrogance and blood lust, and go where gold and magicks avail not.

For as by my reckoning we did near the isles of the Danish Caribees we had of a sudden thunderstorms and heavy rain. At ten o'clock of this morning the weather became so thick that it was as black as night, whiles the violent clashing of the waves against each other seemed to give light from the pale froth. The sea and the wind made a frightful noise, and the ship laboured heavily and pitched so much from poop to prow that each time she fell it seemed to be as from a high tower and so that she would founder in the abyss.

And sorely pressed we were indeed, as without warning a tremendous sea, much higher than the last, bore down directly on us, so black and dark below and so white with foam above, that all those who saw it fully believed that it would bring us all to the end of our lives in a few seconds. This sea, crashing across the bow with a gust of wind, broke over the ship in such a force that it swept away the foremast and sail, yard and shrouds, as well as the bowsprit, and swept many men, Christian and pagan alike, into the raging sea.

Myself swept forward and suffering grievous injury to my leg, I saw breakers starboard, and through the thick sky beheld the darker form of land, rocky and stark like a cruel fortress. Then did the savages bid me make for land, and would have us crash upon the sharp rocks and reef, which the ruin of our sails compelled. We did contrive to make crude running repairs and without hope of escaping the raging of wind and sea I called the crew to carry me below to offer prayer for our souls, as we go to our sure death with the next fury of the storm. For now the black devils would have us on deck again and drive the ruin of poor Phoenix against the island. They say their dark gods have promised them a refuge here, but in this sheer rock and storm there can be none. Never I fear shall she rise from the ashes of this death!

We ask for the love of God that all who may learn of this commend us in their prayers to our Lord. And therefore do I seal this missive in a tube, and which shall be caulked tight and left to the sea, to be taken whither the waves shall drive it.

Last journal entry of Bartholomew Parker, acting Captain of the *Phoenix*, lost with all hands and cargo of 214 slaves on November 24, 1768.

ONE

THE CARIBBEAN — 1980

Wind pummeled the dark clouds, wringing out drops as the storm caught our craft and threw it sideways. We bucked, tossed up into the gray-black commotion and then flung down in a jarring plunge. Blinding rain lashed. Behind me, shattering glass and curses.

"Just a touch of turbulence, folks. Buckle up."

Another slewing plummet left my stomach fluttering under my ribcage as I clutched the armrests. A muttering stewardess knelt to pick up broken bottles. Beyond the rain-streaked window, the world was only gray clouds shredded by wind and wingtip, darker shadows surging in the heart of the storm.

I closed my eyes and a wave of the nightmare memories broke over me:

> *Night sea. A submerged wavering light beam rakes a black boulder carved in crude designs, odd creatures, faces. Etched spiral eyes gleam into life. Hissing shush of the diver's panting breaths, bubbles swirling as he turns, blond hair drifting, glitter of a knife spinning, slowly sinking and the demon faces bulge up out of the stone, summoned. Shadow hands grab him, pull him deeper as he screams into the black waters –*

"That's the worst of it, folks. Just a little tropical squall," the voice over the speakers crackled cheerfully.

"Damn." I shook my head and stared at the blinking light out on the wingtip, mechanically counting the tiny flashes. The plane shot free of the clouds into a harsh dazzle of sunlight. I winced and took some deep breaths. Shielding my eyes, I squinted past the wing's edge.

Islands scattered below, lost pieces of a jigsaw puzzle. The shapes varied – long, short, angular, smoothly rounded, or bent and twisted – but they were all the color of yellowed parchment edged with the deceptive white lace of waves breaking on hidden reefs. Midday sunlight flattened the Caribbean to the two dimensions of an antique map.

I leaned closer to the window. My fingers itched to pluck those cookie-cuttered pieces off the turquoise sea and fit them into a coherent picture. Read their tales of hurricanes, sacrifices to greedy gods pagan and Christian, waves of pillage and pestilence. Did our histories make us what we were? Only flotsam driven by the wind?

An anthropologist wasn't supposed to ask melodramatic questions, just observe. Island after island, they slid off toward the horizon. Hieroglyphs, spelling out a secret message, slipping away before I could translate it.

But I was going to break the code. My research grant was my ticket, and the petroglyphs would give me the breakthrough I needed.

"Sure." Tom Farber, slouching down the hall from Philosophy to wend his way with me through drifts of fallen maple leaves and bewildered college freshmen. He'd squinted at the dog-eared photo I passed him of the boulder with its ancient carved designs. "Truth is one slippery bugger, so don't get too obsessed with this. I heard about your run-in with the Anthro Chairman. You *didn't* accuse him of fossilized thinking in front of all the committee members?"

"Right before God and the committee."

He rolled his eyes. "Still the precocious windmill-tilter of the department."

"No one's precocious at thirty." My chin lifted. "Maybe they need their cozy little cages rattled."

Or was I the one who'd gotten too snug in my teaching position? After I'd broken all the rules by heading solo into the field with my camping gear and almost-PhD, mapping lost Pacific Northwest petroglyphs and documenting indigenous subsistence skills by living them with the help of native elders. That old-fashioned brand of hands-on anthropology was considered suspect by the current academy.

"So maybe you don't blink an eye at cougars and bears and chewing salmonberries and raw whale blubber with your Eskimo cohorts up in the wilderness, but I'm telling you the thorny thickets of academia can be deadly. You'd better work on your survival skills. Like diplomacy."

"Tsimshian, Tom."

"I beg your pardon?"

"Tsimshian, not Eskimo. And they don't chew whale blubber."

"Avoiding the issue, Susan?" He *tsk*ed. "And now you're going out on a limb with this pre-Columbus contact theory. Why?"

I'd only shrugged as he'd handed back the snapshot John had sent in his frantic letter from the Caribbean.

John. Like those islands spinning with the globe below the plane, he always came around again. If my colleagues inside the ivy-covered halls had known the petroglyph photo was from John, they'd have accused me of worse than radical theories. Dr. Susan Dunne, guilty! The ultimate academic sin: allowing emotional factors to influence a scholarly thesis.

Not true. I was a professional anthropologist, trained to look past personal issues to see the big picture. John was *not* going to interfere with my research.

"You all right?" A hand touched my shoulder.

I startled from a blind stare out the window.

"Look like you just saw a ghost. Or a Jumbie." The middle-aged woman who'd been sitting across the aisle dropped into the empty seat beside me, sliding her plastic cup of melting ice into its slot. She craned past me to peer out the window. "Just about there. Don't know why, I always miss the bloody place when I'm away."

I seized on the odd word. "Jumbie?"

"Flying scare you?" She rummaged through a big straw handbag, pulled out a pack of cigarettes, and ran a hand through short, gray-streaked hair that looked like she'd hacked at it with garden shears. "Used to take my Aunt Louise that way, she'd get the screaming heebie-jeebies just thinking about it."

"No, I like flying." I tilted my head toward the window. "I like the big view. Even if it *is* cheating."

"Cheating?"

"My – an old friend always said that about flying. Too quick to be a real voyage. He'd... rather sail."

"Another Romantic type?" Her raspy voice gave it a comic edge. "Auntie insists she'd rather live in the old days, even when I remind her about corsets, scurvy, stinking bilges, and pirates with sharp knives and bad manners who haven't washed behind their ears in decades."

She lit her cigarette and blew a smoke plume. "So what brings you to our island paradise? You on your own?" She laughed, flapping a hand. "I'm incurably nosy. And you're out of uniform for a tourist.

You're gonna melt when you step out of the air-conditioning into our humidity."

I compared her faded sundress, bare legs, and worn flip-flop sandals to my academic camouflage, the neutral jacket, skirt, and flats I'd worn to the seminar I'd squeezed between flights. "I was shivering in Seattle. So what's a Jumbie?"

She shot me a look and blew out more smoke. "Hard to pin down. Like the natives. Some kind of Voodoo thing."

"Voodoo! That wasn't in the brochures."

"Tourist Board makes sure of that. No such thing on our peaceful little island. No fires or riots in the black jungle-towns, either, or Continentals knifed if they wander up the wrong alley." She shrugged. "Bless their propaganda, they keep us in business."

"Your drink, ma'am." A pretty black stewardess offered her tray, and Pat traded cups.

I waved away the offer of a drink. "Are you talking about a cover-up campaign? I didn't think the Vaudun even existed in this part of the Caribbean."

"Whoa! You won't win any popularity contests here if you start asking the wrong questions. The old native aristocracy still has a lot of power, and they like to keep the lines drawn. Which I discover all over again whenever I butt my head up against their Highnesses." She gulped from her fresh drink.

"What do you mean by Continentals?"

"That's island for 'whites.' And don't say 'blacks,' say 'natives.'"

"But that doesn't make sense. The only natives in these islands were the Carib Indians the Spanish pretty much wiped out, and even the Caribs chased out the Arawaks way back when. The blacks are just as much imports as the whites."

"Literally. That's the gripe." She swirled the cubes in her cup, eyeing me. "First thing you better do here is forget about making sense. Second, remember you're minority white. That's been okay as long as you stayed in good graces with the old-family natives, they took over the colonial planter system. But everything's stirred up now, especially with this idiotic Independence Movement. 'Africa Unite.'"

She snorted. "Started with the Dreads. Sort of a violent version of the Rastafarians, live out in the West End rainforest, grow marijuana to sell. Hate Continentals, and they've killed some outsiders dumb enough to go in there. But now the anger's spreading over the island – the town Rudes and all the other natives on welfare squeezed into those godawful jungle-towns. They're getting restless, want a piece of the pie, blame it all on Uncle Sam. Trouble is, they don't realize if the violence gets out of hand and they drive off the blasted tourists, like happened in Jamaica, there won't *be* any pie."

"Sounds like the oven's too hot."

She grinned, hazel eyes snapping with intelligence in the sunbaked and prematurely lined face. Clearly there was more to her than the bag lady accouterments. "If you stay longer than the Glorious Week in Paradise crowd, you'll find it's more interesting than the glossy pamphlets with the palm trees."

"So tourists are basically a necessary annoyance?"

"Don't get me wrong, I wouldn't be mouthing off if I thought I was chasing away a paying guest. I own the Orchid Bay Resort."

We hit another bump of turbulence and the seatbelt light flashed on again. The woman stood up, taking her cup. "Worst of it is the way they water these goddamn drinks. Where's that stew?" She wandered off down the aisle.

Outside the window, a new island was looming. This one was very different from the scattered sunny cays we'd passed. It jutted high out of the sea, deep ravines draped in green and dense shadow, jagged ridges shredding a wisp of cloud. Its sheer dark mass, imbedded in that sunny sea, radiated an oddly oppressive aura. I could feel its stony roots reaching into the black depths.

I closed my eyes and took a deep breath.

My hand was already groping for my briefcase, John's letter. It was getting to be a bad habit, I had to get a grip. But my fingers weren't listening, pulling out the envelope, tracing its history in overlaid *Forwards* that had finally brought the battered envelope to earth in the Tsimshian Cultural Museum I'd helped organize. I didn't need to read the letter. I knew by heart the hasty scribble on a page torn from a spiral-bound notepad, dated a year earlier.

The exact date was branded in my memory: Tail end of Pacific Northwest winter, the muddy trenches of the student dig I'd been supervising on a remote British Columbian island. Dark clouds scudding over the fading gray glimmer of diffuse sunset. Chinook wind sweeping down without warning, churning the Strait to white-lashed fury, ripping up fir trees and banshee-howling around my tent as I drifted into fitful sleep. And then the shocking rage, screaming through me out of nowhere with the nightmare about sea monsters and carved stones and my brother John.

I shook my head and focused on the familiar scrawl.

"Hey, String-bean! This is a rush job while I've got a chance to slip it in the mail. I think he's actually got a tail on me!

"How about these petroglyphs, Professor dear? Get your little butt in gear and come down here to check them out! About time you put up or shut up about that cockeyed theory of yours.

"And maybe you can keep me from wringing Laura's neck. Shit, she knew! I told you I was working with Victor Manden, diving the sunken slave ship for Ye Fabled Tribal Treasure? SOB thought he'd screw me out of my share. Not to worry, I've got it all scoped. The petroglyphs are in the same cove as the Phoenix! It's the goddamn rock! And he has the Parker Manuscript, the old note-in-the-antique-bottle scenario. No shit, there's some wild-ass history for you here. You'll see. I'm going back tonight and –"

The next part had gotten wet. After a few ink-smeared and indecipherable lines, I could make out:

"He'll kill me if he catches me. But no sweat, I'm covered for tonight. This is one Hell of a crazy island, Sweet-cheeks! Tell Mom I'm sorry I never write. I love you. John."

Shaking my head, a reluctant smile tugging at my lips, I laid the letter on my lap and pulled out the snapshots he'd sent with it.

I'd looked at the first one so many times the images had gone distant, receding like those island puzzle-pieces even as I tried to grasp them. The face in the photo could have been a stranger's. A striking young stranger in a faded red Speedo swimsuit, posed on the end of a weathered dock, tanned skin glowing against a topaz cove and palm trees. Fins, mask and Scuba gear slung carelessly over one shoulder, body long and lean with a swimmer's strength. Sunstreaked blond hair, a toothy smile, electric green eyes. Those eyes, and the devil-may-care grin – they gave off palpable sparks of life, laughter, exuberance.

He'd been dead two months when I'd finally gotten the letter.

Blinking back tears that could still catch me off-guard, I thrust the worn photo back into its envelope, scrutinizing the other one like the Rosetta Stone. For me, it was. Taken underwater, its outlines were blurred, colors infused with blue. A striped fish darted hazily across the foreground. Behind it, a flat boulder John must have rubbed free of most of its green algae. In the cleared space, incised designs of birds, fish, a coiled serpent, grotesque capering figures. And a crude face with staring eyes.

Nothing more than spirals carved in stone, those eyes, but they were somehow alive. Those same eyes had stared out of the nightmare a year ago, mocking me. Making me doubt it was only a dream, John screaming his fear and fury at the petroglyph demons attacking him. Attacking us. In the dream, it was *my* throat raw with that raging scream.

I stuffed the snapshot into its envelope. The delayed letter with the photos was postmarked the same date as the nightmare, the night John drowned. Accidentally.

There were explanations. Everyone accused me of being obsessed with the petroglyphs, not so strange I'd dream about them. And the designs were similar worldwide, archetypal images. But some part of me, with a sinking sense of inevitability, knew it was the Link.

If I'd wanted early retirement from academics, and a free ticket to the same institution where they'd treated my poor Granny to electroshock in the bad old days, I'd have rushed right out and told everyone about the Link. My built-in "TV tuner." It mostly gave me static, or garbled bits of people's programs flashing out of the blue – a classmate's sordid fantasies about the teacher, a visceral jolt of urgency as a cop car shot past in a wail of sirens, colored sparks of exhaustion and joy as my sister gave birth to her first child.

I didn't believe in ESP, astral projection, UFOs, or ghosts. I was a logical person. A scientist. I might have dismissed my "tuner" as only an especially vivid imagination if it hadn't been for the Link with John.

At times we'd almost shared the same skin. I always knew when my little brother was in trouble, I could *see* it. I could unfailingly find him when he'd wander off as a toddler. From miles away, I'd seen the truck skid over the center line and sideswipe his car one rainy day just after he'd gotten his license. As I got older, the Links faded, and once John moved to the Caribbean they'd stopped. Maybe the nightmare was the last dying gasp of the Link, a hallucinatory farewell from my brother's drowning brain.

———

"Looks like we're getting the scenic tour."
I jumped.
It was the resort owner, plopping down beside me with her refilled drink.

I blew out a breath and blinked at the window. The pilot was taking us in a wide circle, away from the landing strip grafted onto a crescent bay and the lush foliage between two curved stretches of white sand. The terraced shades of azure in the shallows were so clear I could make out sharp ridges of coral on the bottom, and the narrow beaches were lined with the swaying palm trees my seatmate had mocked. It did look perfectly nice, just like a travel poster.

"Pat MacIntyre here." She stuck out her hand. "You down on business?"

"Susan Dunne, archeology." I returned her strong handclasp. "The pure anthropologists regard us as a sort of subspecies. I'm researching petroglyphs."

"I'll be damned! I was way off base this time. What exactly *is* a petroglyph?"

I pulled out a book and opened it to photos of boulders overlooking my native Puget Sound. Stylized ravens and orcas carved on rocks above cold bays. Crude stick figures dancing in rituals even the local Indians couldn't explain.

"These are Northwest Coast, but a lot of the designs are similar worldwide. No one knows who made them, or why. I'm working on a theory." I shrugged. "And a mystery."

"Mystery?" She cocked an eyebrow.

"My research takes off from some controversial work done by another anthropologist in the Caribbean years ago. He was a brilliant scholar until the old-boy network turned on him, really savaged his new theory. He dropped out. Rumor has it he's 'gone native' somewhere in these islands." I waved toward the window. "Don't suppose you know a cranky old Englishman, maybe living on a sailboat? Dr. Phillip Holte?"

"Never heard of him." She glanced again at the petroglyph photos and handed the book back. "So that's what those carved rocks on Palm Cay are all about. Suppose you'll be studying them?"

I nodded, letting her assume I was interested only in the well-known glyphs on a nearby island. I didn't want word of John's site getting around until I'd documented it. If those lost carvings supported my pre-Columbus African contact theory, I could head home with a significant publication under my belt. I *had* gone out on a limb with the Anthro Department.

"Ladies and Gentlemen," the speakers crackled once more. "There will be a slight delay in landing. Just a little technicality."

Up front, the stewardess hastily finished checking seatbelts. With a nervous smile, she glanced over her shoulder and ducked through the pilot door.

"Hell's bells!" Pat belted down the rest of her drink and shoved the cup into its slot. "Probably the blasted landing gear. Last time we had to circle twice before they got it working."

"What?" The jagged mountain swelled closer.

She flapped a dismissing hand. "Business as usual down here."

We rounded the peak with inches to spare, snagging its clinging cloud and ripping it into swirling ghosts. A deep clunk in the belly of the plane as we circled over the airport again. My hands gripped the armrests.

"Okay, folks," the pilot announced. "We're all cleared for landing now. And welcome to paradise."

I sagged in relief.

Pat chuckled. "So how long will you be basking in our tropic splendors?"

The window still had its hooks in me, that dark rock mass looming almost close enough to touch. The plane banked, throwing a skewed parallelogram of sunlight across my knees. "Umm... just a few months."

"Need a place to stay?" She waggled her fingers. "I'm not pushing my resort. I've got friends with a nice little guest cottage, and they'd like someone in there to make the estate look lived-in while they're traveling."

"Sounds right up my alley. For the first few days, I'll be staying with a friend. Apparently it's an historic home. The Fairview Great-House?"

"Fairview! You've staying with Leon Caviness?" She drew back.

"My friend Laura is his social secretary. Do you know him?"

"Good God!" She stared. "You're his sister!"

I closed my eyes and took a deep breath. "Did you know my brother John?"

A forced laugh. "God, I'm being rude. I just realized why you looked so familiar. I never met your brother, but his picture was all over the paper during that whole.... You know, the accident investigation." She cleared her throat. "I'm afraid the drowning was big news for our little island. I'm sorry, Susan."

I murmured something meaningless as she bent over to forage in her handbag again. Ignoring the *No Smoking* sign, she lit another cigarette. She blew out an explosive gust of smoke. "You know Leon Caviness?"

The way she said his name made me file it under *Remember*, beside the tidbit about Jumbies. "Never met him. I understand he's a... native, family has a lot of property here? Laura didn't write much about her job."

Laura hadn't responded to any of the letters I'd written after the news of John's death. Not until I'd sent a note saying I was coming to the island. Then she'd promptly written back, inviting – no, insisting that I stay with her. And why had John said he wanted to wring her neck?

"I haven't seen Laura in a long time." I'd never understood why John had picked her from his smorgasbord of eager young women. But when Laura decided she wanted something, it was like gravity. She was my age, two years older than John. Before Laura had dropped out of the university, a mutual friend had snidely commented, "So okay, John does use his brain once in a while, passing on all the cute chicks so Earth Mother could take care of him."

Pat blew smoke and crushed out the cigarette. "I'd watch it with her. Some snakes do bite."

"Laura? She's too laid-back to bother."

She said hastily, "I don't really know her, only to speak to, but I've heard the stories." A spluttering laugh. "Damn, I'm doing it again! Look, Susan." She fixed me with a straight look. "I like your style. I don't want to see you get off on the wrong foot here. The island's, well, it takes some getting used to, and it really does matter who you associate with. You can get sucked in over your head before you know it, and you are the perfect target. Young, gorgeous, and blond – bam!"

"You wouldn't be trotting out that line if I were a man."

"But you're not, are you?" She jabbed an emphatic finger. "There's a lot of anger simmering on our rock. And if you're white, everything from slavery on down is your fault."

"Can you blame them? Maybe my research will give something back, if it helps prove the Africans were here first, before Columbus."

"You think the Dreads give a hoot about some moldy old history? Just watch your step."

The stewardess stopped to confiscate another cigarette Pat was lighting. My stomach fluttered with a sudden drop in altitude, the island yanking us down from the clouds with a blur of blues and greens and glaring white pavement. The rectangle of sunlight over my knees narrowed to a blade, sliced blinding over my face. The wheels hit with a jar, bounced, and clung.

Two

Laura was late.

I was the lone passenger left as the dust of departing taxis and shuttles settled over a straggle of palm trees. Blotting my damp forehead with a handkerchief and dragging hot, soupy air into my lungs, I turned back into the airport terminal. The entrance to paradise was a rattletrap metal warehouse, probably some sort of Army surplus, since the island was a U.S. possession. Plywood partitions divided the expanse of cement floor, ratty-looking palm fronds decorating a low fence around a waiting area with rickety tables, sagging cane chairs, and a liquor bar manned by a sleepy black man. A dusty purple satin banner with gold fringe hung crookedly from one of the exposed rafters, spelling out in red sequins: *Hands in the air!* A warning about the hotel rates?

I was Alice in a seedy Wonderland, wishing I'd taken Pat MacIntyre up on her offer to share a taxi into town. She'd departed with, "Be seeing you, it's a small island," and a Cheshire Cat smile that lingered behind her in the humid air.

Head pounding with the heat, I trudged over to the booth covered with more antique palm fronds, returning my plastic cup to the man with the face like gnarled mahogany, who grinned toothlessly above a *Well Come to our I-Land* sign. I'd thirstily gulped one of the drinks he'd handed to all arrivals, minors included, before realizing the fruit floating on top disguised nearly pure rum.

I turned down another cup, blotted my face again, and asked the man where I could find a phone. He looked bewildered. I tried asking the bartender, slumped snoring over the bar, but couldn't wake him.

I sank onto a bench to rub my throbbing forehead and check my watch again.

Laura was really late.

She'd always refused to wear a watch because it would impose false mechanical rhythms and "block the natural flow of the day." Somehow Laura had managed to thrive in a scheduled society by making people feel guilty enough over their own uptightness to indulge her for the sake of Peace, Love, and Freedom.

I was getting cynical in my old age. I was all for Peace and Love, maybe Laura and John had found them here. And lost them.

None of it seemed real. The plane ride. This island. John's death. I kept expecting to turn around and see him laughing at this latest great joke he'd pulled on us all. Closing my eyes, I could see his grin as he popped open the warped door of the old farmhouse he and Laura had rented back home in Happy Valley, one of the last Hippie enclaves dating from the 60s.

"Sue, Sue." Holding me by the shoulders and shaking his head. "You've been holed up in that dusty old library again! Your brain looks tired."

"So let's go jogging tomorrow morning."

"You're on, sweet-cheeks! But hey, look at me, tell Professor Dad I'm brimming with responsibility. Got a J-O-B! So be heartless, you two, have fun while I slave." And he was striding off to one of the brief checkpoints on his eclectic resume, leaving Laura to lead me to the back porch.

The Earth Mother title was purely descriptive that afternoon. Basking in the August sun, large breasts bobbing in a peasant blouse, feet bare beneath an East-Indian print skirt, and long dark hair tumbling loose, Laura exuded lazy sensuality. She refilled my cup with her tangy herbal brew as I admired her organic garden.

Leaves gleamed in the sun. Light and heat pooled, thickening, flooding me with shimmering waves. The plants exploded into riotous growth before my eyes, swelling with fruit and bloom. Their colors intensified to day-glo brilliance. My head swam dizzily.

Laura, shrugging: "What's the big deal? Even you've smoked dope before, haven't you? I brewed the tea from mushrooms I picked myself, it's organic."

I was floating, swooping through the air to perch among the wildly painted dahlias. They were swaying and dancing, grinning faces turned to mine. Together the blossoms and I crooned a medley of Disney tunes. Laura went twirling around the overgrown yard, skirt spinning, colors whirling. She danced, flinging off her clothes, lying back in the tall grass.

"Wow." I stared through the stems at her full breasts and the plump extra flesh pushing against pale skin in mounds and folds of a surreal landscape.

Laura's dreamy voice drifted overhead. "Inner beauty.... Finding a natural balance.... Integrating dualities into a wholeness without needing manufactured rules and logic...."

I finally connected the weird fleshscape with Laura's voice. Naked sounded good, so I stripped in the hot sun, wriggled my toes, flowed into some slow Yoga stretches that melted me right down into the warm earth.

I was a tiny ant, staring up through the grass blades at two huge feet planted before me. It was the titanic Earth Goddess, feet growing out of the fertile soil and head cloud-distant. I'd studied all Her names – Gaia, Pachamama, Inanna, Freya – but I'd never seen Her, felt Her massive power quaking through my bones. I gawked up at Her mountainous peaks and valleys in awe.

But it was Laura's voice echoing down from those heights. "Flaunting it? You've got to transcend, Susie! Just can't break free of the perfection trap, can you?" An immense arm lowered from on high, enormous finger pointing down at me. "It's the pride trip, you think you're immune because it's all so easy for you, it's like you don't even notice you've got all the silver stars for teacher's pet: Thin. Blonde. Track star. Magna cum laude. Daddy's best girl, little brother's idol."

I was baffled. The giant Goddess was crying.

"Go on, be honest for once!" Her voice had gone shrill. "You can't stand it that dumpy old Laura took John away, your darling golden-boy brother."

Dismaying pity and shame stirred me as I crouched naked at her feet in the grass, shaking my head in confusion.

she stirs, the sun behind her head, and she's a dark, ominous silhouette looming over me, blotting out the sky

"Uhn." My head nodded heavily, and with a jolt I snapped upright, blinking in confusion at the shabby terminal. I twisted around on the bench, knocking over a plastic cup that hadn't been sitting beside me a minute before. "What?" I fumbled for it as fruit and bright red juice sprayed across the floor. I retrieved the cup and peered into its sticky, pungent residue. Sharp shards, mixed with dark bits that looked like whiskers, glinted in the red puddle.

I touched them. Broken glass.

The bartender, emerging from his snores to my insistent shaking, threw his hands up, shook his head, swore on his mother's soul he hadn't seen anyone approach me with the drink. "Be dey Rude boy, dey makin' moh trouble here!" He hastily closed up the bar and disappeared. No one else around.

I threw the island's notion of a prank into the garbage can. I needed a cold shower and some sleep. There had to be a phone where I could call Laura.

A red-painted line took me past plywood ticket counters and the roped-off corner where young boys in ragged T-shirts had stacked the baggage that hadn't been misrouted. A few battered boxes and a shiny purple suitcase were the only remnants of the departed tourist horde. The red line died at the back of the building, where I pushed through metal swing doors to the pickup area.

Blinding glare, heatwaves shimmering off cement under the fierce sun. A lone taxi minus driver baked in the dusty parking lot. The heat pulsed, closing around me like a voracious creature determined to suck away even the memory of coolness. I couldn't get a proper breath.

And it was only February. Tightening a sweaty grip on my briefcase, I was heading back for the shade when a battered Jeep careened over the rutted road and jounced to a stop near the taxi.

The cab driver emerged from a cubbyhole off the loading area, throwing up his hands as the dust cloud defiled his glossy black paint job. "You be drivin' dis ting like a crazy mon!" He jabbed a dark finger at the dented gray Jeep.

Its driver stopped bawling out an off-key rendition of *Stairway to Heaven*," pushed back a tumble of tawny hair, and vaulted over the side bar. He reached in back and produced two beer bottles, striding over to lean against the taxi hood. "Cool out, Joe. What's happening?"

The cab owner flinched as the other man lounged against the gleaming paint in his faded shorts and T-shirt. He shrugged, flicked specks of dust from his immaculate trousers and white linen shirt, and accepted a beer.

"Same ol ting. I jus work all de time."

"Car's looking good." He took a swig and poked his head through the window. "New tape system? Put out some sound?"

Joe's impassive face was split by a white grin. "Is de bes."

"Well, don't keep that domino game waiting."

Joe nodded and sauntered back through the dim doorway. The other man took a swallow of beer and strode toward me, stopping to size me up and down.

"Lost baggage?" He grinned through a short coppery-glinting beard. "No point waiting here, could be days. I'll give you a ride into town after I pick up my stuff."

"Thanks, but I –"

"No prob*lem*." Halfway through the door, he turned back. "Want a beer? Cold ones in the back, help yourself. Here, hold this for me."

He was gone and I was holding his half-full bottle. I looked down at it dazedly. I walked over to set it on the Jeep's dashboard and headed back for the shade of the terminal. The tropic sun wasn't kidding around. Time to call Laura.

As I reached the doorway, the man burst through with a large box balanced on one shoulder. A young native boy staggered sleepily behind with a smaller box.

"Ready to go?" He stopped and the boy bumped into him. With his free hand, he steered the boy forward and propelled him gently toward the Jeep.

"Look, you're three or four scenes ahead of me here. Excuse me." I made a move toward the door he was blocking.

He didn't get the message. "If you need the bathroom, it's over behind the bar. What happened to my beer?"

All I wanted was to get inside, out of the sun's onslaught. He was planted tall and solid in the way, teeth flashing through the close-trimmed beard that set off just too nicely the kind of blunt, rough-hewn features that would have labeled a woman homely, but on a man broadcast sex appeal. He seemed to find me vastly amusing. I winced away from the glaring reflections off his mirrored shades, refocusing on a pair of muscular brown legs. This deep a suntan had to be overkill.

"Excuse me," I repeated, edging around him, "I'm waiting for a friend."

"Can't do better than that?" He grinned. "Good luck with the baggage –"

He frowned then, pushing the sunglasses up over his hairline and giving me what seemed to be a suddenly puzzled scrutiny. His eyes glinted vivid blue with the intense sunlight. "Hey, don't I –"

"No. Definitely not." I moved around him toward the door.

He started to reach a hand, then shrugged and slipped the shades over his eyes. "I'd get out of this dive before dark if I were you. See you around, it's a small island."

Inside, I blew out a long breath, sucking in the marginally cooler air with relief. If my first minutes of the island were any indication, I'd have to take Pat MacIntyre's warning seriously. The dull throb of an overheated headache was the worst threat I could cope with at the moment.

I finally found the phone, complete with a faded message scrawled on a dusty scrap of paper sack taped over the dial. *Out of Order.*

"Susie!" Footsteps tappeted over concrete. "How horrid of me, I'm late! I just couldn't seem to get myself organized."

The woman rushing breathlessly toward me must have kidnapped Laura's voice. Slender and tall — no, it was the high-heeled sandals strapped onto tanned ankles — she was wearing a silk designer sundress in soft peach, and a lot of gold jewelry. A floppy shade hat swung from one manicured hand. Her short dark hair was elegantly styled, perfect makeup emphasizing the big brown eyes I finally recognized. She looked like she'd never heard of earth shoes or peasant skirts with elastic waistbands.

"Laura?"

She posed, laughing.

"You've... changed."

"No kidding!" She spun in a circle, grinned, patted her hair, touched her throat.

I blinked, Alice back in Wonderland. The real surprise wasn't Laura's makeover as much as the way she moved. Like she had so much nervous energy she couldn't hold still.

"Laura." I could only stand there gawking.

A flicker of uncertainty passed over the polished pose. "Susie...."

That was when I should have given her a hug, somehow bonded with her in our mutual loss and grief. But I'd never been good at that kind of thing. I never seemed to feel the right sentiments, make the right moves.

"Susie?"

She'd always insisted on the nickname I disliked. "Laura, what's it been? Three years?" I touched her shoulder. "You look terrific."

"Disappointed?" She took a step back, eyes narrowing. "I should be all pale and withered with grief?"

"Laura, why wouldn't you answer my letters? I still can't...." I shook my head. "It doesn't seem real. He was too full of life."

"Yeah. You weren't the one who had to go look at his body."

I flinched and belatedly reached out to embrace her. "It's so hard." She sighed and eased away, biting her lip. "I know." Her face drooped, dark circles puffy beneath her eyes.

She shook her head, and with a brittle little laugh she was dancing back, touching her throat. "Susie – I mean *Su*san — I have to say you look wrecked! You didn't toss off one of those ghastly freebie rums, did you?" Voice shrill. "No sense lingering to absorb the atmosphere here. Let's dig up a baggage boy. They didn't lose it? Airline reserves its own Black Hole for luggage. Come on, the car's outside."

She darted about like a hummingbird on amphetamines, somehow balancing on the spike heels and looking like she'd take flight any second. She buzzed over to inject life into the sleepy attendant, herding me toward the doors as he followed with a cart. "You're the first visitor from back home! I'll give you the nickel tour on the way. You'll get used to the heat, but in those clothes you must be dying."

The smile wavered and blanked out. She turned in a sharp pivot, flicking fingers at the boy with the bags. He followed as she strode on, heels clicking.

"We've really *got* to hustle. I left total chaos up at the estate. Leon has one of his entertainments on for tonight, and I have to drill the servants." She reached into her bag, thrust a sunscreen bottle into my hands, and flew on toward the doors. "Don't you dare step outside before you put some of that on. You don't want to look like a charred marshmallow tonight. Or God forbid, a tourist!"

Outside, she crammed me and my bags into a convertible, one of those racy little cars I probably should have been able to name. Near liftoff as we roared out, dodged potholes, and flew onto a paved road.

Laura accelerated in a squeal of rubber, racing down the wrong lane. Cars hurtled toward us. I braced for impact.

She darted a look and laughed. Everyone was driving on the left, though the cars had standard American drives.

Wind whipped my hair, blurring glimpses of wood and tin shacks, dusty palm trees, piles of rotting trash. Chickens and lithe brown children in dirt yards. A scruffy black goat raised his horned head from a knocked-over garbage can to fix me with his yellow stare.

Laura was forced to stop at a light. "After awhile, you stop expecting things to make sense here." She hurtled toward a mass of oncoming traffic, holding her hand on the horn until a narrow slot magically appeared. We shot through.

Laura's nickel tour:

The harbor, a milky turquoise bowl reflecting painful shards of light. Sky searing blue, with one white puff of cloud. Hills stretching steep green arms above the water, freckled with red-roofed white houses.

Stink of ripe sewage and engine exhaust choked the busy harbor drive. Rusty cargo boats dipped and tugged on lines at the cement causeway, unloading banana bunches, crates, passengers, beer cases, a donkey wearing a straw hat. Beside the boats, shirtless black men whooped and gestured over the slap of dominoes. A pelican fumbled up in a clumsy climb, soared, crashed in a bright spray. I winced at the blinding dazzles, panting under the pressure of heat and humidity.

"It's a duty-free port. Here's the shopping area."

We turned onto a side street and threaded narrow cobbled lanes with tourist-packed sidewalks and pricey shops in converted brick warehouses. Another turn, and we were sucked into the traffic crawling past dilapidated buildings and an open-air market. Laura waved a hand, gold glittering. "Our claim to fame. The first slave market in the new world."

Broken-shuttered windows frowned down past garish signs, graffiti, and bold cartoon figures painted on walls. Sun struck colors from flapping fabrics, piles of coconuts, pineapples, twisted brown roots, odd hairy fruits. Sweet and pungent smells wafted. Waves of mobile dark faces ebbed and flowed around us, crinkled hair crimped and rolled and braided in corn-row patterns with beads, or long and dreadlocked, or piled in hivelike knitted caps. The voices were a sea roar, slurring fast syllables into an almost-foreign patois.

"Watch it in this neighborhood, and don't set foot in jungle-town over there." She pointed. "Suicide for Continentals, and that goes double for a chick."

We lifted away from town and onto a bumpy, tarred road running straight up the side of the steep hill. The car knuckled down and passed a rickety Jeep and an open-air tourist bus wheezing up the grade. The houses clinging to the lower hill gave way to lush foliage.

Laura ran out of guide patter as we turned and climbed and turned again. A fresh breeze hinted at coolness, wafting sweet flower scents. Palm trees, twisted vines, and bushes with red and purple blooms spilled over the road. A bird trilled.

Laura accelerated, soaring over the crest and down the other side of the mountain. She was driving way too fast for the tight curves and narrow, pitted road, her lips pulled back in an intent grin.

Greenery streaked past as she gripped the wheel, pulling in short, panting breaths.

We squealed into another turn, tires screaming.

Thrown sideways, I grabbed the door frame. "Hey!"

"Here comes the best part!" She flashed a challenging grin and accelerated. We shot like a chromed bullet down a straight plunge beneath a mad flicker of sunlight and dark green boughs. The car hit a dip at the bottom, skidded, and bounced up the other side, my stomach flopping like the one time I'd been crazy enough to ride a giant roller-coaster. A car rounded the curve approaching us.

Laura kept her foot to the floor.

Blur of dense green, flickering blue, glinting dark road. And Laura's hands on the wheel, giving it a sharp pull, swerving us deliberately to the road's center as the other car flew closer.

Crimson-polished nails glistened. A horn blared. Dazzle of sunlight off the other car's windshield, blinding me.

red sparks dancing. Hot sharp prickles, a heartbeat drumming faster and faster. A shrill cry, and she's dancing manic glee beside the wrecked and burning car, stamping my charred bones into dust

Tires shrieked, dust plumes choking as my eyes snapped open and the approaching car dodged onto the shoulder. A blurred glimpse of shouting faces. We barely missed sideswiping them. I whipped around to see their car jolting back onto the road, horn still blasting.

"Laura, are you crazy?" I shook my head sharply.

She glanced aside as she skidded around the turn into an overhanging tunnel of trees. Laughter bubbled. "You should see your face!"

"Damn it, you could have killed us!" I shouted against the wind. "Slow down."

A furious glare. Then she shrugged and eased off on the gas. "Admit it, you got a rush."

I took a deep, shaky breath. "I don't need to get my thrills playing stupid games."

"Congratulations." Red-tipped fingers tightened on the wheel. She thrust a cassette into the stereo, and deafening reggae blasted.

"*So if a fire make it burn, An if a blood make it run....*"

Three

Gas torches blossomed on the night, shifting breezes chasing shadows over the vine-covered stone arches and wrought iron balconies of the distant Great-House. A white crushed-shell path snaked through dense foliage to link the big house to the cottage porch where I stood in the dark.

The warm air was thick with overripe scents, heavy in my lungs, oppressively intimate. I fingered the fleshy leaves of the vine strangling the porch rail, broke off a perfumed yellow flower, twirled it in my fingers, and dropped it. Closing my eyes, I pressed fingertips to my forehead. A dull ache pulsed, keeping time to a heartbeat that didn't feel like mine, somehow just out of sync, the humid darkness itself pulsing close around me with its own excessive life force. I was suffocating in its sticky embrace.

I ground my knuckles into my temples and took a deep breath. John had been so jazzed about this island, so insistent I visit. If that final letter had been the last of his outrageous dares, they'd landed me in worse places over the years than this hothouse "paradise." Shaking my head, I headed for the light spilling through the open front door.

"Christ, I'm getting wrinkles! All that fucking sun." Laura was peering intently into a mirror in the entrance hall, fingers on her face. "I'm done for...."

I stopped in the doorway, looking across black-and-white chessboard tiles to her long gown shimmering with pale blue and silvery threads. Laura hadn't heard me. Her reflected eyes were darkly dilated.

"Done primping?"

"Shit!" She whirled, clutching the folds of her dress. "Don't creep up on me like that!"

With a low whistle, I crossed over to her. "You should be on a magazine cover. A very glossy one."

She was polished to a sheen in the designer gown, high heels, sleek coiffure, and perfect makeup. Yet uncertainty rippled over her face.

"Think I'll do?" She touched her neck and turned back to the mirror. "I'm getting age lines already, only thirty! But I can't resist a yummy tan."

"Haven't you heard of character lines?"

"Who are you kidding? Only men get to have those." She glared at the mirror.

"What happened to the natural woman and inner beauty?"

"This is the real world, Professor!" She snorted, gesturing at my plain silk dress. "Look at you! It's a formal affair, I don't know why you won't wear something of mine, let me do your face."

"I can't stand that goo, feel like I'm wearing a mask."

"Christ, why do I bother?" She laughed. "It's such a waste, you could be a knockout if you'd just put a teensy bit of effort into it." She shrugged. "Suppose you're still sleeping once a week with that anemic English prof, if he can get it up. Can't take a shit without writing a thesis about it." She touched her throat again. "Forgot the necklace!" She tapped over the tiles to her bedroom.

I blew out a breath and turned to Laura's mirror.

Typical Nordic stuff. Tall, slender figure toned with all the running, bicycling, and hiking I loved. Thick sandy-blond hair brushing my shoulders, easy to pull into a no-fuss braid. Smooth, winter-pale skin, strong cheekbones, and green eyes that were nowhere near John's high voltage. Mine were Pacific Northwest colors — subdued gray-green like the lichened trunks of ancient cedars, diffused light of the old forests, bracing depths of coldwater bays and mountain lakes.

I'd always downplayed my looks, the same way I'd learned to suppress my emotional biases and become the neutral observer an anthropologist should be. Even as a child, I'd realized my "TV tuner" made me odd. I didn't want to call attention to myself. And the Link with my "go-for-it" brother gave me more than enough emotional thrills and chills.

Laura hadn't transcended the urge to take potshots at my libido, but she was wrong. I enjoyed sex, like other sweaty sports, as long as I could avoid the kinds of messy entanglements I'd inadvertently tuned into all too often. People driven by dark urges, the need to possess more than just the body, digging shadowy fingers into a lover's heart and ripping away with heedless abandon. No, thanks. Michael and I had kept it separate and manageable.

But all at once, studying my face in my dead brother's lover's mirror, I realized how passionless my arrangement with Michael had been. I turned away from my reflected eyes. I'd stopped sleeping with him after the news about John, and somehow it hadn't seemed worth it to start up again.

"Ready? I've got to get over to the house to babysit Leon's millionaire client and greet the guests." Laura shimmered back into the hall, smile flashing, a sapphire and diamond necklace glittering.

"Better check one more time." I tilted my head at the mirror.

Laura frowned, leaned toward it, and irritably wiped the telltale flecks of white off her nostrils. She turned back to me with a sharp little laugh. "What? No lecture, Dr. Dunne?"

"Out of my field."

"So let's get hopping!" Lifting her long skirts, she hurried out the door, wobbled on her high heels down the path to the Great-House. "Damn these shells!"

I caught up with Laura at the pool patio. She was using a lot of gestures to explain something to a young native woman in a maid's uniform.

Blank-faced, the woman let out a big sigh, looking past Laura.

"There you are!" Laura turned to me, flashing her jittery smile.

The maid brushed past without looking up.

"Don't mind her, Susie!" The brittle, false laugh. "They're all like that, it's impossible to get decent help."

The maid paused, back stiffening, then hurried off.

Laura stared after her, biting her lip. "Shit!" She sighed. "They all hate me." She shot me a look and took a deep breath. "You think I'm a bitch, right?" She sounded like the old Laura again. "Sometimes it just gets to be too much, I don't even know who I am any more." She raised her hands, an entreating look breaking through the glittery facade. "Susie...."

"Laura, is something wrong?"

"Wrong?" She produced another fake little laugh, turning with a dramatic sweep of her arm toward the pool, the groomed garden, the lighted Great-House. "What could be wrong with this picture?" She touched the sapphire necklace. "Look, I've got to check the rooms. You coming?"

"I'll be in in a minute."

"Okay. Ciao." She swept off with an airy wiggle of the fingers.

I was tempted to skip the whole scene. Wandering around the pool, I avoided the drowsy pulse of watery light, shook off an urge to curl up on padded wicker and sleep away my jet-lag.

Another shelled path on the far side of the patio led me back into lush foliage. Ducking under a low-hanging palm frond, I followed the faint white glow that petered out past a stone bench into a dirt track. It took me away from the house toward the point of the steep peninsula originally claimed by a Danish sugarcane baron. Now it belonged to Leon Caviness, whose ancestors might have slaved on the plantation.

Laura had introduced me to her employer when we'd arrived at the Great-House. He was a very dark, tall "native," his lean frame elegantly tailored. Close-cropped hair emphasized the strong bones of a classically long African skull. Arteries etched patterns around hollows in his temples, cheekbones jutting above concave cheeks and nostrils flaring over sharply defined lips. To my anthropologist's eye, the furrows in his broad forehead could have been rite-of-passage tattoos. Caviness reminded me of the stylized Ibo sculptures I'd been studying as background research, exaggerated features and large heads symbolizing force of spirit. I couldn't judge his face beautiful or ugly, but it definitely had power.

"Susan Dunne." His deep, musical voice was a liquid blend of accents, British, West Indian, a hint of French. "Anthropologist. Have you come to explicate our quaint folkways, Dr. Dunne? Will you leave us no secrets?"

I ignored his mocking tone. "I'm more interested in your petroglyphs, Mr. Caviness."

He gave me a sharp look. "You've come to visit the site at Palm Cay, then."

"I'm investigating sites on this island."

"I'm afraid you'll be disappointed. There aren't any."

"I have some leads. Thank you for letting me stay a few days with Laura."

He waved that aside, turning to the bookcase lining one wall of the airy study with its high ceiling and open French doors looking out to the sea far below. "Do you like poetry, Dr. Dunne?"

"It depends on which poetry."

He pulled out a volume. "I make a hobby of collecting old books. I acquired this one from a dealer on the island, who had purchased it from a young man with blond hair and green eyes."

He took up a careless pose on the edge of his mahogany desk, swinging one long leg and leafing through the pages. He read in a beautifully resonant voice:

"*No man is an island, entire of itself;*
   Every man is a piece of the continent, a part of the main....
   Any man's death diminishes me, because I am involved in mankind;
   And therefore never send to know for whom the bell tolls;
   It tolls for thee."

He studied me, one eyebrow raised.

I wasn't about to let this arrogant stranger dissect my grief like something under a bell jar. Clenching my jaw, I met his gaze.

He didn't back off, instead he only stared more intently, probing. For a disorienting moment he swelled to fill my vision, dark shape looming over me, invading me through my eyes. A horrible, unsettling sensation of something alien stirring inside me. Almost like the "tunings," except this was different, as if he had reached inside me to trigger it.

I stepped back, thrusting off the disturbing notion and turning away from his rude stare.

A dismissive gesture. "Clearly, the poetry is outdated. Your brother must have thought so. The book is yours." He rose and dropped it into my hands.

It was a slim volume, bound in worn leather, *Selected Works of John Donne*. I opened the cover to find our father's bookplate still there. "*To my son John, on his sixteenth birthday, with love.*"

It had been a treasured possession of Dad's. As a literature professor, he'd clung to the hope John might belatedly take an interest in his illustrious namesake. John *did* share the poet's passionate involvement in mankind. It was just that he'd been more interested in the mailman and milkman, old Florence and Augusta down the road, or how the guys down at Herb's Bait and Tackle had made out on the river, than in "dusty old books."

Still, I found it hard to believe he would have sold the heirloom.

Laura pounced on the book, flipping pages. "Why didn't you tell me you had this, Leon?"

He was still watching me, a supercilious smile on his lips, and I was irrationally certain he'd planned the scene just to see how I'd react. A startling surge of fury washed through me.

"Arrogant bastard." I was rooted on the dark path among shadowed trees, staring into the night, hands fisted. I shook my head and pushed impatiently on, picking my way along the twists of the narrowing trail in the gloom, ducking under boughs. Laura had given me "the spiel" about the plantation's history and the restoration of the eighteenth-century Great-House by her employer's grandfather, but not much about Leon Caviness himself. He was a dealer in rare art, who often entertained visiting clients. Laura hadn't been very informative about her own role as social secretary for the bachelor's estate.

Pat MacIntyre's Cheshire Cat grin floated on the night.

I thrust past it, through a curtain of sweet-flowering branches. The shrouded path ended in an open expanse of dark volcanic rock dropping away over a steep cliff. A nearly-full moon sailed above low cloud drifts, spilling white light and black shadows over the cliff, repainting the night in stark otherworldliness. Darkness seemed to ooze from the rock itself to absorb the moonlight. The narrow point dropped in fissured fault blocks, giant stairsteps down to the restless surf. To the right, a sheltered bay mirrored the shimmering trail of the moon. To the left, the rough open stretch of ocean hurled wind and waves to crash in white foam against black rock.

Something held me motionless in the wild spot, breathing the salt wind, soaking in the night. The place gave me neither welcome nor warning. I was only an insect perching there. The sheer mass of rock, imbedded in water and moonlight, reduced the nearby presence of lights and cars to a fitful dream.

Almost. I belonged to that smaller, civilized world.

In another existence, I might have thrown off my clothes and danced homage to the moon, embraced the stones and flung myself into the cool arms of the sea, seeking their magic release from my grief.

Turning brusquely back to the path, I stopped short. I dropped to my knees near the rocky cliff edge and brushed a vine aside from a flat shelf of the stone.

A glass jar tipped and rolled over the rock with a clatter and the strong scent of rum. I caught it reflexively, staring down at what looked like a freshly-severed chicken head lying on a mound of some grainy flour. Beside it, a crude face stared out of the stone.

A wave of lightheadedness washed through me. There was a disorienting ripple in the moonlight, and suddenly my heartbeat was amplified, echoing in my ears. No, it was a drum, beating out an urgent rhythm, overriding my pulse. The stone beneath me throbbed like a tautly-stretched hide. The beat shuddered through me, demanding, and my blood was pumping to *its* rhythm, not my own. An indignant protest rose up in me, but there was something, some blind force in the night, in the echoing rhythm that brushed this logic aside.

the pounding beat is a live being. It takes my senses, the pores of my skin, opens them wide to greedily drink in the heat and the moonlight and perfumes of rum and flowers. It dances my feet to the driving rhythm

I jolted back from the carving, skin crawling with irrational fear. Slowly I shook my head and took a deep breath, let it out. "Get a grip, Dr. Dunne," I muttered.

Leaning forward, I carefully studied the carved stone. Moonlight and shadow highlighted grooves scored into the rock. It was a very basic petroglyph, one of the common designs found from Australia to Africa to Alaska. Nose and eyes, an elemental watcher looking out to sea. My hand felt oddly detached from my will, reaching down to trace the lines of the carving. The ancient face almost looked ready to find its tongue and speak.

"Wha you do here?" The harsh voice came from behind me.

I lunged on a burst of adrenaline to my feet, spinning around, startled into clumsiness as I stumbled backwards. A man clutched my arm and yanked me roughly from the verge, a glimpse of glinting boulders pawed by the sea below.

The face revealed by the bright moon was not reassuring. It was broad, black, and scowling. Long woolly hair hung over his brow and down to his shoulders in unkempt native dreadlocks. His clothes were patched together from multi-colored rags of shirts and cutoff trousers, and he had thick legs and arms and big hands. A scar ran across his left cheek and pulled his upper lip into a sneer.

"Wha you wan here?" It was a slurred, single-word burst. "You wan trouble?"

Pulse thrumming in my ears, I remembered Pat MacIntyre's warnings about the violent "Dreads." There was no place to go except the path the man was blocking. He stepped closer, the whites of his eyes catching the moonlight.

A crooning noise in his throat. "Liddy missy scare?" He chuckled nastily.

"Mr. Caviness is waiting for me at the Great-House." I cleared my throat, injected some authority. "Now please move."

"Huh." A contemptuous thrust of the hand. "You go. Stay way!"

I needed no urging. The man stepped aside and I hurried through the bushes onto the path, fighting the impulse to run, the back of my neck prickling. I managed to retrace the twists and turns in the dark, tripping over roots in my haste. I stopped at the edge of the pool terrace, heart galloping.

Movement and voices inside the big house. A muted progression of piano counterpoint. Bach. Intricate harmonies, impossibly cool and civilized amidst the hot, humid air, the riotous tropical foliage. Chords spilled through the night, pebbles dropping into a moonlit pond.

Four

"Don't you know the rules? You could be arrested for that, you know!"

"Which rules?" I blinked at the balding little man, rotund belly straining his dinner jacket. Did he think I was trespassing?

He scooped a champagne glass from a passing maid's tray and pushed it at me. "Local ordinance, can't walk around with an empty hand! Arnie Wechsler here." He clicked his heels together, round red face beaming up at me. Tweedle-Dee, or Dum.

"And Susan Dunne here." I shook off the persistent Lewis Carroll images. "Thanks for the useful tip, Mr. Wechsler." I raised my glass, heading across the dim patio toward the verandah.

"Call me Arnie." In the disorienting, submerged glow of the pool lights he bounced along with me like a rubber ball. "Nobody goes for last names around here, and it's better not to ask, since they're usually with somebody else's wife! But you'll remember mine, when you realize you didn't really want to escape everything Stateside. Like batteries and Kotex and mosquito repellant and genuine Kosher dill pickles. Wechsler Marts. Can't miss'em. Welcome to paradise, Beautiful!" He stopped to gulp air and champagne, winking over the glass.

Mr. Wechsler and the brute on the point couldn't exist in the same universe. Sane universe? I decided a drink might help, and took a gulp. "Arnie, you can't mean it. Mosquitoes in paradise?"

I made it onto the verandah before he could do more than call faintly, "See you around, Susan. It's a small island...."

Inside, music and voices drew me down a central hall of the black-and-white chessboard tiles toward open double doors. Before I could register more than a hazy impression of a high chamber, tall iron-grilled windows, and a throng of expensively clad bodies, Laura had seized me and plunged into an endless stream of introductions to bankers, civil servants, merchants, a journalist, and the elderly Canadian guest of honor. My smile went numb through the blur of faces. I nodded finally to a group of dignified native matrons coiffured, painted, gowned, and jewelled to an extreme pitch of elegance.

"Miss Dunne." The last one, stout and haughty, inclined her head and sailed off like the Queen of Hearts in a billow of chiffon skirts.

Laura fluttered over to some late arrivals. A fresh glass of champagne had materialized in my hand. Taking it along, I wove past gleaming mahogany cabinets, a display of Chinese jade snuff bottles, and what seemed to be a genuine Dali. I found a couch in a corner and sleepily sank into it. My eyes glazed, the brightly-costumed guests melting into animated chess pieces.

Tall figure of Leon Caviness, making elegant thrusts and parries, stirring up ripples of unease without altering his sardonic half-smile. Laura's shimmering dress weaving a circuit of the room to resuscitate the wounded and remove the casualties, direct the maids with reviving drinks, and rescue strays in no-man's-land. Painted players, surging forward, ebbing back. One pattern emerged. Laura and Caviness did not really belong.

Her electric blue gown caught a sparkle of light across the room, beside the ebony grand piano rippling a lovely flood of Debussy arpeggios. Her head swiveled. She made a beeline for the open archways onto the back verandah and the glowing pool.

Her abrupt departure opened up a view of the pianist. The masterful musician couldn't have been twenty, and she was beautiful. If Leon Caviness was a nearly grotesque Ibo spirit carving, the girl was the other end of the spectrum, a slender gazelle statuette of a rich wood hue, all elongated curves and glowing patina. Her thick black hair was pulled severely to the nape of a long, graceful neck the color of dark honey. The fingers on the keyboard were so long and delicate they seemed to transcend human flesh and bone. In contrast, her full lips, accented with deep red lipstick, were a jolt of the sensual.

"Which one you got your eye on? I'll tell you about his bank account." Brooklyn accent, right in my ear.

I nearly spilled my glass.

The woman straightened, laughing, readjusting the mounds of breast, hip, and thigh held in iffy control by a tight, taxicab-yellow dress. It clashed with her short, spiky orange hair and pink sunburn. She held a plate piled high with salads, bread, thinly-sliced ham and rare beef.

Her name clicked. "Shelli Carver, isn't it?" The island newspaper's editor, if I hadn't mixed up all those introductions.

She plopped onto the couch beside me, smoke puffing from orange lips. Setting her glass on the floor, she propped her smoldering cigarette on the edge of her plate. "That's right. And you're the sister of the guy who got drowned last year." She shoved in a mouthful of red beef.

My jaw dropped.

"There's plenty over at the buffet," she said around her food. "You look undernourished, suppose you starve yourself. No point here, they like'em plump. Go get a plate, come on back and tell me what you're up to on the island. I could run a story." She chewed complacently.

Alarm prickled. "No story here."

"Sure there is." The woman speared another forkful. "I could run a nice little personal. Sister returns to relive last days of beloved brother, blah blah." She gave me a shrewd look. "I never did swallow the bullshit line the cops fed me on his *accidental* drowning, and the way they kept it all quiet so's not to rile up the dreadlock Brotherhood —"

"Yoo-hoo, Susie Q!" Arnie Wechsler stood beaming before me.

Shelli plucked up her cigarette and blew smoke in his face. "Bug off, Arnie. Susan's giving me an exclusive interview."

He shrugged, winked at me, and took himself off.

I sighed in relief.

Shelli snorted. "Just let me know when the hunks wear you out, I'll take them off your hands. Maybe that gorgeous item across the room who's been eyeing you like dessert. And he's old-family to boot."

Except for Arnie, no one seemed to be watching us. "I take it the *menu's* on your mind here?"

She blinked, then threw back her head and laughed. "Wasn't the editor job brought me to the island. I heard the men were big and liked them big." The cigarette waved in illustration.

"Is it true?"

She grinned. "You bet your sweet bippy."

She was expanding in detail on the theme when Laura landed like a bolt of pale blue lightning on the arm of the couch. Static crackled as she touched my shoulder. "Having fun, Susie? Hi, Shelli."

The journalist mumbled unenthusiastically and squashed out her cigarette on the edge of her plate, renewing her attack on the roast beef.

"Susan, do me a favor?" Laura touched her throat in her quick, nervous gesture, scanning the room. She clutched my arm and dragged me out into the chessboard entry. Letting out a long breath, she sagged inside the vibrant dress.

"Are you all right?"

She shot a look toward the party. "I just need a time out. If Leon goes on the prowl for me, tell him I'm in the powder room, okay?" She darted out the door.

"There you are, Dr. Dunne! Have you seen Laura?"

I spun around to see Leon Caviness standing uncomfortably close, somehow having noiselessly crossed the tiled entryway. "She... mentioned the powder room."

"Arnie Wechsler said he'd seen you wandering the grounds alone. Where did you go?"

"Arnie tells me no one on the island uses last names." Irritated by his high-handed tone, I didn't bother to temper my sarcasm. "Why not call me Susan?"

"Not *Su*sie?" He gave it Laura's inflection.

"I prefer Susan."

A mocking smile. "Very well, Susan, but you must call me Leon." He took my empty glass, handing it to a passing maid. "I should have warned you not to wander in the grounds at night. I can't guarantee we won't have trespassers here, with the Brotherhood territory so close. There have been violent attacks on Continentals recently." He gave me an unpleasant scrutiny. "What makes you think you'll be exempt?"

For no reason, my hackles rose. "I did stumble across something interesting out there."

"What?" His voice sharpened.

"On the point, a petroglyph. Just what I've come to research."

His face froze for a second before he produced a thin smile. "I'm afraid you've spoiled my little surprise. I planned to take you there tomorrow." His eyes glittered coldly.

I'd gone too far. If he wanted to keep the petroglyph secret, it was his land and he could do as he pleased. I cleared my throat. "Would you mind if I made a rubbing of the glyph? It could be an important find."

Again he scrutinized me. "Be careful what you look for here, Dr. Dunne." His voice had deepened, echoing oddly over the tiles.

Then he said curtly, "Do as you like." He strode away.

Was everyone on the island crazy? I could still see Pat MacIntyre's ironic grin. Turning back to the party, I came up short.

A young woman stood in the entrance to the large chamber, watching me intently, dark eyes fixing on mine. An enigmatic smile curved her full, blood-red lips. The pianist. She turned and swept back to the party.

I took a deep breath and slowly let it out. Lightheaded with confusion, jet lag, champagne, and hunger, I decided to remedy one situation.

At the buffet table, Caviness had conjured a feast. Glittering silver trays of fresh pineapple and papaya, miniature pastry puffs with meat and seafood fillings, fragrant wedges of cheese. Local dishes featuring fish, lobster, and unfamiliar vegetables. An intriguingly spiky coconut dessert. Plate filled, I glanced around for a seat and met the gaze of a tall native. He smiled and tilted his head in an urbane gesture, teeth gleaming white against his dark face as he detached himself from a group and made his way toward me.

Shelli Carver's "hunk." He was certainly easy on the eye.

Before I could confirm it at closer quarters, my arm was grabbed from behind and the journalist was dragging me out through French doors to the breezy verandah. She deposited me on a rattan chair and picked up her own plate, this time piled with desserts. "Susan, Deirdre wanted to talk to you."

The middle-aged woman beside her leaned forward. "How nice to meet you, Susan." Voice high and clear, with a pleasant English accent. "I'm hoping you might inject new blood into our book club discussions. Shelli and I were just debating Art versus Function in literature, weren't we?"

The journalist assented glumly.

Deirdre jabbed her fork at Shelli. "Admit it. Anything written with a social or economic agenda is prostituted art and therefore not truly Art."

Shelli swallowed. "Better order a dozen scarlet A's for the office. We can wear'em when we put out the Society page for this crowd. We all know Leon's buying and selling here."

"Selling? You mean his art?" I was watching Leon Caviness through the open French doors. Talking to the exotic-looking pianist who'd given me such an intent look earlier, he suddenly smiled at her, surprising warmth animating his bony face. I pointed them out. "What's the connection between Caviness and that young woman?"

Shelli squinted. "Oh boy, we may have fireworks yet! It's a miracle Pat lets her play piano up here, but if she thought Leon was giving her the eye!"

Deirdre *ts*ked. "Never mind Shelli. That's Adrienne, the adopted daughter of Pat MacIntyre, a resort owner. It's rather complicated, since Pat's a Continental and the girl of course has mixed blood, but she's not native, or even from down-island, even though they moved here from the States when she was practically an infant. So no one knows quite where to *place* her, you see, and the island being what it is...."

A self-deprecating look. "You'll think we're terrible! All this preoccupation with race."

"Preoccupation!" Shelli broke in. "Look, Susan, we're minority whites, so we're targets, especially now with Africa Unite beating the drum on driving out us 'colonialist oppressors.' You're a blonde, and a dish, so it'll be worse. Hit on and shit on, sometimes together."

"Shelli." Deirdre turned to me. "Yes, it's true there's resentment against Continentals. It's hard to break through, so we whites tend to stick together, which makes it worse. And the old-family natives are still determined to keep the lines pure. It *is* changing, though. Witness our Mr. Caviness, who's already bringing some of the fences down."

"Huh. More like having his cake and eating it. He might worm his way back into good graces with the rich old ladies in there, playing the patron of the arts, but not if he keeps a finger in jungle-town, stirring the pot. I'd bet my bottom dollar he's behind Africa Unite."

Deirdre shook her head and glanced toward the crowded room. "Everybody's pussyfooting around, afraid to piss him off. I want to know why." Shelli turned to me. "I'd watch my back, staying up here. Wheels within wheels. Might treat *you* with kid gloves, though, like to have a fancy PhD to parade around while he's politicking." She puffed out her lips, eyeing Caviness and the pianist. "That Adrienne *would* be a plum, add some class on his arm."

"Now you're going too far! Besides, Pat's keeping an eagle eye on her, especially with this land-use dispute with Leon." Deirdre turned to me. "Never mind Shelli's piffle."

I shook my head. "I'm not sure I followed the plot, anyway."

Shelli was laughing. "'Dispute,' my ass! It's a goddamn blood feud. Pat got talked into letting Adrienne take piano lessons from

Leon, since he has this hotshot European training, but you can bet if she wasn't still Stateside, he wouldn't have his protege here showing off for the Upper Crust."

"Pat MacIntyre, you said? But she was on the plane with me today."

"I'll be damned!" Shelli exchanged a look with Deirdre. "So maybe Leon's too busy with Adrienne to notice Laura panting over the little Ludenborg heir."

"Now, really! Susan *is* her guest." But Deirdre leaned forward avidly. "You know Laura likes to flirt."

"Flirt, hah! Never did figure out why John stuck with her, could've done a lot better. Talk about Adonis!" Shelli smacked her lips. "Got any more like him back home, Susan?"

My pleasant buzz suddenly went flat as the champagne in my half-empty glass. I looked down at my plate, set it aside. "No. No more like him."

"Such a dreadful tragedy, Susan." Deirdre's voice was gentle. She patted my knee, turned briskly to Shelli. "I thought *you* were more interested in his partner. You know, the one you described so eloquently as 'one hundred percent beef.' What was his name? Victor Manden, that's it, the one the police investigated about the drowning. You were speculating about his performance, telling me you liked your men a little dangerous."

Shelli scowled. "Give me a break!" She shrugged. "The guy's a jerk. Really twisted." She gave me a sideways look and went on darkly, "He thought he scared me off, but I found out a few things. Like his Army record." She tapped her forehead. "A few screws loose, you know? But the cops didn't bother to ask the right questions, just wanted to smooth it all over."

I sat rigid, seeing the words looping hastily across John's letter. *"He'll kill me if he catches me."*

I changed the subject. "Shelli, you've got your ear to the ground. Is it true the natives practice some form of the Vaudun here?" I absently rubbed my arm where the ragged, scarfaced Dread had yanked me back from the petroglyph. The rum and chicken-head must have been offerings. And that shadowy drumbeat I'd felt pulsing in my blood, had I somehow "tuned in" to the native? If so, it was very different from the tunings I'd long since learned to filter, coming at me through a channel I hadn't known was there.

"The Vaudun?" Shelli frowned.

I cleared my throat. "Voodoo."

The women were staring at me. Deirdre quickly looked away and Shelli laughed loudly. "Don't tell me that's what your research is about? Somebody gave you a bum steer."

"It doesn't have anything to do with my research. It's just... something a taxi driver said."

Shelli gave me a sharp look, then grinned. "Spotted you for a tourist. All they've got around here is some herbal lore that doesn't amount to much. Natives can be pretty tight-lipped, but believe me, if something was going on, I'd know about it."

I murmured dismissively and turned to set my glass aside, but glancing over saw Deirdre tilt her head toward the crowded room and give Shelli a look.

Leon Caviness had moved closer, towering above the group at the nearby buffet table, eyes searching the room. His head swiveled suddenly.

High-pitched laughter crackled out of the dark garden. A gleam of pale blue emerged from the shadows beyond the pool. Laura and a young blond man with shirt and bowtie askew staggered toward the patio, clutching each other in a fit of hilarity. Laura tried to tuck in his shirt, stifling another burst of laughter. He grinned and fumbled at his tie. Laura jigged up and down, still laughing. She choked, coughing.

Her companion looked our way, leaned close to whisper to her. She swung around, saw her audience, and fled up the steps into the house.

"She must be half –"

Shelli broke off as Caviness strode onto the verandah. With an angry gesture, he stalked off.

Shelli grinned. "Laura's little secrets aren't staying so secret any more. She better watch it, Leon'll ditch her if she keeps shoving it in the face of *this* crowd." She jumped up. "Where's my camera?"

"Excuse me." I left Deirdre just opening her mouth. The least I could do was try to warn Laura.

———

No sign of her in the powder room or central hall. I sighed, rubbing my throbbing forehead. I'd had enough of the local festivities.

Looking for a back exit, I followed another hall around a right turn I didn't recall. I was about to retrace my steps when I realized the passage led to Caviness's study. Its closed door was in front of me, where the hall made another jog to the left. A thin line of light glowed under it.

The door swung open. I froze in the shadows.

A white-haired servant paused in the lighted rectangle of the doorway. I could see, past him, the edge of the desk and Caviness's back as he walked toward it. His angry voice carried into the hall.

"...too risky. I don't want us linked. I've told you not to come here!"

The door swung shut and the servant hurried off down the other leg of the hall, but after-images of the brightly-lit office still glimmered in the dimness. Especially the muscular native standing in front of the French doors, waiting for Caviness. Dressed in multi-colored rags, he had shaggy dreadlocks, big hands, and a scar dragging the side of his mouth into a sneer.

Five

I stood naked at the edge of the sea, squinting against sun dazzles. A man stood in the waves, looking out to sea. I couldn't see his face, only a tanned back, hair lit by the sinking sun to gold-coppery flame.

"John?"

He started to turn, but all at once the sun plummeted and a shroud of darkness fell. He moved toward me. Somehow he'd gone dark, too, and stocky, with matted dreadlocks and a scar pulling up his lip. From the shadows, Leon Caviness's mocking laughter.

The Dread grabbed my arm, dragged me under the waves. They were down there, the petroglyph demons, the shadow man who'd killed John. They pulled me deeper as I fought for air. They whispered they'd tell me all the secrets, take me to join my brother in the ultimate revelations. Struggling, I choked on salt, drowning in waves of blood.

A shape surged up through the viscous red sea. Head and shoulders, blood draining off them. John gave me a horrible red-stained grin, beckoning. He rose out of the waves, naked, opening his arms to pull me into his embrace. His flesh was melting, dripping off his fingers, skeletal hands clutching me. It was only an empty-eyed skull grinning at me now. The bones rattled, fell apart into a heap around me as I flailed to collect them, sobbing, trying to piece them back together but they were crumbling in my hands and I was kneeling on stone, my hands empty but for the smell of mould and rot.

I woke sweating and shivering in gray pre-dawn, head pulsing a dull ache. Stumbling into the bathroom, I stared at the pinched face staring back from the mirror, clouded green eyes blurring.

Words swam taunting through my bleak confusion. Dr. Phillip Holte: *"Ambiguous reality."* Kenneth Burke: *"We forget our 'reality' is mostly symbols. If we look beyond them, it is like looking over the edge of an ultimate abyss...."*

Moving like a robot, I dragged myself through the silent cottage, into the kitchen alcove to make coffee. I pulled out John's letter, searching it for the secret that would release me.

"How about these petroglyphs, Professor dear...? He'll kill me if he catches me.... I love you."

I shuddered with the lingering touch of his skeletal embrace. I remembered another bleak morning, years ago, hunched at the kitchen counter of my apartment in the gray winter dawnlight, staring at the wadded-up letter coolly refusing my grant proposal for further development of the Tsimshian Museum.

Rat-a-tat-tat on the horn of a car pulling up outside. My door burst open and John stood there grinning, holding my ski boots and a gym bag. "Hustle your buns, Sis! There's eight inches of fresh powder at the top!"

"John...." I groaned into my coffee cup.

He strode over, plucked up the crumpled letter, and tossed it into the trash. "Wallowing in our misery, are we? Come on, lift tickets are on me."

"No way." He was barely scraping by on part-time waiter work at the local steakhouse.

"Yes, way! I got some fat tips last night, big table of divorcees out for a night on the town, yours truly laid on the famous charm. You've got ten minutes to get into your long underwear. I swung by Mom and Dad's and got your gear."

I leaned over to peer out the window. "His car, too. Thought he said never again after all the body damage last time."

He smirked. "Told him you were driving."

"That was convenient."

He winced. "Hey."

"Sorry." I sighed. "Look, you'd have more fun without me grumping along. I won't rat to Dad, so *mmmph* –"

He'd caught my chin and was pinching my lips together, "zipping" them shut. "Come on, Sue. Your gear's been sitting in their basement all winter, and we don't *get* powder like this every year. What's that line about *'carpe diem,'* Professor?" He lifted an eyebrow. "Don't tell Dad I actually read some of his books."

"I better sit down, the shock may be too much."

We were laughing as we hit the top of the ski lift and paused before our first run down the Chute. "Yes!" John threw out his arms, tilted his face back to catch some swirling flakes, and let out a wolf howl. He shot me his toothy grin. "Catch me if you can!" He was off in a cloud of loose snow. I launched after him, dancing the slope in the spraying powder, the astringent cold tingling to my core.

Smiling now in the damp tropic heat, I could still taste that moment, the mountain air scouring away the sticky miasma of my nightmare.

"Ouch — damn!" The cottage front door slammed. Laura limped into the room, carrying her shoes. She was in worse shape than I was, bare feet filthy and welted with scratches, the torn ruins of the beautiful gown clutched above her knees. Her smeared makeup had caked into lines aging her ten years.

"Coffee?" She pounced on my cup, gulping. "Better."

"I thought I had a bad night." I rubbed my eyes. "What happened?"

She laughed. "Helluva party, wha happened." She waggled a finger. "An I don't mean Leon's." A loose, red-smeared grin. "Can b'lieve you pooped out jus when things're gettin' goin! Poor Harrison, so crushed, pompous sonva bitch."

"Harrison?"

Another high peal of laughter. "Harrison Tyler!" She gave me a reproachful look. "You know, big, black, boo-coo bucks! Where'zat coffee?" She groped along the counter.

"What?" She grabbed the letter I'd dropped, focusing with an effort. She stiffened, shot me a look. "When did you get this?" Her voice had gone sharp.

"Never mind." I pulled the paper from her fingers. "Let's get you to bed."

She lunged to snatch at the letter, and stumbled against me. Straightening with a crafty look, she carefully pronounced, "You came here to snoop around, didn't you? I knew it."

"Laura, you know John. He always carried on that way." An odd, pleading note in my voice.

"I know *you*!" She hissed it, sounding almost sober now. "You'll poke around and dig it up like one of your stupid artifacts. Well, I'm warning you. Don't do it, just go home now and nobody else'll get hurt." She was a cornered animal, eyes shifting fiercely side to side.

"What? Are you saying it wasn't an accident?"

She blinked, said painstakingly, "No, it was. It was only an accident."

I gripped her shoulders, wanting to shake an answer out of her. "John said Manden would kill him if he went back to the sunken ship. Is that what happened?"

She sucked in a quick breath, eyes wide on mine. She slowly nodded, then whispered, "Manden killed him." She shuddered, blurted shrilly, "All right? What do you *want* from me?"

Revenge? I closed my eyes and swallowed. "Why didn't you tell the police?"

"No!" She shook her head wildly.

I held onto her shoulders. "Laura, what was going on?"

She struggled against my grip. "Don't stir it up! He'll kill us both! It's too late, just go away and we'll be safe." Tears spilled, mascara streaking her cheeks. "Susie, please! You don't get it, John tried to mess with him and he paid. He'll kill us, too, he knows I know."

She was sobbing now, and I couldn't get any sense out of her. She clung to me, repeating, "Go away, Susie. Just go away."

No one among the crowded masts at the harbor marina had heard of Dr. Phillip Holte. No one knew about any elderly Englishman living on a sailboat, let alone a self-exiled anthropologist. I stubbornly finished my round of the docks. It was a comfort just to perform a straightforward task, get my feet planted on terra firma and remind myself I was here for a purpose – my petroglyph research.

I repeated the questions, collecting more negatives. The only vague encouragement I got was from a wind and sun-battered Aussie refueling boats.

"Now stands to reason if he liked things quiet-like, he wouldn't be about this end of the island, love. You want to try the East End Marina, they're slow enough to please your bloke. And it's a short kip from there to Coral Bay for a bit of the splash and goggle." He tilted his head toward my net bag of fins and snorkel. "Divers go there, it's an underwater park, like."

Outside the marina gate, roaring traffic, heat glaring off sea and cement. A trickle of sweat crawled down my back. No place under this sun for lurking shadows. What I needed was a long, cool swim to wash out the cobwebs.

Heading toward the marked stop for a beach shuttle-bus, I stopped short at a curbside agency renting scooters and motorcycles.

Susan Dunne, this is lunacy. You haven't ridden a motorcycle since John talked you into that dirt-bike episode....

I wasn't listening. Pulling out a bankcard, I leased a Honda 125. A grin bared my teeth as I buzzed down the curving route to the low-lying East End, wind in my face and the road unfolding before me. The speedometer read nowhere near lunatic, but all the same I felt like I was bursting free of something I couldn't even name. I drank in the hot dry wind and sun-shimmered hills, the glimpses of brilliant azure sea past thorn-covered bluffs. The road dipped through mangrove swamps and climbed across sandy stretches sprouting huge cactus plants. I could hardly believe the contrast to the oppressively humid rain forest of the Northwest End and Caviness's estate. The island was full of surprises.

Like no markers on half the roads. Straddling the bike, I squinted up at a post minus sign, mopped my face, and consulted my scribbled directions. Bouncing on over potholes, I pulled up in front of a thatched building near a rickety wooden pier running out into a channel dredged through a mangrove swamp. The air was hot and still, the mosquitoes voracious, the little harbor sheltered by high arms of land. The Aussie had said it was a good "hurricane hole."

No one was tending a combination office, grocery store, and repair shop, so I climbed to an open-air bar in a thatched pavilion on a little hill. A sign read, *"No shirt, no shoes – no problem."*

I settled on a wobbly stool, grateful for a breeze discouraging the insects.

The bartender was a wiry, monkey-faced man with a bleached tangle of long hair and a gold hoop in one ear. He woke from a doze, scratched his belly, and leaned over the bar with a grin. "Hull-lo, baby! Ain't my birthday, so I must be dreaming. Here," he slapped down a pair of dice. "House rules, I'll take high. You win, the drink's free. I win, the drink's free and I get a French kiss." He laughed, wafting a stale gust of alcohol and cigarettes.

"Sorry, I can't waste all those Gamblers Anonymous meetings." I managed not to flinch from his breath. "Orange juice, please."

He rolled his eyes. "Just my luck, a comedian." He brought me a glass. "Have to charge extra for a 'virgin,' booze is cheaper than juice here. Hey, you derelicts!" He turned to two shirtless, bleary-eyed young men plodding barefoot up from the dock. "Hard night? Here, go for it!"

The blond one caught the dice. They called out numbers and took turns rolling. The redhead with the freckled paunch groaned.

"Show me your money, Stan." The bartender handed them bottles to mix their own drinks. Two big blue and gold macaws sidled along an open beam overhead, squawking. Stan grabbed a peanut from a bowl and tossed it up at them. A noisy flurry, and a feather drifted down.

The bartender meandered back to me, picking his teeth. "You off a cruise ship? This ain't the best area for a white chick. Black bastards eat you for breakfast." His gaze flicked over me. "Not a bad idea." He bared yellow teeth.

I resisted the urge to upend my glass over his head. "I'm looking for someone."

"You found him. I'll close the bar and we'll have a little… breakfast." He winked.

"I'm dieting." I dogged on, "His name is Phillip Holte, but he might be using another name. An Englishman, probably in his seventies." Biographical material on Holte had proven elusive, but I'd estimated his age from the date of his publications. If I could persuade him to discuss his analysis of the petroglyph designs, I'd get a real jump-start on my project. "He might be living on a sailboat based out of the island. Would he come in here for supplies?"

He leaned back and sucked his teeth, eyes focused below my neck. I sighed, laid down some money, and stood.

His hand shot out and caught my wrist. "What's the rush?"

"You tell me."

"Okay, okay." He released my wrist, picked up the money, and eyed it. "Virgin drinks are awful expensive."

I laid down another bill and he stuck it in his pocket. "There's a guy they call His Lordship, anchors his boat the third or fourth cove over, nothing there but rock. Weird dude. Mostly has native kids get his stuff and row it out to him. Boat's got a funny name, *Sirens* or something."

"Could I rent a dinghy here?"

"Down at the office. But don't bother, I heard from a native guy comes in with fish, he took off the other day. Cruises the islands a lot, week here, week there. Always comes back to anchor at that cove."

"Thanks. I'll check later."

"I'll hold my breath." He slouched over to his friends and tossed up a peanut. Another feathered fight broke out.

I'd earned my swim. Headed for Coral Bay, I buzzed across a rocky plateau chopped off in bare cliffs overlooking the sea. The road meandered past dusty clusters of wood and tin shacks, chickens pecking dry earth around rusted auto carcasses. Black men lounged by storefronts with garish signs, drinking beer and casting sullen stares after me. Women walked the narrow edge of the road carrying bundles of laundry on their heads and trailing flocks of graceful big-eyed children.

I rounded a steep, tight curve. Sharp sunlight flashed in the handlebar mirror. A rusted truck hurtled down the grade behind me.

My grip jumped. I edged to the left side of the road. The bike skidded in loose gravel, my gut clenching as the dented pickup skimmed close. A blast of horn and blur of dark faces jeering.

The second time it was a dilapidated, multicolored four-door crammed with dreadlocked young men roaring up behind me on the twisting road, swerving to crowd me nearly off the pavement. I scrambled in a hot clutch of adrenaline to keep the Honda on the road. Through the open windows of the car, pulsing reggae – something about an angry mob – and what sounded like "Muddah scunt" yelled at me.

My arms were still shaking with tension when I turned off at the underwater park, jouncing over the rutted road to a dirt lot. I found a slot in the shade between a battered Volkswagen van and a shiny convertible. Yanking off the helmet, I raked damp hair back and dragged in a lungful of hot, dusty air.

I was a field anthropologist, exploring a foreign culture. It was normal to encounter resistance or hostility.

Gusting breeze swirled a dust-devil over my feet. Beyond a fringe of palm trees and a curve of white beach dotted by towels and sunbathers, a lovely stretch of turquoise water beckoned. Filing away the questions and shadows under *To Be Pursued*, I made a beeline for the sea's cool promise. For the rest of the morning, Dr. Susan Dunne was going to be a tourist in paradise.

Six

I stood at the edge of the sea, squinting against sun dazzles, waves rolling in to fret at the blazing white sand. I was rooted there. Sucked back into my nightmare and waiting for the shadow man to stride out of the waves and drag me into the depths –

A piercing shriek. A pigtailed little native girl ran past, laughing and chasing a multicolored beachball.

I shook my head, slapped on some sunscreen, pulled fins and mask from my carryall. I'd taken the Scuba course after receiving John's letter and the photo of the underwater petroglyph rock.

If only I'd taken him up on his invitations to visit the islands for some diving. Hadn't kept putting it off. Maybe everything would have changed, that would have been the key random event that forked into a whole different set of possibilities. Maybe he wouldn't have died. I should have kept watching out for him. Should have stayed "tuned in."

It kept playing, the endless tape of guilt and anguish.

Wading into the water, I bent to splash my face. Sunlight caught the silver curves of my dolphin pendant. It had been John's, one of the few possessions Dad had collected on his solitary trip to the island to bring his son's ashes home. He hadn't tried to reach me on the Canadian dig. At the time I'd been angry, but now I realized it had been a solo rite.

Water drops jeweled the little charm. I wished I could believe in even the possibility of the dream John had once confided. He'd figured being reborn as a dolphin would be the closest he could come to a heaven.

I dunked quickly into the water, letting it wash over me. Standing, I braced myself against the tug of the waves, adjusted the snorkel, and propped the mask up on my forehead while I struggled with the fins, balancing storklike on one leg.

"You forgot to spit in it."

One fin on and one off, I spun around and lost my balance, sprawling into the surf. I emerged sputtering, lunging to grab an escaping fin.

The man watching me was tall and muscular, with a close-cropped coppery beard and a broad grin. "I see you found your luggage."

It *was* a small island. I found myself regarding the same set of bronzed legs I'd reluctantly admired at the airport. A brief swimsuit did nothing to conceal a narrow-hipped, broad-shouldered physique that would have had Shelli Carver salivating. I grasped my dislodged mask and irritably slicked my hair back.

"I can't imagine you don't have something better to do." I turned my back on him and stuck the mask firmly on my face, grasping the fin.

"You won't see a thing if you don't spit in your mask first."

I pulled it off. He was sitting on the edge of the sand now, sifting a handful through his fingers. A smile tugged at his lips.

"Look, I'm a certified diver and I think I can handle snorkeling." I deposited a glob of saliva in the mask, rubbing it around and rinsing to keep the glass from fogging. His gaze still prickled my back as I finally got the fins on my feet.

"Have fun, then. I don't have to tell you about the urchins and fire coral."

I straightened and met his eyes. They were clear blue and direct, lively with suppressed laughter. I found myself breaking into a grin.

He rolled to his feet with a quick, athletic movement and walked into the water, hand out. "Truce? Name's Vic."

I returned his clasp. "Susan." I looked down at the mask, admitting, "Despite my shiny new certification card, I did forget to spit in it."

The sun sparked copper glints over his tawny head as he laughed. He pointed down the beach, past some teenagers lounging on a blanket, boom-box sputtering reggae. "See that lonely pile of Scuba gear?"

I followed his finger and nodded.

"Funny thing about tourists who sign up for a morning intro dive. They go out for drinks the night before, start in on the shark stories...."

"And the hangover makes a dandy excuse come morning?"

"You got it, no-shows. I'm not a regular instructor, just helping out a buddy who works at Tropic Adventures, so it's been a while since I took a dive for fun." He gave me a quizzical look. "What do you say?"

I hesitated, then lifted my palms. "What's paradise for?"

His teeth gleamed against the beard. "Come help me set up."

He led the way up the beach. A long, ragged scar ran down the left side of his back and around to his belly, standing out pale and angry against the smoothly muscled tan. Turning beside the tanks and buoyancy-control vests, he gave me a head-to-toe appraisal as I caught up. I was starting to regret my impulse.

"Hmm. Tall, but slim. Good to see a person keeping fit. A runner? I'd say a high muscle ratio, not much of a floater. About four pounds?"

"What?"

He held up a webbed belt. "How much weight do you need?"

"Oh." I cleared my throat. "I've only been diving in Puget Sound. Full wetsuit, hood, and gloves. Took fifteen pounds to sink."

"Puget Sound!" He shivered. "Tried it myself, once was enough. You're in for a treat." He gestured at the turquoise bay shimmering with light. "I'll throw the extra gear in the Jeep." He bent to hoist a tank onto his shoulder, grasping another by its valve.

I picked up extra weightbelts and followed him up the beach, lead clanking. He deposited the tanks with practiced ease. I leaned past him to drop the belts.

He was giving me another appraisal. "That swimsuit doesn't cover much."

I looked down at all the pale skin revealed by my one-piece. "I don't believe it's meant to."

"You can get sunburned even underwater." He handed me a rumpled T-shirt.

"Oh. Thanks." I pulled on the shirt, trying to read upside-down some faded printing that ended with "No Prob*lem*."

He was zipping up a short-sleeved wetsuit top. "Wish I had a shorty to fit you. You might think about picking one up if you're planning on diving a lot. How long are you here for?" The question was casual, but his gaze stayed on mine.

His eyes were an unusually vivid blue, striking against the deep tan. I yanked my gaze away. If there was such a thing as "animal magnetism," this beach-hunk had it in spades, and he had to know it.

But it wasn't just the sexy packaging, it was more the kind of energy he radiated. A zest for life. Like John.
I moved hastily toward the shore.
He followed. "Not just on vacation?"
"I'm here on a research grant."
"Figured you weren't a tourist. After a while you get so you can place them too easy." He opened valves, checking air pressure. "Ever used this kind of buoyancy vest? Here's the automatic inflator. You can always go manual if you want, here's the dump valve." He helped me on with vest and tank.
"Here's your pressure and depth gauges. We'll head back at a thousand pounds, come out at four hundred to be safe. You've done all the drills, mask clearing, buddy breathing? Any trouble with your ears?"
"Send me in, coach."
"Indulge me. You know the 'don't touch' sign? I'll show you some fire coral if you've only seen pictures. No fun getting a hit." He handed me fins and mask and marched me into the water.
"Aren't you going to warn me about air embolisms, the bends, nitrogen narcosis, and Great White attacks?"
"They've only eaten two or three people this week."
He sank below the surface. I followed.

The earthbound world and its shadows fell away into stillness. I was floating, drifting down into the sea's embrace, kicking effortlessly above a smooth slope of sand and shifting pattern of lights from above – flying, more than swimming, through crystal clarity. The water somehow amplified details of fish and coral, outlining shapes with a knife edge, infusing colors with their own lights. A cloud of silvery fish drifted past and broke into glittering sparks around me.
The slope plunged deeper, sea taking on a bluer tinge. I rolled over face-up and watched etched-glass air bubbles rise to the surface, dropped back farther to revel in the freedom from gravity. Arching into an open somersault, the tank only a weightless bulk, I drifted down in a slow free-fall past darting schools of fish in colors I'd seen only inside aquariums.
Vic was waiting below, beside a wrinkled brain coral. He gestured, and I followed him deeper over a drop-off. I caught a quick, echoing breath.

It was a lost alien city. A mad architect run amuck with coral. The reef had proliferated into fantastic shapes – tall arches, convoluted ribbons and passageways, pagoda-like spires plumed with delicate fringed plants in muted colors – submerged in flickering bands of surreal light. From out of its watery maze, a huge black manta ray suddenly lifted, flying on rippling batlike wings. The devilfish. It soared overhead, shadow touching my face, circling and gliding deeper, disappearing with a last beckoning dip.

I hovered, staring after it, caught in a disturbing, impossible sense of *deja vu*. Seen before, but not by me. John? A dark foreboding stirred inside me.

A high-pitched sound below caught my attention. Vic guided me on, through a dappled lacework tunnel of coral, lancing lights strobing the dimness inside. Orange blossoms of a feathery creature sucked into its tube on the rock, vanishing like a mirage as I approached. We emerged into a shimmering silver cloud of fingerlings. Vic, peering under a branching coral, waved me over. He pointed at a dark crevice underneath it. I squinted into it.

A mass of slippery-looking pinkish flesh, and an eye staring out at me. The shapeless blob writhed and rolled closer. A tentacle shot out at my face.

I scrambled backwards in a gush of air.

Vic's laughter bubbled. The tentacle had unrolled to reveal the row of suction cups on an octopus arm. With an oddly human gesture, it deposited a beautiful pink, spiral shell. It rolled up again, retreating into its hole.

Vic put the shell in my hand, closing my fingers around it, his hand warm in the cool sea. He gestured, indicating my vest pocket. I peeled open the velcro and sealed the shell inside.

He checked our gauges and shot off along the reef. I kicked hard, but fell behind as a school of large, yellow-tailed fish scattered behind his fins. I turned to watch the fish shoot by, the mask and awkward tank limiting my range to a blinkered forward view. I kicked faster to catch up. I was panting, sucking at the hissing regulator, the water resisting me now. Glancing down to the fanlike growths and fronds of seaweed streaming sideways, I realized I was fighting a current. I looked up. My guide's fins had disappeared. A dark flicker, more felt than seen, moved in beside me. I angled to the side to see.

Six feet of lean, steel-gray, hook-jawed fish had materialized beside me in a glitter of sharp teeth.

I sucked in a shocked breath, coughing on seawater.

The big barracuda fixed me with a glassy stare. I edged around to face it. It disappeared in a flash. I turned back into the current and it was there, hovering inches from my face.

I gasped. The regulator mouthpiece popped out.

Coughing, choking, I flailed for the air line. Finally grabbed the mouthpiece and purged it of water. Took a deep, shaky breath, kicking in a nervous circle. The barracuda was gone. But the current had carried me backwards. I kicked forward again. Couldn't find Vic. I was breathing hard, straining. Checking the gauge, I realized my aimless thrashing was using up the air. I'd lost my bearings, wasn't sure which way to head back. The water was darker out here, murky, oppressive.

I looked down. I'd drifted out over the drop-off, looking down into bottomless deep blue rippling with the shadows of black devilfish wings. I was hovering over the abyss, staring into all that dark emptiness, trying to slam doors against my nightmares.

Something touched my leg.

I kicked convulsively. Fingers slid down my calf, tightened around my ankle.

night sea, a light beam shivers over the creatures carved in stone, stirring into life. Hissing breaths, a spill of bubbles, and the icy hands of the shadow man drag John drag me into drowning depths

Flailing against their grip, pulse pounding in my ears, I wrenched free. My shoulder rammed into a coral outcrop, salt burning scraped skin. Groping through entangling green fronds, fighting the slippery clutch on my leg, I kicked and clawed my way through. I thrashed around in a swirl of bubbles to ward off another attack.

It was only Vic hovering there, eyes closed as he replaced and cleared seawater from the mask I'd kicked off his face.

I shook my head, mimed a mortified apology. He dismissed it with a gesture. Checking my gauge, I saw I'd used up most of my air in my stupid panic. I held up five fingers and Vic nodded, pointing down-current.

We headed in, the current's flow gliding us smoothly over the reef's rise. I hung back over the last sandy slope, unwilling to emerge. Now that the surface was close, I was reluctant to relinquish weightlessness, the clean sea hush, the shallows luminous with wavering sun. I sighed and broke through into the world.

Muffled reggae and hot flower scents enveloped me as I stood waist deep, squinting in the shock of blazing light. I pushed up the mask and filled my lungs. "That was…." Words wouldn't do it. "And the shell!" I pulled the pink spiral from my vest pocket.

His white grin flashed. "He's smart, the way he'll bribe you to leave him alone." He splashed water over his face, slicking his hair back.

"You can't mean that octopus really intended to give me the shell? They can't be that intelligent."

"Sure. Aren't you a marine biologist?"

"Me? What makes you say that?"

He laughed. "I wondered, you looked so surprised at everything. When you said you were doing research, I figured you were another biologist, studying the reef. Here, I'll hold that." He took my mask, steadying me as I removed my fins.

"Thanks. The dive was fantastic." I gnawed my lip. "Sorry I kicked you."

"Was it that barracuda? They're just curious more than anything. I was behind you, trying to get your attention, didn't mean to scare you."

"No, no." I waved a hand in embarrassment, annoyed at myself for losing it out there. "My imagination ran away with me."

He gave me a quick look, then shrugged comically. "I had to stop you before you headed out to sea to join the humpback whale migration."

Back at the Jeep, I leaned against the fender while Vic broke down the equipment. He nodded at a cooler. "Help yourself."

I picked mango-papaya juice and perched on the open tailgate. The dive, the weightless immersion in that dazzling sea, had left me lightheaded and euphoric. Stripping off the T-shirt, I leaned on my elbows and closed my eyes to the sun. Palm fronds rustled, a soft breeze playing over my skin.

"Welcome to paradise." He sat beside me.

I turned my head, saw his cocked eyebrow, and smiled. We touched juice cans and finished our drinks in comfortable silence, as if we'd done all this before. Everything oddly familiar and strange at the same time, echoes of the Alice-in-Wonderland vertigo. But pleasantly so, like the mesmerizing splash and shush of the waves.

I glanced at the man beside me, lost in his own private contemplation of the cove. His meditative quiet convinced me the handsome face and breezy manner only rode the surface over more intriguing depths.

He swung around to face me and I found myself looking straight into his eyes. He contemplated me with the same tranquil look he'd fixed on the distant sea, like a big cat taking in his surroundings. With an unsettling twinge, I recalled our family's ginger tom, crouched in such ease on the lawn, muscle rippling under sleek fur — wearing the same smile. Poised to either flop and stretch in the sun, or launch himself after a sparrow.

Vic asked, "If you're not a marine biologist, what brings you down here?"

I cleared my throat, sitting up. "Archeology."

His open gaze slammed shut. He looked away, asked brusquely, "Shipwrecks?"

I blinked, taken aback. "No, petroglyphs." He didn't comment, so I explained, "I'm hoping they'll provide evidence of pre-Columbian contact from Africa."

He turned his newly-guarded gaze on me. "It won't make you popular. Natives are touchy with outsiders. And anthropologists aren't exactly lining up to cheer people like Fells and Vergara."

"You know their theories?"

A mirthless smile at my surprise. "My specialty was the Conquest era, Central America. Can't say I know much about petroglyphs." He shrugged. "You'll be beating your head against a wall with that pre-Columbian contact angle. What's the point?"

"The point?" I stared at him. "The point is, we deserve the truth. After centuries of Manifest Destiny history –"

"Give the native story a chance? Good luck."

I couldn't tell if he was being sarcastic, or merely dubious. Maybe I was still reacting to Caviness's condescension. I said lightly, "I'll need some luck."

He only frowned down at his juice can.

I cleared my throat. "You mentioned Puget Sound. Were you working there?"

Another uncomfortable pause before he answered. "Just visiting a friend. He was trying to talk me into moving there when I got out...."

"Got out?"

"Out of the Army," he said shortly. "Drafted, Vietnam, same old story. At least the GI Bill paid for my degree." He shrugged again, stiffly.

I found myself glancing at the ugly scar. "It's quite a coincidence!" My voice ridiculously perky. "Running into another archeologist at the beach."

"*Ex*-archeologist." He was scowling at the sea. "If you stay here long enough, you'll stop calling things coincidence. Time and chance don't work the same here. The island has its own rules, you give in to them or you go away."

"What?" I shook my head. "I don't believe in giving in."

"Congratulations." Echo of Laura in her speeding car. "I didn't think there was anyone left to fight for the noble lost cause." The sarcastic edge was clear this time.

"Look, I'm no more tied to lost causes than winning ones. I'm just trying to see from as many perspectives as possible. If I can reach a conclusion, fine. You've been trained as an archeologist, you know there's a lot to be said for the scientific, impartial approach."

"Impartial." He snorted. "You don't know how this place works. You think everything's all clear, but you can't know anything until you dive in and *feel* what it's about. Then it's too late for the scientific method."

I blinked again, straightened my shoulders, and stood. "Time for me to go. Thanks for the dive." I started off.

"No, wait! Christ, I've been on this goddamn rock too long." He jumped up, grasping my wrist.

I spun around, staring at his big hand enclosing my wrist. Heat flushed my face, his pulse drumming through me. I broke free.

He held up his hands. "Sorry. It's the island. Too many shortcuts? Throws you off, right?" Face intent.

"Like that line you tried at the airport?"

"Line?" He frowned. Then he threw back his head and laughed. "That was no line, I swear I've seen you before." He spread his hands, breezy-easy once more. "I promise, before I shove a beer at the next beautiful woman I barge into, I'll introduce myself like a good boy. Truce?"

I was still rattled. Under this tropic sun, I couldn't think straight. "All right."

"I always shake on important deals."

I hesitated, then gave him my hand. He clasped it with a firm pressure, gaze holding mine, holding frank promises.

I retrieved my hand, cleared my throat, checked my watch. "It's almost noon. I should get going."

He tossed his juice can into a box in the Jeep bed. "Guess I better hustle this gear to the shop." He pulled on a pair of shorts and a shirt. "Come on, I'll take you to lunch. You have to try the local conch chowder."

"No, thanks. My friend will be looking for me."

"So there *was* a friend. Will he keep you from having dinner with me?"

"Of course not."

"Good. When?"

"I haven't said yes."

"Okay. I'm trying to mend my wicked ways. I'd just like to get to know you, Susan." He grinned. "Right, you've heard *that* one a million times. Here's my card." He fished in a pocket of the shorts. "Give me a call. Please."

I took the card without reading it. "I'd like to pay for the dive."

"No way. Sure you don't need a ride, then?" He climbed into the Jeep and started up the motor. He leaned over the sidebar. "Thanks for coming along. Showing you the reef was good for me, made me see it new again. See you soon, I hope." He put it into gear and turned around.

I glanced at the card in my hand. *Victor Manden. Underwater Salvage.*

My face froze around the smile, gaze snapping upward.

He waved. "Take care, Susan!"

He rumbled off down the dusty road. I stood staring after the man who'd killed my brother.

Seven

The man who'd killed John. Could Laura be right? I could still feel his big hand grabbing my wrist as he fixed me with his intent stare. His eyes *too* vivid blue.

The spiral eyes of the petroglyph gazed oblivious out to sea. They hadn't changed over the past few hours, the past few centuries. They weren't here to answer my questions.

I pulled out my camera and snapped a lens into place. Set it for a close shot, hoping the light would do. I squinted up at the afternoon sun, then past the rocky point of the Caviness estate, trying to figure angles, figure east and west. Usually I had a strong sense of direction, but here on the island I kept getting turned around, my internal compass off kilter.

Crouching in front of the petroglyph, I focused my camera on the crudely carved face. I kept seeing *his* face, feeling the heat lapping off his bare skin as he sat close on the Jeep tailgate. Feeling his presence somehow here with me now, a shadowy lodestone pulling the compass needle into an erratic spin.

Victor Manden? *"Animal magnetism?"* I shuddered. Gripping the camera firmly, I sighted into it, narrowing my focus to the petroglyph. I shot very carefully from different angles.

Slanted sunlight broke through a gap in the trees, outlining the incised face with shadow and intensifying the image. There was no trace of the offerings from the night before, not even the coarse flour, as if they'd been rinsed away. I took a few more shots and moved cautiously to the cliff edge. Glancing down, I recalled the dizzy glimpse of sharp rocks glinting far below in moonlight. Even now in the sun-drenched afternoon, I felt off-balance.

I snapped another shot to capture the glyph's background, then turned to shoot its view over the sea. The setting for the glyphs often seemed as important as the symbols themselves. Had this watcher witnessed what I'd set out to prove? Had it seen the African traders in their reed boats riding the Atlantic currents to find these islands before Columbus? I wished the stone could find its tongue.

"*Be careful what you look for here.*" Leon Caviness's deep voice echoed.

I replaced the camera in its case, took out a piece of white cotton cloth and a box of charcoal sticks. After whisking away grit with a soft brush and taping a finely-woven cloth over the glyph, I rubbed charcoal over the textured surface. A ghostly image took shape. The ancient face appeared on the cloth like a photo negative, incised outlines remaining white. I blew away charcoal crumbs, sprayed the cloth with fixative, and sat back on my heels as it dried.

The sea pummeled the rocks below in a muffled, rhythmic roar. A breeze made it just bearable on the baking rock, fitfully stirring the bushes crowding the cliff. The carved eyes stared through their cotton veil.

Leaves fluttered in an updraft. I shivered, suddenly understanding why the anonymous petroglyph carver had etched the spirit of this place so long ago – a funnel for the power within the stone. For a frozen moment, I was afraid to touch the cloth shroud, fold it up and carry the potent residue of that power.

I hastily detached the cloth, put it in my knapsack, and started to leave, but then something made me hesitate. Scanning the dense foliage behind the carving, I pushed past a prickly bush. Nothing behind it but more brush and vines beneath the tree canopy. I worked my way through to the trunk of the nearest tree. Papery patches of its scaly bark peeled off under my hand.

Hanging from the lowest branch was a small cloth bag wrapped around lumpy objects, tied with a crimson ribbon, and decorated with bloody feathers. A rust-colored smear stiffened one side of the cloth.

sea roars the drums pounding wind howling, eyes staring from the stone. Shifting, bulging, monstrous faces surging within the blood-soaked rock, swelling rising bursting free, summoned

Alarm heaved up in me, slamming the gates shut, damming off the invading flood of images. I stood rigid, fists clenched, a dizzy mist slowly receding. I couldn't dismiss it any longer. I was "tuning in" to someone – something – on this island, whether I liked it or not.

"*The island has its own rules.*" Manden's assertion.

I was *not* going to give in to those "rules," and I wasn't about to go away without some answers. I squinted upward, studying the bloodstained fetish bag. My head pulsed, hammered by the heat. I didn't touch the fetish. Pushing through the brush, I grabbed my knapsack and slung it over my shoulder. I gave the petroglyph face one more look, turned, and strode down the path.

"Susie!" You've got to stop running around like an idiot in this heat." Laura sprawled in a nest of pillows beneath the ceiling fan. She raised a glass and a lopsided smile. "I mixed a batch of pineapple cooler. In the fridge."

I filled a glass and gulped it. Throat still parched, I took a second frosty glassful to a cushioned wicker couch, finally tasting the juice and rum. Setting the glass on the floor, I sank down, closing my eyes.

"Get what you were after?"

"What? Oh. Yes. The pictures." I winced, rubbing my damp forehead.

"Leon told me you were poking around on the point last night." She groped in an oversized handbag and pulled out a pistol, aiming it at me. Her eyes narrowed, glittering with sudden fury.

"What the hell –?"

"Bang! Bang! You're dead."

"For Christ sake!" I slumped back, let out a shaky breath. "Is that loaded?"

She fell onto her back, kicking her legs and laughing with abandon. "Gotcha!" She sat up, grinning. "Welcome to Paradise, Susie. All the Continental chicks are packing a piece these days. Better get one, there's some bad dudes out there."

I groaned, kneading my forehead. "I know." I took another drink.

Laura put the pistol away and rolled over, admiring her fresh lavender nail polish. Stretching like a well-groomed, expensive cat, she couldn't have been the same woman who'd shaken terrified in my arms only that morning.

I took a deep breath. "Laura, tell me about Victor Manden. What happened between him and John?"

She snapped upright among the pillows. "He's an asshole! John never should have gotten mixed up with him and that fucking ship. One of those Vietnam nut-cases, one minute he's Mr. Charming, next minute he's ready to pound on you."

I could still feel Manden's grip on my wrist, his pulse beating against mine. "What happened that night?"

"John's dead! It's been over a year! I'm not going to talk about it." Laura was digging at an unraveling seam on a pillow, loose stuffing coming out.

"Can't you understand? I have to know what happened."

"Nothing happened! It was an accident." She sat up, clutching the pillow in front of her.

"Damn it, Laura! John said you knew something about the shipwreck cove."

She sat rigid, then suddenly shrugged and flopped down again. "You mean that letter. Well, you're getting all worked up over nothing. You know John, the way he'd talk up his big adventures. Everybody said the cove was too dangerous to dive, but he went alone at night and got in trouble. That's all."

"But you said Victor Manden had something to do with it. What really happened? I swear I'll keep you out of it."

A shrill laugh. "Good old Susie! I was just putting you on this morning."

"Laura, John was my brother!" I blinked furiously, eyes burning. "I loved him. If he was murdered, I have to find out. For God's sake! If you know something about this Manden, something about what's going on here, won't you tell me?"

Back turned, she almost looked like she'd fallen asleep, but her hands were clenched so tightly in the pillows they were shaking. She flung herself to her feet. "What about me? I loved him, too, and it wasn't just the sweet parts!"

Tears glistened in her eyes, and she angrily scraped them away. "You weren't the one cooking and cleaning while he did whatever he damn well pleased. He knew I'd be there when he came home from a night with one of the cute dollies he just couldn't resist. But John never told *you* about them, did he?"

I jumped to my feet, too quickly, dark spots dancing before my eyes.

"I was supposed to be thrilled just to be with the Golden Boy. I even encouraged him. We had to work through our Karma, experience all sides of our totality. If we opened up to the natural flow we'd start living the balance without needing rules. And he *did* tell me things. He trusted me with his dark side, things you couldn't handle, nose buried in your books."

She stalked closer, thrusting her face up at mine. "He never told *you* those things. He even told me he had this dream about fucking you, really got him off, too. And you would have loved it, the way you were always mooning over him, your own brother, couldn't get a real man of your own."

My hand flashed out and slapped her hard on the face. Her head snapped sideways as she staggered back.

I stared at my hand like it belonged to someone else. I shook my head sharply. "You're lying."

She rubbed her cheek. "Why should I lie? Somewhere under all that ice, you've got dirty itches, too."

"You're sick." My hands clenched at my sides. "Are you ever going to get over your jealous –"

"You frigid bitch! If you think –"

"I seem to be interrupting. You were so busy you didn't hear my knock." Leon Caviness leaned in the doorway, watching with his sardonic eyes.

Laura glared at him. "What do you want, sneaking around like one of your snotty servants?"

His nostrils flared. "Since you've seen fit to spend the morning sleeping and the afternoon drinking, what I so unreasonably desire is your time this evening. There are a few items of business we need to discuss."

"Items of business." Laura minced the words. "Sorry, Mr. Caviness, *sir*, but Susan and I have plans for tonight. We're getting ready to go out."

I shot her a surprised look.

Caviness stepped closer. "You'll have to change your plans."

"Shove it, Leon. You don't own every minute of my life. And if I ever catch that Leroy of yours spying on me again, you'll be sorry."

"That's absurd."

"Sure. Well, you can skip the lecture. Susan's dying to meet John's lowlife buddies."

"Laura, I've told you not to go to that place." He turned to me. "Can't you leave Laura alone and let the past be past? She's suffered enough over your brother."

"That's between Laura and me." I started toward my bedroom, but he was blocking the hall. "Excuse me."

He didn't move.

Laura scowled at him. "We're leaving, Leon, we need to get changed."

"Not tonight. Remember who pays your wages."

She snorted. "Suit yourself, hope you get your money's worth." With a parody of a seductive smile, she tore open her blouse, tossed it aside, and performed a crude bump-and-grind as she peeled off her shorts. She sauntered past Caviness in lacy purple panties and bra.

His bony face was a mask around his glinting eyes.

Laura unhooked the bra, dropping it slowly to the floor and smirking up at him. She turned to me. "How do you like them, Susie? They're even better than your perfect little Ice Maiden tits. Leon bought them for me."

She'd had some kind of surgery. The large, pendulous breasts from the Happy Valley days were high and firm now, too perfectly round.

She started past Caviness, but his hand shot out and caught her arm. She didn't seem surprised. He was clearly used to touching her whenever he wanted. She glared up at him, breasts rising and falling quickly.

It had finally dawned on my dull senses that she was his mistress. I made hastily for my bedroom.

Behind me, Laura's pealing laughter. "Susie, you are such a wuss! Don't you want to watch?"

Caviness's voice penetrated my closed door. "One day, Laura, you'll push too far."

"So what are you going to do about it? Why don't you call up your feathered friends and see if your recipes work on me?" Her bedroom door slammed.

A heavy drumbeat nearly drowned out the rumble of a gas-powered generator, saxophone and electric guitar reverberating through the night forest. The wooden building perched like an overgrown treehouse on thick poles, patched together with scraps of plywood. Over the edge of the shored-up dirt yard, a vertical plunge to a moonlight-shimmered cove.

I was turned around again, didn't know which direction I was looking. Laura had driven me around too many mazelike twists and turns to a nearly-deserted peninsula, and we'd walked the last stretch on a rough trail to this "party-house."

"Come on!" Laura grabbed my arm and dragged me through an open doorway into a wood-floored room making up most of the shack.

Candlelight and an oil lamp fought a losing battle against a fog of smoke and incense curling past the vague crush of bodies toward open windows on the cliff side. The drummer, a stocky native with enormously muscled arms and shaven head, presided in one corner.

The guitarist, wearing one of the hivelike crocheted caps, slouched against a wall in bored contemplation of his fingers writhing over the frets. A gaunt man with a straggly beard and hair like bleached straw swayed in a sexual rhythm with his screaming saxophone. Dim forms of couples lounged on cushions against the opposite wall, and a knot of cross-legged Continentals with punk haircuts went through complicated maneuvers with a glass pipe, oblivious to the sweaty mass jostling around them.

Laura thrust a beer into my hand, shrieking over the din, "Wild, huh?"

She turned to a young native man, long hair braided in precise rows studded with colored beads, T-shirt artfully ripped to emphasize a muscled torso. His dark face was as arrogant as it was handsome. He watched, expressionless, as Laura gestured, laughed, and jigged restlessly. Whatever she was high on tonight seemed to be kicking in.

The native tilted his head toward the windows and sauntered off. Laura pulled me over outstretched legs and through a doorway onto a rickety deck running the length of the building.

I looked over the edge to the cove far below. "Is there such a thing as a building code on the island?"

She tugged my arm. "Frank's a no-show tonight, but some of John's other pals are here. I'm sure you'll find them charming."

"Frank Savetti?" John had mentioned him on a postcard. They'd taught Scuba together at a local resort, before John went to work for Victor Manden.

Laura dragged me over sagging floorboards humming to the band's soundwaves, toward a shadowed group sitting on the deck passing a pipe around.

"Fucking-A, it's Hot-Lips herself! What you got for us here?" The man leered, slouching against the wall, Hawaiian-print shirt exposing pale paunch.

Laura shoved me forward. "Guys, this is John's sister. Have fun." She was gone down the deck, leaving me facing a row of upturned faces.

Score one more for Laura. I worked on a smile and sat down. They shifted, eyeing me, and the one holding the pipe finally offered it. I took a token puff and passed it on.

Hawaiian Shirt growled, "Don't waste it, that's good shit!" He snatched the pipe.

The man beside him barked, "So what are you doing here?" He had close-set eyes and a beaky nose over dirty-looking stubble.

"I'm planning to do some diving."

Looks passed. "There's better places for Scuba." The beaky man scrutinized me.

"John loved it here."

A buxom platinum-blonde snickered. "That's not all he loved."

"No one could complain about the scenery," I answered, poker-faced. "Did any of you go diving with him? I was wondering about —"

"Climate here ain't too healthy for *some* people." Hawaiian Shirt heaved himself to his feet, spat over the rail, and thudded off.

The beaky man stood. "That bitch Laura! She think this is cute?" He stalked down the deck, followed by the others. Inside the shack, cymbals crashed.

Maybe I forgot to brush my teeth. I climbed to my feet, peering in through the doorway where the group had disappeared.

Beak-Nose was yelling at Laura, chopping a hand. "...trying to get the narcs sicced on us again, you cunt?" Drums and guitar pounded, deafening. Laura jabbed her middle finger at his nose. He grabbed her arm.

Two big natives moved up behind Laura, one of them the handsome young man she'd talked to earlier. The beaky man backed off, scowling, and pushed roughly through the crush toward the other door. A smile curved Laura's lips. She turned to the handsome native, tugging him into a dance.

I turned away from the door and leaned against the deck rail. The music beat at my back, shivering the boards under my feet. Patterns of reflected moonlight scattered and reformed and scattered again behind the waves below.

What was Laura's game this time? John may have sampled some weed now and then, but he'd never been into heavy drugs. Was Laura's involvement with this crowd why he'd wanted to "wring her neck"? What was it he was going to "bust wide open"? If only he hadn't been so damn cryptic in that letter.

More waves crashed through the moonlit mirror below. I sighed and turned to peer in through the open window, hoping to persuade her to call it a night. Her T-shirt appeared through the smoke haze, the crowd shifting her closer. She was still dancing with the young native, his face aloof as a polished statue's as he moved his body sinuously against hers. She straddled his bare thigh, bunched with muscle as he swayed his torso back, thrusting his pelvis in the rhythm of the most ancient dance. The drums pulsed. Laura's face was flushed, eyes closed.

The saxophone wailed into a sustained high note. Laura opened her eyes and smiled up at the man. She reached out, one sharp crimson nail running down his arm, pressing until it drew blood. His arrogant mask didn't flicker. Laura held his arm and licked the blood.

The drums beat insistently, throbbing through the hot night. The muscular native pulled Laura away toward the door.

"Laura!" I couldn't get through the packed dancers, so I leaned over the corner of the deck rail to see if I could climb down that way. Moonlight sifted through the leaves. Laura and her partner threaded a path away from the shack.

"Laura, wait!"

"She don' stop now." A high, slurred voice next to my ear.

The boy was thin and gangly, around fourteen. He was trying for cool, lids drooping over big dark eyes. "Dey goes secret place. My brother Dwayne."

"He looks strong."

"You bet he bad. No body mess wi' Dwayne."

"Does he always bring you here with him?"

"Nuh." He spat. "Say too young. Huh!" He gave me a sly look. "I hears bout you, study on dem ol' rock. Me, I knows some ting big. You come?"

"Where?"

He was already squirming down the side of the deck.

"Hold on!" I hurried to catch up, slithering down the bank below the deck, grabbing branches and shrubs. He didn't slow down. Cursing, I stumbled in the dark across a steep rockslide, heading in the opposite direction from Laura and his brother. Ahead, the boy plunged into the deeper shadow of trees. I trailed his white T-shirt's ghostly glimmer through the maze of trunks.

Breaking into an opening, he squirmed without pause up a nearly vertical rock face. He waved me up. It wasn't as bad as it looked, volcanic rock giving a good grip for my running shoes.

I crawled over the lip, looking out through a gap in the trees. Silver light spilled down the steep fall of leaves, mirrored moon sailing the dark surface of the cove below. A breeze rustled leaves, carrying a sweet flower scent.

The boy's hushed voice, close to my ear, "Dis power spot way back. Look."

I followed his pointing finger to the top of the rocky outcrop. "Oh!"

My guide crossed his arms over his chest.

I knelt to examine the worn carvings in the stone, tracing the grooves with a finger. Two figures, one like a peach with an inverted stem that branched into two circles within the larger circle. The second was almost effaced, a curve with wiggly lines raying.

"These are terrific. Thank you." I looked up. "I don't know your name."

"Samuel." He crouched beside me.

"What do they mean? Why do you call this a power spot?"

He shrugged, scraped at the rock with a twig.

"They've been here a long time, Samuel. Maybe a thousand years ago your African ancestors sailed their reed boats here and carved them. There's power in that. Is that what you mean?"

He snorted. "Don' know dat stuff." His eyes glinted as he looked from the carvings to me. "You feels it. Old herb-lady, Granny, she say you hang ouanga-bag near dem rock, make strong med'cine." He glanced around edgily, couldn't resist showing off. "See." He pulled a leather thong from under his loose T-shirt. A lumpy little cloth bag hung from it.

I reached out to touch it, but he yanked it away and stuffed it back inside his shirt. He looked around again. I could smell his sweat. He caught the tip of his tongue between his teeth and reached out to run his hand over my hair.

I moved back slightly. "That's not what this place is for."

He narrowed his eyes and tried to look tough. He was still holding the bag through his shirt. "Dis my secret place. I be strong like Dwayne, he say womans likes it."

"The right one will."

He gnawed his lip and shot me an appealing look. He started to speak, then froze. His eyes widened. Breath hissing sharply, he scrambled backwards, skidding down the rock. He bolted away into the dark.

I twisted around. Pale eyes burned in the night.

My heart lurched. Moonlight shimmered over the rock, and the figure on the stone glittered silver within sharply shadowed outlines. The eyes pinned me.

*sharp sweat, panting breaths as my/his thin dark arms launch us down the rock face, scrambling, fleeing through the night the trees our hand grips the ouanga-bag. "Mama Loa! Gimme guard,

Granny," we run but the eyes follow shadow beast howling gloating.

A knife slashes, crimson flood and his eyes go blank. The boy's lifeless face turns to me, glassy eyes mirroring the moon. Limbs moving stiffly, puppet dance grotesque cemetery dance his arm jerks, finger points the way flesh melting to the bone, the skeletal hand points over the edge. I follow, staring into the abyss*

I crouched on the rock like a rabbit hypnotized in headlights, arms and legs gone stone, fused with the boulder. I stared into those cold, glowing eyes, atavistic power throbbing behind them, pulling me down to merge with the dark heart of the island.

Shadowy shapes inside the rock whispered seductive secrets, voices washing through me with contempt for mortal life. I stopped breathing. I didn't need air any more. The voices drew me deeper, molten stone lapping over me, flowing into my lungs.

I choked and gasped, sucking in a harsh breath. Tearing my gaze from the carving, I forced my heavy arms to push, propel me slithering over the boulder into a heap at the bottom. Scrambling through the trees, I made it to the rockfall and picked my way across it.

Music throbbed on inside the party-house. Heaving myself up the bank onto the dirt yard, I saw Laura gesturing angrily at an evasive Samuel.

He shot me a guilty glance, then stared at his shoes.

"It's all right, Samuel."

He melted into the night.

Laura turned on me. "Jesus, look at you! What did you do, crawl back? What the hell were you doing?"

I looked down at the dirt smeared over jeans and shirt, produced a feeble smile. "Research."

Eight

"When can I move in?"

Pat MacIntyre paused on the path from the drive. "You haven't seen inside."

"It's perfect." The cottage sat back from the road and apart from the main house, screened by a tangle of flowering shrubs and two thick mahogany trees. Pale-pink stucco winked in sifted shade. "I assume it's got a shower and a stove. That's about all I need."

She crushed her cigarette beneath her heel. "Never assume anything on this rock. You're in luck — a shower, hot water no less, and a stove that works. Even a bed."

"I'm used to working out of a tent. I'll get spoiled."

"Let's take a look." A brief smile, the closest Pat had come to her friendliness on the plane since I'd called and she'd agreed, after a pause, to show me the cottage.

Ducking under the fronds of a stubby palm, I followed her onto a stone-flagged patio. The stucco walls had peeled in patches to reveal aged brick beneath, and a sprawling broadleaf vine was determined to consume the rest. The wooden door had faded to soft silver. Nestled in the lush foliage, the cottage radiated a homey welcome.

Pat unlocked the door and led the way inside. "Nothing fancy, basically one room, plus the bathroom at the back." She flicked switches. A naked bulb lit up and a ceiling fan reluctantly shed a sprinkling of dust. "Good." She wandered about the room, poking and peering.

A woven-rag rug covered part of the tile floor, its colors warming the plain walls. Tree-filtered sunlight through a window screen laid a glowing rectangle on the floor, dust motes dancing. The low bed, wooden table, and crooked cupboards of the kitchen alcove had a comfortably lived-in feel.

"It's perfect," I repeated.

"I don't think anyone's been in here since the Jorgenson kid left for college." Pat's voice echoed from the bathroom, was drowned by a sputtering shower. "It works." She emerged dusting her hands. "You'll be getting water from the main house cistern. Don't wallow in it, we haven't had any rain since Christmas. If we don't get some pretty soon, we'll be into the dry season and they'll have to start trucking up barged water from Puerto Rico. Expensive, and so thick it stands up by itself. Thank God I finally got enough ahead to put in a de-sal unit at the resort."

I pushed on the mattress and it sprang back. "Can I move in today?"

"You're not enjoying the splendors of Fairview?"

"Laura's lifestyle is way too fast for me. And I didn't exactly hit it off with Leon Caviness."

"What a surprise." She wandered out to the patio. "Did you see the latest *Tattler*, the Africa Unite agitators trashing a hotel in town, knifed a tourist?"

"I haven't seen the paper."

"Things are getting touchy, so watch your step. I'll introduce you to the neighbors, good to stay on friendly terms and they'll keep an eye out for you. It's a pretty safe neighborhood, mostly old-family natives and a few established whites."

I took the key she dangled. "Am I wrong, or is the island an incredibly snobby place?"

Pat flashed strong teeth. "Of course it is! Won't do a bit of good to fight it." She pulled a cigarette pack out of her shirt pocket and lit one. "You'll be much better off associated with the Jorgensons than Leon Caviness."

"Literally or symbolically?"

She chuckled and sat on a wooden bench at the edge of the patio. "You're wondering why I warned you about Leon. Now you've met him, you get the picture, but you want to know what my beef is."

"Pretty much sums it up." Noting the switch to "Leon," I sat beside her.

She blew smoke. "We're butting heads over development plans for the Northwest End. I want it rezoned for recreational building, and he's trying to get that end of the island declared a cultural preserve or some such b.s."

She tapped ash onto the stones. "I sound like one of the bad guys, trying to exploit the islanders? There's no choice. I live with the West Enders, I can tell you they're not going to make it much longer as fishermen. The areas close in are cleaned out, and they're having to go out too far in those little boats. Tourism butters everyone's bread now. Hell, buys the bread. If we start in with an intelligent plan, we can do it attractively, provide jobs for the locals, instead of the way it's sprung up haphazard around the harbor and crowded the natives into those godawful jungle-towns."

"What does Caviness say?"

She snorted. "You can bet he's behind the scenes on Africa Unite. Egging on the Dreads and the town hot-heads, knows there's a snowball's chance in hell for independence. Meanwhile he keeps his own hands clean, up on his high horse about preserving the native heritage, maintaining cultural authenticity, and some bilgewater about public domain of historical sites. *Sounds* impressive. But the only thing out in the rainforest," she waved vaguely in the direction of the steep peninsula where Laura had driven me to the party-shack, "is some ruined Great-Houses burned in the slave uprisings. Now the land's just free territory for the Dreads."

She shook her head. "And it just so happens Leon's estate runs right next to the Brotherhood enclave. He loves playing lord of the manor with his own little wild kingdom."

"I have to say, I'm not crazy about condos taking over the rainforest. Part of the West End *should* be left wild."

"So you're on his side, too!"

"Hardly. He went out of his way to be disagreeable. But couldn't there be a compromise, like making a park out of part of the land?" If developers were moving in on the West Side, it was one more reason to locate John's petroglyphs quickly, document the historical site for a preserve.

"Suicide Park?" She snorted. "You go in there, you better have a small army. Matter of fact," she stared at the smoldering tip of her cigarette, "I think that's just what Leon's got. His own little army of Dreads."

"You can't be serious." But I remembered the threatening, scarfaced Dread at the Fairview petroglyph, who'd later met Caviness secretly in his office.

"Look, everyone knows they're growing marijuana, it's what they live on. So how do you think they sell it and never run into the police or shore patrols? Leon's rolling in dough, he has the perfect cover with his art business, and he's probably got the police in his pocket."

"Do you have any proof?"

A short bark of a laugh. "Try to make anything stick. That man has a lot of power around here, even if his name was mud for a while with the old families. He's got the poor natives behind him, with his 'back to our roots' hype, and that cult of his that he *claims* has nothing to do with Africa Unite."

"Cult? Is that what you meant on the plane when you mentioned Voodoo?"

She sighed, tapping off a long ash. "Just don't say it came from me. He claims he's only holding 'native awareness' meetings, but they're at night in the forest, and they get pretty wild. If you're out in a boat off the resort at night, sometimes you can hear the drums. I don't blame you for getting out of Fairview." She shrugged. "Probably wake up with a doll full of pins on your pillow."

I shot her a look, thinking about the bloodstained fetish bag.

"Kidding! I don't suppose Leon would be that tacky, though I wouldn't put it past Laura." She made a face, waved the cigarette. "So maybe there's nothing wrong with dancing to drums at night. But it's more than that. I know the local fishermen, and some of them have changed...." She gave me a defiant look. "If I point a finger, everyone will say I've got a grudge against him."

"Is it more than business?"

She dropped the cigarette and ground it under her heel. "I barely know the man, from planning-committee meetings. That's enough. He likes to push people around." She shook her head. "Word is, Laura's deep into that cult of his, too. Apparently your brother tried to keep her out of it, but a couple weeks after he died there she is, living up at Fairview."

"How did you know John tried —?" I was cut off by the growl of a car pulling into the drive beyond the strip of trees and brush.

"Who could that be?" Pat climbed to her feet and headed toward the path.

"Pat." I followed, throwing out a wild card. "What do you know about Victor Manden?"

"Manden?" She spun around. "That man your brother worked for?" She shook her head. "There were lots of wild stories flying around after the drowning. The police investigated him, but of course it was only an accident. Why do you ask?" She stood still, watching me.

"I'm not satisfied with the police investigation, and I'm not the only one."

"Who've you been talking to?" She was watching me too closely. Even on the plane, it had been obvious she knew more than she was admitting.

"Shelli Carver, for one."

"Shelli." She rolled her eyes. "She had the hots for Manden, got miffed when he turned her down. So all of a sudden she's pushing her deranged Vietnam-vet murderer theory."

Manden's behavior after our dive had certainly been erratic. It would be easier to label it, not have to wonder what was behind his intense eyes. I cleared my throat. "What did *he* say? I guess I should ask him."

She snapped, "Don't do it!" Then she flapped a hand. "He's got a bad rep, nothing to do with your brother. People are saying Manden's salvage business is a cover for cocaine-running, and that means guns and –"

"Pat! You know that's not fair!" A longlegged young woman strode through the gap in the bushes.

"Adrienne! What are you doing here?"

It was the young pianist from Caviness's party. Even in a plain blue sundress, she looked like she'd just arrived from some exotic other world.

Chin lifted high on her long neck, she fixed a smoldering look on Pat. "Why do you repeat that nonsense about Vic Manden? It's just a vicious rumor."

"Ri, Ri." Pat laid a hand on her slender brown arm. "When you've been around as long as I have, you won't be so quick to trust men."

"Meaning Leon, too?" Her nostrils flared. "Time for *that* lecture again?"

Pat sighed, turned to me. "Susan, this is Adrienne."

"Hello." I smiled, not mentioning our encounter at Caviness's party.

A faint blush had crept under the warm complexion. Her gaze flickered from Pat to me as long fingers tightened on a rolled-up music score. "Forgive me. It was rude to barge in this way." Voice a rich alto.

"Isn't today your piano lesson?" Pat indicated the sheet music.

"I'm done. Leon suggested I meet you here, since he was sending his chaffeur down with Dr. Dunne's luggage."

"My luggage?" I turned, startled, as a heavyset native in a uniform and cap puffed up the path, a bag in each hand.

"He told me you were moving in here."

"I am, but I didn't –" I stepped back, gesturing the man through. "Thank you, drop them anywhere inside."

"You don't waste time, do you?" Pat cocked an eyebrow.

I'd told Laura only that I was going to look at the cottage, I hadn't packed my bags before I left. I shrugged. "Guess I wore out my welcome at Fairview."

Adrienne was watching me, smooth face expressionless. "He said you were abandoning them in search of phantoms." Voice remote, inflectionless.

Then, as if she hadn't made the odd statement, she was stepping forward with a graceful gesture, handing me the sheet music. "Leon told me you play classical flute. If you like this Mozart duet, maybe we could play it together."

Pat suddenly remembered they were late for something and hustled her adopted daughter off down the path. Doors slammed and a motor revved. I stood staring at the score in my hands.

The three-hundred-year-old fortress was a highlight of the tourist attractions along the harbor drive. The hideous stone hulk squatted on prime bayview property, pierced with thin slits of windows and surrounded by a fence of anchor chains and ancient cannons tarred for preservation. It was now the island jail. A modern cement building, just as ugly, glowered at it across a crowded parking lot. *Police Headquarters.*

I couldn't waste any more time locating John's petroglyph site. And it was long past time to put a stop to the nightmares, sweep out the shadows clinging to his death.

The receptionist, a formidably fat woman with a beehive of lacquered black hair and cloying perfume, sniffed disdainfully as I requested an interview with a detective. "You waits." She flicked a daggerlike fuchsia nail at an empty bench.

She picked up the phone and started a long conversation about plans for dinner, if I understood her thick Carib patois. I waited. A young native couple came up to her desk. She greeted them with a vivacious smile, directed them through a gate and down a hallway. I waited. A middle-aged native woman in a flowered dress approached the receptionist and was quickly sent down the hall. I waited. An older native man was guided past me to the offices.

I walked over to the desk. "How long will I have to wait?"

A gloating smile. "You waits."

Half an hour later, a uniformed policeman jabbed a finger at me and led me down the hall to Lieutenant Leland, who presided over a partitioned corner of a large, noisy room. A sluggish fan barely stirred the sweltering heat. As I approached, the official straightened in his chair and laid his hands flat on his desk, starched shirt cuffs sharp white against blue-black skin. He stared blank-faced and silent, not offering an introduction or a seat. I pulled out the empty chair and sat.

Leland maintained a fixed look of boredom as I explained about John's drowning, the letter, my questions. Only when I mentioned the *Phoenix* shipwreck did his eyes flicker.

When I finished, he pronounced in a schooled voice with only a suggestion of the musical island lilt, "Quite a story, Miss Dunne. But you're wasting my time. Do you really expect us to reopen an investigation closed a year ago?" He referred to an open file on his desk. "According to this report, your father accepted our findings. Why wasn't this letter brought to our attention sooner?"

"As I said, I didn't receive it until two months after John's death. At first, I didn't think...."

"Yes, Miss Dunne?"

I sighed. "I didn't realize the implications at first."

"And why was that? What made you overlook the phrase –" he peered at the smudged letter – "'He'll kill me if he catches me'? According to these statements from acquaintances, your brother was an excitable young man." He consulted the file again. "One who could 'make an adventure out of a trip to the grocery store.' One who enjoyed taking risks like going alone to dive that wreck at night. Who would have enjoyed exaggerating the danger and inflating his daredevil reputation."

"You certainly were thorough."

"Surprised?" His voice picked up a scornful sting. "I can assure you we are professionals here, with serious work to do. You only make it harder, you Continentals, thinking you're free to flout our laws because you have white skin. Your brother broke the rules against diving alone, and he paid for it. Of course it's *our* reputation that suffers." He jabbed a finger at me. "We've had enough colonial arrogance in these islands, Miss Dunne, enough of being Uncle Sam's stepchild. Attend to your own work, and leave ours to us." He snapped the file shut.

"I'm afraid you've misunderstood, Lieutenant Leland." I tried to maintain a civil tone. "I came here for your expertise. My brother's letter is connected to my research, which is far from a defense of colonialism. I believe Africans were the first explorers to discover these islands, and the petroglyphs John referred to may help prove that. They could be an important discovery, a source of pride for your island. You could contribute by telling me the location of the shipwreck cove."

"That's impossible."

"Pardon?"

"Forget about Ship Bay, and your brother's wild stories. There are no petroglyphs there. Mr. Manden should never have been granted his salvage permit in the first place. It's a dangerous cove for boats, and it's been claimed by... a radical element on the island."

He cleared his throat. "This is an unstable time for us, Miss Dunne, and no one will thank you for your patronizing attempts to rewrite our history. What concerns us is the present, and the future. Change is coming, whether you Continentals want it or not, and we can only hope it won't be violent."

"Like Africa Unite? The attack on the tourist hotel?"

His nostrils flared. "That gossip sheet posing as a newspaper is doing its usual job of sensationalism! If you'd prefer facts, the supposed Africa Unite strike was actually just two burglars with prior convictions. They thought they'd cover their tracks by spray-painting a political slogan on the wall, and the tourist was unlucky enough to catch them in the act. But as usual, you Continentals would rather twist the facts and play up the violence."

"But the Dreads and Africa Unite do support violence if it takes that to drive out the whites, don't they?"

"How would I know? Are you accusing me, a police officer, of collusion in revolutionary activities?"

I sat back, startled by his vehemence. "I'm just trying to understand the political situation here."

"Save your curiosity for your research. Don't intrude in our affairs and stir up more anger."

"But —"

"We can offer you no protection if you should be foolish enough to try to find that cove. I will add this letter to the file, but that's the end of it. We can't reopen the case on the basis of these... fantasies."

I gritted my teeth. "What about Victor Manden?"

"I suppose you've heard about his prison record." He didn't seem to notice my surprise at this revelation. "That doesn't make him a murderer. We found no evidence against him."

"John must have had a reason for saying what he did."

He shrugged. "You should accept your brother's death."

"Then you don't need the letter."

As I reached for it, he pulled it away. "You've offered it as evidence."

"But you're not going to reopen the case. It has personal value to me." Again I reached for the letter.

He slipped it into the file, smiling nastily. "Regulations, Miss Dunne."

If he said "Miss Dunne" one more time, I was going to scream. "Very well. I'll speak to your superior officer."

His eyes narrowed. "Captain Wilkes is on vacation."

"Then I'll talk to him when he gets back."

A curt gesture. "As you wish. Waste your time and ours. Good day."

I stalked out the door and started down the hall, then suddenly checked and hurried back. Leland snapped his face toward mine. He was gripping John's letter, and I was certain he'd been about to rip it up.

I slapped my hands onto his desk. "I'd like a receipt for the letter."

"That's not necessary." He shoved the page into the investigation file.

"I'm afraid it is."

He shot me a venomous look and wrote out a note.

I took my time reading it, placed it carefully in my briefcase, and stepped back. "Good day, Lieutenant Leland. Thank you so much for your helpfulness."

Nine

"No body go dere. You fool you stir bad Jumbie."

That seemed to be the consensus. Spurred by my outrage at Leland's obstructiveness, I'd scoured the marina and commercial docks for a boat I could hire to take me to the notorious Ship Bay. All I'd come up with were uneasy evasions, outright denials it existed, and the hints about Jumbies.

John's petroglyph cove had fallen off the map. Literally. No map of the island showed Ship Bay.

The policeman was right about one thing, the *Phoenix* was a touchy subject. From what I could see, it was a local legend from long before John's drowning, the wreck and fabulous sunken treasure intertwined with ghosts of vengeful slaves and black magic and curses. Giving up on a straight answer, I finally retreated to the island archives and the sanity of scholarship.

The building crouched behind the converted warehouses of the shopping district, an antique stone structure with thick walls, narrow grudging windows, and the inviting air of another prison.

Gripping the motorcycle helmet, I mopped my sweaty face with a kerchief and tried to ignore the steady beat of a persistent headache. The muggy heat was wearing me down. For a moment I wavered, tempted to call it a day and head for a cool swim. *Not* at the beach where I'd run into Victor Manden.

I pulled my sagging shoulders straight. To top things off, I'd had a cheery telephone conversation with the head of my grant committee. Miller, the Anthro Chair I'd so brilliantly antagonized, was not behind my project. Surprise, surprise. And with the budget cuts, my leave might be curtailed unless I could come up with a progress report. I'd be lucky to have a teaching position to return to. It was "publish or perish" with a vengeance.

"Damn." I trudged up the steps, scowling down at cracked marble.

"Uhn!" Startling back, I teetered off-balance. I'd nearly bashed into a man descending. I stumbled down a step, goggling at an elegant apparition out of tropic *cine noir*.

His spotless white suit gleamed in the sunlight. With a mockingly debonair flourish, he swept off his broad-brimmed planter's hat and gestured me past.

Face flushed with more than the heat now, I muttered an apology and scuttled by in my rumpled culottes. Hasty impression of thick gray hair, deeply tanned square-cut face, bushy brows lifted in ironic amusement. The whole bloody island was getting its jollies from the travail of Dr. Susan Dunne.

The dungeon-like stone entrance to the archives building opened welcoming arms, sucking me down to its dim lower floor, a public library where children in school uniforms hunched on stiff wooden chairs and two native women patrolled a grim silence. Up a back staircase, I took a deep breath and plunged into a replay of the Lieutenant Leland Experience.

A bald native guarding a chained gate, slurring incomprehensible responses to my queries. A long, sweltering wait in a tiny cubicle where I perused a fascinating pamphlet on "Communicable Diseases and Hygiene for Schools in the Tropics." A march down the hall to the office of Miss Martin, Senior Archivist. Another mandatory waiting period on her hard wooden chair before she scanned my letters of introduction with a look of distaste on her smooth brown face.

"You've wasted your time." She adjusted the snowy starched frills on her blouse. "Try the Geology Department at the Institute of Caribbean Studies."

"As I explained, they don't have information about petroglyphs. What I'm looking for are clues to Pre-Columbian African influence here. If I can find supposedly indigenous design parallels with African tribal motifs, it could be very important, and the slave populations would have been a microcosm of West African tribes. I'm particularly interested in information about any wrecked slave ships."

"Shipwrecks! I might have known. Another treasure hunter!" Her nostrils flared. "They've wreaked havoc with our records."

It took me some time to convince her I wasn't intent on pillaging the archives, all the while hoping she didn't connect me with John and the *Phoenix*. She refused me access to the catalogue, claiming it was "policy" that she'd pull relevant materials for me. Head spinning with the Alice-in-Wonderland feeling, I gave up and followed her to my assigned desk in a stuffy, narrow cell with closed windows. The other inmate was a white-haired native man in a linen dress shirt, absorbed in a spread of documents and old leather-bound books.

I wrote up my queries for Miss Martin, who grudgingly doled out books two at a time. After an hour of futilely exchanging romanticized pirate stories for daily journals of eighteenth-century sugar mills, I was beginning to lose hope I'd exhaust the archivist's patience and win a glimpse of the fabled catalogue.

Sweat prickling my back, I defiantly opened a window to let the faint breeze in. I sat tapping my teeth with a pencil.

I was getting nowhere fast on this island. I'd been pigeonholed even before I arrived, and all the natives could see was a nosy Continental to resent. I hadn't appreciated how lucky I'd been to be accepted so easily by the Tsimshian in Canada. Maybe it was just dumb luck that I'd run into old Willie Raven while I was out scouting petroglyphs, and he'd invited me back to the village. Maybe it was simply that the tribe's Northern ways suited my temperament. Willie's laconic, circuitous conversation, laced with meditative silences, was worlds away from this island's feverish beat.

Or it was the visceral bond I felt with my Pacific Northwest homeland, like the link with their land celebrated by the Indians. Willie Raven had told me I had "affinity." Why hadn't I asked what that meant?

I took a deep breath, straightening in my wooden chair. Affinity with these tropics or not, I had a job to do. And I was a guest here. I rose and approached the white-haired scholar. "Excuse me, sir. I should have asked if the open window bothers you."

He looked up from his papers, blinking. "I beg your pardon?" He glanced at the window. "Oh, yes, that is, no. The fresh air is welcome." He rose and extended a hand. "I beg your pardon, Miss. I should have introduced myself earlier. Edmund Lallas." His voice was soft and musical.

I smiled and clasped his hand. "Susan Dunne. I'm an archeologist, investigating petroglyphs."

"How fascinating." A self-deprecating gesture at his pile of documents. "I dabble in the history of these islands, but I fear I am abysmally ignorant of petroglyphs. I would be interested to learn how your investigations progress."

I lifted my palms. "I'm afraid there's not much progress at the moment."

He glanced at the two closed books on my desk, and a smile flitted across his lined face. "You seem to be experiencing some difficulties with our... system here. You must forgive our Miss Martin, an admirable woman, if a bit severe. She has taken on the formidable task of reorganizing these archives. Her predecessor was terribly lax with his catalogue." As he talked, his hands rose and dipped like eloquent bird wings. "Come, allow me to be your guide."

A gentle word from Dr. Lallas earned me admission to the inner sanctum of the catalogue cubicle. My initial search through the riotous disorder in a stack of dog-eared notebooks left me feeling more sympathetic to Miss Martin. I hoped her new catalogue would dispense with the last archivist's whimsical categorization in favor of some attempt at cross-reference.

She looked surprised when I returned with a list of documents, but promoted me to three at a time.

One was a paper I'd already read back in the States, by the controversial Dr. Phillip Holte. It described the carvings on nearby Palm Cay, now an historical park. Holte had attempted to trace some of the symbols to a Libyan alphabet used between the first and thirteenth century, suggesting they had been carved by visiting Africans before Columbus. I might be excommunicated, too, if I tried to build on the heretical theory.

I was still hoping Dr. Holte could be persuaded to work with me on the linguistics – *if* I could find the old scholar who was proving as elusive as John's petroglyphs.

I stepped to the window to stretch, gazing absently out at a weed-choked courtyard. Late afternoon simmered in the deceptive quiet before rush-hour traffic. Below the window, a pitted stone cherub danced on the edge of a dry fountain, head tilted up at me, eyes empty.

I couldn't shake a growing certainty that John had sent me a message in that last nightmare Link, imprinted on my nerves in hieroglyphs I couldn't read. Something more than sunken gold had called him back to Ship Bay. The petroglyphs themselves?

Grabbing my notebook, I headed down the stairs to the public library's card catalogue. I flipped past *Volcanoes* and *Voltaire* and stopped at *Voodoo*.

"The Bocor, Haiti's Faustus," by Phillip Holte, PhD.

"A caveat to the traveler to Haiti, from one who has gone before: I fear you will fail to find throughout this entire exotic island a single doll impaled with pins, needles, or related domestic weaponry. Further investigation along these lines is best pursued within the archives of the Hollywood moving-picture industry...."

I was briefly disappointed to discover that the travel article by a young Dr. Holte, in a tattered regional collection, described only the Haitian Vaudun. Holte had apparently carried out field work there before turning his attention farther south to these islands and the petroglyphs. The article echoed the accepted wisdom that the Vaudun had not spread to this part of the Caribbean.

It was a hybrid religion, rooted in both the ancient snake worship of the West Africans and the Catholicism of new-world slave owners. These more southerly islands had been Protestant-controlled, so hadn't developed the colorful pagan *loa* corresponding to the Catholic saints.

"My first foray to the houngfor came admittedly as something of a shock, since I was at the time a practising vegetarian....

"We're summoned by the swelling throb of drums through the night, the eerie flicker of candlight in the cavelike houngfor. The altar is cluttered with bottles, pictures, offerings, and the richly cloaked black Stone. The houngan, swaying to the beat of the big drum, traces the sacred veve design over the dark stamped earth, white corn flour glowing in a geometric tracery of spirals, diamonds, curves, filigreed spikes. A gust of wind streams the torches. The loa has arrived! Sweat springs on the skin of the white-clad dancer as she shrieks. The loa enters her to 'ride the Horse' in feverish exaltation, celebrants stamping the earth and crying out with her ecstasy. A scream, flashing knife, and the salty taste of the sacrificial cock's blood —"

I stared at a black-and-white photo of the torchlit ritual yard, the *veve* patterns rippling dizzily. The designs were somehow familiar, as if I'd seen them before, but I couldn't remember where. I blotted my damp face and read on.

"But this was only the Arada form, 'white magic' performed for healing and spiritual sustenance. I was determined to penetrate the secrecy shrouding the outlawed Petro, 'black magic' used by a Bocor to lay curses.

"I had circulated the story of a hated rival I wished to destroy, providing a description of my old Latin tutor. In Haiti, where paid curses and revenge poisonings are everyday affairs, no one found my story particularly surprising. Finally my guide whispered that a Bocor had agreed to see me, if I would pay for the proper sacrifices. Judging by the sum, it would be an impressive show. However, when I had been blindfolded and led via mule to

his compound, I discerned no preparations for a ceremony and was forced to conclude that I had been duped once more.

"As it was a pitch black night and I'd no idea where they'd brought me, I thought it wise to humor them, especially the large chap with the sharp machete. He led me into a thatched hut to meet the infamous Bocor.

"At first glance, he was not an impressive sight, this graying fellow dressed in stained trousers and little else save shell and feather necklaces. He sat on a low stool in front of a table littered with the same paraphernalia I'd seen in the houngfor. I sat on the dirt floor. He stared at me silently for several minutes without blinking. I began to experience a disagreeable chill down my spine, despite the hot, humid night.

"I couldn't let him win the upper hand, so I stood and demanded the charm I'd paid for. He blinked then, gave me a smile I didn't half like, and told me to take the little bag on the table.

"The poison would kill my enemy slowly, without trace, assuring me success and wealth. He told me how he'd made it, after extracting a solemn vow of silence. After he'd explained what happened to his enemies, I deemed it prudent to honor that vow.

"He warned me that if I used his charm, I would gain power and riches through it, but that finally one of the dangerous loa would come for payment. He himself had postponed the inevitable by offering a cousin and later a sister, but eventually he would run out of relatives and the spirit would demand his own soul.

"He seemed quite philosophical about this outcome. I told him about Europe's own great Bocor, Faustus, and how he'd made a pact with Lucifer to possess all the knowledge and riches of the earth. The Bocor nodded approval. When I told him of Faustus' later remorse, he shrugged and said Faustus was not a great magician if he let his fear master him. He himself would never regret the payment demanded, for he had become something greater than men who let fear nag them like a fat wife.

"I was impressed with the Bocor, but on second thought politely declined the charm. I went away, blindfolded as I came, and forever blind to the dazzling riches I might have possessed, of which my nagging good-wife, Mrs. Fear, will doubtless never tire of reminding me. However, I am content to pursue my humble course among those who tremble at the name of the terrible Bocor. These poor folk are indeed wedded to Fear, but I have seen no envy in their eyes when they look to the hills at the sound of the distant Petro drums."

I closed the volume, smile twitching my lips. I was becoming quite fond of Dr. Phillip Holte.

Reminding myself I might be in for a disappointment if I did finally track him down, only to find a cranky and befuddled old man, I trudged up the steps to collect my papers. I couldn't face more digging in the dusty archives. It was a pretty slim chance I'd find clues to the shipwreck cove, anyway. Had I come this close, only to fail?

It was time to go to the source. Victor Manden.

TEN

"Susan?" Victor Manden, crouched on the dock to lift a rusted chunk of metal, turned to squint under his lifted hand. He stood and headed toward me, a dark silhouette against the glare of the lowering sun.

I wove cautiously around heaps of corroded cables, fittings, and engine parts toward the dock at the end of his salvage yard. Beyond a couple of tethered motorboats and some sailboat masts, the clutter of small waterfront businesses gave way to the deepwater port and a docked container-ship. A crane swinging slowly over it, and a turquoise-painted fishing boat chugging across the flat water, were the only signs of life. The breezeless air shimmered with heat, sun poised for its plunge below the waves.

As Manden reached the head of the dock, a balding Continental in swim trunks, Scuba gear slung over one shoulder, strode out of a quonset-hut office to cut him off. Short and stocky, he squinted up at Manden, gesturing.

Manden nodded at him, moving on toward me. "See you tomorrow, Bill."

The diver gave me a curious once-over and strode past my parked bike to the chain-link gate. I nearly ran after him. There was no one else around.

Manden stopped a pace away, glanced at the helmet in my damp grip, and flashed a grin. He radiated the vitality of a healthy animal. His sweat-stained T-shirt strained over biceps and pectorals as he pulled off a pair of leather gloves and stuck them in a back pocket of rust-streaked shorts. His sea-blue eyes hadn't faded any.

I cleared my throat. "Hello... Vic. I hope you don't mind my just showing up like this. I've never seen a salvage operation before." Voice absurdly bright.

"I don't mind, Susan."

"Is that your office over there?" I waved at the quonset hut by the fence.

"Part of it. I share building space and the dock with a couple of other guys. That your Honda over by Wally's truck?"

"I'm leasing it." I poked my toe at an assortment of cleats.

"Just don't let the maniacs run you off the road. Are you planning an excavation there?"

I glanced up from the cleats and couldn't help smiling.

He looked amused. "We'll do the grand tour later. Come see my home first. I'll mix you a drink and you can relax while I clean up. Looks like you've been working too hard, you know that's a violation of local ordinance."

"Your home? But I can't —"

"This is home." He waved toward the boat with the winch.

"Oh." I could hardly refuse to follow him down the dock. Passing another parts heap, I stopped short. Propped against the metal scraps was a big antique anchor with the classic flukes and cross bar, pitted and corroded. The cross was topped by a white blob of dead coral, roughly the size and shape of a human skull. Slanted sunlight cast shadows like two empty eyes.

Manden chuckled. "You don't like my prize?"

I shrugged, images from the Vaudun journal lingering.

"Gaylord, my yard man, won't touch it, swears it was a skull the coral grew over. Jumbie in it. Probably get a good price for it, put it in the garden for shivers."

"I'll stick to petunias." I turned away from the grisly-looking relic, following him down the dock toward the big power boat, seizing on the first thing that met my eye. "Is the winch for raising things off the bottom?"

"I generally use lift bags for that. Winch is mostly for transferring loads onto the dock. For scouting and small jobs, I use the Whaler." He indicated a smaller motorboat farther down the dock. "You can leave your shoes here." He was barefoot.

I pulled off my jogging shoes, glancing at the stern above a wooden dive platform. For the boat's name, there were painted hieroglyphs.

"Mayan." He paused beside me. "Supposed to mean calm seas, safe harbor, something like that." He started to say more, then clamped his jaw and turned away, climbing into the boat.

I followed him aboard, squelching my curiosity about Victor Manden's troubled psyche. I was here to collect hard data. "Salvage work must be something like archeology. Do you actually raise sunken boats?"

He shrugged off the mention of his former profession. "Mostly just recovering things lost overboard. Motors, anchors. A car someone drove off the dock after a few too many. Sometimes I get a contract for a complete wreck, but usually we just take them apart for scrap and expensive pieces like fittings."

"We?"

"I hire help when I need it. No problem finding divers around here."

Like John. "So... how do you work down there? What are the lift bags like? Could I see one?"

"Whoa! You must be Hell on the job." He laughed. "Why don't I get you a drink and I'll jump in the shower, then I'll bore you with the deadly details. I've got some good local rum and fresh juice."

"Light on the rum, please."

He ducked into the cabin and was back quickly with a tall, moisture-beaded glass. He tilted his head toward a ladder. "Go up and catch the breeze. Choice sunset coming on."

Cushioned benches lined the railed cabin roof. Sinking down with my back to the dropping sun, I watched it plate the shabby warehouses with gleaming copper. A thankfully cool breeze ruffled the flat bay. I took a long, thirsty swallow of my drink, and the flavors of mango, papaya, and lime blossomed on my tongue, igniting down my throat. He'd been generous after all with the rum.

I leaned back just for a moment, closed my eyes, and rocked with the tug of the boat against its lines. Another long, cool swallow. The rum on an empty stomach probably wasn't smart. Waves slapped against the boat to a lulling rhythm, and even the birds had fallen silent in the prelude to sunset.

The gentle swell lifted and dropped, sea hissing softly, sleepily. The sound of rain, a pattering shower, surf on sand.

blood-warm waves lapping at my legs, I stand in the sea, holding a glistening pink spiral shell. My hands caress the smooth curves inward turning, savoring the touch. I look down at my hands dizzy surge turning inside-out and they're his hands big powerful, I'm flexing those thick male fingers cupping the shell, palm flattening over the curves, but it's soft warm skin my skin pale ivory in the sunlight he's stroking, smiling, sunlight glinting copper in his beard

The boat dipped suddenly beneath me. I snapped upright on the bench, shaking my head sharply, face flushed. Manden climbed up in a clean shirt and shorts, wet hair slicked back, moisture glistening red-gold tints in his beard.

I shook my head again and took a deep breath.

Manden raised his glass to the flaming sky and to me, sitting with one knee cocked, facing me too close on the bench. He brought with him the faint aroma of soap, a tangy scent of skin. He eyed my depleted glass and my face. "Doing okay? You've got to get the island rhythm. Keep rushing around in the heat, you'll make yourself sick." His gaze held mine. "Seriously. These tropic fevers can be killers."

I yanked my gaze away, face still burning. Had I "tuned in," on *him*? "I'm... just tired. Spent the day in the archives."

"No wonder! You must have met the Dragon Lady. You do need another drink, then we'll go get you some dinner. I know a great place for native food."

"No, really." This was not going as planned. "I just stopped by to say hello, not invite myself to dinner."

"I invited you, remember? Hand me your glass." He started down the ladder.

I managed, "Just juice, please."

He paused before his head sank below the deck, and shot me a grin. "Okay." He disappeared.

Impossible. He was Victor Manden. Even if he hadn't killed my brother, he was probably selling cocaine, maybe worse. Was he connected to those lowlifes Laura had tossed me to at the party-shack? Some kind of drug ring operating out of Ship Bay, that John had threatened to expose? I raked back my hair and took another deep breath as I heard him climbing up again.

He sat back as I sipped, at ease in a silent contemplation of my legs. I tucked them under me on the bench.

"So what were you doing in the archives?"

"Looking into slave records."

"Our glorious island had the biggest slave market in the new world for a while. Some claim to fame." He shook his head. "Thought you were after petroglyphs."

"I am. But I'm expanding on Phillip Holte's work. You said you'd heard of his theory?"

"Vaguely. All I know is the academics won't buy it, too many tenures built on Isolationism and separate continents. Besides, you're the wrong one to start tilting at that windmill."

"Why?" I frowned.

"Same thing I ran into in Central America, natives here don't want some Continental — gringo, white, whatever — poking around their turf, taking their voice. You didn't get hit with that in your Northwest Indian work?"

"Of course." I gestured impatiently. "But other Indians were cooperative. A lot of them are just starting to realize what they lose every time new technology replaces an ancient craft, new beliefs take over old worldviews. There's always a tradeoff. So if some whites want to help them recover part of the culture the colonials wrecked, maybe there's a balance in that."

"In some best of all possible worlds. This island ain't it." He shook his head. "So how do your petroglyphs prove pre-Columbian contact?"

"I'm trying to connect design motifs with African elements."

"Sounds like a stretch."

"That's what the old boys say. But there *is* other evidence for early contact. The Libyans were taking their reed boats around the tip of Africa to trade in East India, and that was a hell of a harder sail than sliding into the Atlantic currents."

"It's no proof."

"Then look at the Toltec monument variations in Mexico."

He licked a drip off the outside of his glass. "I thought Fleming and his crowd put that one to rest."

"I'm not convinced." I pursed my lips. "Anyway, it's the linguistic angle that should clinch it, and the new designs, if I can locate —" I bit it off, took a hasty sip of my juice. I was getting way off track here.

"Find what?"

I waved a hand. "I'm boring you with all this stuff."

A slow smile, his gaze holding mine. "I'll tell you when you start boring me, Susan."

Face flushing again, I looked down at my drink. "You don't want to hear a bunch of shoptalk. I thought you were done with archeology."

"So that's it." Voice suddenly brusque. "Slumming here?"

"What are you talking about?"

He scowled. "You don't have to talk down to me and my junkyard." He gestured toward the enclosure and the vague beast shapes of rusted metal lurking in the twilight. "Archeology's just glorified garbage, anyway. At least in the salvage biz I'm my own boss, I don't have to kowtow to bullshit academics, some stuffed shirt's ego on the line if my results don't support his theories. People aren't stabbing each other in the back to make black-market bucks off artifacts. Here, I'm accountable to myself and I don't have people accusing me of –"

He stopped short, staring at his big hand gripping the glass. He made an aborted movement, as if to throw it overboard.

I edged back on the bench.

He gave a short, rueful laugh. "Damn. How do you push my buttons?" He blew out a breath, gave me a straight look. "There's something about you, Susan. Like I can cut to the chase, skip the polite doubletalk. Like I know you."

Disturbing echo of my own sense of the familiar/strange. He was watching me, gone still, waiting, and our gazes locked for what could only have been a few seconds. The moment was frozen like a jammed film frame, plucked out of time and charged with a free-fall vertigo.

I desperately battened my hatches, couldn't face such intimate contact with the man who could have killed John. I might start understanding the mind of a murderer, might find him not a monster, but all too human, all too familiar. I wrenched my gaze from his. Cleared my throat. Gestured toward the darkening sea that had swallowed the sun with a voracious haste very different from the leisurely northern settings.

"You said before you'd excavated sunken galleons. I... suppose there are some around here, too? Have you done any diving on them?" I had to find out about the shipwreck cove and get away. Dusk gathered around us, the wharf deserted except for our lonely pool of light on the boat deck.

Face gone shuttered again, Manden answered brusquely, "Spanish weren't that active in this area. We're not on the main trade routes. The island was important later. Danish, Dutch, English shipping. And the slave trade."

I managed a neutral tone. "So what about the slave ships?" My heart was beating fast, palms damp.

"Sure. But nobody's interested in them because they didn't carry much in the way of other valuable cargo."

"It must be exciting just to dive on one of the old wrecks."

"You'd be disappointed. Only the recent ones have any structure left. On the old wooden ships, all you can see is maybe an encrusted anchor and a cannon or two, and nine people out of ten would miss those. The rest would be disintegrated or covered with coral or sand. Takes a lot of boring work to get through to any artifacts."

"Pretty much the same on the Indian digs I've done. Mostly dull routine." I had to fill up the tense silence. "But when you find something important, it's that much better, isn't it? You know — holding it in your hands, bridging that gap."

After a moment, he nodded. "The maker's long gone to dust, and there you are with his clay pot or pewter spoon. No idea what it meant to him. Some immortality." He was watching shreds of purple cloud fade into darkened sky.

The last thing I wanted was to hear Victor Manden's views on immortality. I cleared my throat. "So you've done some shipwreck diving here? Do you know anything about a slave ship wrecked in a cove called Ship Bay? I've found evidence connecting it with a possible petroglyph site."

He swung slowly toward me, blunt face unreadable in the dim glow of the boat lights. "Where did you find out about the *Phoenix*?"

"In the archives." I gestured vaguely.

"What is this, Susan?" An edge to his voice. "I happen to know there are no records of that ship left in the archives."

"But I —"

"Don't bother, you're a lousy liar." A jerky movement of his head, like he was shaking off an irritating insect. "No wonder you've been acting so nervous. You came here to find out about that wreck and the rest of it, didn't you? You've heard all about it by now. I should have known." Voice bitter.

"Stealing those documents was just one more thing I've been accused of. God only knows why I'd bother, when I already had the salvage permit. Maybe just for the fun of it, you know a criminal like me will stop at nothing. Even murder. They told you that, didn't they?"

I couldn't answer, throat gone dry.

His eyes narrowed. "You're like the others, came for a cheap thrill?"

I said carefully, "Aren't you overreacting?"

"For the hundredth time. Everybody knows my partner got killed looking for the treasure on that damned ship, and everybody *knows* I had it in for John. Sure, he was a sneaky little bastard and he was ripping me off, but you don't go killing people for that."

I caught a sharp breath, swallowing an outraged retort. "Why don't you tell me what happened?"

"I might have if you'd asked me straight out." He scowled. "What's happened to your academic impartiality? Or am I an interesting study for you? The mind of a murderer?"

I flushed with a crazy certainty he'd read my mind.

He stood, shadow falling over me. "You're afraid, aren't you?"

He was right, but I'd be damned if I'd let him gloat over it. I pushed to my feet and moved past him to the ladder, convinced he could hear my heart pounding. "Good night, Mr. Manden." My chin thrust out in my family's stubborn habit.

"Christ!" His eyes widened in shock. "You're his sister!"

If he was angry before, he was furious now. "Jesus! Playing me for a sucker again, does it run in the family? No wonder I thought I knew you. You're just like him, a sneak." He moved closer, fists clenched. "Get off my boat."

"Then they're right about you." I held my ground, deliberately provoking him. "What did John find in that cove? Why did you kill him?"

He looked down at me and jabbed a finger. "Get off."

I'd hoped his anger would explode into a revelation, but his face had gone cold and hard. He looked like he wanted to kill me.

I forgot my pathetic pride, scrambling down the ladder and onto the dock. Grabbing my shoes, I ran for the Honda, past the vague lurking shapes in the yard. The skull-shaped coral glimmered through the dusk.

Eleven

I'm running. Lost, naked, blind, can't see in the dark. Drums pulse. Behind, before. *"License my roving hands, and let them go, Behind, before, above, between, below...."* I keep running, the drumbeat's pulling me now, I have to find the source.

Thick vines, serpents brushing me. Hiss of flaring torches, shadows leaping. Backlit palm fronds. Flames licking with the drumbeat, gilding my skin. Leaves entwine me smooth and whispering, and I dance, feet pounding the hollow earth, reverberating. The beat quickens and I dance faster, heat flooding my limbs, flushing my face.

A shadowed figure moves slowly toward me. Big hands grasp my waist. Pulling me, eyes vivid sapphire a glint of teeth and copper gleam fire as we dance the drums alive. He rips away the clinging leaves. Skin slippery his palms glide down my hips cupping buttocks pressing me tight his tongue laps, the snake laps my breast sharp sting and he sucks, sweat springing, serpent sliding over my belly slick glistening he bends me back into the leaves the night the pounding drums thrusting inside me darkness opening to swallow him swallow me –

I jolted upright, face damp with sweat, heart flailing against my ribs.

White room luminous with morning, walls glowing like sun through an eggshell. Warm air drifting scents of soap, mildew, overripe fruit. Bird trills beyond an open screened window.

I scrubbed at my eyes. *Victor Manden?* I groaned.

Levering myself out of bed, I strode barefoot out the door and around the side of the cottage to raise my face to the sun. Eyes closed, I took slow, careful breaths. I didn't know if the images came from Manden or from myself. Didn't know which was worse. An earthy fragrance simmered around me, teasing elusive recognition. I plucked a sprig of the perfumed white blossoms from a bush beneath one of the mahogany trees, stood absently shredding the flowers. I looked down at the stripped twig, flung it aside.

Feathery mimosa leaves rustled overhead. A big lizard clung to one bobbing branch, blinking beady eyes beneath a scaly forehead. Skin of gray plate-armor, spikes down its spine, whiplike banded tail a yard long. But the iguana looked peaceful enough, content to drowse in the sun.

"Hope your dreams are better than mine, Granddad."

The jeans hung on the clothesline stretched from the iguana's tree to the gatepost were still damp from a scrubbing the night before. When I'd finally unpacked the bags Laura or a maid must have packed to deliver here, I hadn't found the shirt I'd worn to the party-shack and muddied in my scramble from the petroglyph rock. It was a favorite casual shirt, cool white cotton with a thin striping of lavender.

Back inside, I picked up the note Laura had left:

"Susie, I don't know why you went running off to that grubby little hut! You'll miss out on all the fun. Seriously, you should come back and stay here, let me show you the ropes. Give me a buzz, Laura."

I'd assumed she'd be eager to get rid of me. Shrugging, I dropped the note on my table. The *Island Tattler* lay open there, where I'd thrown it down the night before in my agitation. Sport pages, a spread on the local karate club. Dark men snapped mid-kick, punching the air with powerful fists. A gaggle of grinning native kids in loose gees, a big, bearded Caucasian laughing as he tousled a pigtailed head. *"Vic Manden coaches the Junior Karate Kids."*

I couldn't align the face in the photo with the furious man who'd thrown me off his boat last night. With the violent ex-con, Vietnam-vet wacko, maybe drug-dealer, maybe murderer everyone was warning me about.

My head hurt. I paced the tiny room, sat with a cup of coffee at the table, stared at the newspaper, shoved it onto the floor. Plucking up my flute, I felt out a passage from the sheet music the mysterious Adrienne had thrust into my hands. How had Caviness known I played? Why would he bother to mention it to her? Mozart sparkled in the air with the random dust motes stirred by the ceiling fan, as good an answer as I was likely to find.

I put down the flute and picked up a framed family snapshot I'd set on the windowsill. Years-ago Christmas tree. Mom in an armchair, smiling, slender nervous hands for once still in her lap. Dad's lanky height behind her, pipe between his lips and a smile quirking the corners of his mouth. One hand rested on Mom's shoulder, the other on my older sister Ellen's. I stood a little apart, gangly teenager, chin set unattractively in what Dad called "the stubborn mode." John lounged on the rug at Mom's feet, head propped lazily on one forearm, lock of bright hair tumbled over his forehead. About to spring up, grab my hands, and dance me around the room as he improvised nonsense lyrics to a carol tune.

Eyes vivid with life. Like Vic Manden's. Too much? Life/Death. Some kind of equation? Did you always have to pay for pushing the limits? Manden *would* pay.

I smacked the photo face-down on the table. I had work to do. I'd made a vow on the plane, no ghosts would come between me and my work. Looking down on those sharp-edged islands, it had all seemed so clearly defined, the division between mind and heart so reasonable.

Laura's lazy voice as she stretched plump and naked in the summer grass at the Happy Valley farmhouse, "Integrating dualities into wholeness...." Had Laura known she was challenging a basic tenet of Western thought since Descartes? At the time, I hadn't realized what a perilous proposal it could be.

I shook my head impatiently, stuffed camera and tracing gear into the knapsack, threw on some clothes. There was one answer I was going to find that day. I was going to the party-shack and the petroglyph boulder Samuel had shown me. Back home, I'd watched rabbits cowering in fear, paralyzed by a hawk-shaped shadow. I wanted to know if I was only a rabbit.

Trapped air vibrated with the intense heat distilled by the black boulder. Above the distant barking of the big chained hound who was the only one home at the party-shack, a drone of mosquitoes circled and homed in. The forest pressed close with its green excess, leaves hanging limp, waiting for overdue rain. A tiny chartreuse lizard clung to the rock, doing lizard push-ups as it pulsed its scarlet throat pouch. With a flick of color it was gone.

The scarred rock face was twenty feet high, a nearly vertical curve to the ledge where Samuel had shown me the petroglyphs. I grasped the sharp edges of a diagonal crack, scrambling for leverage with my toes. The black surface seared my palms. I slipped once and slithered down partway before I caught myself, hands scraped and burning.

Drenched with sweat, I reached the top in a cloud of mosquitoes. I shrugged off the knapsack, wiped my face, and looked out over the trees. The rocky rim of the circular cove below enclosed a glimpse of dark blue water. Deep. The cliffs plunged almost straight down.

The petroglyphs were badly worn. My finger traced the incised lines of the peach-like face with its circular eyes. The rock burned in the noonday sun. There was power here. Only the power of the ancient and mysterious to create wonder? I wanted to know who had carved them, and why, wanted to trace their obscure links to lost cultures and secret rites. The carved faces kept stubbornly silent, guarding their knowledge.

Challenging the rock, or myself, I deliberately called up that night — the chill closing around me, carved eyes glowing into life, shadow men summoning me over the precipice.

Silence. Only the stone, waiting.

I scowled at the carvings. "You only come when my back's turned? Cheapskates!"

Dr. Phillip Holte: *"The ancients understood the power of the inexplicable, and gave room in their lives for it. The petroglyphs remain testimony, a gateway to the force residing in the rock and sea, mute only to our insistence on logic and the safety of a rigid order to reality...."*

I examined the carvings. The peach-like figure was clearly outlined, but the other was so worn it was barely recognizable as a circle with squiggly rays from the upper curve. A sun design. I doubted it would make a decent rubbing or photograph, but I went through the procedures on each figure.

Camera and cloth packed up in my knapsack, I stood, sweat crawling down my back. About to climb down, I turned to check under the brush for offerings like I'd found by the glyph at Fairview. In the tangle overhanging the exposed outcrop, a white thread clung to a bramble, one end stained rust-brown. I pushed past thorns and flowering vines to a glossy-leafed tree, partly-exposed roots clinging to the meager soil.

This time there were two of them. The little bags hung from the tree's lowest limb. The first was white cloth, smeared with dried blood, tied with a leather thong and feathers. The other was tied with a red ribbon, no stains on the feathers or cloth.

My pulse thudded in my ears, echoing the drum of my heart. The sun was blinding, unbearably hot. The second fetish bag was made from torn white fabric with a thin striping of lavender. The missing shirt I'd worn that night.

Fists clenched, I refused the reflexive jolt of alarm, of dread. Whatever was going on here, it was human work. I would simply not participate.

Pulling out the penknife attached to my keys, I stretched up, barely reaching the striped cloth. I jumped and grabbed the squishy bag, pulling the branch down to cut the red ribbon. A smell of rotted meat wafted. I stuffed the fetish into my knapsack. The mosquitoes were back with reinforcements.

The distant barking suddenly swelled. A heavy crashing through the brush near the outcrop. The barking became an exultant howl.

Ripping aside vines, I pried at a point of rock, tore it free of the dirt and hefted its weight. The hound burst into the opening below. He was a huge thing, brown and hairy. He hurled himself at the rock face, snapping in fury, claws scrabbling at stone. Momentum carried him up.

Teeth sliced air. He fell back. Again he howled, hurled himself up the steep wall, fell back. I gripped the jagged rock.

The dog snarled and barked and tried again. He found a grip with his hind legs, scrambling nearly to the top. He slid back. The barking picked up a deep tone of rage. He readied himself for another lunge.

"Down! Bast'dog, down!" A big man with matted dreadlocks strode out of the trees. The hound cringed against the rock, snarling. The man kicked him in the ribs and he cowered lower, teeth bared.

"Back you!" He pointed toward the shack. The animal skulked into the trees, waiting there, snarling fitfully.

The Dread tilted his head on a thick, powerful neck and glared up at me. My fingers tightened on the rock.

"Wha you do here?"

I swallowed, throat parched.

"Down you!" An angry scowl. "You! Down now!"

Reluctantly I dropped the rock, shouldered my knapsack, and crawled down.

His tangled hair glistened with sweat, hanging heavily over bloodshot eyes. "Wha you do here?" He pushed closer, cornering me against the rock. A sharp sweat smell closed around me with the heat off the stone.

I cleared my throat. "I came back to look at the carvings. I was here at a party the other night."

He grabbed my arm, shoving his face close and barking out the same question. "Wha you do here?"

I stiffened, made my voice assertive. "I told you. I was looking at the rock carvings. Now let me go."

He tightened his grip, hurting me. He bared crooked yellowed teeth. "Why you want dem?"

"I'm a scientist. I think they were carved by your African ancestors."

He snorted in contempt, pulling me closer until I could smell the marijuana in his breath. "Who bring you here?"

"A young boy. Well, actually, Laura Frankel. Leon Caviness's woman. Now let me go. You'll make trouble for yourself."

His fingers dug painfully into my arm. "Laura! *Erzulie Rouge!*" He spat and flung me away.

I fell against the rock face, knapsack slipping to the ground.

"You go!" He pointed toward the shack.

"After you."

He smiled nastily and whistled. The dog bounded from the trees as I bent to pick up the knapsack. It leaped to sink its teeth into the nylon bag and tear it from my grip, shaking it.

The camera. Without thinking, I grabbed a strap. The animal growled and tore at the knapsack, released it to take a swipe at my hand. I snatched the bag away as the sharp teeth closed over air.

"Down, you! Kill you, bast'dog!" He yanked it by the collar. I grabbed the knapsack, moving back until the rock stopped me. The hound lunged against the man's arm, growling, eager to get at the bag I was clutching. The fetish inside?

The Dread scowled. "Go now!" He pointed to the path.

"After you," I repeated.

He spat and dragged the dog into the trees. I followed at a distance, waiting until he had the brute chained before I climbed onto the dirt yard. The dog hurled himself to the end of the chain, barking hoarsely as I started up the steep trail.

"You!"

I looked back warily.

"Who boy?" His eyes narrowed.

"Just a young man. I don't know his name." Too late, I regretted mentioning Samuel. I turned and scrambled up the steep trail, the space between my shoulder-blades prickling. I could feel the man's stare on my back, piercing through the knapsack to the fetish hidden inside.

Twelve

"Like I said, better get one of these." Laura sat crosslegged on her beach towel, bare breasts tanned and gleaming with oil. She groped in her bag and flourished the pistol she'd aimed at me before.

I sat up, squinting against dazzles off the cove, and pushed the barrel down. "That's not a toy."

"You're telling me. This baby has some stopping power — three-eighty, semi-automatic. Here, take it, Leon'll buy me another one."

"No thanks. I don't want to become part of the problem."

"You're already part of it!" she snapped, tossing the pistol into her bag. She jammed on a pair of sunglasses and turned to bake her naked brown back.

I shook my head and smoothed sunscreen on my own deepening tan, gazing over the crescent of white sand, nodding palms, and scattering of nude sunbathers at Laura's "tourist-free" beach. I'd analyzed to pieces the few petroglyph designs I'd collected, brain numb with beating my head against research dead-ends, so I'd taken Laura up on her invitation to "cool out" with a swim. I was already starting to regret it.

"Well shit, Susie!" She rolled onto her side, facing me. "I'd have taken you back there if you had to see that rock again. I can't believe it, *you* finding Voodoo hexes under every rock! Get serious." She plucked up my notebook, reading quotations from the archives in a melodramatic voice.

"*Damballah! Damballah! The drums beat. Dancers ripple in torchlight like the serpent's back, and the drums become the dancers, the dancers the drums. Head darting from side to side, tongue flickering, the boy, the Horse, slithers past the drummers, rubbing out the veve patterns that had called the god....*

"The Bocor rules the cemetery with the help of black Baron Samedi. Someone may suddenly die, and the night of the funeral, the coffin is broken open and the body spirited away...."

She made a face and dropped the notebook. "Cheap movie."

"It's a religion in Haiti, it's not a joke."

"This ain't Haiti. What's got you so hot on the trail?" The sunglasses fixed on me, mirroring my warped image.

If she didn't know about the fetish bag made from my shirt, I wasn't about to fill her in. "I told you what Pat MacIntyre said about Caviness's cult. Laura, if he's got some kind of hold on you—"

"Pat!" A scornful twist of the lips. "I'd take it with a bucket of salt. She's gunning for Leon, just because he's trying to keep the natives from getting screwed one more time. So lay off him, he can be an arrogant prick but he's basically okay. He's done me some real favors. Cool out and catch the rays." She flopped onto her back.

I leaned on my elbows, staring over the cove. Turquoise water glimmered with sunlight and a swirling cat's-paw of wind.

Laura was an expert at rationalizing, but she was right about one thing. In the last few days, I'd exhausted local sources on the Vaudun and found nothing to indicate the cult existed here, or could be connected to the petroglyphs. Still, I couldn't shake the bone-deep feeling there was a hidden link. I kept on reading about Haiti, couldn't resist the stories of the many *loa* and their powers, the ecstatic ceremonies, the drums, the dances. The secret *Petro* societies headed by terrible Bocors who could create *zombis*, the living dead, or provide curses and poisonings with arcane ingredients like dried toads or chopped horse tail.

Crimson residue in a juice cup, glinting with broken glass and black whiskery bits — only a prank, at the airport? The dark magic could "put a power" on a victim, using fetishes made of clothing, hair, fingernail parings.

Or a torn shirt with lavender striping?

I couldn't ignore that fetish made from my shirt. It was real. I'd opened it to find a dessicated chicken foot, black pebbles, and a smelly goo smeared on leaves. If it was only an "herbal charm," who made it? Caviness? Why?

I sighed, sat up, and dabbed sunscreen on my shoulders.

"Do it right for Chrissake, you'll fry yourself out here." Laura took the tube and rubbed some onto my back. "Lie down." She pushed me down onto my towel. "Murder to burn your tits." She squeezed more cream on my chest and breasts, rubbing it in, hands sliding lower over my navel.

"I can manage." I took the tube, edging away.

"You're so uptight!" She slapped my hip and laughed. "What a waste, with that killer bod. Thought the tropics might thaw out that frigid little heart of yours."

"Drop it, Laura."

"Touchy, are we? S-E-X beneath you?"

I tossed down the tube. "Since you're so bothered about my sex life, yes, I do happen to enjoy it. Just because I don't go losing my mind and getting all tangled up in —"

"Losing your mind? Like John?" She pushed her face close. "Like me?"

"All right. Like you and Caviness. Now there's a healthy relationship."

"Healthy relationship! Sounds like some kind of house plant you're watering. Listen, Leon and I know how to play games, how to keep it hot. 'Nice' sex is a big fat bore, like that tame prof of yours. Admit it."

She was right, damn her.

"I could still set you up with Harrison, he'd show you some moves. Give him a whirl, Susie! He'll knock your socks off, I guarantee it."

"I'm not having this conversation." I rolled over onto my belly.

"So what *does* push your buttons?" Laura was relentless. "This Voodoo stuff? Kinky serpent gig?" She laughed. "Always said you were all airy fairy, but maybe John was right — said inside you were earth and fire, just needed opening it up. Brother and sister, ultimate elementals, him with his mutable water. Wanted to go with the flow, be a trip to take it all the way and fuck you —"

"For Christ's sake!" I sat up. "What is this incest obsession of yours? I can come up with a list of more interesting taboos, if you want to branch out."

Laura did have a gift in going for the jugular. Maybe my link with John *had* been a form of incest she couldn't imagine, an intimacy deeper than sex.

I still flinched at an old, queasy memory. Jolting awake one night in my teens, face burning as I futilely covered my eyes against a flash of visceral participation in what was clearly John's first sexual encounter, with a young divorced woman down the road from our family. After that, I'd gotten more disciplined about blocking off parts of my "tuner."

I hadn't wanted to look too closely at my first shocked reaction to that night's Link. I'd felt betrayed.

"Wake up, Susie!" Laura was shaking her head. "I've been trying to show you the scene, but you don't want to hear it. *Feel* it." She crouched on the beach towel, fingers digging in. "Let's get this out once and for all. You don't give a damn about me! You just want your golden-boy brother all tidied up in your mind like some goddamn file card. I fucked John, so I've got a piece of him you never had, and you want it, put everything in a little box all perfect. Well, you can't! My memories are *mine*." Her voice had gone shrill. "Trust me, you don't want them!"

"Laura." I caught her wrist. "What's wrong? What's going on here?"

Her hand was shaking in my grip. She wrenched free to face the sea, arms clasping her knees. Waves hissed over the sand.

Finally she sighed. "Okay. O*kay*. It's... maybe it's the island itself. It started out fun. So John and I were into partying, but it was under control. Until he got in with that Manden creep. He had John all pumped up to find that sunken treasure and be rich for life. Things changed then. I mean, it was a lark before, and now it was too intense. Manden had some big-time drug deals going...."

"I'm tired of all these vague hints."

She scowled. "John's the one who told me, Professor. Manden was torqued when John got wise to his cocaine deals, looked like Manden might be setting him up to take the heat. All I know is we were at The Keg one night and he comes in acting crazy, grabs John, shoves him up against the wall."

"Did he say anything?"

"He thought John was going to turn him in. 'You little shit!' He was screaming in his face. 'Think you're going to blackmail *me*? My boat ID'd on that delivery? I'll take you apart with my bare hands!'" Laura was staring past me, face gone blank. She shuddered. "Some guys pulled him away from John, and he took off."

"Who else saw it?"

She shot me a look. "Shelli Carver, for one. Ask her, you don't believe me. I think she tried to tell the cops later, but they just buried it like the rest of it."

"Those guys at the party-shack. Were they involved?"

"Them?" She waved a dismissing hand, watching the waves. "They're peanuts, cops questioned them after the drowning, didn't even bother with their penny-ante operation. Everybody here uses a little, it's like candy, no big deal."

"All that nose candy is taking its toll, Laura."

"So, okay, I've decided to cut down." Another shrug. She fixed the mirrored sunglasses on me. "Look, I don't have any proof about Manden. But if he thought I was going to rock the boat, he wouldn't blink about offing me. You know how some of those guys came back from Vietnam, killed so many people it doesn't mean a thing."

I couldn't make him add up. Dr. Jekyll, or Mr. Hyde? "If you're convinced Manden killed John, how can you ignore it?"

"Wise up! You'll only get us in trouble if you go stirring him up. You went to the cops, right? Big help." Her voice had gone shrill again, cracking. "I don't know what happened that night, but what good will it do now to find out? John's dead, damn it! He's *dead*!"

She ducked her face, shoulders shaking.

"Take it easy." I rose to my knees and put an awkward arm around her.

The shaking subsided. Pulling away, she scrubbed her face with a towel. She turned back to me, eyes finally naked, afraid. "Susie, stay away from Manden! We'll both end up like John."

"Laura, I have to know the truth."

"The truth! What the fuck's the truth? Christ, why do I even *try* to clue you in?" She pressed her balled-up fists against her head, hunching, making a strange, animal sound of pain. She straightened, leaned close to stare into my face.

Her eyes widened, pupils flaring dark and then shrinking to pinpoints. "That's it! You know something, don't you? Something you're not telling me. Don't you?" She grabbed my shoulders, nails digging in. "I can see it all over you. Now listen, bitch." Her lips pulled back in a snarl. "He's watching me, watching you, too! You keep poking around and get me killed, I swear I'll come back and haunt you. I'll make real sure you know what it's like to live in hell."

A dizzying blast of fear and rage hit me, and for a moment I was spinning into darkness, feeling my crimson-tipped fingers flex with Laura's desperation as they dug into my shoulders. Hot blood flowing over my hands.

I wrenched free.

Laura gave a harsh laugh, snatched up her things, and stalked off down the beach.

"Damn it!" I grabbed my swimming goggles and turned to the cool clarity of the sea.

Splashing through the shallows, I plunged in. Clean blue washed over me. I headed out from shore in a fast crawl to get the heart pumping, skin tingling. Rippled lights flowed by on the sand below as I loosened into rhythm, pulling in deep breaths. Rounding the breakwater, I swam parallel to the rocky shore, waves slapping against my face now. I stroked harder, deepening my kicks until I finally reached that perfectly weightless, flying place where muscles and breathing and air and water are all one seamless whole and time is only the present.

I swam, surrendering myself to the effort and the rhythm, until I was tired — the good, clean tired of physical work. I rolled onto my back and floated. One far, gauzy shred of cloud drifted through hot blue.

Taking my time on the way back, I savored the sliding coolness of the sea, the luminous clarity, the darting shadows of fish below. I'd tasted Laura's fear, it was genuine. But she was hiding something. And how had she known about my visit to the police? Only the island grapevine? Or was someone pressuring her to keep me quiet, stop me asking inconvenient questions? Why was everyone so insistent I stay away from Manden?

I filled my lungs and pushed toward the bottom, wishing the sea could wash away all the questions. I was sick of the whole mess. Maybe Laura was right, I should drop it.

A gleam of color on the rippled sea-bed caught my eye. Nearly buried, the yellow spiral of thin-walled shell pulled free with a trailing glitter of sand. Holding it, I surfaced and kicked in to the shallows, stood hip-deep to examine my find. The globe of the largest spiral filled my palm almost weightlessly, smaller twists narrowing to a fine point unblunted by the waves.

Sunlight ignited the shell's golden curves as I held it up. Warm caress of the breeze, whispering, *"All right!"*

"All right! What took you?" John's twelve-year-old voice trying for cool but cracking, grin crooked, mud-streaked face pale with pain. "Knew you'd come, Sis," he whispered.

He was lying in the mud and brush beside his flipped dirt bike, leg broken, partly sheltered from the cold rain by the overhanging cedar tree with the distinctive twisted branch that I'd seen so clearly from miles away in a vivid flash of urgency.

"You know you're not supposed to be riding these trails by yourself."

"Yeah." He snorted, then winced. "Same way you're not supposed to ride your horse by yourself out here?"

"Little snot!" I eased around his outstretched leg and hugged him. With a funny little catch in his throat, he hugged me fiercely back. "You'll always be there, won't you, Sue?"

I stood in the lapping waves, blinking against the salt sting, breathing in the bright hot air, feeling the silky kiss of the shimmering sea he would never swim again.

The sun-gold shell glowed in my palm. I'd been blessed or cursed with the Link to John ever since I could remember. I was meant to watch out for my brother, it was a sacred trust. And I'd failed. I'd lost him, lost a piece of myself. I owed us both those answers.

The *Wechsler Mart* was impossible to miss. Identical to the others of the island chain, glaringly lit in red-white-and-blue, it sprouted among the twilit palms and hibiscus like a toadstool. Open in the evening, a convenient breach of island etiquette, it offered such essentials of life as barbecued potato-chips, disposable lighters, and popsicles, just as the bouncy Mr. W. had promised. Returning from the swimming beach where I'd lingered until sunset, I pulled into the parking lot.

The cashier ran true to form, ignoring me and my can of fruit juice while she flirted with the young man slouching over the register. I started to count change, then picked up a copy of the biweekly *Tattler* I'd missed when it came out the day before. I left a dollar on the counter.

The girl finally noticed as I reached the door. "You got change!"

"No prob*lem*." I pushed through the door from air-conditioned chill to the muggy evening.

Sitting on a concrete wall to drink my mango-papaya juice, I glanced through the paper. The front page pursued the ongoing controversy over the local garbage dump. There was an amusing editorial by Shelli about Congressional committees that always met here in the dead of icy winter back home, accompanied by scantily-clad "aides" and generating a lot of "hot air," which the island already had, and ignoring "trivial distractions" like a twenty percent unemployment rate and welfare fraud.

A turn of the page, and the pretty young faces running for Carnivale Queen smiled up at me. I skimmed the cartoons, was about to throw the paper away when a photo on the back page grabbed me.

"Family grieves over sudden tragic loss of thirteen-year-old son.... Emergency staff labored in vain.... Unexplained fever.... Survived by

parents, Mr. and Mrs. H. Benjamin Simmons, brother Dwayne, 21, and sisters Lisette, 18, Marie, 16, and Clara, 15.... Funeral tomorrow at 2:00 pm."

Today. They'd already buried him.

"He's dead. It's too late, he's dead...." Laura's outburst rang silent echoes.

Samuel. The news photo was blurry, but it was the same boy. Crouching beside me on the petroglyph rock, trying to look tough. Gripping his fetish-necklace through his T-shirt, leather thong creasing his neck. His "ouanga-bag."

Two cloth bags hanging from a tree limb in the sweltering forest. The white one, smeared with bloody feathers, dangling from a leather thong. Samuel's? Had he hung it there for "power," or had someone taken it, smeared it with blood? Why hadn't the one made from my shirt received that bloody baptism?

I shivered. No Voodoo on this island?

There was a pay phone in the store. It worked.

"Susan! Ready to talk?" Shelli's voice boomed in my ear. "Hear you already moved. Too hot for you up at Fairview?"

"Shelli, I just picked up yesterday's paper. What do you know about Samuel Simmons' death?"

A pause. "You get around, don't you? Don't tell me you knew the kid?"

"I only just met him. But it's crazy, he looked perfectly healthy just a few days ago. Sweet kid."

"Nothing strange." Voice brisk. "These tropical fevers. Main thing is not to get a panic going. E.R. at the hospital's probably fighting them off with a stick right now, every kid with the sniffles hauled in with all the sisters and brothers and Grandma screaming she's gonna die, they should take her first for a magic shot."

A breathy snort. "Matter of fact, I'm on their shit-list. I let that article get by me without checking the wording."

"What was the diagnosis?" No magic shot for Samuel.

"Oh, they gave me a lot of smoke about chemistry tests and waiting for pathology reports from Puerto Rico. I wasn't exactly in the running for Miss Popularity over there, anyway, on account of a piece I ran about staff padding." The line crackled. "So pay up."

"What, you're wearing your Scarlet Letter?"

"I scratch your back, you scratch mine. I want to know what you dig up, and I don't mean old rocks. You've been asking around about Vic Manden and the cove where your brother got drowned. So guess what? I followed up on Manden's medical discharge out of Vietnam, he *was* in the Psych Unit. Think about it. Radical mood swings, uncontrollable temper, paranoia. Have to admit, I didn't figure it at first, he's a charmer when he wants.... Susan? They cut us off?"

"No." I cleared my throat. "Shelli, do you recall Manden threatening my brother in a bar?"

"Sure. At The Keg. Manden grabbed John, said he'd kill him. No joke, John was sweating all right. *I* was. Tried to clue the cops in after the drowning, but they just pooh-poohed it. Listen, kiddo, you and I should have that talk."

I gnawed my lip. "I guess so. I'll call you."

"Make it soon. Remember, no freebies. You owe me a story."

The connection died. I stood staring into the twilight. The phone started wailing and I hung it up. I took another look at Samuel's photo in the *Tattler*. The cashier and her boyfriend were still carrying on their lazy flirtation. I fished out another dime.

The switchboard operator at the hospital sounded swamped and irritable. I finally got connected to a night clerk when I said I was calling from the Health Science Department of the Caribbean Research Institute. An exasperated male voice with a Texas twang picked up. Before I could ask, he informed me they already had my message and the medical librarian would get back to me during the day shift. "I've got enough to do in the lab without taking these frigging calls."

I cleared my throat. "I'm not exactly thrilled with putting in a double shift! We've got to finish this study and you people keep saying you'll call back but you never do. Can't you give me a diagnosis on the Simmons case so we can close up the report?"

"So that's it. You'll just have to wait."

"Sounds familiar."

"Look, this time the docs really don't have a clue. Symptoms didn't add up, must be something bizarre. So we have to wait for those path reports, we're not equipped here to handle the exotic stuff. They're pretty sure it wasn't contagious, that's the main thing. Now if those screaming mamas in E.R. would just get the message...."

"Good luck."

He hung up.

I looked at the obituary one more time and laid the paper gently in the wastebasket. Heading for home on the Honda, I stopped at the crossroads. A magnolia tree, branches drooping with thick, creamy blossoms, hung over the road. I jumped from the bike, broke off a branch, and wedged it into the carrier. I took the turning for town.

The shops along the waterfront drive were shuttered and bolted, only the bars spilling music and tourists onto the shadowed wharf. The bay reflected faint purple to the darkening sky. I followed its curve past deserted dim streets, an empty schoolyard, a closed automotive center. I parked next to a wrought-iron gate set in low masonry walls.

Inside them, a miniature city of white houselike monuments. The cemetery lay hushed in the fading dusk. Stone glowed pale against pools of black shadow in the aisles between crypts.

In Haiti, if the family could afford it, they installed heavy stone crypts to keep a Bocor from stealing the body to make a *zombi* slave, one of the living dead.

I hesitated at the gate, glancing back at the deserted street. My fingers slipped into my pocket to touch the can of mace I'd bought after the encounter with the dog and the hostile Dread. Was it my fault, mentioning the boy? Had they gone after him, poisoned him?

"Slow down, girl," I muttered. Taking a deep breath, I pushed through the gate.

I wasn't alone in the cemetery. Along the far wall, where the tall, ornate crypts thinned out and gave way to simpler monuments, a low shape rested on freshly disturbed earth. The coffin and ground around it were covered with flowers. Two men sat on folding chairs, drinking from cups. I clutched my armful of blossoms, easing through a shaded alley between high, ghostly-white boxes. A whirring sound passed overhead, a bat making passes through the night. Despite the sultry evening, the shade in the narrow passage felt dank and cold. I walked faster.

Emerging into the open, I let out my breath. The bat swooped by again. The men looked up.

They froze, one crouching to light a lantern, the other with his cup raised to his mouth. The one with the cup dropped it, stood, and picked up a karate weapon, two short sticks connected with a chain.

"Who you come for?" The man by the lamp stood, too, voice gruff. The whites of his eyes glinted in the dusk.

I stepped from the shadows, holding out the waxy pale blossoms. "I'm a friend of Samuel's."

"Huh." A match scraped and the lantern flared, lighting a cooler and radio beside their chairs. They were both big men, dressed neatly in khaki pants and work shirts rolled up to reveal muscular arms.

"Who you be? Why you come now?" It was the man gripping the weapon, giving me a once-over as I stepped cautiously closer.

I cleared my throat. "I only just now read about him in the paper." I laid the magnolias among the other offerings, a pitiful gesture after all.

"You fool, gal. Lucky you find us, not dey Dread, not dey Rude town-boy."

I looked up to meet skeptical dark eyes. Suddenly I felt very small. The man could have modeled for a statue of an epic hero, everything on a giant scale and not an ounce of fat on him. He radiated power, but not the threatening, violent aura of the Rudes strutting around town.

I made a rueful gesture. "Guess I lost my head."

A dazzling smile, startling in the dimness. "You bes keep dat pretty ting." He picked up a chair, offered it to me. "You sit now, drink a rum foh Samuel."

I offered my hand. "I'm Susan."

"James." His huge hand engulfed mine. "Dis here Frederick."

The other man, burly but not on James's scale, wiped his hand on his pants and gave mine a brief squeeze. "You frien' of de family?"

I shook my head. "I'd just met Samuel. I couldn't believe it when I saw the newspaper." Or had it only been the jolt of recognition? Those swirling images out of the blue, stone demons and the boy's eyes gone blank glass, death finger pointing over the brink of the abyss –

"His mama like to lose her mind." Frederick poured some rum and Coke into a paper cup and handed it to me. "Now she got jus dat Dwayne." He snorted. "He be grief and moh grief."

"Don' got flap lip like some." James crossed his arms, gave Frederick a narrow-eyed look.

Frederick shrugged. "No secret he mix it up in dat bunch over West End. No good coming in dat, sure. See what come to young Samuel, he follow on Dwayne."

"You talkin' like ol' granny, you got Jumbie on de brain." James shook his head, raised his cup. "Now you drink up, gal."

I sipped, coughing on fiery rum.

"Hoo-whee!" A rumbling laugh from Frederick. "Dat de cure."

"What you do here on you own at night? You bes stay safe at de tourist place." James was sprawled on the grass, eyeing me.

"I'm living up on the mountain. I'm an archeologist, investigating petroglyphs."

"Dem ol rock to Palm Cay?"

"I see dem carve rock!" Frederick nodded. "Granny say dey power spot."

"Power spot?" I leaned forward. "What do you mean?"

"Dey say —"

"Huh!" James cut him off. "Don' you listen on Frederick, he jus 'fraid on dark, 'fraid on Jumbie hide under every little pebble."

Frederick scowled, massive fist pounding the flimsy armrest of his folding chair. "Now you diss me, dat one ting, James! You mind you mouth, you diss ol' Granny! Maybe Jumbie come foh you, maybe soul-stealer, he creepin' in de dark to take *you*, and you not be minding de ways!"

"Hssst!" James made a dismissive chopping motion.

"Frederick." I cleared my throat. "Are the carved rocks connected with Jumbies? What are they?" I wasn't sure, with the fast patois, if I'd heard him right. *Soul-stealer*?

James rolled to his feet, leaned over, and tuned in a local radio station. Reggae crackled. *"Jump, jump! Hands in de air...."*

He flashed white teeth, sliding into a dance step. "Carnivale song! Come now, Samuel not likin' all dis fool talk. We send him off right, raise a little party here." He reached down to take my hand and tug me out of the chair. One hand on his belly, he danced some swivel-hipped steps, pulling me toward him.

I shook my head, stepping back. "I'm not much of a dancer, I'm afraid."

"No fear, gal, you makin' bold tonight! You dance now foh Samuel. How you go Carnivale, you don' shake it up a little?" He tugged me closer again.

I gave in and started swaying to the lively beat.

"Hoo-ha! Dat de way!" Frederick raised his cup to us.

"Dat right. Here, you got to get moh loose, gal!" James laid his huge hand on my hip, guiding me into his movements.

"Jump, jump, every-body...." Tinny drums pulsed out of the radio, swelled our little circle of light, glimmering on rum-soaked waves, holding the dark night and the pale stone monuments at bay.

I danced, sweat springing on my face in the damp heat. Another song picked up the pace, drums pounding, claiming my feet. Hot surge up my spine to the serpentine sway, flash of James's glistening grin, *"Dat it, gal!"* and I was flowing with his loose-hipped lead, flowing with the rhythm pulsing up from the dark earth.

"Dance, dance, Hey!" A final crash of cymbals and steel drums.

"Hey, gal, you showin' dat big-head James how!" Frederick crowed.

Laughing, dizzy with the rum and a final spin from James's arm, I staggered, pushing my tumbled hair from my eyes. I came up short before the flower-covered coffin, the open earth grave.

I sucked in a shaky breath. "I guess I should get going."

James touched my shoulder. "Dat mighty fine send-off foh poor Samuel."

Frederick stood, beaming down at me.

I shook his hand. "Thank you." Turning, I peered past our fragile circle of light at the night settled over the tombs. I wasn't eager to retrace my steps through those dark aisles.

James stepped beside me, touched my arm. "No fear, Sweet Sue. Where you car? No body mess wi' you when James walkin' longside."

His powerful presence steered me through the rows of boxes shimmering dull silver in the night. No sign of the swooping bat. James, karate sticks and chain in his grip, chuckled when he saw the Honda. "Gal, you a case sure."

"James, why are you and Frederick staying by the grave?" *Soul-stealer*? Were they guarding the body from a Bocor?

"Don' you listen on dat Fredrick. We jus shows respect on dead."

"I see. Well, good night."

"Now you take care dat pretty little head, Sue." Teeth flashing, he touched me under the chin. "Come see me down de harbor. My boat, she *Sea Maid*."

"I will."

He stood tapping the wooden sticks against one leg as he watched me start up the motorcycle and ease forward.

I turned to wave. "Good night!"

He was already gone, melted into the shadows of the cemetery.

Thirteen

"*No problem*, bullshit!" I spun around, kicking the door to Police Headquarters as it slammed shut behind me.

This time Lieutenant Leland had had me bodily thrown out by a patrolman. He'd angrily dismissed my evidence about Samuel's death and Leon Caviness's cult. And confiscated the fetish bag made from my shirt. Right now he was probably sticking pins in it.

"Get a grip, Susan Dunne," I muttered, stomping down the steps. A young native woman in a poplin dress and matching hat pulled her children aside, shooting me an alarmed look.

I closed my eyes and bit my lip. *No ghosts would come between me and my work.* The puzzle pieces were only proliferating.

"There is no such thing as Voodoo on our island, Dr. Dunne!" Leland's scornful voice, lashing.

I took a deep breath of hot, asphalt-scented air. Now I had two reasons for finding Dr. Phillip Holte.

The decrepit outboard coughed as I throttled down to peer over the side of the rental dinghy. Only a thin veil of water covered the razor coral. I threaded a twisting path of deeper water, emerged between two exposed coral heads, and swung wide around a jutting headland.

Sheer cliffs dropped straight into deep turquoise water, sunlight inking shadow along fissures in bare rock. A lone sailboat lay at anchor.

The outboard sputtered and died as I let up on the throttle in surprise. No battered wooden boat weathering along with its eccentric old hermit. *La Sirene* was a sleek fiberglass vessel gleaming in reflected sealights, tugging in the swell at twin anchor lines and swaying a tall mast as if eager to be racing between islands.

An inflatable dinghy bobbed on a line behind it. Dr. Holte was home. I yanked on the cord, and the motor finally belched into life again. Chugging closer, I wondered if the old scholar would come out hostile like most of the islanders. Or, worse, feeble and forgetful.

A cat's-paw of wind ruffled the cove's clear blue. The stone walls towered close overhead, blazing with harsh light and black shadow. Rippling with watery reflections, the rock itself melted into dizzying waves. Shapes in the rocks heaving to the surface, looming over me, shadow hands reaching down.

I winced away from the blinding sun-dazzles and eased closer to the sailboat. "Hello?" I glided in toward the stern.

The boat rocked, a head appearing in the low hatchway. A man swung himself up onto the deck. He was average height, with the sort of blocky build that tends to go to fat in middle age, but hadn't. His arms and legs had the strong, corded look of a dedicated sailor. He was deeply tanned, barefoot, dressed in loose shorts and shirt, thick gray hair combed straight back off a square face. He stood feet apart, rocking easily with the boat, expression neutral.

Disappointment bit. The man looked to be in his fifties, and well-preserved at that. He couldn't be the elderly eccentric I was looking for. Counting on, like an idiot, to fill in some gaps in the petroglyph puzzle.

My dinghy slowed to a stop a few feet from the sailboat. Now the sun was behind the man. I shaded my eyes to peer up at the solid figure tilting with the swell. Dark, then a flare of sun rays, then the dark silhouette again. *Backlit shadow man turning in the waves, stalking me –*

Exasperated, I shook off the nightmare images, stuffed them, stomped them down. "Hello. I'm looking for Dr. Phillip Holte. Do you know him? Does he anchor near here?"

My dinghy drifted closer and I could see the man more clearly. If Leon Caviness was an intricately carved and elongated ebony statue, then this face was an oak block shaped with a few skilled cuts of an ax. It did not look welcoming.

The voice from that rough-cut figure came as a surprise, a tenor, syllables clipped and very British. "Be careful what you look for, Dr. Dunne. You just might find it."

"Pardon?"

"You've taken some pains to find me, and I don't fancy it was strictly for the pleasure of gazing rapt at my inspiring features. What is it you want?"

"Dr. Holte? But I thought you were.... I've read your papers."

He waved off the non sequitur. "Now that you're here, you needn't sit gawking. Hadn't thought I'd decayed quite to the museum-exhibit stage. You may as well come aboard."

With an agile thrust, he was down the metal ladder and standing on the narrow platform suspended from the stern. He gestured and I threw him my bow line. He tied a quick knot and pulled the dinghy to the platform, handing me out with a briskly formal air. He stood back, gesturing at the ladder, sketching a suggestion of a bow.

"Thank you."

"The pleasure is all mine, Dr. Dunne." A corner of his mouth quirked as he followed me up. "I say, it's just time for a gin and tonic. You'll join me?" A mocking undercurrent to the ultra-refined accents. The gray eyes under ironically tilted brows were somehow familiar.

Another little bow, and he retreated down the hatchway, to reappear in a moment with an elegant silver beverage tray. The Alice in Wonderland feeling was back. I nearly obeyed a ridiculous urge to curtsy as he displayed the tray with a flourish and set it on a stand. Tongs, flask, and seltzer bottle came into play to fill silver-rimmed crystal tumblers with an effervescent concoction. The deft motions of his weatherbeaten hands on the delicate crystal were incongruously fascinating.

"If I may propose a toast? We'll take 'God save the Queen' as assumed." His lips twitched as he raised his glass. "To the fruitful issue of your dreams."

I looked down at the cocktail in my hand, at my grubby shorts with the grease stain from the ornery outboard. I couldn't help it. I burst out laughing.

Unperturbed, he sipped his drink. Finally I caught my breath. Flushed, I leaned back against the cushioned bench, closing my eyes and wishing I could sink through the hull to the bottom of the cove.

"That's better. You looked so grim when you motored up, as if you'd girded your loins for tigers and lions at the very least." He raised his glass again. "Drink up, it'll help. I expect you've had a rough time of it on the island."

"It hasn't exactly been open arms. How did you know who I was?" I still couldn't believe this was the elusive Dr. Phillip Holte.

"Spies, Dr. Dunne. All over the bloody island." He chuckled. "I must say, if you've encountered one-tenth the resistance to your research that I found when I arrived here, I admire your persistence. Of course, you've already run the gauntlet at the archives."

"The archives! That's it, you were the man I barreled into that day!" I squinted, clothing him in an immaculate white suit and planter's hat.

"Of course I'd no idea why that young woman was storming the archives like Joan of Arc."

I was still shifting gears from my preconceived portrait of Dr. Holte. He seemed to be taking a perverse delight in further confounding the clueless Yankee with his Lord Peter Wimsey routine. I took a cold, bracing sip of the cocktail. "So you know why I'm here?"

"Dr. Dunne, you'd be surprised at all I know about you. I've been through it, you know. It's a thankless effort that will earn you only disappointment and derision. You've seen the reception awarded my theories. 'Biased and unfounded' was one of the milder attacks. Bloody fools, the only thing that could change their minds would be a lobotomy, if it weren't superfluous." A bitter note underlay his banter. "And, of course, there's the very real element of violence these days. If I may offer a purely clinical observation, you're precisely the sort of target the militant natives would choose. Young, fair, and very lovely."

Before I could protest, he continued, "You have no idea what you're getting into. A pretty smile won't help you here. The only advice I can give you is to leave, now, before you have to regret the wasted effort, or worse."

I stiffened. Setting the glass aside, I stood. "I'd hoped you might be interested in seeing your theory supported, but I'm prepared to continue on my own, of course. Thank you for your time, Dr. Holte." I turned to go.

"No, no!" He jumped up, gesturing. "Please, sit down. I was being bloody insufferable. Do tell me about your work. I understand your field has been Pacific Northwest tribes?"

"How did you —?"

"I told you. Spies." At least he hadn't said, "It's a small island."

There was nothing feeble or forgetful about Phillip Holte, as he mercilessly quizzed me on my research. I didn't mention John's glyph site. I wanted to verify it first, and I had to admit I'd enjoy surprising those skeptical gray eyes.

"Dr. Holte, I haven't been to Palm Cay yet. I've seen the pictures, of course, studying your paper on the parallels with Libyan script. Are you still working on your theory? Have you discovered anything new?"

A decisive motion with the blunt hands. "No, no, I'm done with all that. I'm just an old war horse, content to be put out to pasture." He gestured at the glimmering cove.

"I expected someone much older. You must have begun publishing in the cradle."

He looked disconcerted, then laughed. "You flatter me! I was one of those brats who enter university at a tender age." He shrugged. "Now, about those design correlations...."

"Actually, I've stumbled onto something that suggests an entirely new approach, but I'm not sure what to make of it." I told him about Samuel's petroglyphs and his "ouanga-bag," and my excursion to the cemetery where the men had mentioned the "soul-stealer."

"I've read your article about the Haitian Vaudun, and the Bocor –"

"That silly old piece of travel fluff?"

"Do you think there could be a connection between the Vaudun and the petroglyphs here? A local cult?"

He set his glass down, leaned back against the side of the boat, and closed his eyes for a moment. A warm breeze ruffled the clear surface of the cove and lifted a steel-gray strand over his forehead. He brushed it back impatiently. "I do hope you won't give in to the temptation to romanticize the native beliefs. Surprising how those Saturday matinee images survive the shell-fire of education."

"All the drums, snakes, and the doll with the pins? But surely you, of all people, can't deny the real Vaudun."

I wasn't about to share my nagging alarm about the other fetish made from my shirt, and the dark vibes I was tuning into here. Then he *would* think I was a silly Yank.

He was studying his steepled fingers. "It's difficult to convey to an outsider what Haiti was like back then, and the ceremonies."

"I've been wondering about the writers who claimed to have become Vaudun initiates. Could their observations ever be objective?"

"Shall we open that can of worms already?" An ambiguous smile. "The nature of reality? Do we know with our heads, or our hearts, our blood...?"

Disturbing echo of Laura's outburst at the beach. And Victor Manden's odd statement about diving into experience until it was too late to escape.

"We'll have none of it." Voice brisk. "Let's stick to scientific method, Point A to Point B." His eyes glinted under the shaggy brows. "Of course, I never immersed myself in the cult the way some of our colleagues *claimed* to have done." His lips twitched. "But I'm certain a grafting of the Vaudun wouldn't take here, with the Protestant heritage. All they have is a mild form of Obeah."

"Just herbal 'magic' and cures?"

"Quite so. The practitioner is generally a strong Grandmother figure. Fits the lingering matrifocal orientation, adapted to the modern welfare system and the absent male syndrome."

Holte was equally dismissive of Caviness's "cult." "Nothing more than theatrics to cement his influence among the poor natives, with the independence movement. He's an ambitious man, rather ruthless in using people for his own ends. Power can be a potent addiction." Glimmer of an ironic smile, then he was leaning forward, intent. "If you *do* come up with a significant find, you'd be wise to be circumspect, or you may find yourself a political pawn of Mr. Caviness."

"I certainly wouldn't advertise it."

"Good." He rubbed his hands briskly. "When shall we visit the Palm Cay petroglyphs? I'm afraid I'll be tied up with business for a few days. Damn nuisance, but I keep a demanding mistress."

I must have looked startled. He laughed and slapped the gleaming wood trim beside him. "This charming lady demands regular offerings and as much devotion as her namesake."

"*La Sirene*. One of the loa, isn't she? The spirit of the sea, the one the fishermen offer presents?"

A quick glance. "You've done your homework." He rose. "When I'm free we'll sail over to the cay. Bring along your photographs of the glyphs you've found so far." He frowned. "I do wish you'd let me accompany you on further forays into the bush. There *is* a real danger from the so-called 'Dreads' these days."

"I'll watch my step."

"Undaunted, I see." He lifted his palms in surrender.

I reached out to shake hands. "Terrific to finally meet you, Dr. Holte."

"Phillip." He held onto my hand. "May I call you Susan? Ours seems destined to be more than a formal relationship." His gaze lingered on mine.

"Of course." I retrieved my hand, wondering if he was tweaking me again.

"Good. Here you go." He handed me down the ladder and into the dinghy, gave it a push into the cove. "Until our little adventure then, Susan. I'll look forward to your charming company."

Drifting off, I bent over the outboard. He was watching from the top of the ladder, again a dark, blocky silhouette. A glint of teeth. The motor miraculously caught on the first pull.

I waved and chugged off through the razor-coral maze, humming the cheerful Mozart flute theme.

Fourteen

"Lookin' good, Babe. Hot hot."

Buoyed by my discussion with Phillip Holte, I cheerfully ignored the bleached-blond bartender lounging against a piling, picking his teeth and leering as I docked the rented dinghy at the seedy East End Marina.

A big iguana drowsed on a thorny branch overhanging my parked Honda. He could have been a twin to old Granddad, who'd climbed down from his mimosa tree that morning to investigate a piece of mango I'd set out for him. He'd accepted it with dignity, wattles bobbing as he moved ponderously to the cottage doorway to peer inside with heavy-lidded eyes.

"Lookin' good, Babe!" Imitating the bartender, I winked up at this iguana as I climbed onto my bike. He blinked and licked his scaly lips.

Humming Mozart again, I dipped and climbed the dry hills of the East End, spiky shrubs and stony outcrops sharp-edged in the shimmering sunlight. As I rounded a turn, heading down a steep hill, a glimmer in my handlebar mirror caught my eye. A rusty pickup, speeding down the slope at me, swelled in the mirror.

Used to the scare tactics by now, I edged closer to the left shoulder, keeping an eye on the mirror.

The pickup barreled closer, veering toward the shoulder, right behind me. Light lanced off its windshield. It was closing in on me fast. Heart leaping, I tried to pull onto the shoulder, started skidding, got back onto the pavement, shot a glance at the mirror to see the pickup almost on me. It wasn't swerving around me like they usually did at the last minute.

A side road appeared ahead. I managed to pull into it, skidding, pulse pounding in my ears as the pickup roared past in a cloud of dust. Glimpse of the dark driver, a bald head, gold chains.

Coughing, arms shaking, I waited. Cautiously I edged toward the main road. I pulled back onto the pavement, climbed the next hill past another side road, and picked up speed down a dip to a mangrove swamp.

Sharp flash in my mirror. My grip jumped on the handlebars. Rusty pickup. Same one? Hurtling even faster down the slope at me this time.

The truck bore down on me. Dense green and black shadows closed in with the ripe stink of the swamp. A sickening slide as I skidded in loose gravel on the shoulder, leaning, losing my balance but somehow recovering. The bike careened over potholes. Salt taste of blood as I bit my tongue. The truck's horn blared in my ears, almost on me.

In a startling green flash, a young iguana darted ahead of me onto the road, then froze.

I jounced the bike off the edge of the road, lurching up and over lumpy roots and in among sheltering trees. The dented pickup blasted past, bulky metal cargo shifting in the back. Impassive dark face behind the wheel, shiny bald head, glinting gold. The big lizard was still frozen on the right side of the road. The truck veered right to hit the iguana, then left again, screaming on up the hill and around a curve.

Jolting to a halt, barely missing a tree trunk, I straddled the bike, gasping for air and straining to hear the pickup return. Killing the iguana must have satisfied the driver.

Shadows shifted under the mangroves, my heart hammering. One vivid glimpse was stamped on my nerves. The cargo in the pickup bed: a corroded, antique anchor, cross-bar topped by a chunk of dead white coral the size and shape of a human skull. The same anchor I'd seen in Victor Manden's salvage yard.

The bike died, ticking into silence. Leaf shadow flickered, pulsing with the damp heat of the swamp.

I threw off the helmet, scrubbed a forearm over my sweaty face, and strode into the sunlight blazing over the road. The iguana was barely clinging to life, back broken and hind legs crushed. Its scales shimmered a complex pattern of bright greens that should have faded later into mature gray. Opening and closing its mouth in silent cries, it tried to drag itself along with its front legs.

If I moved it, I'd only hurt it more. Blood pooled, thickening on the baking road.

The lizard finally went still, and I pulled it into the mangroves. I didn't want to touch the mangled body, but it had been a beautiful animal, I couldn't leave it to be pulped into the road like another tossed paper bag or beer can.

The dense silence mocked me. The merciless sunlight pounded down, mosquitoes closing in with the overripe stink of the swamp. I could smell the iguana's blood. I wanted to wash my hands. Wanted to race to the sea and let the waves wash away the presence of the island. Heat haze shimmered off the paving, the red pool shivering into life. It suddenly surged, gushing over the road toward me.

*earth groans sky splits and the crimson deluge pours down. Shadow hands seize the iguana, sharp blade slicing its throat and red drops spray over the mob, avid faces tongues lapping the blood.

Drums pulse to a feverish beat. Strong hands crush roots, mix powders, place the flask on the cave altar with the smeared feathers and bones and shells, cloaked black rock and gold coins winking in torchlight with the white veve patterns.

The Bocor's face is a glinting gold mask, carved mouth gaping on darkness. He lifts a hollow skull brimming with blood, tilts it to my lips gagging hot sweet stink forcing it down my throat*

Waves of pain beat through my head, red sparks dancing. The blood tide was swamping me, pulsing against my dams. They were cracking. I could taste the primal glee as I struck back at John's killer, clawing his flesh to ribbons and wringing his pain and death into the steaming flood.

Maybe Laura was right — you could never be whole until you threw open the doors and embraced the darkness. Was this the shadow side of the Link? Had I made some blind Faustian bargain long ago, and now I was paying the price?

Shuddering, I pried my eyes open. I was sitting on the edge of the road, huddled with my head in my arms. I straightened, dreading to see my hands dripping with blood.

The fierce sun beat down, Mozart flute theme ringing an endless loop in my ears, transformed to a sinister minor key. Civilization was a joke. A rickety dam of sticks and rocks and concrete and steel alloys bulging before the mounting flood, little people running around frantically tacking on patches of poetry and penicillin and symphonies and martyrdoms across the pathetic shield. What was it for? What did it matter?

"*No man is an island.*"

With a shaky, rueful laugh, I pulled myself to my feet, patching together my own little rituals of purpose, blotting my forehead with a kerchief, pulling on the helmet, sipping tepid water from my plastic bottle. I had work to do. Somewhere there were answers. Starting up the bike, I eased onto the road.

Stop.

Sunlight stabbed reflections off the road sign, the harbor a blazing sheet of light in the midday heat. I couldn't remember taking the turnoff for town.

The Caribbean Research Institute. I'd planned to try them one more time. But the morning's enthusiasm had dried up. What difference did it make whether or not I found a sunken rock with some crude pictures carved on it?

The trickle of traffic swelled, sweeping me into town and the dusty crawl around the harbor. I passed the mast-choked marina, the Sea View Hotel, the graffiti-covered walls of the jungle-town on the other side of the road, simmering in the stink of ripe garbage and overflowing sewers. The police station's scowling bulk. A fitful breeze snagged a paper sack from the litter in the ditch and harried it across the street. At the intersection, a heavyset woman in a dark blue polyester uniform stopped me with her raised white glove. Over the rumble of motors, I heard my name called.

There, where sunburned tourists from a cruise ship overflowed the sidewalk. Victor Manden.

He hadn't seen me. Why would he call to me, anyway? He was stepping out of a bookstore with a package and a rolled paper tube under his arm, looking back at the doorway. A tall young woman in a white dress stepped into the sunlight. She was shaking her head, amused. Adrienne, Pat MacIntyre's adopted daughter.

The intense sunlight did nothing to diminish her exotic beauty. Her skin glowed golden-brown and her smooth face swayed to a graceful rhythm above the crowding tourists. She tilted her head close to Manden's, whispering.

He nodded, gesturing with the paper tube. Adrienne gave him an intent look and reached out her long fingers to touch his arm. She dropped her gaze, a smile curving her full lips.

Manden shook his head, an oddly gentle smile on his bearded face. He was opening his mouth when he abruptly stepped back, raising his face in a startled movement. His gaze locked on mine.

The smile was wiped off his face. I couldn't look away. I was flushed with the heat, with the electric punch to the gut the man could somehow send me even across the noisy traffic. His gaze stayed level on mine, lips compressed.

Honking behind me. Shouts. White gloves gestured impatiently. Lurching forward on the Honda, I glanced back to see Adrienne turning with surprise to Manden. She saw me then, fixed me with a penetrating stare, and raised one hand in a strangely hieratic gesture. The traffic swept me past.

I numbly followed the harbor's curve until the flow of cars let me pull off into a parking lot. The bay shimmered before me, boats trailing white wakes across turquoise water, ripples fading behind.

A steep, loaf-shaped little island sheltered the harbor from the open sea. Treasure Island. John had worked at the resort that owned it, teaching Scuba with Frank Savetti.

I'd already taken the shuttle boat over there, only to learn that Savetti was gone on a sailing trip "down island." He was probably my last contact to John here, my last chance to find out about the petroglyph cove. Maybe I was glad to postpone one last disappointment. I'd never find out from Manden, I'd burned that bridge. Maybe he *was* crazy. Why had he looked so startled to see me? Why had his anchor been in that careening truck? No such thing as coincidence here, he'd said. And what was he doing with Pat MacIntyre's beautiful daughter, smiling so –

"Sweet Sue!"

I spun, squinting over the crowded quay for the source of the deep voice.

"Sue. Hey, gal!" A big native man lounged against the gunwale of a wooden cargo boat with bright blue paint and *Sea Maid* in yellow. Flash of white teeth against skin so dark it gleamed polished blue-black in the sunlight.

"James!" I waved at the man who'd danced with me beside Samuel's grave. Sidestepping a truck backing onto the quay with a towering stack of beer crates, I eased through launch passengers and native crewmen unloading banana bunches and straw baskets of coconuts from local cargo boats.

"You come foh you next lesson, gal?" James ran a hand over his close-cropped head and did a swaying dance step on deck. "Got to be set foh Carnivale."

Punch-drunk from alarm, adrenaline, and confusion, I found myself beaming up at the big native, grateful for his friendly grin. "James, it's good to see you."

"Dis de happenin' place, gal." A dazzling smile. "You like fresh?" He pulled a plump mango from a basket and held it up. "Fine as Sweet Sue." Whipping out a knife, he sliced the fruit in half, handed down a dripping piece. "You eats dese fruit, dey *talkin'* to you. Tell me I lie."

The fruit was warm, lush, scented sweetness curling around my tongue and sliding indecently delicious down my throat. I licked my lips.

"So! What she say inside dere?" He wiped juice from his chin and cocked his head, listening.

I shrugged. "Don' you worry 'bout no ting."

He threw back his head and laughed.

I had to laugh with him. It didn't matter, he couldn't be real. Rising and dipping with the boat's sway, he towered above me, sunlight pouring over him to emphasize the sheer scale of his giant frame. On a purely esthetic level, the man could only be called gorgeous.

"All right! We get you fix up here." He whipped out a burlap sack and vaulted over the boat's rail. "Come, gal."

We were off on a tour of his friends' boats, the sack loading up with mangoes, three kinds of bananas, coconut, pineapple, and some sort of hairy oversized berries.

"Sweetest fruit, you finds it right here!" Rocko, the last one, slapped a callused hand on his boat's stern. "You come see me, gal! Dat James, he jus break you heart." He winked.

"No breakin' cept I break you fool head, Rocko." He escorted me back to his boat, swinging the heavy sack onto its deck as if it were filled with feathers. "Now you an me go get us lunch. You lookin' puny, gal."

James was an inevitable force of nature. I found myself being shepherded through the shopping district and into the native jungle-town behind it, threading narrow cobbled streets between peeling plastered walls. Sauntering along, he grinned down from his height at the natives who paused suspiciously to eye me. He called out greetings to women in upstairs windows and teased the big-eyed kids playing games in the streets. Even the packs of prowling Rudes, with their dreadlocks and hivelike knit caps, boom-boxes blasting reggae, and slit T-shirts showing off pectorals and gold chains, parted like the Red Sea before him. James was my ticket to the neighborhood that was officially "suicide for Continentals."

We passed through a crumbling brick archway and down a stifling passage between buildings. A faded wooden sign, *Le Lambi*, pointed the way up plank steps onto a thatch-covered landing. An old dugout *pirogue*, hacked crudely from a mahogany log in the style of the original Caribs, hung from the rafters. Beneath it, an elderly man snored on a bench, face the color of the age-blackened wood.

Past him, a dim room with five assorted tables. A plump, sleepy young woman in a tight red sarong presided over the bar.

"Good day, Lisabet. An how you be dis fine afternoon?" James gave the curvacious bartender his heart-stopping smile.

She sniffed at me, shrugged, and picked up a glass to polish with a towel.

He sauntered over to the table beside the one dingy window, pulling out a chair for me. "I go talk to de cook."

I sat fanning myself with a cardboard beer ad. The decor featured grass thatching hung from the bar and ceiling, a tinseled rope looped around the walls and wound with blinking Christmas lights, a poster of Superman (Caucasian), dusty plastic flowers in Dixie cups, and a jumble of dried puffer fish, shells, sea fans, and liquor bottles on the bar. Among them, what appeared to be a genuine human skull grinned over at me.

From a couple of tables filled with native men, fast patois and snorting laughter. It cut off as James reappeared from behind a plywood partition screening the kitchen area of the dim room.

"You in foh a wake up, gal," he announced.

I swung around, eyes widening as I took in the white designs painted on the partition beside him. Geometric shapes — diamonds, interlocking triangles, filigreed spikes, dotted spirals.

Veve patterns. Voodoo.

James stepped closer, towering over me and reaching down a huge hand. The one naked overhead bulb and the twinkly little Christmas lights suddenly died. The room plunged into darkness.

For a black moment, I ricocheted wildly among generic scare stories for women, and the island warnings about jungle-town. I jumped up in a general clatter of chairs. Hysterical vision of flinging off my clothes in a convenient phone booth to emerge as Superwoman.

An enraged shriek from the kitchen. James chuckled, patting my arm.

I sat with a thump. My eyes had adjusted to the sketchy window light. An enormous shape engulfed in a ghostly apron flew out from behind the partition, waving a wooden spoon. The men at the other tables struck matches to candles stuck here and there with wax globs. A red candle flared, crimson dripping down the cheekbones of another empty-eyed skull. Wavering lights threw grotesque shadows of the cook and bartender carrying on a heated exchange in what sounded like a French dialect. The cook finally retreated behind the partition. The bartender flounced back to her bottles.

"Every body come home foh lunch, turn on de stove, and boom out go de power. Dey cook on gas here, we be fine."

The sulking bartender eventually brought us warm Elephant Beers. She smacked the bottles down and turned away with a peevish twitch of the hips.

James looked pleased. "Drink up, gal. You gon' eat de bes food on de island."

The big cook swept out with a tray and laid heaping platters before us, plenty for four or five people. I looked up from the dishes, glancing at the smirking men across the room. "You invited your friends?"

"Eat up, little Sue! You lookin' puny. How you find a man watch over you, an you not got plenty soft pillow foh his weary head?"

I picked up my fork. "Guess I'll have to find a man who's not so weary."

He looked taken-aback, then slapped his leg and laughed. "Whoo-whee! You a case sure." He touched my arm. "Now you dig in."

I didn't need urging. There was a rich soup with conch and "root" and "kallaloo." A huge pile of seasoned rice with round black peas and pungent bits of peppers and chicken. A mound of "fungi," a firm mixture of corn meal and okra that looked terrible but tasted wonderful with fish sauce spooned over it. Fried little pastry pies with "salt-fish" inside. Cooked plantains with a syrupy coating.

"Ooph. I just died and went to Heaven." I leaned back in a daze of beer and gluttony.

"We jus startin' on you, gal. You gon' lively up here." He flashed a lot of white teeth.

I smiled back, allowing myself the added indulgence of a frivolous fantasy or two.

He leaned forward, suddenly severe. "Now you tell James. What you do in dat bone yard, why you askin' dem question? What got you spirit all confuse?"

I studied my hands, finally lifting them. "It's a mess."

"Dat de way with life. Plenty messy." He sat back. "You carryin' a heavy load. You let James help."

Maybe I was more like John than I'd thought. My instincts told me I could trust James, so I decided to "go with the flow." I told him about the threatening Dreads, the rumors of Caviness's cult, and the pickup nearly running me off the road.

"And poor little Samuel!" I dug knuckles into my throbbing forehead. "Maybe it was my fault for going back to the petroglyphs he'd shown me."

"Fool talk! An worse fool you, goin' roun lone like dat. You find ting you don' want."

"James, what are those cloth bags for?"

He picked up his fork. "Jus ol' herb-granny charm."

"But why would someone make one from my shirt? Why was Frederick afraid of the 'soul-stealer' that night in the cemetery?"

He set down the fork. "Fredrick, he jus open mouth and mind be sleepin.' Me, I don' look trouble in de face, he don' come foh me." He gave me a shrewd look. "You maybe jus too curious, like de cat."

"Maybe I am. But my brother died here, supposedly drowned by accident. Now I'm not so sure it was accidental. I have to find out."

He looked surprised, reaching out to squeeze my hand. "You be sorrowin'."

Eyes stinging, I looked down. "Sometimes I still can't believe it. John was so *alive*."

"John? John Dunne? You brother?"

"That's right." I raised my face. "Did you know him?"

That too-familiar, guarded look had come into his eyes. What the hell was wrong with this place? He looked away, looked back, laid his hands flat on the table. "I hears 'bout he be drown, all de island talkin.'"

I leaned forward. "He was excavating a wrecked ship in a cove here called Ship Bay, but it's not on any map. I have to find it."

"You stay 'way from dat cove!" His vehemence made the tinsel ceiling strips shiver. "Dat one bad place. You brother he lookin' foh trouble, divin' there and no body foh help when he drown."

"I *have* to find Ship Bay, there are important petroglyphs there."

"You jus bound, gal! Member dat cat what too curious. Dat de Brotherhood place, dey mad since you brother go dyin' dere, you got to stay clear."

"Do you think there are bad Jumbies there? Frederick seemed to think they lived in the carved rocks."

He snorted. "Don' know Jumbie. Be powers all 'roun, us namin' good or bad, who say? Maybe dey live in dem stone, maybe not. Dey be plenty moh carve rock, I know one bro he take you 'roun."

He jabbed his fork at my half-emptied plate. "Now you stop broodin' on crazy notions. You don' eat up —" he tilted his head toward the partitioned cook's domain — "dat Francine she put a wrath on us. *Dat* one bad power, you be sure!"

I pushed away my plate, groaning, head swirling from a second potent Elephant Beer. The cook waddled out, shaking her head over my pitiful efforts as she cleared the table. A couple of men wandered over with a box of dominoes. I leaned back and drowsily watched them slap the counters around as they tossed outrageous insults back and forth in their fast patois.

Rubbing the persistent ache in my forehead, I went over to the bar. "James was right. That was the best food on the island."

The young woman sniffed, pouting over her nail file.

"My name's Susan. You're Lisabet?" I glanced from the grinning skulls to the *veve* designs on the room divider. "Are you from Haiti?"

She looked up, startled. "Wha' dat James talk?"

"Nothing. I've seen pictures of designs like those before." Some Haitians decorated their houses with the patterns, too. "Have you been on the island long?"

She gave me a suspicious look and bent over the file, casting a smoldering glance at James.

He looked up, gaze lingering on Lisabet's curves in the crimson dress. A slow smile spread over his handsome face.

I was suddenly very far from the stifling little room, floating among cool clouds, looking down on the scene. Dark men in unbuttoned work shirts gleefully slapping down dominoes, shouting, punching each other's arms. James dwarfing the wooden chair, throwing back his head to laugh at a fast-slurred insult. Lisabet shifting sensuously on her stool, brown breasts straining the tight sarong, full lips pouting. Pale and cool among my northern clouds, I was no match for their tropic heat.

I shrugged and smiled, turning back to the bartender. "If I were you, I wouldn't let that one get away." I tilted my head toward James snapping a domino onto the table.

She gave me a look, glanced over at James, and laughed, her whole body participating. "Wha' you drinkin,' gal? On de house."

"Do you have any coffee? Aspirin? I can't seem to get rid of these headaches."

She pursed her lips. "Dat no good, chile." She spooned some instant into a cup. "Got no med'cine?"

I took a sip of tepid coffee. "I tried the clinic. They just told me to take aspirin and rest."

She snorted. "Dey fool doctor don' know nuthin.' Puff-up foolish. Now Granny she cure all ting wha' dey jus throw up dey hand."

"Granny?" I looked up. "Do you think I could see her?"

She shrugged, picking up a glass to polish with her towel.

I sighed and rummaged in my bag for an aspirin.

She glanced over at the table, leaning close to whisper, "You go ask Willy. He de boy to ice cream stand, nex' de big store, DeGraf by park. You say Lisabet send you." She straightened with a sly smile. "You go see Granny, you find wha' you askin' foh...."

"Who talkin' dat ol' Granny now?" James was standing behind me, smacking a hand onto the bar. "What you talkin,' Lisabet?"

She tossed her head and cast him a heavy-lidded look. "Never you mind. We jus' talkin' gal talk."

Fifteen

"So that's who made these murderous trails." Puffing and sweat-drenched, swatting at mosquitoes, I pushed through pink-blossomed brambles onto the high rock outcrop.

The spotted goat lifted his triangular head, fixing me with a yellow stare. Kneeling beside him, Conrad echoed the movement, raising his light-brown freckled face and hazel eyes. Man and goat merged for an eerie moment in the same watchful expression. I stopped short.

Conrad patted the goat. Bleating, it scampered off through the brush.

"Friend of yours?"

Conrad chuckled and stood, long reddish dreadlocks swaying. "Jah say bless all de creature and de plant. I-an-I all come to Zion." He gestured east over the panaroma of distant sea.

I dropped my knapsack and stepped down beside him to look out over the steep flood of green to waves crashing on black rock far below. I took a deep breath of hot flower scents. My guide smiled and turned to point behind me.

"Conrad! It's a beauty."

For the past week, I'd followed him up and down countless steep, overgrown paths crisscrossing the mountain. I hadn't managed to coax more than a few words out of the young man. He didn't seem to require many. But I had a nice collection going, a variety of petroglyph designs from small, isolated carvings, most of them with a view to the sea. Conrad specialized in high, lonely places.

He'd saved the best glyph for last. A little gem of a bird figure, well-preserved, etched in lively curves.

I finished taking a rubbing and sat down on the warm rock, leaning back into feathery mimosa shade. Hidden birds rustled and chattered among the leaves.

Conrad sat cross-legged and pulled off his damp shirt, dreadlocks dangling over bony shoulders as he strung crimson seeds on a nylon line. He sold the pretty shell and seed necklaces at the tourist market where James had introduced us, telling me, "He be study on dey Rasta-mans, but he no Dread. He keep you out of trouble you be nosin' like dat cat."

I offered Conrad my water bottle and he smiled, nodding thanks. Setting the string aside, he pulled out a fat reefer and lit it up, inhaling with a sharp hiss. He raised it with a questioning movement toward me.

I started to refuse once more, then shrugged and accepted it, taking a musky pull. I settled back on my elbows in the drowsy heat, smoke easing through me. Silence but for the rustle of boughs and lazy bird-chitter. Lacy leaves glowed vibrant green against searing blue sky. Scarlet blossoms glimmered in sunlight. No trace of cloud. I sank lower against the warm stone, its deep mass cradling me.

low hum, distant shush of the sea, dark stone soaking in the sun's power. Light shimmering. Leaves sprouting, bursting lush from the plateau and its whispering secret springs. Burgeoning in Her hands the giant rock figure cups the vines and dripping blossoms, the goat, Conrad, me, the shiny red seeds. Immense carved face lifts to the sun eyes bottomless wells the leaves ferns trees clothing Her mountainous mass, flowing down Her flanks, rich green, rocking to the pulsing deep hum

"Hmmm." I blinked, drowsily sat up to see Conrad giving me a slow smile.

I rubbed my eyes. "Do many people visit these carvings, Conrad?"

A shrug. "Some do."

"Is this a power spot? Do Jumbies live here?" I hadn't seen any more ouanga-bags hanging beside the petroglyphs.

He grinned, shook his head, spread his hands. He rose to his feet and took my hand, leading me through the underbrush beneath the trees. He showed me how to pick pods for the crimson seeds he'd been stringing. Rooting through the bushes, he beckoned me closer, breaking open another pod. He held out two handfuls of the shiny red seeds.

As I reached out to touch them, he shook his head, holding up his hands side by side. The second handful had a tiny black spot on each seed.

He held up that hand. "Crab eye." He threw them away into the bushes and wiped his hand down his pants. "Dey bad, dey poison. Make necklace and dey slow can kill. Chew one seed and die. But leaf foh cold be good tea, hot bath foh soakin' ache." From Conrad, it was a long speech.

I pointed at the handful he'd kept. "And these?"

"Foh Missy Sue." He gave me a sly look. "Keep mischief clear. Jumbie seed."

He chuckled and ducked his head, leading the way back to the petroglyph. He sprinkled the seeds over the bird carving, red gleaming wetly on dark stone. He murmured, "I-an-I do praise."

With a shy smile, he lifted the necklace he'd strung that day, scarlet Jumbie seeds set off by flat black pods. He draped the strand around my neck. "Jah bless. Keep she safe."

Main Street was a hot blaze of color and noise outside the air-conditioned camera shop where I'd dropped off my petroglyph film to be developed. The flow of shoppers swept me down the narrow sidewalk and through an archway onto a bricked passage between buildings, a shortcut to the harbor. Along one side, mimosa saplings in planters shaded wrought-iron tables. Neon pink ruffles overflowed one of the chairs, dripping off freckled shoulders.

"Shelli."

She craned sideways, revealing the woman sitting with her. Pat MacIntyre.

"Susan! Take a load off." Shelli pulled her straw bag off an empty chair. "What did I say, Pat? You sit here long enough, the whole damn island cruises past. I always get a story." She flagged down a waiter and ordered more drinks.

Pat drained the one she held. "Solve your mysteries, Susan? You know, carved rocks, eccentric old hermit scholars?" She pulled a cigarette from a pack on the table, tamped and lit it, fingers fumbling. She blew out a cloud of smoke.

The waiter set something frothy with two straws, a paper parasol, and a chunk of pineapple in front of me.

Shelli helped herself to Pat's cigarettes, glance jumping from the resort owner to me. "Pat here's giving me the skinny on the West End rezoning effort, looks like Leon Caviness is pulling some slippery moves on the committee."

"Slippery moves, my ass! He's outright passing our plans straight to the Independence agitators. Fanning the flames."

"Sure you don't have anything to add to the record, Susan?" Shelli leaned toward me. "What's going on at the Great-House?"

"I've already told you, I'm not involved."

"Bullshit!" Pat smacked down her glass. "This is an island, Susan, everybody knows what you're up to. You've got to make up your mind whose side you're on."

"I'm not on any sides." I took a sip of the overly-sweet rum concoction.

"Don't play innocent." Shelli's eyes narrowed between stripes of bright blue liner. "What's your connection with the Simmons family, and those other natives you've been hanging out with? What's your angle on the latest newsflash?"

"Which news?"

Shelli tapped a folded *Tattler* on the table. "Check out today's edition. Another death in the Simmons family. Dwayne, the big Rude brother."

I stared at her. "Maybe Samuel had something contagious, after all."

"That's one way to put it." Pat's raspy voice was heavy on the irony. "Seems Dwayne got his throat cut."

"What?!"

"So what do *you* think's going on, Susan?" Shelli leaned closer. "Come on, level. I know he was one of Laura's little diversions. Drug dealer. Liked to flash his muscle at that same karate club where...." She was looking past my shoulder. "Well, speak of the devil."

Pat peered around me. Face gone blank, she plucked up her glass.

I turned on my chair and met Victor Manden's gaze. He came up short, flushing darker beneath the deep tan. He shot a glance over Pat and Shelli, spun on his heel, and started pushing through the crowd.

"Manden, what's the big rush?" Shelli was out of her chair and across the bricks with surprising speed. She grabbed his arm. "Sit down and have a drink, tell us how's business. A little advertising never hurts. But then maybe in your line you don't want any?" She grinned up at him. "What's your take on our latest island murder? Or should I say *accident*?"

He swung around, lips pressed into a scornful line behind the beard. He glared at me, shook Shelli off, and strode away.

"Frank, she looks just like John!" Tears sprang into the pale-blue eyes of the wispy blonde. She darted around the counter of the Treasure Island dive shop and threw her arms around me, leaning her head against my chest as she sobbed. A cloying cloud of coconut oil and patchouli enveloped me.

I fell back a step with the woman still attached, making ineffectual patting, warding-off motions.

Frank Savetti laughed heartily. "Mary likes to emote." The wiry diver peeled her off me. "That horse's ass John never told me his sister was a knockout!" He grinned through a dark bandolero mustache.

"We heard you were here, Sue." Mary smiled through her tears, rushing on in a high, little-girl voice, "We really miss John." She sighed. "He had such a fresh, young soul, I knew he wasn't destined for this world."

Behind her, Frank rolled his eyes. "Mary's into past-lives."

She grasped my hand. "You have to come up for dinner! I'll do my lobster curry, it was Laura and John's favorite. In the evening, we'd all cool out on the big mattress on our deck. You'll love our place, Sue, it's like a treehouse out on the West End, perched up looking out, we even get a breeze. Sometimes when I'm quiet there, I can still feel John hanging around." She sighed. "He was such a dreamy fuck."

"Pardon?"

She smiled beatifically. "He was so totally *in* his body. And he had such a beautiful cock, too, pure light inside me. Like riding a dolphin. Tuned into the joy of it, never trying to rush things. Not like Laura, I know she's really hot, all that serpent energy, but sometimes she was so, I don't know, *driving* about it...."

I stood goggling down at her.

Frank laughed, tugging her back. "Chill, Mary, maybe she's not into the group scene."

She looked puzzled. "You're not into sharing?" Turning to Frank, she put her hands on her hips. "But I can *feel* it in her! Powerful kundalini all coiled up. I bet if we all laid back with that fantastic new bud you got from the Dreads —"

"Come on, Mary. You've got to get the afternoon divers signed up, remember?" Frank steered her back behind the counter. "Now what the hell did I do with that...." Ducking under a draped fishnet filled with snorkels and beach balls, he groped through drawers. Behind him, the wall displayed T-shirts with the Treasure Island skull-and-crossbones logo or cute native sayings. SEX IS A MISDEMEANOR – *de more I miss it, de meaner I gets.*

"Ha!" Frank pulled out a small object wrapped in a kerchief. "Sue can help me deliver the demo gear." He shot me a wink.

"Oh. Okay!" Mary gave me a dazzling smile. "We'll do it soon, Sue!"

Outside the red-painted door with the white diver's slash-mark, I blew out a long breath.

Frank squeezed my arm. "She's revved, seeing you. She really dug John."

"I gathered."

He eyed me. "Man, this is a weird trip! You look so much like him, but...."

"I know."

"Hey, no complaints!" A comical leer, brown eyes dancing in his sunbaked face. "Island'll shake you loose. C'mon." Barefoot on the searing concrete quay, he hustled me past the departing resort ferry sporting shiny crimson paint, a red-and-white striped awning, a Jolly Roger and Muzak Calypso trailing off the stern. Frank climbed behind the wheel of a mini pickup, waving me around to the other side. I was closing the door as he shot into reverse, burned rubber out of the lot, and tore into a steep road winding up the hill to the hotel.

"Here." He reached into a picnic cooler, thrusting a couple of Elephant Beers at me. "Opener in the glove compartment." He careened around a switchback.

Taking the opened bottle I offered, he tilted it in a long swallow, propped the bottle between his bare thighs, and dug into a crumpled bag of peanut candy. "Balanced lunch — vitamin 'B' and protein."

With a shudder, I popped the other beer. "How long have you been on the island, Frank?"

"Six or eight years, I guess." Swigging, he squealed through a turn.

"You don't get 'rock fever'?"

"What's to get tired of?" He swerved past a startled gardener. "Always something wild going on. You drive as fast as the roads let you, work when you want, forget about shoes. Never run out of sun, cheap booze, parties, good diving, lobster and conch. And pretty ladies." He raised his bottle to me and drained it.

"Look." We'd come over the crest onto a parking strip with a view over the outer side of the island. Below, the brilliant sea pawed at the rocky shore and a breakwater shielding a golden curve of beach. "Welcome to paradise."

He pulled to a stop and turned to face me. "So, okay, we've got a big mark against us since John bit it. But he was having a blast here. He could've bought it just as easy, getting hit by some old fart with cataracts and a Rambler in good old Straightville, Washington. He was *alive* here."

I bit my lip and nodded.

"Hey, I hear Laura and her crowd's been giving you the royal runaround. Fuck-heads. Here." He fumbled on the seat, pulled out the little bundle wrapped in a red kerchief. "You should have something good to remember John by."

Wrapped in the cloth was a delicate little perfume bottle, clear glass curved into a graceful hourglass shape. Each flattened side had a different design pressed in, on one side curling vines and flowers, and on the other a geometric lattice. Sunlight sparked iridescent rainbows in the antique glass.

"It's beautiful."

"John found it on one of our dives in the harbor. Bunches of ships got wrecked in a hurricane a couple hundred years ago, now they're all ground up after they dredged the harbor for the cruise ships. Once in a while you get lucky and find something choice. Illegal as hell diving there, don't advertise it." He winked.

My finger traced the curling glass vines. "It really should be in a museum."

"Bingo!" He slapped his thigh. "That's what he said you'd say. I remember, we were having a blast, John really got stoked diving those wrecks, had the treasure bug bad. He was laughing, showing off that bottle and a silver piece of eight he'd found. Then all of a sudden he went serious on me, mooning over that bottle, said he wished he could give it to you, but you'd probably just hand it over to some moldy old museum where it'd sit locked up in a cabinet with the life sucked out of it. Knew you'd really want to keep it, use it."

Throat tight, eyes stinging, I gripped the little bottle, the first solid artifact of John I'd found on the island. Suddenly his life here was real.

Frank touched my shoulder. "No crime in crying. John was a good man."

Closing my eyes, I swallowed the surge of grief. I held the bottle up to the light. "Thank you."

"Hey, it's from John."

"I mean for talking to me. No one else will."

"Yeah, I heard you were asking all kinds of questions. About that shipwreck cove, and Vic Manden. Buzz is, you think Manden offed John."

I turned quickly. "Frank, what happened between them?"

"Shit, I don't know for sure. John got tight-lipped toward the end, tripping out over that treasure, goddamn Laura pushing him into it. All I know is he was smokin' over Manden double-crossing him somehow."

"Was Manden running drugs?"

He eyed me and sighed. "Where's this gonna get you? Won't bring John back. You don't know the scene here, you'll just stir up trouble for yourself."

"I need to know what happened. He was my brother. Your friend. Doesn't that mean anything?"

He stared out over the sea.

"You know something, don't you, Frank?"

He finally turned to me, spreading his hands. "All right. I know a guy who might have something to tell you." He glanced at his bulky dive watch. "Shit! Got to get this gear to the pool." He jumped out of the truck. "Come by the shop next week."

Sixteen

Willie was finally on duty at the ice cream stand, making change for some tourists off a cruise liner. A thin little boy in ragged shorts and outgrown T-shirt, he eyed me with an oddly adult skepticism when I mentioned "Granny," the herb woman Lisabet had told me about the week before. He snapped up my five-dollar bill and found another kid to watch the kiosk.

Willie led me through twisting, pot-holed alleys squeezed against the base of the mountain, between houses in peeling stucco and warped wooden shutters. Flies swarmed in the stewing stink of sewage and garbage. He stopped at the foot of a rickety wooden stairway climbing the side wall of a two-story house.

"Upstairs?" I turned to the boy. "You can go, I'll find my way back."

He gave me a sly, quicksilver grin and vanished into the winding lanes.

I had to pound on the door at the top of the landing before it finally cracked open in a swirl of spicy cooking smells and an indefinable pungency. A tiny girl in an oversize polka-dot dress let me in. She led me through a livingroom with frayed furniture, droning TV, a shirtless man snoring on the couch, and magazine pictures in pink plastic frames on the walls. In the kitchen, a woman turned from the stove, wiping hands on her apron. "Fifteen dollah."

The little girl tugged me down a hall to a closed door, opened it, and gave me a push.

The pungent smell engulfed me, foreign and overwhelming. Through the haze, candles vaguely illuminated pictures crowding the walls. Christ images, from innocuous blue-eyed Jesus sitting with a lamblike smile among an adoring flock of children, to bizarre red and black renditions like Picasso on LSD. Surrounding them, painted directly on the wall, geometric *veve* patterns of spiky stars, triangles, filigreed curves, spirals.

On the opposite wall, rosaries. A chipped plaster statue of the Virgin Mary smiling gently from the corner, hands reaching down. Beneath her, on a cloth-covered table, a wild clutter: candles, a cross, seeds, dried plants and roots, feathers, corked bottles. And a big chunk of black rock, "dressed" reverently with a gold-fringed sash and silver chains.

The paraphernalia registered only for a moment. She moved, and there was no part of me that wasn't tuned in on her.

She was enormous. Her sturdy wooden chair creaked as she rose ponderously to her feet. I'd never seen a woman so tall, sheer volume of flesh overpowering. She stood and I looked up into a broad shield of a face, full dark flesh in a fine net of wrinkles, age capturing only the outermost layer. A turban-like wrapping bound her head. She wore a loose white cotton dress, thick strong arms bare. She wasn't swollen with fat, but packed solid, cast in a giant's mold.

Towering carved stone face, immense hands cupping lifeblood, a cascade of vibrant green down Her mountainous flanks. It was this woman's face I'd seen in my vision on the mountain with Conrad.

She didn't speak. She grasped my wrists and turned my hands palm up, studying them. Her opaque gaze lifted to mine. I was pinned by her stare, wrists held in a grip I could never break.

The pungent smoke swirled, and all I saw were her eyes, ancient stone eyes carved in infinite spirals. I was spinning down a blind whirlpool, following John, and I couldn't breathe, swallowed by the choking blackness.

*night sea hisses with my panting breaths, John's breaths, my/his heart pounding, bubbles bursting up as he spins around, fins kicking. Knife knocked away glinting, drifting down. Hands grab him masked faces mocking laughter ringing as he fights useless he's caught he's drowning.

Rage screams down his throat my throat. The heavy anchor crashes down on us, cold blue eyes watching behind the mask.

Devil fish manta swoops up eerie silent bat wings undulating through red waves, horned beast circling me, spiraling down. I follow beckoning black wings into the abyss, into the pulsing bloodbath, deeper*

"Viens!"

Hands gripped mine. I gasped, fighting them.

The grip tightened, holding me there. Warmth spread through me, suddenly intensified to a hot pulse. I shuddered, icy darkness melting out of me. A touch on my forehead. I blinked. I was sitting in a chair, the woman looming over me.

"C'est un bete, un bete noir, que t'a pris."

"Comment?" *A black beast*?

"Tu comprends."

"No, I *don't* understand!" I wrenched my hands free. I didn't understand anything any more. I'd thought I could keep it all straight, but now nothing made sense. Maybe Manden was right, that first day at the beach, I couldn't know until I plunged in, but now everything was out of control.

A sharp sting on my scalp. The woman was stepping back with startling quickness for her bulk, clutching strands of my hair glinting in candlelight. She turned to the cluttered altar, laying the hairs on it and picking up a smoked glass bottle. "You drink."

I shook my head.

A fleeting smile curved thick lips. A low chant rose, swelling to reverberate through the dim, smoky cave of a room.

Rhythm of the sea. Day and night. Waxing and waning moon....

I sighed as it faded.

The enigmatic smile again, fingers touching my forehead. "You drink. Good foh pain. Fever."

I took a swallow. Sharp alcohol bite and aromatic herbs. The astringency flared through me, scouring away my nagging headache, snapping me into clarity.

"So." She took the bottle, stood watching me. "You be tinkin' on put a power on some body. Eye foh eye, blood foh blood?"

I gawked at her.

"You temptin' de powers." Slow shake of her headdress. "Some spirit dey quiet in heart lak whisper, lak soft wind in tree, lak tide she come an' come in own time ripen. Yes and be some spirit dey summon easy, make big promise fast, big power, dey always come back takin' more dan give. You fool chile. Don' know de price. Dey bring all you nightmare come sure."

She could see the visions invading me. This was real. My stomach flopped like I'd just stepped out into free-fall.

"I didn't ask for this." My voice cracked. "But someone murdered my brother." Finally I *knew* it. "I want justice. The truth."

"Truth." She snorted. "You taste blood, you get a thirst don' quench. Hand grasp knife, blade turn two way."

"Is there a Bocor behind it all? Who is he?"

"Dem ting no matter foh you. You look inside, ask you heart."

She turned to the altar. More incense, more chanting, as she put my hairs and other things into a small cloth bag. She moved ponderously to me, touched Conrad's Jumbie-seed necklace, and draped her bag on its leather thong around my neck.

I touched it gingerly. "Did you make one of these for Samuel Simmons?"

A crooning moan, her broad face stricken with grief. In place of the impassive oracle stood a sorrowing grandmother, bowed under the weight of her immense frame. Somehow she was even more powerful.

She sighed. "Chile he need help. He start messin' in de powers, don' know to stop. Too late now."

"What about his brother Dwayne? What happened to him?"

"Bad seed." She spat. "Now you, chile, you got powers, an dey drawin' powers you don' want. 'Cept you study deep on de ways, you bes leave dis island. Run 'fore you drown, too." She thrust a paper packet into my hands. "You shake dem seed roun house. Mischief spirit stop, pick up every seed, be too weary foh comin' in."

"Thank you." I braced myself, gripping the packet. "But I need to know about the petroglyphs, the carved stones. Are there Jumbies in them? Are they power spots?"

The woman drew back, towering grimly over me, thick finger jabbing. "Stay clear dem stones, dey drawin' you. Too strong. You ign'rant drawin' powers, you drawin' trouble foh more dan self. No place here foh you."

"But —"

"You go."

Steel drums, ringing overhead, woke me in the middle of the night.

"What?" I bolted upright, straining.

Rain pounded the corrugated metal roof, sloshing down the gutters into the cistern beneath the cottage. My persistent headache was gone.

The darkness was heavy with moisture. Pulling in a muggy lungful, I swung open the door to a cool mist fuming off the patio with the force of the cloudburst. Frogs sang madly through the thrumming downpour. Thick flower scents simmered, rivulets racing over the cobbles into the thirsty earth.

Deafened, still half-dreaming, I lifted my hands to slide my nightshirt over my shoulders and let it drop around my feet. I stepped out into the blinding deluge. Tilting my face up, eyes closed, I opened my arms to the rain.

Seventeen

"Sorry I'm late, Phillip." I dropped into a chair at the wrought-iron table, blowing a loose strand off my face. Behind me, past the entrance to the cobbled breezeway, Main Street jostled taxis and tourists off the cruise ships. "I keep forgetting about rush hour in paradise."

Phillip, dapper in his white tropic suit, nudged a tall drink toward me. "I took the liberty of ordering for you."

I sipped, squinting at the sun beating down with a concentrated fury after the night's brief shower. "That little spit of rain just made the drought feel worse."

"Susan, I'm afraid I must apologize." He'd pulled out an antique pocket watch. "Some urgent business has come up at the last moment, and I've a plane to catch. We'll have to postpone our cruise to the Palm Cay glyphs a bit longer."

"Damn." I sagged in the chair.

"I was looking forward to it, too." He smiled, lifting his palms.

"Guess I better get creative with the grant committee. The vultures are circling." I'd been counting on Holte's offer to explain his analytic theory, planning to compare the Palm Cay styles with the glyphs Conrad had shown me, and putting off the progress report the committee was demanding.

"I daresay I'll be able to wrap up this nuisance quickly, with a minimum of blood spilt." A wry look. "Meanwhile, have a look at these notes on my linguistic system." He handed me a manila envelope.

"Thank you!" I peered into the envelope. "Now I can feed the number-crunchers something to chew on." I knew it was Miller, the Anthro Chair, behind the sudden pressure.

I pointed at my briefcase. "I already started a design analysis with photos of some local petroglyphs I've found."

"Good show. To a fruitful collaboration." He raised his glass to me and sipped. Then he stood and took my hand. "How I loathe all this tawdry bustle and hurry!" He raised my hand to brush it with his lips. "'*Verweile doch, du bist so schon.*'" His mouth quirked. Pulling out the watch again, he exclaimed, "I'm late, I'm late!" Clapping his Panama on his head and grabbing his walking stick, he cut a swath through the crowd, coattails flying like the White Rabbit's.

"'Oh, my ears and whiskers.'" I raised my glass to the swirling vacuum he'd left behind.

It was too hot and noisy to concentrate on Phillip's notes, so I slipped them into my briefcase and headed for the Honda. I pushed through the crowds toward the back street where I'd parked it, blotting my face and neck with a kerchief as I waited for a break in the traffic. Across the busy street, a flare of bright color, thin dark-haired Continental in a bold flower-print dress whisking through sunlight and into the mouth of a shadowed alley.

"Laura?" I hadn't seen her face. She was gone.

Some native kids were jostling around my parked bike over there, two little girls perched on it licking dripping ice-cream cones. Behind the laughing kids tossing a ball, one thin, shirtless boy stood ramrod stiff against the brick wall by the alley entrance. Arms hanging straight at his sides, he stared blank-faced at my motorcycle. A bulky pendant hung on a thong over his bony ribcage.

Stepping forward to cross the street, I froze. "Samuel!"

The boy didn't move, dark eyes staring fixedly. The pendant on his chest was a red-smeared ouanga-bag. "Samuel!"

A car roared past inches away, horn blaring. I stumbled back. Samuel. He *hadn't* been buried in that coffin. A chill raced down my back.

"Samuel!" I repeated stupidly, craning across the rushing traffic. The blank-faced boy was gone.

"Shit!" I caught a sharp breath and dashed in front of a delivery van, behind a taxi, made it to the other curb in a fresh blast of horns. The kids were laughing, cheering me. No sign of the boy.

Glassy blank eyes. Thin hand clutching the ouanga-bag, running in terror, "Granny gimme guard!" Too late. *"On the night of the funeral, the Bocor may steal into the cemetery and take the body...."*

Sweat broke out on my face, ice in my gut.

"Did you kids see where that shirtless boy went, the one standing over there with that little bag around his neck?"

They rolled their eyes, shook their heads, made the loco sign. Even some dollar bills passed around produced nothing but shrugs. I gave up, peeled the little girls off the Honda, and started to climb on. I stopped short.

Back of my neck prickling, I checked over the bike. Nothing missing, tires okay, gas tank still full. The brake lever had too much give. I traced the lines. Shiny fresh cuts, the cables sliced nearly through, holding by a few thin strands.

I closed my eyes, rocked by a sickening flush as I felt myself swooping down the steep curves of the mountain roads, felt the empty clutch of the brake lines snapping. Felt myself flying, plunging, spinning faster and faster out over empty space.

By the time I jumped out of the cab at the Fairview gates, I was boiling mad. I was sure it was Laura I'd glimpsed in town. Had she seen someone mess with the Honda? *Had* it been Samuel, standing there? Somehow I couldn't bring myself to believe the boy would sabotage my bike. Would Laura go that far? I could still feel her desperate fury washing over me at the beach when I refused to drop my questions about John.

"And maybe you can keep me from wringing Laura's neck." At the moment, I would have cheerfully assisted him.

"She just come back, she cool out to de pool." The gate guard pointed at the shelled path.

Pushing up my sleeves, I stalked fuming past Laura's hot, ticking sports car, a fresh dent creasing the passenger door.

She was perched beside the pool on the edge of a chaise lounge, leaning over an end table. Her short, tropic-flowered dress shimmered bright colors in the sunlight.

"Laura."

She sprang to her feet, whirling around. A hand whipped over her mouth, eyes widening, pupils flaring darkly. She coughed, looked down, fell back a step to conceal the little table. "Susie...."

She took a deep breath then, and shrugged, dropping back onto the lounger to finish laying out lines of white powder. "Prime stuff here. You're always sniffing around, try some of this." She bent over, inhaling a line of the coke.

"Damn it, Laura! It *was* you in town, wasn't it?" I strode over and yanked her to her feet. The table tipped, scattering the coke and an uncapped vial.

"Fuck!" She broke free, dropping to her knees to scramble for the vial, licking her finger and blotting up bits to suck. "You know how much this shit costs? What's *wrong* with you?"

"What's wrong with me? Other than getting my brake cables cut?"

"What are you talking about?" She was searching the ground, groping for the vial, and didn't look up.

"You were running off from my bike. That's the dress, I saw you."

"Shit, every tourist in town's wearing this style." She twitched a fold of the flowery fabric, leaned forward, grabbed the vial. "So what did I do this time, other than blow too much money? You sound like Leon. Now he's threatening to take my car keys away, just because I had another fender-bender." She peered into the vial, capped it, and stuck it into her purse.

My anger deflated. She couldn't want me off the island *that* badly. And I just couldn't see her wielding a tool so efficiently to slice my brake lines. I sighed. "I thought you were cutting down on that stuff."

"I did." Still on her knees, she shrugged, licked her fingertips, and sniffed.

"What happened to Samuel and Dwayne, Laura?"

"What?!" Her face snapped up to mine, nostrils flaring.

"You heard me. Who killed them?"

She looked down at her shaking hands. She jumped to her feet, started gathering up some packages piled in a wicker chair with her shoes. "You are out of your fucking gourd, girl! What are you talking about?" Her voice cracked.

"Laura, is it the Bocor?" I stepped close to grip her trembling arms, the packages scattering. "I saw Samuel in town, he was wearing that bloodstained ouanga-bag. What's going on with this cult?"

"Samuel?" She whispered it, rolling her eyes.

"They didn't bury him, did they, Laura?" I leaned closer, tightening my grip. "He's not really dead, is he?"

"No, Susie, don't!" She wrenched in my hold. "I told you, he'll kill us! But you won't stop poking around, and now he's...." Her voice broke, tears streaking her mascara.

"What? What's he going to do next, Laura?"

She shook her head, trembling.

"Should I go ask him? He's here, isn't he?"

"Here?" She gasped, twisting out of my grip, staring around in alarm. "Here? No, he's —"

From inside the house, harsh piano music suddenly spilled over the patio. Waves of staccato arpeggios and atonal chords pounded through the heat.

Laura tilted her head, listening. She frowned at me. "The cult? You want to talk to Leon?" A short bark of laughter. "All right, let's go."

She grabbed my wrist, nails digging in, and dragged me toward the back verandah. I pulled free, suddenly reluctant to face Caviness.

The piano hammered into a crescendo, my hackles rising. Fight or flight. It was the rhythm, alien but somehow familiar. Like a nightmare, two different forces fighting each other in the music. A splintered treble jumped from threads of a haunting melody to atonal chords, rejecting but tethered to the deep bass forcing a different rhythm, driving the cresting waves of sound.

It was like breasting a heavy tide, pushing onto the verandah after Laura. I stopped beside her in front of the open French doors.

Leon Caviness, shoulders heaving as he attacked the keyboard of the ebony grand, was looking straight toward us, but he didn't seem to see us. His bony face, beaded with sweat, was perfectly blank, dark eyes glassy.

Samuel's eyes. I dropped back a step, head ringing with the harsh chords and the plaintive, fading lament of the treble motif. I couldn't tear my gaze from Caviness's skull-like face, his eyes set deep in shadow.

His long fingers – *Ansi the black spider loa* — played me with the piano keys, plucking the web strings dancing his puppets. A tugging, wrenching inside me, shock of an overpowering sexual surge. Something was shifting, opening, *being* opened inside me, blossoming wide to drink in the perverse music. That dark greed opening inside me, sucking it up, rocked me with revulsion.

The music crashed to a stop without even an attempt to find a tonic resolution. Silence rang in my ears. I shuddered, turning toward Laura. She stood swaying, a dreamy smile on her lips.

"Dr. Dunne. To what do we owe the honor of this visit?"

I jumped. He'd come silently around the piano to stand beside me. One eyebrow raised, he gave me his mocking smile.

I cleared my throat, shook my head. After that music, after whatever it was he'd been pounding at me, words were ludicrous.

"Come, now. You've been so busy here on our lovely island. Surely you have some questions for me." He was leaning over me, a parody of solicitousness.

Anger flared. "What do you want as the Bocor? What are you trying to do with your cult?"

His eyes narrowed. "The Bocor? The priest who works with his left hand?" His long fingers reached out, made a plucking motion in the air.

My gut clenched.

He chuckled unpleasantly. "My followers call me Houngan, but I must admit the distinction is spurious. Every Houngan is also a Bocor. We must embrace the shadows in order to know them, embrace the light to summon it from the clouds. It is all the same in the end." A dismissive gesture. "Surely you're not so childish as to insist on good and evil?"

"So it's all the same to you whether Samuel's dead or alive? Is that what you're trying to do to her, make her into one of your zombis?" I pointed to Laura, who was still standing with a vague, bemused smile on her face.

"Zombis?" He straightened and laughed. "From petroglyphs to zombis! Have you captured the *Ti Bon Ange* of my victims in your test tubes, Dr. Dunne? Have you found my secret altar with the graveyard dirt?" He snorted. "You scientists, you think if you dice the world into bits and examine each piece under your microscopes, you will understand the songs that move the wind and waves, the drums that pulse in your own blood. You see nothing."

He turned and strode over to Laura, said something to her in a low voice. She blinked, nodded, laid her hand on his arm. He guided her into the house, and the door closed behind them.

The Mozart duo was a fresh breeze, sunlight dancing over Orchid Bay beyond a flickering screen of palm fronds and hibiscus. I finished a trill and lowered the flute. Catching my breath, I watched the hands at the piano, long supple fingers conjuring life from the black and white keys.

For a moment, they were Caviness's hands, spiders dancing discord to a lash of dissonance. I shook my head and raised my instrument for the final passage, flute and piano weaving a sparkling web that slowly dissolved into silence.

Adrienne dropped her hands into her lap and turned on the piano bench, smiling. "I knew we'd play well together." Her rich alto carried a hint of a schooled British accent, spiced with the island lilt.

"I'll never be near your league. But now I can tell my friends when you're out there packing the concert halls, I actually played with Adrienne MacIntyre."

A throaty laugh. "You have the music in you, Susan. You just need to practice more."

"I'm sure there are better flutists on the island. Why did you want to play with me?"

She lifted a graceful hand to run a finger over the keyboard. "Music. It's my way to know things." She rose with a sweep of pale-coral skirt, stepping close to touch my hand and look down into my eyes. Her smooth face went eerily blank for a moment.

She stepped back. "Leon's wrong about you." A frown creased her forehead. "Why?"

I started putting away the flute. "I'm not crazy about him."

"Everyone has blind spots. Sometimes our powers make us too proud. He told me that."

I swung around. "What kind of powers is Leon playing with, Adrienne?"

"It's no game." A smile ghosted. "I myself have danced over fire when the *loa* enters me. I have taken a live coal between my lips with no harm. The spirits give me strength. Why don't you welcome your own powers, open up to see where they could take you?"

I blinked. Her face was serene, eyes clear.

"Adrienne, have you ever read *Faustus*?"

"Of course. Leon thought I should study German, as well as French, but I don't like it. Those ugly gutturals." Her brow furrowed again. "And the story is so naive, really, all that nonsense about Lucifer and damnation. Goethe didn't have a clue what spiritual powers are really about."

"Heavy on the black and white?" My lips twitched. "But there's a truth to it. Maybe there are forces we shouldn't mess with. We'll get sucked in...." Caviness's dark music still thrummed in my bones. "There have to be limits. Some things are wrong."

"Of course. But how can we know the right paths if we won't see? If we blind ourselves in fear of our true natures?"

"Leon's words?"

"He's my teacher." A fluid gesture toward the piano. "I could never play the way I do if Leon hadn't taught me to explore different ways. He's shown me how to go beneath the surface of the music, root it deep in the rhythms, draw on my power. Sometimes it's hard. Sometimes it's frightening. It takes courage to accept the truth. If you want his words," her voice deepened, eerily capturing Caviness's cadences, "'Harmony and resolution are only illusions. Music — life — is the violent dance of oppositions striving for unity but never unified.'"

Her face glowed. "I'll never be a true musician if I always follow the safe path."

I touched her arm. "Stick to it, Adrienne. Just... keep your eyes open."

She tilted her head. "You're like Pat, you believe Leon is plotting some sort of evil, don't you?"

"Is he the Bocor?"

"Is that what she said?"

"Not Pat. I've been talking to some of the natives. A young boy was killed, and it has something to do with black magic. Do you know about an herb-woman called Granny?"

She shook her head, moving to a louvred window to gaze out over the turquoise cove. "There *is* something wrong. Off-balance. The drought, and Africa Unite, everyone's stirred up. But you don't understand, Leon is trying to help the people. It's time they found their own voice, their own power. Pat refuses to try to work with him, she just fights everything he suggests."

"That's not the way she tells it."

"She's so stubborn." Abruptly she turned, opened the piano bench, and pulled out some papers from the piano music inside. "This is one thing he's trying to do for the island." She handed me the top page.

It was a petition, partly filled with signatures. It described boundaries of a large chunk of land on the West End, demanding it be declared a public preserve and calling a halt to further development. Adrienne's signature headed the list.

I whistled. "Pat's going to blow a gasket. Has she seen this?" I handed it back.

"Not yet. We want to get enough signatures, then present it to the Land-Use Committee. Leon's tried to work with them, but he finally decided it's a sham, the other members are all pushing the developers' agenda." Her teeth caught her lower lip. "I know Pat thinks she's helping the locals, but she won't look at the big picture. It's only the businessmen who would benefit from more resorts."

Still reciting from Caviness? "I'd like to see an historical park over there myself."

"Leon told me you've been researching petroglyphs on the mountain. It would help if we could count on you for testimony about the historical value. He suggested I ask you for your signature." She offered the paper again.

"He suggested you ask *me*?" I shook my head. "I can't sign, anyway, I'm not a resident. I don't have a vote."

"No one does, that's part of the problem. That's what the Independence Movement is about. Everything is decided back in the States, or by special committees here. We want to change that."

The puzzle pieces were shifting. Caviness? This was the kind of power he was trying to give the people? Or was it only window-dressing for his cult? I couldn't shake the visceral memory of his fingers plucking the air, plucking shadowy web-strings.

I cleared my throat. "I'm an anthropologist, I'm supposed to be a neutral observer. I shouldn't get involved."

She stood offering the paper, gaze holding mine.

I sighed and took the petition, signed it. "Be careful, Adrienne." With a reluctant grin, I handed it back.

A vibrant smile, white teeth flashing. "You're very like him, you know."

"Who?"

"John. When you move just so, or smile like that, it's like looking at him."

"You knew John?"

"Of course. Didn't Pat tell you? He worked here with Vic Manden, raising a sunken barge in the bay."

"Here? With Manden? She said she'd never met either of them."

"Oh." She sat abruptly on a wicker couch. "I see." She gnawed her lip, suddenly looking young. "Susan, I'm worried about her! She's getting obsessed about this feud with Leon, it's almost like some kind of vendetta, and she's been drinking too much...." She shot a glance out the window. "I was expecting her back for lunch, and she's gone again. She's letting things slip at the resort."

She sighed. "And this thing about Vic. She actually tried to forbid me to see him."

A painful smile compressed her lips. "I suppose she's denying he and John ever worked here, maybe that will make everything go away. Make sure I stay here forever with her." A short laugh. "She doesn't have to worry. He's never...." She shrugged. "He's a good friend, he's always sweet when we meet in town for lunch once in a while. But he's never looked at me that way. Don't worry, Susan, I don't mind, really."

I stared, wheels spinning. "Adrienne, what are you talking about?"

"Vic, of course. The way he looked at you in town that day."

Eighteen

Victor Manden. Underwater Salvage.

I took a deep breath and knocked on the door of the quonset hut office.

Inside, a muffled, "It's open."

He was leaning back in a swivel chair, feet up on a desk covered by a nautical chart held flat with leather work gloves, a conch shell, and an antique bottle. Grease smudge over one eyebrow, coffee mug halfway to his lips, he toyed with a pink spiral shell, thumb slowly tracing the inward-turning curves.

He dropped his feet to the floor and looked down at the shell. "You forgot it. Your present from the octopus." He tossed it at me.

I caught it reflexively. Now. Say something. I had to find John's glyph boulder soon, or I might as well pack up my PhD and head home with my tail between my legs. But all I could do was stand there holding the shell while he watched me with a face like a stone wall.

I walked over, set the shell on the desk, and turned for the door. "This was a mistake."

He whipped out of the chair and put himself between me and the door, shoving it closed. "Let's skip the hunt and chase. Tell me what you want."

"Apparently there's no point." I made a motion toward the door.

He didn't move. "Try me. You must want it bad, to come back here."

I stiffened. "All right. I want you to take me to Ship Bay. I want to see where John drowned. I want to see the rock with the petroglyphs."

"And no one else will take you there."

"That's right."

"So now you step in where angels fear to tread, and prove I killed John. Got to admire your guts, Susan."

"I'm not asking for your admiration."

"No, you figure all you have to do is walk in here, smile pretty, and I'll fall all over myself. You and your spoiled brother."

It was ridiculous to stand by the door letting him trap me. I walked over to the desk and sat down. "Well? Will you take me to the cove?"

He returned to his side of the desk. "Tell me why I should."

"It's your business. I'll pay you."

He flushed angrily beneath the deep tan. "I don't come cheap. Boat and diver for half a day, two hundred bucks."

I gritted my teeth and nodded.

A mirthless smile. "Since you're hiring me, I have to tell you I don't know anything about a petroglyph rock. Knowing John, it could be on the moon."

"Fine."

"I always shake on a business deal." He rose and reached across the desk, mouth pressed straight behind the beard.

I rose stiffly to shake hands. His palm was warm and dry, mine damp.

"Okay, let's not waste time. If we leave now, the tide will be about right to make it over the entrance reef."

"Now? But.... I need to rent an underwater camera."

"No problem. I've got a good setup."

"I can't pay you today."

"I'll bill you later. Let's go."

"Wait." Things were moving too fast. "Why did you agree to this?"

He turned abruptly, knocking the pink shell onto the floor. "Shit!" He scooped it up like it was alive and wounded. Then, with an irritated gesture, he thrust it at me. "Can't you hang onto this thing?"

I took it. "Are you going to answer my question?"

"I don't trust you any more than you do me, so I might as well keep an eye on what you're up to and save myself getting broadsided later. Does that make it all clear?"

I was looking at the gleaming smooth curves of the shell. "I guess so." I stuck it in my pocket.

"Let's go then. The tide won't wait."

"I have a lunch date." I'd finally arranged a meeting with Shelli Carver. "I'll call her and put it off."

"Laura?" He sounded disgusted.

"No."

He shrugged and pointed at the phone. "Be sure to tell them you're going out with me. We don't want any more unsolved murders, do we?"

"That's a sensible suggestion." I picked up the phone as he strode out the door.

Shelli's laughter crackled over the line. "You *are* crazy, Susan! I'll be waiting for a blow-by-blow." She hung up.

I gripped the receiver like a lifeline. A beautifully preserved, unglazed terracotta jaguar head snarled at me from a shelf above the desk. Mayan. I hung up the wailing phone and headed outside. No sign in the yard of the antique anchor with the skull-shaped coral. I was still wondering about coincidences.

"Let's go." Manden strode between two rusted mounds, trailed by a shirtless native. He turned back to the man. "Go ahead and sort those cables. We'll search for the hull section tomorrow."

The man ran a hand over his close-cropped head, sweat gleaming. His eyes rolled from me to Manden. "Why you go dere? Why you mix it wi' she? You jus find moh grief."

"Gaylord, the customer is always right."

Manden threw the throttle forward as we rounded the Treasure Island breakwater. The Whaler shot ahead, sea-spray splintering off the bow. Glitter of white teeth and mirrored shades.

"Little rough today," he shouted over the roaring motor and waves slapping the hull. "Got to move it or we'll miss high tide."

The boat's surge shoved me into the seat. Big waves rolled in, and we seemed to be jumping the watery peaks instead of climbing them. I clung to the console, foam spattering over its sprayshield as the Whaler crashed up and down and wings of churning white swept back from the bow.

Manden spun the wheel, swerving around a coral head. I let out a pent-up breath as we shot through a stretch of deep blue, swung around another shallow formation. After a while I stopped straining and decided to enjoy the scenery.

We were rounding the West End cliffs, sheer rock climbing to lush green, threaded by a narrow ribbon of falling water. No sign of people, but this was Brotherhood territory, the Dreads who claimed Ship Bay. What did they know about the *Phoenix* and its dangerous Jumbies? What did Manden know?

No clues in his blunt profile. The work-roughened fingers rubbing his beard, gripping the wheel. Grabbing my ankle as I hovered over the watery abyss, shadow man dragging me deeper. Maybe I'd gone as crazy as everyone else on the island. It was more than the petroglyph theory now, more than John's death. Manden was right, I had to dive in and find out –

"Look!"

I jumped.

"Dolphins." He slowed the Whaler.

I squinted under my hand, saw them farther out. Two, no, three sleek curves, leaping the waves. They flung themselves in acrobatic twists into the air, plunged in a burst of sun-dazzled spray, raced on out to sea.

"The way they move, it must be magic."

"That's what —" He shook his head.

"What?"

"John. Said the same thing. No matter what he was doing, if he spotted dolphins, he'd take off after them. Jump in to swim with them."

I could see him leaping with a whoop into the sea, trying to out-swim a dolphin. "Thank you."

"What for?" He was peering over the side, steering around shallow banks.

"You didn't have to tell me that."

He shot me a look through the mirrored lenses. He pointed up at the cliffs. "This is my favorite part of the island. Still wild, still itself."

Another waterfall, this one higher, plummeted off the green-fringed black rock. Rainbows sparkled the mist over boulders below. I took a deep breath of clean salt air. Deep blue sea rocked us, white crests fretting at the foot of the cliffs and sun burning away the shadows.

I turned to Manden. He smiled.

I smiled back. Out here, I couldn't hang onto the reasons why I shouldn't.

"So why did you decide to try me again? You've heard it all by now." He nudged the throttle up to speed, glancing over the side.

I hesitated. "Adrienne gave you a sterling character reference."

"She's an incredible kid."

"Hardly a kid. Don't tell me you haven't noticed she's a knockout."

The mirrored shades swung towards me. He pursed his lips, shot the throttle forward to make the Whaler leap. His white grin flashed.

The waves were rolling in white-frothed now, stronger wind from the open gulf lashing spray. "Could be rough!" he shouted. "Hang on."

The sea was darker here than on the east side. Waves slapped with building force, the Whaler dipping and plunging. Manden abruptly cut speed, spinning the wheel, heading straight toward the cliffs. The wind was behind us now, pushing damp strands over my face.

He pointed. "Through that gap."

I'd seen the cove before. Round bowl cupped by steep green hills and stone walls. High in the dense forest above it, barely visible, a wooden railing and wall. The party-shack where the druggies hung out. It couldn't be coincidence.

"What?" His mirrored lenses reflected my face gone wary.

I pointed. "All this time I've been searching for the cove, I was looking right at it. Laura took me to a party in that shack up there."

"I'd watch it with her."

"She says the same thing about you."

"Big surprise." He angled the boat into the entrance gap, waves boiling over shallow rocks.

I grabbed the console as he shoved the throttle and we leaped into the churning cut. The Whaler rolled sideways, bucked, tipped wildly, was spewed into the calm bowl of the cove.

Manden slowed, watching over the side and steering around a barely-covered rock. He waved at the encircling walls. "No way to get down here from land, and no beach. So don't worry about the Dreads hassling us, anyway they're afraid of the cove.... What I pieced together, the slave ship was driven up against the island in a storm. Northers come up fast around here. They had to chance the cove, couldn't have known how shallow the entrance is."

"So it broke up there?" I glanced uneasily around the rock ramparts, hoping he was right about the Dreads.

"Tore apart into two main sections, got carried out into the middle." He gestured with his chin. "Some pieces scattered, but the two hull sections are still close together. Overgrown with coral now, not much to look at, except where we worked the anchor and part of its chain free."

"The anchor." I swallowed. "That's where John drowned."

He nodded curtly. "I found him pinned under it." Voice flat. "He must have tipped it over on himself, looking for that damned treasure."

"Or someone else tipped it." No response. I cleared my throat. "You never found anything valuable?"

I thought he wouldn't answer, but he finally said stiffly, "Probably nothing *to* find. Just a lot of old stories that had Laura and John all whooped up, talked me into it. Some taboo about the cove, the *Phoenix* wreck, forbidden gold guarded by Jumbies who'd put a curse on the place. People who'd tried to find the treasure kept getting killed."

I watched the submerged coral slide by beneath us. "If it was a slave ship, why would it have had treasure on board?"

"Exactly." He shot me a look and shrugged. "Supposedly they were renegade slaves, took over the ship and killed the captain, some kind of down-dirty 'pagan sacrifice.' Story goes, they had this mythical magic treasure stashed on board. There was a key document I never could find. Some ship logs in the archives mentioned it, like it explained the whole show. The 'Bartholomew Parker missive.'"

Another puzzle piece from John's letter: "*He* has *the Parker Manuscript.*" I cleared my throat. "I couldn't find anything about the *Phoenix* in the archives."

"The documents disappeared after I got the permit. I stole them, remember?" Voice lashing. "Then I killed John."

He cranked the wheel sharply, craning over the side, boat chugging forward in tense silence. He straightened, said brusquely, "We won't waste time with the ship. As far as your glyph rock goes, I'd say if it's here, it's along that cliff edge."

His arm chopped out an arc. "Where it looks like big bites out of the edge. If there are glyphs underwater, nobody held their breath to carve them. Rock was probably up on that cliff and a slide took it down. There's a lot of limestone around here, gets weathered into caves and cracks, pretty unstable."

Throat gone dry, I nodded.

"Okay, the dive plan. We'll anchor by that wall. Shouldn't have to go down more than fifty feet, run a search pattern. Currents won't be much problem on the slack tide, but stick close to me and do what I signal. Don't get any fancy ideas."

I braced myself. "I want to see the ship."

"Take a look. We're above it now."

Climbing off the chair, I leaned over the side. The glassy water revealed only masses of coral. The sea here looked unnaturally dark and stagnant.

"*Death place.*"

"*Dey bad Jumbie.*"

"*Stay away from that cove. And Victor Manden.*"

"*Un bete noir....*"

I shook off a heavy foreboding. "Anchor here, over the ship. We can swim over to the cliff after I see the wreck."

Manden turned from the wheel, flashing my distorted reflection in his mirrored shades. "That what you want?"

"Yes."

He shook his head, brought the boat around until it faced out to the cut, and killed the motor. There was no breeze in the cove. Heat hammered down, sun stuck at its zenith, sea and air quivering with compressed stillness.

The anchor cut through it, splashing off the bow. Manden started setting up regulators, vests, and tanks. The gear was all marked with his initials, *V.M.* "Here. Put it on." He thrust a rolled-up wetsuit at me.

As I pulled on the short suit, he strapped a sheath to his leg, thrusting a serrated dive knife into it with a snap. "We'll take a quick circle of the ship, then head over to the wall."

"I want to see the anchor."

"The anchor?" He swung around. "What is it with you? What will it prove?"

"I want to see where he died."

A muscle in his jaw jumped. "Don't do it. You'll be sorry."

"Are you going to show me or not?"

His hands clenched. "Just remember, you asked for it."

Nineteen

Cool depths closed around me with the echoing *sshhh* of my breaths, bubbles trailing toward the light. The water was very clear, but there was a strange, subdued tint to it, not at all like the bright turquoise bays or deeper blue of the open sea.

Manden hovered by the coral clumps. He gestured curtly, leading the way around encrusted shapes that looked like nothing manmade. 'Christmas-tree' plumes fringed the cream and rust coral, vanishing at our approach. Tiny fish darted in and out of crevices in sparks of orange, yellow, and neon blue. I hovered in weightless suspension to watch the spiderlike progress of an arrowhead crab across a brain coral. Now that I was finally down here, I wasn't so sure I wanted to see the anchor where John died.

Manden pointed at his watch. He gestured me over to a long protrusion of coral, taking my hand and guiding it toward the rounded end. Feeling the raised rim, I realized it was a hollow tube, nearly filled in. A cannon. On a cleared plate near the base, engraved letters. *Phoenix*.

Teeth clamping on the rubber mouthpiece, I turned quickly away. No rising from the ashes here.

Manden was pointing out shapes in coral where they'd been working, cast-like impressions of now-disintegrated beams. Blue-green bits of corroded copper lay scattered among the debris. He was right, there wasn't much to excite visions of treasure. We dropped deeper, colors leaching away into blue-gray dimness.

The snakelike shape of a chain solidified out of the shadows. Huge links, blotched and encrusted, twined over a leaning boulder that cut off the light. Below it, the flukes of the anchor stretched taller than me, freed from their two hundred years in the coral.

I'd seen it before. Shadow man grabbing John, pushing the anchor onto him. He rages helplessly, pinned as his air runs out and he's drowning.

I blinked quickly, taking a deep breath, regulator hissing. Manden was watching me, eyes cool blue behind the mask, face expressionless.

I swam to the anchor, touched the corroded shaft where it rose from its solid-looking bed. It shifted under my hand. Like a sleepwalker following a nightmare script, I raised my other hand to grasp the rough surface and pull. Metallic breaths echoed. The anchor rocked, started a ponderous dip toward me. He'd pulled it over on top of John this way, making it look like an accident.

I pushed the anchor and it rocked back, moving heavily in its bed. I turned, and sucked in a startled gulp of seawater.

Manden was rushing at me in a swirl of foam, kicking hard. He grabbed my arm and yanked me toward him. Choking and coughing, I struggled for air, trying to break free. A spill of bubbles burst up between us. He wrenched me around, jabbing a finger toward the anchor.

It was rocking forward in its bed again, rebounding quickly this time, tumbling over. Manden tugged me back. The anchor crashed in a cloud of silt onto the coral where I'd been hovering.

His fingers dug in on my shoulders, shaking me roughly, masked face furious.

*gold mask of the death god, cruel face glittering over me, over John, mouth dripping blood –

A screaming gale rips the sails to shreds lashed by driving rain. The frigate heaves and shudders in the crashing waves, pitching, flinging outward limp arms of a body lashed to the mast, grotesquely beckoning. Lightning strobes dark bloodstreaked faces, teeth flashing, howling with the storm, arms waving glitter of silver and jewels. Demon face hard gold the sharp stab of devil horns —

Manden's ice blue eyes behind the Bocor's mask. Hands clutching John clutching me as we fight blindly, drowning, screaming our fury*

Past, present, future blurred into the nightmare pulling me deeper. Manden was shaking me, making me look at the anchor, making me relive it. John, myself, pinned beneath the anchor, our hands tearing uselessly at the massive bar, shredding our skin on the corroded metal and raging at death. Those eyes coldly watching.

Hatred flamed. The air feed hissed faster and faster in my ears. John's killer. Shadow man. I thrashed and kicked at him. His grip tightened. Panting, breath gusting in swirling bubbles, I raised my fists to batter Manden's face. He brushed my fists off. I pounded his chest, snatched for his air hose, clawed at his face.

His arms were always there to block me. Finally he spun me around, twisting one arm behind my back and forcing me up against his body. His other arm crossed over my chest and squeezed.

He pressed harder against my windpipe. I thrashed desperately, but couldn't get any air. Red swam in my eyes. *"You taste blood, you get a taste don' die."* The fury abruptly drained, leaving me limp in his grasp.

The choking pressure eased. I dragged in a harsh breath. Manden still held me against him. I sagged, gone numb.

Then, with an odd hesitancy, he touched the top of my head. Everything was off-kilter, unreal in the floating, flickering shadows leaching color away into monotone. He held me as we hovered in the depths, stroking my shoulder like he was soothing a frightened animal.

A shudder rose through me and escaped in a bubbling swirl. He turned me and peered closely at my face. Drifting in the surreal suspension of time and gravity, we stared through our masks, deep into each other's eyes.

Manden abruptly released me. He shook his head, made the diver's hand signal: *OK?*

Like a robot's, my hand returned the signal. He swam away from the wreck of the *Phoenix*. I followed.

I numbly followed Manden's search pattern over submerged rock faces. We found nothing. I felt nothing. My eyes scanned the rocks for carvings, registering only blank surfaces. Every detail was etched in my memory like a photograph in sharp black and white. *Deja vu*, but not by me. I floated somewhere above it all, watching the two divers move slowly among the darting fish. The rhythm of distant breathing *sshhh*'d hypnotically.

Manden, face blank behind his dive mask, gestured a halt. There were no petroglyphs here. Maybe John had taken the photo somewhere else. Maybe it was all just a dream.

I was kicking along the wall, following his faster pace back to the boat, when a big silvery fish suddenly swam up in front of me. It gave me a challenging stare, flicked its tail in my face, and disappeared below.

Grabbing a rock, I wrenched myself up short. This was my only chance to find the petroglyphs. I couldn't give up. I kicked hard to catch Manden's fin.

He brusquely showed me his watch, flashing fingers for fifteen minutes. I turned back to the most likely section, swimming closer to the surface this time.

Nothing. Only the same cracks and fissures I'd checked the first time. Manden flashed ten fingers. We were close to the decompression limit. He jabbed a finger toward the boat.

I ignored the order, peering into one last crevice, a dark dead-end I'd already scanned. This time I leaned into it. Deep inside, a flicker of light.

Manden's flashlight revealed a crude tunnel of fallen rock slabs. I eased around a sharp turn, tank scraping. Breaths hissed to a faster rhythm, silver trail streaming up in oozing blotches under the black stone ledges, quivering like live things. I squeezed out into an enclosed well of water twenty feet across, open at the top where rock slanted toward the cliff face but didn't quite meet.

Shadows swirled in the trapped sea, suspended silt glinting. A startled fish whipped past. A horned demon leaped out of the gloom.

Flashlight jumping, I eased closer. Petroglyphs covered the broad, flat rock making up the inner side of the well. It was bigger than I'd guessed from the blurry portion John had snapped. I stared at the strange/familiar designs. Bird and fish and man-shapes danced in the submerged light, rippling into life.

A wing-spread bird, talons extended. Curled serpent. Dancing figures. A sharp-horned goat. And spiral eyes, whirlpools into darkness.

Head throbbing, I floated forward, braced myself, and reached toward the boulder, half-expecting it to suck me inside. But I needed to know. I'd been lying to myself, it wasn't only for my research I'd needed to find this glyph rock. The carved figures had called me through the Link, just as John had. Flinching, I flattened my palm over the stone.

A hand touched my shoulder. I flailed around, face to face with Manden.

His eyes were wide, startled-looking in the jittering swerves of the flash. I wrenched free, gestured curtly at his camera. He gave himself a shake and drifted over to the farthest point from the wall, fiddling with the camera. My teeth clamped on the mouthpiece, pulse pounding.

Maddeningly slow and painstaking, Manden took a full roll of film. Closeups. Distant shots. Different angles. Finally he looked at his watch, beckoned sharply, and headed out the tunnel. A last glance at the carved stone rippling with light and shadow, and I hurried after him.

His fins disappeared around a narrow turn. A spotted eel poked its head from a crevice beneath me, needle fangs flashing. I dropped the flash, and it swung down on its cord. The light caught a metallic glint in the crevice.

The dive knife was coated with algae, blotched with a crusty growth. I worked it free, rubbed off the slime, and flashed the light over initials etched in the metal handle. V.M. Manden's knife, marked like all his gear. He was lying. He'd been here, seen the petroglyphs before.

Hands shaking, I slipped the knife inside my wetsuit. I kicked hastily out of the rock tunnel.

He was waiting outside the crack. With an impatient gesture, he set a fast pace to the boat. The water tugged against me now, resisting as I thrashed to keep up. A shadowy current pulled me back toward the petroglyphs. The sea darkened around me.

The bulk of the boat loomed overhead, and I broke free to the surface. The sky mirrored the sea's deepening gloom. Scudding clouds spattered rain, a rising wind stirring the cove's surface and tossing whitecaps outside the cut. More clouds piled up from the north, building into a dark mass overhead.

"Shit!" Manden tore off his gear and hauled up the anchor. "Came out of nowhere. Better get back before it really hits!" He jerked his head at a storage cubby. "Rain slickers in there." He spun the wheel and headed for the cut.

"Nothing." I slammed the cubby shut.

"Great. Keep your wetsuit on, you'll stay warmer. Strap those tanks in and get up here. Could be a wild ride."

I staggered into my seat just as we shot out the gap into a frenzy of wind, rain, and chopping waves. Manden settled into the pilot seat, weaving the wheel back and forth to climb the waves racing in at an angle. We plowed, crashed, and slithered into the storm. Spray flew, the Whaler plunging. Manden laughed.

He was jazzed. Jaw clenched, I gripped tighter to the seat as we thrashed and climbed and dropped with a sickening plummet into a steep trough. Rain and cold spray lashed, stinging. We crashed jarringly into the next mountainous wave, and the next. The wind and the motor roared. Manden laughed again, shouted something.

I clung grimly, thoughts churning like the storm-wracked sea. Nothing to grasp but the boat crashing and jolting through drenching cold spray, dark clouds boiling in, the wind howling, and my life in the hands of Victor Manden, grinning madly in the teeth of the storm.

Twenty

"What next? Shark-wrestling?" Shaking her head, Shelli Carver set her napkin beside her half-eaten sirloin, rare. She reached into her voluminous purse. "Damn, out of smokes. Here, take a look at this while I go scrounge some." She pushed a manila envelope at me and made her way between restaurant tables, swinging broad hips in a clinging skirt.

Inside the envelope, photocopies. On top, a Honduran newspaper article in Spanish, with two grainy photos. The first showed blurry trees and dug-up earth around an intricately carved stone stela. In the other, two uniformed Latinos were tugging at a tall man straining back toward the camera. Manden. His beard and hair were longer, but the photo had caught a familiar rage in his eyes.

Shelli plopped into her chair, flicking a lacquered fingernail at the page. "Good shot, huh? Guy's an animal." She lit up, blowing smoke. "Hondurans nabbed him for smuggling. He was down there working with a U.S. university group, excavating a Spanish ship. Caught him siphoning off Spanish gold, along with some Mayan artifacts, to a fast cigarette-boat for the States."

She set the smoldering cigarette aside, picking up her fork. "Hondurans made a big stink about exploitation by imperialist gringos, but he got deported to the States. Only served a year up there. This other article came from the university newspaper where he was originally funded." She pointed to the next page, an editorial on "the tarnishing of academic ideals."

"What I couldn't figure when they found your brother —" she forked in a mouthful of steak — "was why the cops didn't press Manden." She waved her fork, chewing. "They knew this stuff, at least they did after I tipped them. But they just put the lid on it. That snooty Lieutenant Leland was a royal pain in the ass. You ask me, the whole thing stinks. Maybe Manden paid them off. Or there's somebody behind him, somebody they don't want to mess with."

She picked up her wine glass. "I think he's the front man for a drug operation. Why wouldn't the cops follow up on that lead about his boat, when he threatened John at The Keg? And now there's fresh buzz flying around. Something's up, more than the usual penny-ante drug deals. A lot of activity in the West End, over by that cove you were so hot to see." Her eyes narrowed. "Come on, Susan, what's going on over there? Pat MacIntyre and Leon Caviness are at each other's throats, and you can bet it's more than the land-zoning tiff. She keeps hinting she's got something on him. I bet he's behind Manden *and* Africa Unite. You've got the pipeline to Laura. Dish me some dirt."

I pushed my plate aside. "I tried to talk to Pat about Caviness, but she didn't seem to know anything concrete. Laura won't talk. She's terrified, and I think it's Caviness and his cult."

"I wouldn't trust that bitch." She stabbed into her steak. "She likes to play her little games."

Like cutting my brake lines? I told Shelli about the ouanga-bags, the Dreads guarding the petroglyphs at the Great-House and the party-shack, what I knew about Samuel and Dwayne Simmons.

"I can't prove any of it's connected to Caviness." Just talking about it made it all sound unreal, outrageous. And if it hadn't been for Manden's roll of film in my purse at that moment, I could have doubted the trip to Ship Bay even happened.

"There's no such thing as coincidence, Susan." Shelli gave me a straight look, as I tried not to flinch at the echo of Manden's pronouncement. "It's all connected. Better keep me posted, you know the press does have some power. Think of it as insurance."

She leaned toward me, slapping her palms onto the table. "I'm going to blast this thing wide open."

"And you want a story from me."

"Damn right! We scratch each other's backs."

"All I have are questions." My gaze flickered toward the envelope with the news clippings on Manden.

"I have a feeling you'll get hit with some answers real soon." She smiled and speared the last chunk of red meat.

Shelli's fingers waggled through her open car window as she peeled out of the seaside restaurant's parking lot, dust settling over blackened bricks and boards of a fire-gutted house along the dirt road. Beneath planks slanted across one corner of the weed-choked foundation, a man slept on a blanket beside a dented cooking pot, empty beer bottles lined up meticulously. The shoreline's curve took me past houses in peeling pastel stucco and curlicued antique grillwork clinging haphazardly to the steep hill of the former French Quarter. An old woman smoking a pipe waved to me from a hammock. Two men, one black with a wrinkled bald head, one tanned to leather under a straw hat, trailed fishing lines among bobbing garbage. A black goat raised its satyr's face to watch me go by.

Heat quivered, dust puffing with each step. Leaves hung limp and parched from scraggly boughs. The storm hadn't dropped more than a sprinkle, and the island cisterns were nearly dry.

Sparks danced and dazzled on the milky bay. Melting, shifting into elusive kaleidoscope patterns over the shadowed depths. Across the harbor, Treasure Island shimmered in the heat waves like a mirage.

"Blackbeard's Castle?" I squinted up at the antique stone tower rising from the crown of Treasure Island.

"What's left of it."

"Um-hm."

"He did visit the island once or twice." Frank Savetti gestured at narrow slits in the rock walls. "Colony honchos fired cannons down on the pirates from up here." He waved me toward a crumbled gap in the tower. "Cool out, I'll go get Bill at the pool. He can tell you what he saw at Vic Manden's place."

Inside the jagged doorway, flowering weeds sprouted between broken rock flagging. Stone steps spiraled around the inside wall. Testing them, I climbed. The stairway broke off halfway up the tower, beneath one of the slit windows, a stiff-leafed bromeliad clinging to crumbling stone.

A cowardly little voice told me to run before Frank came back with whatever new revelation he had for me, like Mary's "group sharing."

After another bout of sticky hugs in the dive shop, her coconut-oil and patchouli scent still clung to me. I'd tried not to cringe from the forced intimacy, but it was a reflex, like damping the random flashes of my "tuner." If I hadn't learned to block the invasive waves of strangers' passions, I would have lost my mind. My self. Could I afford to fling open the doors now?

Moot point. The island was set on tearing them off their hinges.

"*A-plus for dodging, Professor.*" John's quirky grin hovered Cheshire Catlike. "*Mary too low-rent for you?*"

I bit my lip. John could always prick my bubbles. Who was I to judge Mary, or Frank, or my brother? Whatever his faults, John had no pretensions, he'd truly enjoyed people. So what was wrong with taking those earthly pleasures as you found them?

"*He shared it all with me, his shadow side, too.*" Laura's face thrust close, challenging. But somewhere paradise had gone wrong. If I'd been trying to stuff John into a tidy little box, maybe Laura had tried to lock him into a different one.

Closing my eyes, I took a deep breath and tried to stop the futile merry-go-round. A fresh, spicy scent was wafting in through the window slit of the tower. Peering out, I saw a mat of small yellow flowers on the outside wall, busy with bees. I reached out to pluck a sprig and hold it to my nose.

"Ginger John."

"Damn!" I spun around, losing my balance on the narrow step.

"Gotcha." Frank caught my shoulders, pulling me in toward the wall and pressing his body against mine. "Mmmm. Hot."

"Too hot." I pushed him back, moving down the steps.

"Ginger John." He shrugged and pointed at the yellow flowers. "That's what they're called. Ho, Bill," he called as we reached bottom. "In here!"

A man in flowered swim trunks stepped into the tower. Short and muscular, with a balding head and a mat of hair on chest and shoulders, he looked familiar.

He grinned. "Hey, we met at Vic Manden's, right? Well, he didn't introduce us, not that I blame him." He winked, looking me up and down.

"Keep it in your pants, man. Tell her what you saw."

"Well, I didn't think it was any big deal at the time, right? I mean, I wondered...." He spread his hands. "I was helping Vic on a job last week, see?"

I nodded.

He cleared his throat. "Look, I don't want to get him into trouble or anything. I mean, he treated me decent." He shrugged. "Anyway, one night Vic wants to wrap up early, but we're running late, it's getting on for dark. He tells me and Gaylord to take off, he'll put the gear away."

He ran a hand over his face. "I'm on my way home, and Shit! I remember I left my mask and fins in the Whaler. Got the next day off, going lobster diving with some guys. So I head back, it's dark by then. I park on the street since he has the gate shut, but it's still unlocked. There's this big black Rolls parked inside."

He frowned. "There's a light in the office, so I walk over. Door's open a crack and I can see Vic's in there talking to somebody. Then I feel funny, like I'm sneaking around, you know? So I just tiptoe over to the boat and grab my stuff and head back. Get as far as the gate. Office door opens and they come out."

"Who was with him?"

"Guy's turning in the doorway for a sec, so I get a good look. Native, real dark. Kind of a bony face, tall and skinny, taller than Vic, dressed real sharp. Deep voice, that kind of snooty talk the rich ones do. He's no Rude."

Frank put in, "Had to be Leon Caviness, that Rolls."

I asked Bill, "Did you hear what they were talking about?"

"Vic walks him to the car, and I slip through the gate." Bill looked at the ground. "Like I said, I'm feeling kind of funny, I just hug the wall there and hope they don't see me. Vic says something I don't catch. Then this guy Caviness says low, but I can still hear him, he maybe should've had Vic come up to the Great-House, somebody might recognize his car. Vic says not to worry, there's no one around. Caviness says he wants Vic to be extra careful."

Bill looked up and met my eye. "He says the deal's worth half a million."

Twenty-One

Underwater, in the agitated swerves of the flashlight beam through the gloom, the carved bird had looked predatory, threatening with its extended talons and wings lowering over me. Now, captured on a photo, the glyph was neutralized. The spread wings could have been ascending.

Kitchen chair tilted back, feet on the table, I balanced my coffee mug on my stomach and studied the Ship Bay prints from Manden's film I'd gotten developed the week before. I hadn't seen Manden since blowing into port with that storm, more tempest-tossed inside than out. I didn't want to see him, didn't want to *think* about him, or his involvement with Caviness. I had work to do.

I frowned, scrutinizing the next print. The stylized dancing man was part of what looked like a fertility group fractured when the boulder slid from its original location up on the cliff. Light glimmered over upraised arms, the thrusting spear of an exaggerated phallus.

A shadow darted across the image. I lurched forward, photos scattering. A tiny lime-green lizard froze on the window screen, bead eyes glittering and scarlet throat puffing. It skittered across my treasure collection on the sill.

Conrad's Jumbie-seed necklace, my family snapshot, the golden shell I'd found at Laura's nude beach. A jam jar with a wilting hibiscus. The empty hourglass curves of John's antique perfume bottle sparkling in the morning sun, beside the pink spiral "octopus shell" Vic had tossed back at me.

"Hello? Susan?"

I crouched hastily to retrieve the fallen photos.

"Susan?" Pat MacIntyre peered through the open doorway.

"Pat!" I shoved the photos under some papers on the table. "Come in."

"Scorcher today. Phew!" She plopped down in a chair, hiked up her rumpled skirt, and squinted at the ceiling. "We don't get some decent rain before summer, we'll have a real drought on our hands. Why didn't you tell me that fan wasn't working right?"

I glanced up at the slow rotations stirring dust motes. "I thought that was how it was supposed to run. Walk."

A thin smile. "I'll get Harry to fix it."

"Thanks." I picked up my mug. "Coffee? Orange juice?"

"Juice." She lit a cigarette, blowing smoke toward the fan. "Throw in a shot of rum, will you? It's gearing up for one of those days."

"Don't have any." I banged the ice-cube tray on the counter. "If I have to taste one more rum-spiked drink or ice cream or cake, I'm going to throw up."

"No problem, got my emergency rations." She dug in her purse and pulled out a flask, pouring dark amber into her juice. "This is for you. From Adrienne." She pushed a paper-wrapped package at me.

"What's the occasion?"

"Beats me, we're not talking. She's on the warpath."

I set the package aside, asked cautiously, "Over what?"

She ran a hand through her cropped hair. "It's that bastard Leon, putting more ideas in her head. Talked her into applying to some snooty French music conservatory."

"Oh." I cleared my throat. "What's wrong with that?"

"She's still my daughter, damn it, and I don't like them sneaking around behind my back! She's already been accepted, for Chrissake. Now she wants to go running off, just when I was training her to take over some management at the resort. She's got a career lined up for her here, she doesn't need to go chasing some silly fantasy."

"Pat, she's a gifted pianist. Don't make her choose between you and her music."

"You mean between me and Leon!" She ground the cigarette furiously into a saucer and gulped her drink. "I never should have let him get his claws into her with those lessons." She scowled. "And that's just the start. Now he's brainwashing her about the land-use debate and the goddamn Independence Movement, he finally came out in the open supporting it. You heard about his petition?"

"Matter of fact, I—"

"He's playing the islanders for bloody fools! Sabotaging the committee's due process, trying to force some kind of popular vote."

She emptied her glass. "He knows there's no chance, island economy depends on Uncle Sam's support, who the hell does he think's gonna feed all the unemployed if we can't build more resorts? All he wants to do is tear things down, wield his bloody power! He's even got Adrienne talking about a union for service workers, go on strike if they don't get the vote. Do you have any idea what would happen to this island if it shut down in the height of the tourist season? Not to mention *our* resort she's ready to flush down the toilet after all our work!"

"Pat, slow down. Natives claiming their rights doesn't mean everything's going to fall apart." I was starting to sympathize with Lieutenant Leland and his anger at the "colonial powers."

"Slow down? I haven't started. Look at this!" She threw her bag onto the table and pulled out a dishtowel, slapping it onto the table and unwrapping it with shaking hands. Inside was another ouanga bag, tied with red string and feathers, smeared with blood.

"Found it hanging on my bedpost this morning. Sure as hell wasn't there when I went to bed."

"Pat! Someone got in while you were sleeping?"

"I pinned Adrienne down this morning." She scowled.

"You can't mean she did it."

"Of course not. But she knew what it was, seems Leon's been teaching her more than music up there." She pounded her fist on the table. "He won't scare me off! I can see him gloating, you know he can move like that, quiet as a snake. Well, this time he's gone too far, I'm taking this to the cops."

"Pat." I poked a fingertip at the bag. "What's between you and Caviness?"

A sharp look. She blew out a breath and sat back. "Guess it won't make any difference." She lifted her empty glass, set it down. "Look, he may play lord of the manor and the poor man's hero around here, but I knew him back in Florida, after his family gave him the boot. He'd gone to that ritzy school in Europe and blown the money they packed him off with after the scandal here. He'd gotten a young girl from a good family pregnant, and she killed herself. Anyway, he was playing piano in the resort where I was assistant manager. But he had connections with some shady types, people in the drug and illegal gambling rackets. Oh, he had a smooth act. Mister Aristocrat." She lit another cigarette, fingers fumbling.

I drummed fingertips on the table. What to do with Bill's story about Caviness and Vic Manden? Pat would run wild with *that* ball.

Pat blew a gust of smoke. "My roommate got pregnant by him, they were talking marriage. Then the news came about his parents being killed, he'd inherited. He was off in a flash and she never heard word one. Guess he didn't want to know he had this fantastic daughter."

She shook her head. "At first she thought she'd keep the kid, even though her family would slam the door in her face if they knew. But after she had the baby, she... it all fell apart. She couldn't cope. She left the little doll with me, went home to Louisiana, just for a visit. An old boyfriend came back into the picture. No one there knew she'd had a baby. No way could she go back with an illegitimate child fathered by a black man."

She tipped ash into the saucer. "By that time, I'd really fallen for the kid. So I adopted her."

"You're telling me Adrienne is Caviness's daughter?"

She mashed the cigarette into the saucer. "It was almost funny when the chance to manage Orchid Bay fell into my lap, with an option to buy in, and I realized it was Leon's island. I couldn't afford to let the opportunity go by. Now you tell me why I should tell her all about her wonderful father."

"He doesn't know?"

"Are you crazy?" She snorted. "Let him really get his hooks into her? Should've had my head examined for letting her start those piano lessons in the first place. If I'd had any clue about this cult, that he'd try to get her into it...."

"If you're that worried, why not send her off to the music school? I take it you don't intend to tell her about Caviness."

She looked alarmed. "You won't spill the beans?"

"That's up to you." I took a deep breath. "Pat, I should tell you something. I signed the petition." I pulled out the copy among my papers on the table.

"What!"

"I was planning to try to get some West End petroglyph sites protected as an historical preserve, anyway."

She launched to her feet, smacking her palms onto the table. "God damn it, you're playing right into his hands!"

I didn't want to remember Caviness's fingers plucking invisible strings. I stood to face Pat. "You can't make it go away."

She grabbed for the petition, jostling my notes aside to reveal the petroglyph photos I'd concealed under them. "What's this?"

I gave a resigned shrug.

She squinted, then caught a sharp breath, gripping a shot of the boulder. "This is what you were after, poking around the West End, asking all your questions." Her eyes narrowed. "What did John tell you?"

I met her intent stare. "What are you hiding about John, Pat? I know about that job he did for you."

"What? What are you talking about?" She backed up a step, face blanching.

"Adrienne told me."

"Adrienne! But she can't...." She shook her head back and forth.

"Here. Sit down." I tried to take her arm, but she shook me off. "Did something happen at the resort when John and Vic Manden worked there? All Adrienne said was you thought Manden was going to take advantage of her."

"Manden?" She frowned. "If that slimeball tries to get his hands on her.... Why are young women such idiots about men?" She ran a hand through her hair, leaving it sticking out wildly. "You're just the same, think you're tough. You're a fool to get mixed up with that man. Look at your brother, for heaven's sake! No honor among thieves."

I stiffened. "What the hell is that supposed to mean? I'm sick of these innuendoes! If you think you know something about John and Manden, just tell it to me straight."

"Now aren't *we* the righteous one!" She snorted, threw down the photo and the petition, snatched up her fetish bag. "I've been trying to help you, Susan! This is the thanks I get." She shoved past me and stalked out the door.

Dust motes swirled to the thresh of the ceiling fan.

I picked up the saucer to dump the cigarette butts, and saw the package from Adrienne pushed to one side. A folded note was taped to it.

"Susan, thank you for sharing the music. I've never worn this dress, but I saw you in a dream, wearing it and dancing with Vic."

I ripped open the package and pulled out a soft cotton, thin-strapped sheath in a bold print of sunshine yellow with big green banana leaves. I frowned. Turning to the wall mirror, I held the skimpy short dress up against my tank top. The supple fabric clung to my tanned skin, leaves twining over my contours like a jungle vine. My face looked startled. I recalled my own dream – running through the rain forest, leaves and vines twining around my nakedness, Vic Manden's hands ripping free the clinging leaves.

I backed away from the mirror, wadding the dress up and throwing it into a corner.

"Where is she? I know she was here. I just talked to her a couple weeks ago."

"Don' know nuthin.' No Granny here." The young boy looked sullenly at the warped linoleum, scuffing it with his bare foot.

I turned slowly in the stifling little room, staring at peeling papered walls. A few tattered posters of musicians and athletes. A narrow metal-framed bed and a wooden chair. All that was left of giant Granny and her altar was a whiff of distinctive pungency.

"Here. She de one, she push in here hollerin' bout some Granny!" A gaunt, middle-aged woman in a stained apron jabbed her finger at me, gripping the arm of a big, paunchy man.

He scowled. "Who you be, bustin' in here? You after my boy?"

The kid smirked, waving the five-dollar bill I'd given him.

"You gimme dat!" The woman grabbed it.

The boy swore.

"Where did she go? You know, don't you?" I caught the woman's arm. I was sure she was the same one I'd seen here before. "I need to talk to her."

Granny had seen it all. My nightmares, the shadow men, the *bete noir*. She could tell me more about the cult. About Caviness, and Adrienne, and Vic Manden. About John, and poor little Samuel. Had I really seen the boy in town? Was there an empty coffin in that cemetery? "Tell me! Where's Granny?"

The woman shrieked, tearing free of my grip. "You crazy! You go 'way! Al*fred*, you make she go!" She scuttled off down the hall.

"I'm not crazy. She was here. I talked to her."

The man dragged me down the hall and shoved me outside. The door slammed.

"*You run 'fore you drown, too.*"

I sagged onto the steps and sat taking deep breaths, head pounding.

Below, in the alley, quicksilver movement. I squinted through the blinding sunlight. A thin little boy in a striped T-shirt, big eyes gleaming, was grinning slyly up at me.

"Willie?" It was the boy who'd guided me here the first time.

My eyes stung and blurred in the harsh glare. I blinked and squinted again. There was nobody in the alley.

Twenty-Two

"Just bring her up closer into the wind." Phillip lounged against the rail in faded khaki, steel gray hair whipped off his craggy face. "Tighten up the jib a bit. There you go."

White sails snapped and bellied in the wind. The hull plunged, spray flying in a sunstruck dazzle. I squinted up at the jib and nudged the wheel. Canvas tautened as *La Sirene* heeled and surged forward, rising, dipping, racing into the wind over the turquoise sea.

I grinned, riding the plunging rhythm. "This is much better than a motor."

"Quite right," he shouted over the wind. "There's been the devil to pay since the invention of the infernal internal combustion engine."

"Phillip." I tweaked the wheel. "I'd like to ask your advice about some problems I've run into on the island."

He shot me a look. "Thought you looked a bit strained." He stood and touched my shoulder. "Let's save it 'til we've had our picnic, shall we?"

He waved a square hand at the clear sky, the stretch of shimmering blue sea. "Glorious morning! I'll go below and pack up our lunch, just keep bearing for that end of the cay." He pointed toward the swelling, humpbacked mass of Palm Cay, then ducked down the hatchway.

La Sirene curtseyed and flew over the rolling waves, responding to the slightest touch. No noise but the hiss of water and slap of sails in the wind, sun and salt air scouring away the cobwebs. Just what the doctor ordered.

"It's a mirage."

Sheer black rock towered overhead, sheltering a gemlike green oasis, grass and low trees clustered around a stone basin fed by a spring. Behind me, Phillip puffed up the last sunscorched grade of the steep goat track. We'd been slogging through choking dust and prickly dry scrub for the last half hour.

"The sacred pool." He came up beside me.

Leaves shimmered, cool and beckoning in the heat. I cleared my parched throat, dropped my knapsack, peeled my damp shirt from my back, and started toward the pool.

"Wait." Phillip took my arm, turning me around. "Look. You see why they chose this spot?"

Beyond the high cliff edge at the peak of Palm Cay, the sea stretched flat to the horizon, dotted with distant islands. Far below, waves crashed and foamed at the base of a jagged fang of black rock thrusting out of the offshore depths. Pale birds glided around it.

"They had water two ways."

"The outlook and the spring itself. Come." He led the way to the spring.

The ceremonial pool filled a natural rock depression beneath the stone wall. Wild tamarind crowded around the basin, thorny creepers twining thirstily over the rock. A row of deeply etched dots and curves decorated the rim. On the inner wall, climbing the rock face, more dots and carved figures.

The familiar stare of carved eyes met mine. There were several pairs, unadorned or enclosed by circular heads. Some of the petroglyphs appeared to be merely geometric designs, but there was a personified sun and a comical bird with a squiggly crest, studying its reflection in the brackish dark water.

Phillip was pointing out a large character on the edge of the group. The man, stick legs and arms akimbo, had an animal head with pointed horns. His straightline torso sported a superimposed belly circle and an exaggerated phallus.

I sat beside Phillip on the basin rim and reached across to trace the line of one carved leg. "This character is a different style from the others, isn't it?"

"If only those arrogant asses at the Institute could see, but they'd have to be bludgeoned. 'No compelling evidence!'"

"It's the dating problem. Nothing organic connected with them, not even earth layers for a relative age."

A contemptuous chop of the hand. "With the establishment stake in the Anglo-European-supremacist Isolationist dogma, they'd ignore a Carbon 14 dating."

I traced the figure's triangular head, distinctly goatlike. "But the lines are so much better defined and deeper than the others. And you'd have to be blind to miss the resemblance to West African fertility figures."

"It's nearly line for line."

"And there was nothing even resembling a goat, indigenous to this area."

"They'd argue the head is only a spirit-design. That's why I didn't bother bringing it up, without more supporting data. You've seen how they attacked my absolutely conservative treatment of the script."

He pointed below the figure. "These marks represent rain. Now, look closer here. What do you see?"

"Rain. Fruitfulness to the earth, offering of a heavenly coupling.... Of course! I assumed it was just a male figure, but now I see it. The circle on the straight belly, like a pregnant womb. And the triangular tip to the phallus is the universal vulva symbol. It's a coition, a synthesis-figure."

"Susan, you're a treasure!" He beamed. "The Libyan-Egyptian influence on West African style is striking when you accept the possibility."

"But with all the evidence of Libyan and West African trading and exploration, how can they all ignore it? The Africans must have adapted this place to their own worship. Like the Spaniards, with their little chapels stuck like warts on top of the Mayan and Aztec temples."

"Yes, yes. Now look at the script." He reached along the back wall to pull away a vine and trace the lines of dots and curves along the pool's inner rim. "Remarkably like Medieval Libyan script: 'Plunge in to cleanse and dissolve away impurity and trouble. This is water for ritual ablution before devotions.'" His moving hand reflected darkly in the water below.

I leaned over the pool, knocking in a pebble. Mirrored silhouettes dissolved into grotesque shapes with the ripples. A pale floating face, sharp talons reaching out for it. I pulled back hastily, blotted my forehead, and studied the hieroglyphs. *Cleanse and dissolve away impurity and trouble.* "Too bad the magic is gone."

"Surprising, how many natives still see Jumbies under every rock. But you and I are anthropologists, immune to that sort of thing." He lifted one thick brow.

I touched fingertips to ripple the dark-mirrored surface. "Suppose the petroglyphs were created as some kind of funnel for the power of the stone? Should we close our minds to trying to understand that?"

His lips twitched. "Spoken like a true scientist." He touched the rain dashes with an absent finger. "It *is* a pity there's no magic here, we could use the rain. See how low the pool is. The water is usually at this mark." He indicated the dark line above water level. "There's generally quite a clear reflection of the script characters. I even toyed once with translating the reverse-image characters, searching for an alternate meaning —"

He turned abruptly back to me. "Very well. You've bewitched me into helping you on this benighted project. *Are* you committed to collecting the facts and judging them with an impartial eye? To maintaining the proper detachment of the anthropologist? You're not going to muddy the waters by invoking some shadowy link to the Vaudun?"

He was giving me a look all too familiar from my run-ins with condescending faculty committees. Maybe Holte was still closer to those "conservative asses" than he'd admit.

"Phillip." I'd been planning to ask his advice about Granny, the ouanga-bags, and Samuel. Lousy timing. "I know the difference between speculation and scientific proof. But if I find evidence of local involvement with something like the Vaudun, I'm not going to overlook it because it smacks of spiritualism or is inconvenient to accepted theories."

"Of course, of course!" He raised placating hands. "You're quite right. I've no intention of trying to straitjacket your findings, as those barbarians did to mine."

"Did they attack your work in Haiti, too? I wanted to ask about your field work there, that's one reason I mentioned the Vaudun. What do you think of the recent ethnobotanic theories about the Bocor potions? The psychoactive zombi powders producing a deathlike hypnotic state?" I still couldn't shake my glimpse of the blank-eyed boy in town, my gut-level certainty it was Samuel.

"Zombi powders?" He frowned. "This new crop of analytical scientists! Don't forget, it was decades ago I did that field work, Haiti was a different world then. A chapter I've no wish to reopen."

"But surely you encountered stories about the zombis, and the curses —"

"Still set on Caviness as the evil Bocor, Susan?" With a dismissive gesture, he rose to retrieve his knapsack. "Let's start with the petroglyphs, take this one step at a time, shall we? But first, some fortification."

With one of his mock-courtly gestures, he indicated a spot of flickering shade beneath the trees. "Shall we dine?"

"Not another bite." I waved away an offering of sliced mango and leaned on my elbows, gazing sleepily over the linen cloth and remnants of the surprising array of delicacies Phillip had packed into his knapsack — elegant little cucumber and lobster sandwiches, cheeses, caviar, sliced fruit, fancy chocolates. "You didn't warn me we'd be roughing it this way."

"My dear, one *must* be civilized about these things." He chuckled, leaning over to pour the last of the Zinfandel into his crystal wineglasses. "May I propose a toast?" He lifted his glass. "To the fruitful issue of your desires, Susan. Pardon me if our lusty friend by the pool has colored my metaphor." He tilted his head at the fertility carving, his gaze lingering on my face. "The vintage becomes you."

I set aside my empty glass. "The only thing I'm becoming is fuzzy around the edges."

He snorted. "Very well. But it's time to 'fess up."

"Confess what?"

"You didn't tell me it was your brother who was drowned here last year."

I sat up abruptly. Looked out over the cliff to the distant waves and wheeling shorebirds. "Did you know John?"

"Of course not." He cleared his throat. "I told you I have contacts on the island, Susan. They inform me you've been asking a lot of questions about your brother's accident."

I turned sharply toward him. "I don't like being spied on."

"I'm sorry." He lifted his hands. "But if I'm to help you, I must know if you're truly dedicated to this project, you're not going to be distracted by some personal quest here."

Reaching into my knapsack, I tossed down my prints of the Ship Bay glyphs. "This should prove I'm serious."

Phillip plucked up the top print and sucked in a startled breath. "Bloody Hell!" He stared at the photo of the entire boulder. Hastily he thumbed through the close-ups.

His stare snapped to my face. "Where did you get these?"

I blinked, taken aback. Was he jealous of my discovery?

He was flipping through the prints, face stunned. "So this is it. This is why you wouldn't give up." He shook his head and gave a short, apologetic laugh. "I *am* sorry! You've given me quite a turn. I'd no idea you'd found anything this spectacular."

"I believe your theory can be proven if these glyphs support it stylistically. And from what I've correlated so far, I think they do. Look." I leaned forward, spreading out the photos. "I wanted to show you this one in particular, now that I've seen the fertility figure here." I handed him the print of the male and female dancers from the sunken rock. "These two. Don't they show the same influence as the newer ones here?"

"You're right!" He'd recovered his poise. "Look here, this headdress. The pattern of rock pecking for these feathery bits looks identical. Difficult to tell from a photograph, shame they're underwater. How did you find them?"

"It was a lead from my brother. Apparently he came upon the petroglyphs when he was excavating a sunken ship."

"The *Phoenix*? What did he tell you?"

I shrugged. "John was... a little haphazard. He just sent me a semi-coherent note, along with a snapshot. Right before he drowned." I poked at the photos. "I had a hard time locating the boulder."

"You do realize how dangerous it was to go to Ship Bay, with the Brotherhood nearby?" He shook his head. "I wish you had asked me for help."

"You were so skeptical, I wanted to verify the site first."

He rolled his eyes heavenward. "A fit epitaph: 'Died a skeptic.' Susan, please don't think of going back there on your own. I do have contacts in the Brotherhood, they might sanction a visit if I approach them carefully."

"Phillip, I didn't dare hope you'd help me this way. Of course, your name will come first if we publish."

"Oh, no, I'm done with all that. This is *your* project. No, I mean it. My reward will be seeing those sacred bloody cows led to the slaughter." He cleared his throat. "I do think we'd better keep it under wraps for now. Could be touchy. You know about the land-use dispute?"

"Pat MacIntyre dropped by this morning to talk about it."

"Pat MacIntyre! You didn't tell her about your find? She might try to block your access, since she's promoting that odious tourism development there."

"She saw the photos."

"Damn. No one else knows?"

"No. Except Victor Manden. He took me there."

"Manden? Don't you know he was a suspect in your brother's drowning?" He leaned forward, laying his hand over mine. "Now listen to me, please, I'd never forgive myself if you were to get hurt. I'm serious, you've been tempting fate. This is the Caribbean, there's a different order down here. Piracy, slavery, violence – it's soaked into the stones of these islands."

"I'm aware of the risks." I pulled back.

His grip tightened on my wrist. "You *are* after more than petroglyphs here, aren't you? What is it? Revenge?"

His eyes were intent. "You may end cursing the day you came here, Susan. You may make discoveries you'll wish you hadn't. I've seen it. The dark heart of the tropics may trap you, and then there's no going back." He lifted a hand, made a cutting motion. "You could stop now. Go home and forget all this."

Goading me again with his dramatics? He was watching me closely. Maybe he wanted the discovery for himself.

My gaze fell to the photos spread on the cloth. I rose and sat on the rim of the pool, meeting the ancient gaze of spiral eyes. A ripple of vertigo washed through me, shadows stirring inside me, part of me now. The back of my neck prickled with a premonition of danger.

I pulled back from the pool, the dim reflection of carved raindrops. "Too late, Phillip."

Twenty-Three

"Mango shave ice! Rum ice cream!" The sidewalk salesman waved balloons in my face as I stepped out of the post office.

"No. More. Rum." I sidestepped him, groping for my sunglasses.

The heat in town was frightening. Flags and sails along the waterfront hung limp and listless. Dark faces crowded the streets, taut and tense, blinds lowered behind their eyes. In the native market, beneath a hand-lettered Independence poster, a restless crowd cheered and jeered a man shouting through a megaphone. "Africa Unite" graffiti overlaid older slogans spraypainted on brick and stucco walls. On Main Street, tourists scuttled through the glare between dim oases of import shops. Gray dust hazed the parched air.

The people at the camera shop needed only the negatives to duplicate my petroglyph photos, so I could keep the working prints. I breathed an absurd sigh of relief as I stepped back into the cobbled street. I'd been lax about backing up my efforts, but that morning, working alone at the cottage, a sudden uneasiness had seized me. I'd sent copies of my notes home for insurance.

"Hot shit! Knew I was on a roll today!" A hand grabbed my shoulder and spun me around. Frank Savetti flashed a grin through his bandolero mustache and gave me a sweaty hug. "Where you been, babe? Said you'd call, you know Mary's pining to make that lobster curry and do a past-life reading on you."

"I've been working. My grant deadline's getting too close for comfort."

"You got to get on island time, gal. Let's go snag a fruit cooler over at The Wave." Gripping my arm, he towed me down an alley, through a market arcade, and in the back gate of an open-air cafe along the harbor drive.

"This'll cure what ails you." He came back from the bar with two tall, frothy drinks, and plopped beside me.

I sipped with resignation from the overly sweet concoction. "Is there some kind of law requiring rum in everything?"

"Mon, dey be no virgin drinkin' on dis I-*land*." He nudged the glass closer to me. "Drink up, rum's just tropical medicine."

"Now there's an inspired line."

"Hey, it worked for John every time. Not that he needed it, chicks were on him like flies. He ever tell you about that first Carnivale he was down here, we hooked up with that female drill team up from St. Kitts for the parade? Now *those* gals knew how to party...."

He stared past me, then jumped up. "Shit! That's the ferry casting off. Gotta make tracks, if I'm late for another afternoon dive, my ass is grass."

He was weaving through the tables toward the quay and the striped awning of the Treasure Island shuttle. Darting through traffic, he made it across the boulevard and jumped a watery gap onto the disembarking ferry. I crossed the street to check out the native fruit stalls on the docks, waving across the wake as the shuttle chugged off.

Frank grinned, shouted, "So give me a call, Hot Stuff!"

The squat ferry churned past docked native cargo boats, the nearest one rising and dipping on its swell. Bright blue paint gleamed. *Sea Maid*.

"James!" I headed over.

He was standing on the deck crowded with wooden crates, staring at the ferry. He spat over the side, turned toward me. Handsome face oddly expressionless, he looped a line with practiced thrusts of his muscular bare arms. The boat's motor was running, fumes bubbling from the stern.

"James, how have you been?" I smiled, squinting up at him.

He shook his head, stowed the rope, stood towering over me. "Gal, you go ask on you self, you don' know de score. You takin' a wrong turn here." He jumped down to the quay, jerked his boat's line free.

I fell back a pace. "James, what's wrong?"

"I say, you bes askin' you self. Why you tink you so rock hard? You jus ridin' foh a fall." He threw the line onto the deck and leaped on board, gunning the motor and swinging away from the quay in a churning wake.

The repaired Honda ticked into silence, dust settling, heat closing in with the trees and bushes surrounding the cottage. I pulled off the baking helmet and blotted my damp face. Feathery mimosa fronds hung limp over the path, beaten down by the fierce sun. Even the lush greens looked drained, color leaching in the drought.

Lifting my key to the lock, I froze. The door hung ajar, wood splintered where the lock had been forced.

Silence buzzed in my ears. Edging away from the doorway, I set down the knapsack, groped for the can of mace I'd bought. Snapping off the guard, I eased back to the door and put my ear to it. No sound inside. I nudged it open, gripping the spray can.

Nothing but the wreckage of my cozy retreat. Table thrown over, clothes flung around the room, gaping closet, broken drawers. Stifling a curse, I checked the bathroom. No one.

I sat abruptly on the bare mattress hanging half off the bed. The sheets had been torn from it, ripped in apparent fury. Broken dishes littered the kitchen floor, scattered into the sitting area. Books were dumped from their splintered case. It must have taken a long time to do so much damage. I sat gaping at the wreckage, trying to comprehend the pointless destruction, still stupidly gripping the mace can.

A glimpse of blue caught my eye. Dad's heirloom volume of John Donne had fallen behind the tipped nightstand. I leafed through it.

"...and in the shadow of death, if thou think to wrastle and bustle through these strong storms and thick clouds with a strong hand...."

I spun toward the windowsill and my little collection of treasures. Swept bare. Dropping to my knees, I plucked up a shard of curved iridescent glass. Elusive rainbows glimmered in the base of John's antique perfume bottle. The rest was only shattered bits on the floor.

I huddled over the fragment, anguish heaving up from deep in my gut, wrenching in its suddenness. Scrubbing at my eyes, I groped through the rubble for my family snapshot. There was still a world out there where my family laughed and smiled in front of a Christmas tree. I couldn't find the framed photo.

Like flicking a switch, grief turned to rage. I pawed through the spilled books, flung aside my scattered clothes, picked up and threw down discarded, ripped petroglyph photos. It was gone. They'd stolen it.

"Bastards!" I pounded the wall. "This goddamn bloody island!"

I threw the tipped chair aside, stormed through the room kicking shattered dishes, flinging aside a broken drawer in a clatter of flying cutlery. My head throbbed with a swelling pressure, shadows swimming before my eyes. I grabbed up a butcher knife and stabbed it deep into the chopping block.

— — —

Stumbling back from the kitchen counter, I stared at the knife handle swaying above its impaling blade. The butcher knife melted, metamorphosed: *serrated dive knife stabbed into a dresser in a dark room, shadowy mirror reflecting red Jumbie seeds like drops of spilled blood* –

I backed away, hands lifting, fending off. Turning stiffly, I strode out the door and headed for the phone at the main house. I called the police more from some stubborn sense of order than any hope for help. At best, the sulky switchboard operator might connect me to someone other than Lieutenant Leland.

"Miss Dunne?" A deep voice tinged with the island lilt. "Susan Dunne? Captain Wilkes here. Pat MacIntyre's been bending my ear about it. Come on down tomorrow morning and we'll talk it over."

I frowned at the phone. "Pat MacIntyre? How did she know?"

"I got it wrong?" Voice lazy. "Didn't you find one of those charm-bags, too?"

"Oh. I see. No. That is, yes." I cleared my throat. "That's not what I was calling about. I just got home to find my cottage broken into."

"Are you all right?" The voice became brisk. "Anything stolen?"

"I don't think it was burglary. They've torn everything apart."

"We'll be right up."

I hung up, paced the stuffy livingroom, dialed the Orchid Bay Resort.

"Susan!" Adrienne sounded harried. "Have you seen Pat?"

"A couple days ago. Why?"

"She told me she'd talked to you the other day, about the music school. We had a terrible fight about it this morning, that and the petition. She stormed off, said she had to meet someone." A pause, the connection crackling. "She was... awfully wound up. Said she was going to get the ammunition she needed to stop Leon." A distant sigh. "I got the impression she might be going to meet you."

"Oh. No. That's not what —"

"Is something wrong?"

Motors rumbled beyond the trees. As I walked down the front driveway, a big native was unfolding his height from a dusty compact. He slouched over to me in rumpled slacks and linen dress shirt, dark scalp gleaming above a graying frizz, face drooping in folds like an intelligent basset hound.

Hostess of the disaster, I guided Wilkes and two patrolmen through the highlights of the wreckage. The three big men and the mess overwhelmed the tiny cottage. Harry, the resort handyman sent by Adrienne, squeezed in to exclaim over the splintered door, smashed dishes, broken shelves. "No good trash do such!"

Wilkes stroked his jowls and shoved an enormous shoe at the rubble. "You're sure nothing was stolen?"

"Not that I can tell, except...." The ouanga-bag Granny had given me was gone from its peg. I wasn't about to discuss that with the police. Spying a gleam of crimson, I crouched to scoop up Conrad's Jumbie-seed necklace.

"Except what?"

I slipped the necklace over my head. "Just a framed family snapshot. No value to anyone else. They could have taken my typewriter or flute instead of dumping them on the floor."

He muttered something. "I was hoping it was just another burglary — the usual outbreak before Carnivale, what with so many transients from down-island. Multiply by two, with the Independence rabble-rousing."

"They were after my research material. The way they ripped up those extra photos and old notes, tore through the cottage. I think it's connected to the fetish-bags and my investigation of Ship Bay. Someone wants to scare me off."

"Cap'n." One of the men was pulling something from behind the tilted bookshelf. He stepped over to hand Wilkes a short metal pry-bar.

"Yours?" Wilkes tilted his head at me.

"No."

"Must have used it on the door, got lost in the action." He turned it over, squinted at peeling, blue-painted initials like construction workers used to identify their tools. He pursed his lips and set it aside.

The other patrolman straightened on his knees beside the bed. "Here be one ting. Dey no break him." He held up the pink spiral "octopus shell" from that first dive with Manden.

I shook my head curtly and he shrugged, setting it on the windowsill.

Wilkes, leafing through his notebook, glanced up from under his brows. "Looks like we'll have to reopen the file on Ship Bay. Sorry about Lieutenant Leland. He can get a little high-handed."

"That's one way to put it."

"He's touchy with Continentals. Thought you were trying to nail him with some connection to the Africa Unite crowd."

"Why would I care? It's no crime to be involved in the Independence Movement, is it?"

"Not quite the same thing. If the word got out, it wouldn't help his career any." He pulled out a folded paper. "Here, I made a copy. You can have this back."

John's letter. I laid it carefully on the righted bookshelf. "Thank you."

He took my elbow and guided me to the door. "Let's go outside."

I sat on the wooden bench beneath Old Granddad's mimosa tree. Wilkes gave me a pensive look. "Who knew about the photos from Ship Bay?"

"Pat MacIntyre."

"What if she staged this production? You two had an argument about the cove, right? You and Leon Caviness are standing in the way of her development plans. She's been pretty vocal about his 'cult.' You might almost say she's acting a little unhinged about it."

"But that's crazy! Someone broke into her place, too, and left that fetish." I rubbed my aching brow. Pat's ouanga bag had looked a bit different from the rest.

Quick gleam of his eyes beneath the lazy lids. "Who else?"

"Phillip Holte. He's an anthropologist who's been helping me with my research. It may help prove his own theory."

"Okay. We've checked him out before, all those trips on his sailboat. Consults on the British islands, advisor for the resource management office."

Phillip had been so mysterious about his trips, part of his dramatic persona. The "cranky hermit" was starting to look downright respectable.

"Anyone else?"

"Victor Manden. He took the pictures for me."

His pen tapped the notebook. "Manden. You hired him to take you out there? The man you accused of killing your brother?"

"No one else would tell me where the cove was."

"Too many people are interested in Ship Bay all of a sudden. Looks like –" He frowned. "Hold on." He ducked inside, reappearing with the pry-bar they'd found. He squinted at the peeling paint, wordlessly handed it to me.

The marks were badly eroded, but I could still make out *V.M.*

"Victor Manden?" Eyebrows raised.

I frowned at the tool. "All his dive gear was marked with his initials, but they were engraved, not painted." Too easy? I cleared my throat and told him about Manden's dive knife I'd found by the glyph boulder. "And there's something else." I repeated what Frank's friend Bill had said about the secretive meeting between Manden and Caviness, the "deal" worth half a million.

He looked up from his notes, an odd expression on his rubbery face. "Huh." He scribbled.

"So what about Caviness and his cult? Aren't you going to question him?"

"If you knew Leon Caviness, you'd realize he's got no need to become involved in some drug ring."

"Phillip Holte said something that made sense. 'Power can be a potent addiction.'"

His nostrils flared angrily. As he opened his mouth, the two patrolmen came out the door.

"No find nuthin,' Cap'n."

Shooting me an irritated look, Wilkes followed them back inside.

Overhead, Old Granddad had crawled onto his favorite branch to watch.

"What did *you* see, old guy?"

Wilkes and his two uniforms filed out the door as a car grumbled up the side drive. A door slammed. Shelli Carver huffed through the bushes, camera slung over a billowing orange blouse. She tossed a cigarette stub onto the patio.

"I just heard, Susan. Tough break." She glanced eagerly around, grinning up at Wilkes. "Captain! Nice surprise."

He grunted and turned to me. "Be sure Harry puts in a decent lock with a deadbolt." He scowled at Shelli and lumbered toward the main drive.

Shelli called after him, "Don't you want your picture taken?"

A car door slammed, motor revving.

"We're having a feud." Shelli grinned. She waggled a ring-encrusted finger. "Why didn't you call me? Remember our deal?"

"This was just burglary."

"Right." She gave me a scornful look. "They knew all the fancy silver would be in here instead of the estate house. Do they figure it was Manden?"

"I don't know what Captain Wilkes thinks. He doesn't seem to take me very seriously."

"Yeah, he's a load of laughs. So what did they get?" She stuck her head through the doorway. "Holy shit!" She raised her camera.

I stepped in front of her. "No pictures, Shelli. Wilkes wants to keep this quiet while they're investigating."

"What about freedom of the press? All right, all right." She retreated to the patio. "So level, what's going on?"

"Looks like someone trying to scare me off. Maybe there *is* a drug ring operating out of the West End. Wilkes pooh-poohed questioning Caviness, but I guess he's going to question Victor Manden again. I'll let you know what they find out."

"By that time the whole island will know." She scowled. "Okay, so I'll sit on it. But remember — you scratch my back, I scratch yours." She shrugged. "Gotta go. Hang in there, kiddo." She headed down the path.

I was contemplating the splintered door frame when Shelli called back from the bushes, "Hey!"

I whirled around to see her camera aimed at me.

"Cheese!"

My jaw dropped in dismay just as she snapped the shot.

Twenty-Four

The Honda skidded on spurting gravel as I shot out onto the mountain road. I roared around aimlessly, taking the steep turns too fast, leaning into them, losing myself in the rhythmic flicker of sunlight through leaves. My head pulsed to its beat.

I hadn't come up with anything missing from the cottage besides the family photo, a nightgown, my hairbrush, and Granny's ouanga-bag. I refused to wonder what they'd do with those things. I didn't believe in their magic. Didn't believe in Granny's magic, either, as I'd tiptoed around the cottage perimeter, sprinkling her packet of anti-Jumbie seeds I'd found forgotten in the rifled cupboard.

After cleaning up the mess, I'd tried to get back to work. But the petroglyph photos and my notes kept blurring to a meaningless hodgepodge. Random hieroglyphs. I didn't know how to assess data any more, how to weigh its importance. Maybe Phillip was right, I was losing my objectivity.

The stifling air of the cottage forced me to breathe in the lingering exhalations of my intruders. Somewhere I'd read how the cells of our bodies are continually casting off their old matter, rebuilding from the new bits of our chance encounters, our old selves doomed to be lost. I didn't want to incorporate the shadowy stuff of this island into what I was.

The walls closed in. They'd been transformed, too, the pores of the plaster soaking in the rank sweat of urgency, violence, the crude glee of wrecking. They pressed closer against me in a repulsive damp embrace.

"Damn." Yanking back on the throttle, I broke out into bright light, squinted, realized I'd taken the road to the Fairview Estate. The gates were closed. The guard called the house, told me Laura wasn't home but Caviness wanted to talk to me.

He received me in his airy office with its view over the sea. "Doctor Dunne, please sit down. How splendid you could make time in your busy schedule. I understand you've made an important petroglyph discovery."

"I've found a few glyphs."

"Come now." He waved a long-fingered hand as he sat behind his desk. "Surely you don't imagine your forays into the West End have gone unnoticed? Now it becomes clear why you were questioning Laura so insistently about the cove where your brother drowned. Obviously the danger from the Brotherhood, and the delicate political balance, haven't daunted you."

I ignored the taunt. "Where's Laura? I'd like to talk to her."

"She's out." He rose abruptly, stood gazing out the French doors for a moment. He turned back to me. "I would like to ask your cooperation, Dr. Dunne. Laura has become increasingly agitated since your return. She suffered a nervous breakdown after your brother's death, and those feelings have been haunting her again. I'm trying to persuade her to begin a therapeutic program. In the meantime, please stay away from her, she doesn't wish to see you."

"I'd like to hear that from her."

An impatient gesture, mouth tight. "At the risk of upsetting her further?"

"I have only your word for that."

"How much evidence do you need, Doctor?" The sarcasm was clear this time. "Oh, yes, I'm forgetting. Godfrey Wilkes tells me you think I broke into your cottage. I'm honored to be promoted from Bocor to burglar."

Great. They were thick as thieves. "What do you want from me? I admit I'm baffled. You've tried ridiculing me, intimidating me, accusing me of stealing the native heritage with my petroglyph work. Then you want my signature on that petition, enlist me as an expert witness for the West End preserve."

He studied me, one hand making that disturbing plucking motion. "You are a dangerous young woman, Miss Dunne," he said slowly. "Dangerous because your ignorant meddling may cause more damage than you suppose. There are complex forces at play on the island now, and the balance could easily be tipped toward violence. Whether you wish to court that risk for yourself is your own affair, but your blundering may well hurt many others."

"It's easy to toss vague statements around." My fingers gripped the chair arms. "It's not that I'm becoming inconvenient to your plans with your cult?"

His nostrils flared. "You've been listening to Pat MacIntyre, her ridiculous accusations. But that's irrelevant now." A gesture of dismissal. "She was right about one thing, Ship Bay is dangerous. Stay away from it."

"You think you can use my testimony, then tell me to drop my research project?"

He slapped his palm onto the desk. "I'm *asking* you to wait until the political situation has cooled off! Can't you see past your own agenda?"

"Can you see past yours?"

His eyes narrowed, then he sat, steepling his fingers. "As you wish. At any rate, Wilkes has decided to institute shore patrols along the West End and keep people out of that cove."

"Wilkes decided? Or you decided for him?"

He gave me a slow smile.

Furious, I headed for the door. Before I could reach it, there was a loud knock, a voice calling, "Mist' Cav'ness, she home." The door pushed open.

I stepped aside from its swing as a big native strode into the office, towing Laura by her arm. Head down, she was pulled along and planted in front of the desk. She shuddered, didn't look up.

Caviness gestured sharply for the man to release her. "Laura, look at me."

She shivered, slowly raised her face. She looked somehow shrunken, pulled in on herself, rumpled shorts and blouse hanging too loose on her thin frame.

"What did I tell you?" He drilled her with his dark eyes and deep voice. "Laura?"

Staring at him, unblinking, she lifted her hand in a jerky motion, held out her car keys. She dropped them into his upraised palm.

"Good. It's done, then." He tilted his head at the servant. "Take her to Imogene, she'll put her to bed."

Wordlessly, Laura turned. She saw me standing in the shadows by the door and gasped, stumbling back with a horrified look on her face. "John! No, don't, it wasn't my fault —" She choked, hands coming up to fend me off.

"Laura, take it easy." I stepped forward, raising my palms in reassurance.

She flinched, squinted, caught a sharp breath. "Susie! It wasn't...." She shook her head quickly, darted a look at Caviness, back at me. "Oh, God, I'm so fucked!" She burst into tears.

"Laura." Caviness didn't move, his voice stern. "Go with William. Now. You need to rest."

She nodded, ducking her head and bumping blindly against the man as he guided her out the door.

"Laura, wait!" I started after her. "We need to talk."

Caviness caught my arm from behind, pulling me up short. I spun around, ripping free of his grip.

"Don't." He was gazing down at me, and I couldn't move. I stared with revulsion and fascination into his deep-set eyes.

"No man is an island?" he whispered.

The room was spinning dizzily around the dark pools of his eyes. They were fixed and blind-looking. His hand lifted, summoning. Deep in his eyes danced tongues of flames, a pale face drowning in silver moonlight, the pulsing rhythm of the sea pounding the shore.

I fell back a step, raising a hand to my throbbing head.

"Remember, Susan Dunne." His voice resonated through my bones. "A blade cuts two ways."

I winced. Hadn't Granny said that?

"If you must fight my black magic, why not arm yourself with knowledge? I perform a ceremony for the water loa on the night of the full moon. Take part and see. Perhaps you will find those answers you think you want, perhaps you will find what the questions should be."

I eyed him warily.

"Surely you're not afraid? You don't believe in my powers, do you? Come, walk where angels fear to tread."

"I'll come." I turned stiffly and walked out the door. Behind me, dry laughter.

The echo of his laughter pursued me to the driveway, past Laura's dust-covered sports car back in its slot. The "fender benders" hadn't been repaired. I revved the Honda and roared out the gate into the leafy tunnel of the mountain road. I couldn't face the cottage yet, the presence of my intruders oozing from the walls. I headed over the crest to Orchid Bay. Maybe Adrienne could shed some light on Caviness's Byzantine plots.

Baffled by the maze of unmarked roads, I finally found the right turnoff. It took me winding along the crest of a high ridge, then swept down in steep plunges. Lowering sun threw the tree-lined road into shadowy gloom. The rain forest still simmered with heat, thick silence pierced only by the Honda's racket.

Another precipitous drop ended in a sharp curve around an exposed rock outcrop. Far below, scattered houses, a strip of beach, darkening sea. I slowed for a tight curve, skid marks onto the narrow shoulder the only caution signs for the straight drop off the verge. No guard rails on the island roads.

I almost missed it, just happened to glance at the view opened over the shadowed hillside as I took the turn. Something shiny and light blue glinted among the green and dried brown.

I pulled a U-turn and parked on the edge of the drop, heat and silence dropping over me. I peered down.

Shredded plants and shattered boughs ripped a swath through the dense foliage. At the bottom, caught and twisted against thicker trunks and almost hidden in the branches, a car. What I'd first glimpsed was a crumpled fender, wedged above the wreck in some bushes, still gleaming light blue with what looked like a fresh wax job.

Easing over the rocky outcrop, I slithered and groped my way down through the tangle of bushes and trees, grabbing at shattered branches, fresh rivulets of sap just starting to harden.

I was still feebly hoping that help had come and gone, the driver had already climbed to safety, when I got close enough to see into the shadowed interior. There was someone slumped behind the wheel. I caught a branch, bracing myself. The car was a compact wagon, common on the island. I dropped lower over the slope, tripped over a vine, tore free and fell against the tilted car, paint warm against my palms. Shattered windshield glass glittered over a motionless body.

"Oh, no. No." I yanked at the door on the driver's side. It scraped open in a screech of bent metal.

A mangled mess where the driver's legs had been crushed when the front of the car folded around the tree. Blood everywhere. Spattering the seat, splashed on the door panel, pooled on the floorboards. The woman's hands were still clutching the wheel, bones standing out sharply against the skin, head slumped forward. Smell of hot metal. Sickly-sweet alcohol fumes from a broken bottle wedged in the empty passenger seat.

I touched the woman's inert shoulder. Still irrationally hoping, refusing recognition, I pulled her back against the seat.

Her head lolled, lifeless and grotesquely loose. Her face was gashed, hair blood-matted, eyes staring glassily. Pat MacIntyre.

Twenty-Five

"She, she is dead; she's dead: When thou knowst this, Thou knowst how lame a cripple this world is."

The pages turned, whispering.

"And there rises a kinde of Phoenix out of the ashes...."

I closed my eyes, rubbed my aching brow as the ceiling fan vainly stirred the muggy heat.

"If the calamities of the world have benumbed and benighted thy soule in the vale of darknesse, and in the shadow of death....

"What is there then that can bring this Nothing to our understanding?"

I dropped the volume of Donne on the table and picked up the Island Tattler again. Front page photos, a black and white turmoil of shapes and faces radiating urgency. Harsh contrasts of bright light and shadow caught squad cars, policemen, ambulance, white-coated aides frozen on the edge of the cliff. Shelli had snapped me beside slouched Captain Wilkes, my face haggard and staring.

The raw urgency was only an illusion. By the time Shelli and the rest had arrived, the need for hurry was long past.

"Another tragic accident on the Crown Mountain Road.... Evidence that Miss MacIntyre lost control of her car while intoxicated...."

I tossed the paper down. At least Shelli had waited until after Pat's funeral. But the article promised "continuing in-depth coverage." She was champing at the bit for her big story.

From the windowsill, my family in miniature smiled through cracked glass. The police had found the stolen photo in Pat's car.

None of it made sense. Had she really been that desperate to prevent me from investigating the cove? Captain Wilkes seemed convinced she'd been my "burglar." When I'd asked him why she hadn't left a bogus fetish to warn me off, he'd shrugged. Maybe she ran out of time. Maybe she was drunk and forgot it. Maybe she meant to make up a fetish from my stolen nightgown. But the police hadn't found any sign of it, or my missing hairbrush, at the wreck site.

I knuckled the painful pulse in my temples. The headaches had disappeared for a while after Granny's "cure," but now they were back. With a sigh, I turned to John Donne, leafing through his poetry as my fingers absently traced the smooth curves of a seashell from my dwindled collection on the sill.

"*License my roving hands —*"

I looked down at the pink "octopus shell" in my palm, hastily pushed it aside and turned the page.

"*That I may rise and stand, o'erthrow mee, and bend*
Your force, to breake, blowe, burn and make me new....
Take mee to you, imprison mee, for I
Except you enthrall mee, never shall be free,
Nor ever chaste, except you ravish mee —"

A sharp knock on the door.

I slapped down the book. "Who is it?"

"Vic. Manden."

I stared transfixed at the closed door. Like a robot, I rose to open it.

He stood in the searing sun, face a blank mask. In vivid contrast, the light intensified the color of his eyes to electric blue, tension snapping in the air. Heat and sunlight shimmered over him, sparking coppery glints I was sure would crackle static shocks on contact.

Sweat broke out on my back, face flushing.

"Are you going to let me in?"

I cleared my throat, moving back.

"Pretty Jumbie-beads." As he stepped inside, he tilted his head toward Conrad's necklace I was wearing. He plucked up the book I'd dropped face-down, glancing at the passionate sonnet. His gaze snapped to my face.

I took the book and smacked it shut.

"John Donne? 'No man is an island'?" He shook his head. "We all are. Just damn lucky if we manage to get any kind of signals across the gulf."

I blinked.

He turned, studying my family photo, John grinning distantly behind the cracked glass. He picked up the gleaming pink shell and weighed it in his big hand.

He set it down, turning back to me. "I've been down to see Adrienne. She's taking it hard."

"It's all so senseless...."

"I know the feeling. Hear you had a break-in."

"Did Captain Wilkes talk to you?"

"The cops?" He frowned. "They haven't accused me of *that* yet. Why?"

I cleared my throat. "It wasn't the usual burglary, looks like they were after the petroglyph photos."

He gave me a sharp look. "Stolen?"

"No, luckily I had them in town, being duplicated. But Wilkes seems to think there may be something going on over by Ship Bay. I... thought he might ask you about the photos." Either the Captain was biding his time, or he'd just been humoring me about investigating Manden. After Caviness's revelations, I didn't know what to think. It was possible that pry-bar with the initials had been deliberately planted. By my intruders, maybe even the police. My fingers absently kneaded the annoying ache in my forehead.

"What?" He was watching me.

"Nothing. It's just this island."

"You'll get used to it." Glimmer of teeth. He took a breath. "Look, Susan, I think you've got guts. So what if you're dead wrong."

"What are you talking about?"

"I didn't kill John. I know you don't believe it, so you better come with me today." His lips twitched. "You've been slacking off on me, I kind of miss the excitement. Aren't I still the number one suspect?"

I stood gawking at him.

"Grab your dive gear, I've got a job you can help me with. You might find out some things." He lounged arrogantly against the wall, crossed his arms, gave me a taunting look. "You want to know what happened with me and John, or not? Better make up your mind. Maybe I won't be in the mood tomorrow." He met my gaze, all his pent-up energy crackling in the crowded little room, another invader in my space.

"*I'm* not in the mood." I strode to the door and held it open.

"Forget it, then." Mouth tightening, he started past me. He spun around, frowning, reaching to grab my seed necklace. "Where did you get this?"

Startled, I pulled back, jolted to a stop by his grip on the strand. He yanked it over my head.

"What the hell are you doing? A friend gave me that!" I grabbed at it.

"Some friend." He twitched it out of my reach. "You need to take a shower. Now."

I fell back a step. "Are you crazy?"

He was scowling down at the red seeds. "Crab eyes."

Backing away, I came up against the wall.

He raised his face. "Shit. You're really afraid of me." He held out the seed strand. "Look. They're not Jumbie seeds, they're crab eyes, you can tell by the black dots. Poison, absorbed through the skin."

"What?" I stepped reluctantly forward to squint at the loop. There was a tiny black dot on each seed. It wasn't the necklace Conrad had given me. A wave of dizziness passed over me.

Manden touched my shoulder, voice gone quiet. "You really should wash it off. I'll go." He tossed the seeds in my wastebasket and headed for the door.

"Wait."

He turned, gaze locking on mine. Another ripple of dizziness, and I was lost in time and place, back in the drowning seas. Suspended in the surreal depths where John died, these same eyes probing me intently through our masks.

"All right. I'll go with you today. Maybe I'm as crazy as everyone else on this goddamn island."

His white grin flashed. "Now that's John's sister talking."

―――

The battered gray Jeep growled down the switchbacks off the mountain, Manden silent at the wheel. I touched my neck where I'd scrubbed off the poison of the crab eye seeds. How had he known about them? The necklaces must have been switched during my break-in.

I glanced over at him, blunt face masked by his mirrored shades. It was like peeling an onion. How many layers were we going to strip off each other before we got to some core of truth? *Was* there a core, or only layer after layer, wrapping empty air?

The road took a last turn, and we broke out of tree shade into blazing sunlight, swooping into the straight plunge toward town and a dark pall hanging over the harbor. I swallowed, tasting smoke. "What's going on?"

He snapped out of his fixed stare at the road. "Another fire."
The smoke was thicker past Main Street, in one of the native jungle-towns. "This is the third one in the past two weeks."
"Bad season."
The grass and bushes along the road, brown and withered now, had been rich green when I moved in. "Shelli came out with one of her subtle editorials, hinting it's the Africa Unite agitators starting the fires."
"Ms. Ethical Journalism?" He snorted. "Maybe it's worse this year, with the drought and the Independence Movement, but shit always starts happening in the spring." He glanced at me. "The old pressure cooker just gets too hot, people go a little crazy. Good timing, Carnivale coming. Release valve."
"Like the ancient rain rituals. Leon Caviness is planning to perform a ceremony for the water spirit." I glanced aside at him. "Have you seen the fetish necklaces he makes for the natives?"
He eased around a tourist bus wheezing uphill. "That where you got your crab-eye seeds?"
"No. I'm talking about cloth bags, made from a person's clothes, with magic objects inside, used for protection or 'putting a power' on someone."
"Sounds more like Voodoo than the Obeah they have here. This tied into your research?"
"In a way. You've never seen one?"
He shook his head, swerving around a pothole as we swooped down the last hill. The stinging smoke haze closed around us. "So you think Caviness is into black magic? I've heard the buzz about his so-called cult. That's the island for you, start casting stones, ask questions later. Me, I don't know the guy." He turned onto the busy harborside drive.
What about his "deal" with Caviness?
He shot me a look. "Funny you mention him." He stopped for a red light, heat pulsing in the breezeless glare off concrete and chrome, simmering the acrid smoke. "Just met him a couple weeks ago. Hired me to look for a yacht wrecked in a storm last year, he bought the insurance rights for salvage. I'd about written it off, but I think I stumbled onto it yesterday. So we're working for Caviness today."
"Oh." Truth? Lies? If I collected enough stories, maybe the puzzle pieces would fall into place.
The light turned green and the Jeep moved forward, bringing us below the fire. Red lights flashed, sirens wailing through smoke. Muffled voices shouted, surging closer through the haze.

"Steal we island, burn us out!"

"We drivin' out de slavers!"

A shrill whistle, shadowy shapes running, boiling out of the billowing smoke. Taillights flared, traffic crunching to a halt.

Another loud whistle, someone shouting through a megaphone. Sirens wailed up behind us. The mob was pouring downhill from the fire, natives darting between cars ahead. Police cars were blocked behind us, sirens shrieking, lights flashing. Native cops with helmets and billy clubs advanced past the jammed cars.

A wild-eyed, dreadlocked native in ripped T-shirt grabbed the Jeep door and thrust his face up to mine, shouting, "Fuckin' muddah scunt, you suckin' off us!"

Vic leaned across me, pushed at the man's chest. "Get going, man. Cops coming."

The man's eyes rolled. He whirled and ran.

An angry roar broke out. The crowd surged uphill again, running back into the twisting lanes of jungle-town. I coughed, squinting through the haze. Ahead, a policeman was waving the traffic on.

We rolled slowly forward, past more cops handcuffing a couple of Dreads. A knot of women and children watched, one woman screaming at the police. Uphill, beneath the smoke, flames leaped from a two-story building, water spraying, lights flashing. The cop directing traffic waved again, and we were past it, picking up speed along the harbor boulevard.

I cleared my parched throat. "Looked like an apartment building. I can't believe the natives would burn their own homes. Where will they go?"

"Who knows, with the housing crunch. More of a mess, everybody on welfare, plus all the illegals, crammed into those godawful jungle-towns. Nowhere to go, no way out. Don't even have a vote."

He shot me a look. "At least Caviness is speaking out for the people. Government and the Continentals are screwing them over, same old colonial bullshit, same old mess just like over in —" He bit it off, chopping his hand through the air. "Our glorious white man's civilization has managed to royally fuck up the world, so maybe Caviness is going to Voodoo us all. Why the hell not?"

The sea stretched prostrate beneath a merciless sun, ruffled only by a fitful breeze. Manden pointed over the bow at a triangular chunk of rock thrusting through haze in the distance. "We'll head past French

Cap. There's some shallow reef out there where the yacht hit. Then it got carried into a trough. Wind and currents must have been a weird combination that night, what with the storm, to carry it that far. Probably why the insurance company couldn't find it."

We picked up speed, and I raised my voice above the motor's roar. "How did Caviness come into it?"

"Guess he heard about the gold and emerald jewelry the insurance company coughed up for. I've bought salvage rights myself, generally for boat parts after the companies settle."

"How did you find it if they couldn't?"

"Started looking in the directions that didn't make sense. Towed a magnetometer and got lucky. I only had time yesterday to check it out and clear off some of the mess."

"Caviness trusts you to bring him whatever you find? What would stop you from just keeping it?"

"Are you naturally suspicious, or do you practice?"

French Cap swelled closer across the deep blue, loomed jagged over us, and fell away behind. Manden pulled into a slow circle, our foamy wake smoothing out. Dark sapphire gave way to light turquoise and brownish shapes of submerged reef.

"We're close." He took bearings from land and swerved, slowing over an apparently empty stretch of deep water. "To starboard. There's a ridge and a trough. Climb up on the bow, would you, drop the anchor when we get over the ridge?"

When I dropped it, he cut the motor. We drifted back and then held.

"All right, it's a deep dive, about a hundred feet, so we'll have to watch our bottom time. All you have to do is stand backup from the upper salon while I go below." He reached into a storage niche for a piece of nylon line and briskly coiled it. "Yesterday I cleared most of the junk away from the hatchway and braced it where the roof had caved in, so I can get down below to look for the jewelry box in the hidey-hole Caviness told me about."

He tossed a set of coveralls at me. "They aren't glamorous, but they'll save you scraping yourself up."

I zipped the suit over my shorty wetsuit and tied my hair back. "Why did you want me to come along?"

He turned from the tanks, glittering lenses fixing on me. "Maybe I need to find out some things, too."

Shadows and the weight of depth pressed in on me. My breaths echoed to the hiss of sharply-etched rising bubbles. I felt as hollow and fragile, the distant world of sunlight and air unreachably remote. The dark sea pulsed in my veins, singing, calling me deeper.

I shook my head and pulled in a deep, slow breath. Nitrogen narcosis. Rapture of the deep.

My light jittered over the wreckage of the yacht's main salon, a disintegrating couch, a smashed television set, what must have been a built-in bar. Shattered glass gleamed among the rubble and the squat shape of a bottle furred in silt. I finned over to pull it free. The paper label was gone, but the distinctive shape was still intact and full of amber brandy.

Already tipsy with the nitrogen effect, I held up the bottle and raised two fingers for victory. Manden's eyes crinkled behind his mask. I stuck the bottle inside my coveralls, weight belt holding it in place.

He beckoned me toward the top of a descending spiral staircase. Broken pieces of cabin roofing and remnants of crushed furniture were piled to one side of a narrow, cleared opening. He pointed out the beam he'd placed the day before to support the crushed ceiling.

Indicating his watch, he flashed fingers for "fifteen." He pointed at me, held out his palm in the "stay here" sign, gave me the end of his coiled line. I signed "OK," and he squirmed headfirst down the opening, tank barely clearing.

Hovering with the line in my grip, lightheaded, I swept my flash around the salon, caught a flicker of movement across an empty picture frame hanging askew on one buckled wall. A tiny octopus, crawling across it, froze in the light.

Bubbles oozed up from below, through cracks in the flooring. Manden's air trail moved beneath the rubble of the wrecked bar and stayed there. It seemed like a long time. I chewed edgily on my mouthpiece, remembering the limit on bottom time at this depth.

Hovering over the cleared stair, I flashed my light down into the wrecked spiral. I couldn't see much through the cleared gap. Shining the beam over the salon, I saw bubbles moving back toward me. I let out a relieved lungful of air.

In the next moment, it was all turned inside-out. Dimness swirled over my eyes, and *I* was the diver at the bottom of the spiral staircase. I was drowning, claws of the *bete noir* tightening around my throat, my lifeline snapped.

I took a shaky breath and shook my head, staring in confusion at Vic's cord still intact and slack in my grip.

Then the shadows exploded around me. A muffled *whump*, and trapped water surged, tumbling me back in the wrecked salon. I scrambled, hit something spinning past, groped blindly. A cloud of silt billowed, pressure like a giant hand swatting. Air boiled up from the stairwell. Flailing upright, I grabbed my flash on its wrist cord. All I could see was swirling silt. I kicked forward, knocking my shins against a hard edge. The spill of air finally carried off the silt. The cleared stairwell had caved in.

I dropped the useless line. Clawed at the rubble blocking the stair, ripping out pieces and throwing them behind me, oblivious to the tangled mass shifting above me with each piece I grabbed. Air gushed up through the debris. His tank valve must have been knocked off. Even if it was only a broken hose, he couldn't last long at the rate his air was pouring past.

I tore at a twisted metal bar, slicing my hand through the glove. Yanked the bar free. Flung it away. Blood drifted, swirled by the rush of air from below. Sharp metal taste in my mouth. Would I clear an opening only to find him dead? Not again. Glassy eyes staring up at me, blank windows onto nothing.

I couldn't let him drown. Vic. John. Not that horror, again, staring into the abyss through his eyes while his air ran out, and he was trapped and screaming.

Air hissed, pulse pounding in my ears, terror echoing me to him, he to me. I could feel his useless struggles twitching in my own muscles. I ripped my way through. Almost there. The stream of air trailed off. A few stray bubbles. None.

I tore aside a thin sheet of plastic. His eyes stared, glazed, through a cracked mask. Too late. They'd gone empty.

I stared at his glassy blank eyes, cold despair settling in my gut. Was this what I'd wanted?

The eyes blinked. I gasped.

Vic focused on me. His eyes crinkled in a strange smile.

I grinned back, weak with relief. Then I saw his arms and body were pinned by the supporting beam fallen onto his back.

I yanked the useless regulator from his mouth and pressed mine into his lips. Somewhere a pedantic voice recited passages from my diver's training manual: *"When buddy-breathing, always purge the regulator and allow your partner two breaths...."*

The voice didn't tell me how to free him. I pushed and tugged at the beam. It wouldn't move. Vic grimaced. His shoulders strained, but he couldn't free his arms. I wrenched at the stubborn beam.

A high-pitched sound caught me up short. Vic spat out the regulator, giving me a pale imitation of his cocky grin. I dragged in a couple of breaths and stuck the regulator back into his mouth. He jerked his head and spat it out, mouthing words, gesturing with his head.

Finally it penetrated. I took another shot of air and gave the mouthpiece back to him, pulling off my buoyancy vest with its tank. I positioned it under the beam where it wouldn't slip free. Pressed the inflator button.

The beam shifted a little as the vest ballooned with air. It stuck again. I made a despairing gesture. Vic only nodded. I added more, then stopped, afraid the vest would rupture. The beam shifted slightly. I tried to pull him free by his shoulders. He shook his head.

We were running out of air. Out of time. I gave the beam a furious shove. It slipped to the side, rose slowly above the vest.

I gripped it, afraid to move. Holding the wobbling beam, I braced my legs apart in front of him. He squirmed and pulled. Yanked at a strap. I couldn't hold my breath much longer. He worked his arm out of his trapped vest and tank, pulled himself free with a heave. I couldn't let go of the unstable beam.

My lungs screamed for air. Biting back a desperate urge to gulp water, I hung on as Vic eased himself up against me. He pushed the regulator into my mouth.

I gasped in a breath, nearly choking on seawater. He raised his hand to hold the beam and vest in place, jerked his head upward. I hesitated, suddenly terrified to leave the mouthpiece. I sucked in a last breath and shot up through the stairwell.

I waited forever. No air, dark depths crushing down. A faint thump below, more felt than heard. Silt cloud bursting up. Hands appeared, clutching the ballooned vest and tank flying up as the beam and debris crashed in to close the passage. The freed vest flew upward, nearly past me before I grabbed the hose and hit the deflate button, releasing air. Vic floated beside me, grasping the tank. He passed me the mouthpiece. Hands shaking, I pressed it into my mouth and breathed deeply.

Vic gave my shoulder a squeeze, flashed his watch, pulled the vest over my arms. He beckoned, swimming out the broken cabin roof. I swam after him, shooting up toward the gleam of light at the far surface.

He grabbed my hand, slowing me down, pointing at the glistening stream of bubbles drifting toward the surface. The diver's manual was droning again: *Air embolisms. The bends.* Vic gripped my wrist as we drifted slowly upward, staying safely behind the slowest air bubble. My pulse drummed in my ears.

As I passed Vic the mouthpiece, he grabbed my wrist, pulling my hand in front of his cracked mask. I'd forgotten my gashed palm, haze of blood drifting.

Worried frown in his eyes. I shook my head, made the *OK* sign. He grasped my shoulder and pointed past me. I turned and saw the shark.

Big. Ten, twelve feet long. Dark stripes. A picture from my fish guidebook leaped alive in sinuous threat and rows of teeth. Tiger shark. Known man-eater.

It circled, testing for the blood that had drawn it.

Vic pressed his hand against my cut palm. He pulled me toward the boat, keeping submerged and close to the ridge. The shark followed, swimming faster now, circling us with sinister grace.

It stared glassily as it whipped by. Eyes flat, dead-looking. No spark of intelligence, only the raw instinct to kill and feed.

We reached the shadow beneath the stern of the boat. Vic gave me a hasty ascent sign. The shark made another quick pass. In a flash of gleaming stripes, it whipped around to circle back. Vic grabbed my arm and shot for the surface.

The last of my air escaped as I raced upward for the boat. A gray streak shot past. The shark darted in again.

Blur of bubbles. Glinting teeth. Vic kicking his fin at its nose. Long sinuous shape twisting. Barreling back at us. Silent scream ringing. Surface breaking over us. Sunshine, air, blessed blue sky. Water heaving, boiling beneath me. Monster hurtling up out of the depths. Bobbing stern platform. And the weight on my back, holding me down.

A splash. Something heavy, rough, slamming against me. I scrabbled for the platform. The waves jerked it out of my grip. I screamed.

Twenty-Six

Vic grabbed my wrist. I gasped. He tugged. Somehow he flew out of the water, dragging me and the heavy tank out with him onto the platform. Beside us, a splash. A triangular fin cut the surface, circling the boat.

Vic pulled me into the Whaler, tore the vest and tank off me. I sank onto the bench, legs gone rubbery, dragging in heaving breaths of warm air. The fin circled again and disappeared. I shuddered.

"Jesus!" Vic paced the cramped deck. Looked over the side. Slapped off water with quick, charged movements. He dropped his weight belt to the deck. Peeled off his coveralls and wetsuit, flung them aside. He leaned over the side of the boat again. Straightened. "I guess it's gone. You don't see many Tigers around here. Not aggressive like that one." He slicked back his wet hair and rubbed his beard. Finally he planted his feet before me. "Are you okay?"

Shivering uncontrollably, I managed, "You c-certainly get your money's worth out of a diver, d-don't you?"

"Let's get that coverall off you." He crouched in front of me, fumbling with the zipper. He unbuckled my weight belt and the brandy bottle tumbled out.

"What?" He caught it with a startled movement.

Relief, absurdity flooded. I started laughing and couldn't stop. "If you c-could see your face!" I struggled out of the sodden coverall and my wetsuit, teeth still chattering. "I c-could use a shot."

Vic handed me a towel. "Let's take a look at that hand first."

I studied my palm, the gash oozing blood. "Not so b-bad."

He nudged me onto the bench, dropping to one knee to grasp my wrist and examine my palm. "Guess you won't need stitches."

But he kept hold of my hand, staring down at it. Closing his eyes, he took a deep breath, suddenly raised my palm and pressed it hard against his forehead, bowing over it. A strange, keening sound rose from his throat.

Startled, I yanked my hand free. He slowly raised his face, brow and cheek branded with my streaked blood. Raw emotion transformed his face to the mask of a primal rite. Unmasked? Stripped of another layer.

I closed my eyes, shivering.

His hands, surprisingly gentle, tucked the towel around my shoulders. "Here. Hold out your hand. Got to disinfect it." A popping sound.

I opened my eyes to see him tilting the brandy bottle. "Wait!" A generous splash poured over my palm. "Ouch!" The flame in my hand burned off my chill.

He pulled out a first-aid kit, dabbed on gooey cream, and pressed wadded-up gauze against the cut, wrapping my hand.

I peered over his shoulder at the open kit. "I'm sure you've got some kind of antiseptic in there that wouldn't sting. Sadist."

He sat back on his heels and gave me a sober look. "You saved my life down there. I owe you."

My eyes suddenly filled with tears.

"Hey." He stood, pulling me to my feet, wrapping his arms around me and holding me close. "It's all right. Just let it out."

I gripped him, leaning into his bare chest, had to feel us both here in the flesh. He was warm, solid, tangy with the scent of sea and skin. Alive.

His arms tightened around me, heart beating deep and fast against my ear. A low hum as he rocked me slowly. His lips brushed the top of my head.

My body blindly curved into his, felt the heat of his skin through my swimsuit. I caught a sharp breath and raised my face. He was flushed, eyes bright against the deep tan. That electric connection crackled between us. Alive. We were alive.

My hands moved in a dreamlike motion, reaching up to touch his coppery beard, pull his face down to mine. I licked my salty blood off his cheek.

A strangled sound in his throat as he gripped my head with his big hands and kissed me hard. My mouth opened to his tongue searching, sharing the taste of my blood. He groaned, pulling me closer.

I was licking his salty skin, biting his neck, digging my fingers into the thick muscle on his shoulders and chest, grabbing his head and drawing his mouth back to mine. I wanted to consume him, be consumed. High-pitched animal sounds were coming out of me. He was hard, pulsing against me, his heat swamping me. I gasped in a wave of blind panic, drowning.

"I'm here. Hang on." He pulled me in tighter, mouth finding mine again, tongue probing, demanding.

My palms slid over his slippery wet skin, muscled contours, pulling him against me, pushing against him until the boundaries of our skin melted and fused. I panted, sinking deeper into his scent and taste and feel.

He ripped off my swimsuit – *torch flames licking shadows in the night forest, leafy vines entwining me, his hands ripping them free* – and pushed me down onto our towels, kissing and biting, sucking my breasts, rubbing his hard penis over my belly slick with our mingled sweat. *Drums echoing snake sliding thick and slippery over my belly, thrusting into me –*

I cry out as he thrusts into me it's his cry I feel in my throat his throat, my big callused hands sliding over her shoulders and breasts we're melted together in the drumbeat and fire. He's inside me, groaning, pushing deeper. The rhythm pumps faster, harder. Plunging to the core of me/him and it's too much I climax unable to bear it but he pushes on, relentless, taking me with him ever deeper into the redhot dark, searing through the walls, the limits and I'm lost.

"Susan. Stay with me."

He's there with me, inside me, turning me inside out I'm inside him and we're going together. He's pushing, making me give him give myself more and I suddenly hate him, fighting it he has no right to do this to me. My eyes snap open, see his straining, bloodstreaked face above me. Mask of a stranger. Animal eyes glinting fierce grinning rictus skull beneath the skin. Always. Claiming us, the elemental powers.

I close my eyes and I *am* the power racing us on. The pulsing beat, faster, the rhythm driving our mingled heartbeats and blood. Pounding to a final impossible pitch before we're thrown free.

A sticky tangle of limbs. Vic, beneath me, still inside me, lying slack and staring glassily at the sky. A pulse slowing, diffusing the aching fullness in my groin, *his* groin –

I wrenched away from him, fists pressed against my pounding head.

"What? What?" Scrambling sounds, and he was beside me, arms around my shoulders.

I shuddered away from his touch. "I don't know who you are. Who *I* am. I felt you calling me down there in the yacht, you were drowning, only it was John, calling me again. The Link? I'm losing it, this bloody island —"

"Susan!" He shook my shoulders.

I flinched away.

"Susan, damn it, look at me!"

I scrubbed at my damp face, met his eyes, vivid in the blazing sunlight. "Vic, it's too much." I shook my head. "I can't —"

"Can't trust me?" Face naked, chest rising and falling like he'd been running.

"It's... more complicated than that." I rubbed my eyes. "I can't explain."

"Try me." Voice lashing.

He was kneeling, naked, holding up his empty hands as if to show me he had no weapons. "Susan, after everything we've been through, you have to at least explain."

I took a deep breath. "You're right. That's fair."

"Good." He squeezed my shoulder, stroked the hair back from my face. "You feel feverish. How long were you wearing that crab-eye necklace?" His palm rested on my forehead. "Here." He grabbed a towel and dunked it over the side, offered it dripping.

I rinsed my face and wrung the welcome coolness over my back and chest.

He silently handed me my swimsuit and a towel. As I dried off and slipped on my suit, he climbed onto the rail, dove in with a splash. I craned over the side, gut clenching, expecting the shark back.

Vic emerged with a smooth heave onto the stern platform, shook off water, and pulled on a pair of shorts. Leaning against the gunwale, he crossed his arms. "Okay. Tell me." Face gone neutral.

I cleared my throat, tugging the towel around my shoulders and sinking onto the bench to stare out to sea. "You'll think I'm crazy."

"I've given up expecting things to be sane. Just be straight with me for a change."

Watching the smooth swell, riding it as it rocked the boat, I told him about John's letter, Laura's fearful behavior, Leon Caviness and his cult, Samuel's death and the ouanga bags, all the fingers pointing to Vic and a drug ring.

"I figured most of that. But what were you talking about, you *felt* me down there? Felt John?"

I stared into the sea's blue shadows. "I always called it the Link. I'd tune in bits from other people sometimes, but with John it was loud and clear. From when we were kids, I could *see* it when he was in trouble, or really excited. Feel it." I shot a glance at him, his face still neutral.

"I had a nightmare about him the night he drowned, only it wasn't a dream. I saw... *felt* it happen, from inside his eyes."

A startled movement. "You think you saw me, killing him?"

I shook my head. "It was a shadow man, no face. And since I came to the island, I've been seeing...." My shoulders hunched. "I don't know. Visions. Tuning in on people? Down there, today. It was John drowning again, I was inside him, he was inside me. Only it was you. And when you *were* inside me, just now, I didn't know any more. Where my skin ended, whose voice was inside me...."

Or if I was opening those doors to my brother's killer. "So. You think I'm crazy?"

"No." He shook his head. "I've been in some weird scenes before, but this may take the cake. Why are you so scared?"

"You don't understand. If I let all those voices in, I'll lose myself."

"Maybe not. Maybe you should stop walking on eggshells, worrying you're going to crack. People get busted up all the time, they put the pieces together."

"Like you?" I'd felt the jagged ridge of the long scar curving around his back to his belly.

He turned stiffly away. Bending abruptly, he groped among the tossed gear. He straightened holding up the brandy bottle. "I don't know about you, but I could use a drink."

Hands shaky, I accepted the bottle, tilting it to my lips. The brandy burned down my throat. "At least we came back with some kind of treasure." My voice was still quavery. Solid ground was too far off.

He took the bottle and swigged. Crouching, he fumbled through his discarded coveralls to pull out a flat, corroded case. He pried it open with his dive knife and held it up. "Ta-dah."

Gold and emeralds blazed with sunlight, dazzling my eyes. "You found it!" I started to reach for the jewels, then pulled back.

"Go ahead. Here." He grinned, took out the diamond and emerald-encrusted necklace, and draped it around my neck. It was surprisingly heavy.

I ran a finger over the cool green fire of the emeralds. "Gorgeous."

"Let me take a picture."

"No." I fumbled with the clasp.

"Please." Voice quiet.

I looked at him, then finally lifted my palms. The Alice in Wonderland feeling had me again.

He pulled out his camera. "Sit up on the rail. Good. Perfect, with the sea behind you, your hair slicked back that way." He sighted through the lens, shifted position. "Like a mermaid swimming up with the sunken treasure. Just turn a little toward the sun, pick up the green in your eyes...."

"Can we get this over with?"

"Look past me, over the bow. That's it." He clicked a few shots. "Okay."

Relieved, I climbed down and handed over the necklace. "Maybe we should get back." I cleared my throat. "This jewelry must be worth a fortune."

"Caviness said half a million."

"Half a —" So that was the mysterious deal between Vic and Caviness. "Vic." I cleared my throat again. "I answered your questions. Now will you tell me why so many people think you killed John?"

He shot me a look, crouched to strap in the tanks. "I've got a record." He'd gone wary again, voice brusque.

"I know that."

He tightened the strap with a jerk, started gathering up the other gear. "Since I killed in the war, I guess that makes me a murderer."

"Does it?" Somehow it seemed perfectly reasonable to be asking this man, whose taste and smell still clung to my body, if he'd murdered my brother.

"No. It's not the same. I...." He shook his head. "And the Honduran gig, suppose you want to know about that. Stealing artifacts. I was framed, took the rap for the other guys. If I'd kept my stupid head, hadn't gotten so goddamn pissed off...." A choppy gesture. "They reversed the conviction on appeal, let me out, but of course nobody bothers to look at the whole record." His stiff shrug. "So now I'm a drug dealer, offed John because he was sniffing around?"

I nodded.

He stood. "Some people like to throw blame around, maybe you should ask why. I didn't kill John."

"But you threatened him in The Keg. What *did* happen between you?"

He looked down at me, pulled his mirrored shades from his shirt pocket, and stuck them on. He climbed onto the bow, dragged up the anchor, started the motor. "Better get back before somebody tries to liberate our treasure. I think someone might have followed me yesterday, gone down there afterwards. I know I had that beam in securely. Maybe they shifted it."

"Oh." I swallowed, looked nervously around.

"I've got a rifle, but I'd rather avoid a hassle." He climbed into the pilot seat and nudged the throttle.

"Are you going to tell me about John?" I shot a jittery look over my shoulder, pulled on a sweatshirt, climbed up beside him at the console. I glanced at his profile, strong hands on the wheel. I wanted to touch him. Wanted to run and hide.

He swung the Whaler past the sunken ridge. We picked up speed, foam surging off the bow. "Let's drop it."

"If you didn't kill him, why won't you talk about it?"

The mirrored shades flashed toward me, turned back to the sea. "Because you don't want to hear it."

Twenty-Seven

I steered the rented dinghy through the razor coral maze, picking my way between barely-submerged shoals. The sun beat down, glittered blinding off the surface. I winced and swerved around a sharp ridge.

"You don't want to hear it."

What was Vic hiding? I *didn't* want to listen to more innuendoes about John. None of the stories were about my brother. I was the one who'd really known him, from the inside out. From the Link.

Linking me now to Victor Manden? The maybe-murderer, maybe-crazed drug dealer, volatile walking wounded. Shelli was right, the man was capital T Trouble.

I yanked on the throttle, the outboard sputtering, then roaring around the headland into the next cove. Phillip was up on deck, leaning over the far rail of *La Sirene*. He turned and waved, climbing down the stern ladder as I glided in.

"Susan, where have you been? Here, toss me your line."

I smiled in a rush of gratitude for his craggy face and incisive gray eyes.

He handed me onto the platform and gestured me up the ladder. "I heard the news while I was off-island. Terrible. Do you think Pat MacIntyre was behind your break-in? Please don't tell me there was any damage to your research material."

On deck, I shook my head. "I'd just taken everything to town to have it duplicated and sent back to the States."

"That was a stroke of luck, then — Susan!" He caught my left arm and turned the bandaged hand palm-upwards. Grasping my right arm, he turned it up, too, revealing the bruises and scratches from my assault on the caved-in stairway of the sunken yacht.

"Good god! Don't tell me you were attacked!"

"No." I reclaimed my hands. "I was diving with Victor Manden yesterday, helping him salvage a wrecked yacht."

"He did that to you? I swear I'll —"

"There was an accident, a beam fell in."

He frowned. "You *are* determined to get to the bottom of your brother's drowning, aren't you? You've been awfully reckless." He shook his head. "Just a moment, I'll pay this fellow for the fish and send him off." He stepped around a plastic bucket, striding over to the far rail.

Fins flapped listlessly in the bucket of water, sunlight gleaming over scaly bodies and dulled eyes. Phillip was leaning over to talk to a man in a dinghy. He handed some money over the rail. I skirted the dying fish and joined him.

"Susan, meet my traveling fish market. Susan Dunne, Ngembe Kono. That's his Brotherhood name."

The man was standing in one of the native wooden fishing boats, the size of a large rowboat, net piled in the bow. He was very dark and powerfully built, dressed in ragged shorts and a torn T-shirt, unkempt dreadlocks hanging to his shoulders. A scar pulled up one side of his lip.

The Dread who'd threatened me that first night on the cliff at Fairview.

He recognized me. His eyes rolled startled, yellowish whites, then his face went expressionless, closed-off. He glanced at Phillip, grunted something, and sat abruptly, roaring off in his battered boat.

"He was in a rare hurry!" Phillip rubbed his hands briskly. "Now. If I hadn't already prepared a shrimp mousse for lunch, I'd grill one of these fish for you. You look as though you could do with some nourishment. Shall we eat on deck?"

"I didn't expect...." I was watching the boat speed away.

"Susan, what on earth?"

"That man. He's the one I told you about, the one who met secretly with Leon Caviness in his office."

He whipped around to stare over the rail. Then he turned back to me, raising an eyebrow, guiding me with one of his mock-formal gestures toward a cushioned bench. "You're sure? You couldn't have gotten a clear look at the man that night."

"It would be hard to mistake that scar."

"He seems a decent sort, though we've only discussed the merits of grouper versus amberjack."

"I'm sure he was the one. He recognized me, too."

"Very well, dear. Sit down, please, you're agitated." He sat beside me. "Perhaps I could make some discreet inquiries. Kono might provide us more insight into the mysterious activities of Mr. Caviness."

"I might have a chance myself to find out more. Caviness asked — no, he challenged me to attend his ceremony for the water *loa* tonight. Maybe I'll learn more about his cult."

He pursed his lips. "Suppose it's no good trying to dissuade you?" I shook my head.

"Very well, then, it may be a good opportunity to observe. Stay with the crowd, and you should be safe." He rubbed his hands. "Now, what do you say to that lunch? I seem to be possessed of a ravenous appetite today."

I helped him set a small, hinged table with a snowy linen cloth, china, and gold-rimmed crystal. He brought up a silver serving tray, displaying several dishes with a flourish. "*'How am I glutted with conceit of this!'*" He set the tray on a stand, watching me expectantly.

I eyed the elegant feast he'd conjured, dredging up another passage from the tragedy, one of Dad's favorites he was always quoting around the house:

"*Go forward, Faustus, in that famous art*
Wherein all Nature's treasure is contain'd:
Be thou on earth as Jove is in the sky,
Lord and commander of these elements."

Phillip looked taken-aback, then laughed. "A foe worthy of my mettle! Come, try my *'pleasant fruits and princely delicates.'* I crave a victim for my experiments."

Phillip's banter, along with the food, settled my queasy stomach. I hadn't gotten a bite down since the day before. Leaning back with a wine glass, I eased into *La Sirene*'s gentle rocking.

"That's better." Phillip settled onto the bench next to me, raising his glass. "To solving all your mysteries."

I squinted over at him, wondering if it was another of his double entendres. But he was gazing across the cove, a cat's-paw of wind ruffling clear turquoise.

He turned toward me. "Susan, I've been rethinking the questions you've raised about Caviness and his 'cult.' Perhaps there's more to it than I thought."

I sat up quickly. "I forgot to tell you. When I talked to Caviness, he told me to stay away from Ship Bay. His friend Captain Wilkes has started police patrols offshore along the West End, to keep boats out of the cove."

"Bloody hell!" Phillip pounded his fist on the gunwale. "They think they'll keep us out?"

"That's the idea. But I'm going to go over their heads, try to get a permit to continue the research."

"Don't bother, waste of time." He chopped a hand. "I'll talk to my connections, find a way to get in there. We need to examine the glyphs more carefully." He was agitated, face flushed.

"I think you're as excited about this find as I am."

"Of course I am! We've got to get Ship Bay exempted from resort development, give you a chance to fully document the find and publish your paper."

"Phillip, you really should be listed as co-author. Your career isn't over."

"No, no. Naturally I've retained my interest, matter of fact I'm pursuing what you could call my own brand of experimental anthropology." He chuckled. "But I'm done with academia. I'll be happy enough to see you expose those ignorant asses, braying over their petrified theories."

I shook my head. "You know, maybe your earlier advice was right. Things are getting pretty complicated here. Maybe we should go through higher channels."

"Don't expect any official help with this project. You'll encounter indolence and incompetence at best. I know how the local bureaucracies function."

"So I hear." I couldn't resist a dig. "Captain Wilkes revealed your dark secret, Phillip."

"What on earth?" He laughed. "I've committed my share of youthful follies, but lately I've been deadly dull."

"He told me about your work for the British government."

He threw up his hands. "Unmasked! How can I redeem myself?"

"Too late."

He smiled, clear gray eyes holding my gaze. Sobering, he plucked up my hand to examine the bandaged palm. "Susan, have you told me everything about Victor Manden?"

I pulled my hand free. What was there to tell? Maybe our sweaty tangle in the Whaler had been only the adrenaline-pumped release of survivors. He'd seemed relieved to get away, brusquely dropping me at home on his way to Fairview with the jewelry.

"He's got under your skin, hasn't he?" Phillip was watching my face. "I do hope you're bearing in mind all those unanswered questions about him. I'd hate to see you hurt." He lifted an eyebrow. "But it's rather nice to know the fire is there, after all."

I looked away, shaking my head.

He leaned closer. "I'm ready to give Victor Manden a run for his money."

I stood up, gripping the rail and watching the patterns of wind ruffling the turquoise waters. I'd been counting on Phillip as an ally, a haven of rationality amid the island insanity. This could screw up everything. "Shit," I muttered.

"An elegant summation." He lifted his palms, gave me his ironic smile. "Just remember, I'm a persistent man. You've enchanted me, my sorceress, and I swear I *will* see your face return passion for passion."

"Phillip, please."

"Only giving fair notice." His lips twitched. He made a dramatic, sweeping gesture. "'*Shadowing more beauty in her airy brow than have the white breasts of the Queen of Love....*'"

"Right now I'd settle for the Ace of Spades, if I could just dig up the truth about that petroglyph site."

He laughed, sitting back. "Very well! But beware, my dear, I thrive on challenges. Now," he picked up my glyph design notes, "prepare to defend your thesis!" He gave me a menacing scowl over the papers. "I'm feeling quite merciless."

Twenty-Eight

Headlights stabbed the night, flickering leaf shadow over the high stone wall of the Fairview Estate. A rumble of motors converged on the closed gate. Natives in white milled restlessly outside it, shirts and dresses ghostly pale in the dark. Beyond, in the forest, a muffled drumbeat.

More cars arrived. I was surprised to see a few Continentals among the natives. The drum beat without pause, people shifting edgily. Another set of headlights raked the wall, dancing shapes of light and dark across the stonework, carved faces peering out and melting away. The drum pulsed. My heart thudded, keeping time. The heat and the rhythm and a sickly-sweet smell of blossoms and overripe fruit closed in.

The gates swung open. A cry rang out, the crowd surging inside. The back of my neck prickled as I followed the stragglers. Of course this ceremony to the water *loa*, the spirit of the rain, could only be a cover for the more secret cult gatherings deeper in the rain forest, where the Dreads lived. The drum mocked me, beckoning.

I followed the celebrants down a leaf-shrouded path skirting the estate house, winding downhill through dense foliage. The drum swelled louder, a deep, resounding tone that never faltered, pulsing out of the dark forest. *Dread. Dread.* Pulsing inside me.

Despite the stifling heat, a core of ice in my belly refused to thaw. My heart beat fast against my ribs. *Dread. Dread.* I didn't know if it was fear of Caviness's black magic, or my own blind compulsion to follow that pounding summons.

Chanting swelled around me, people stepping and swaying in rhythm to the drum, bars of cool white light glittering over us as we passed into a clearing.

"*Damballah Ouedo He! Kelemanyan Oh!*"

"*Dameci Ouedo Oh! Kelemanyan Oh!*"

The moon had floated free above the hill, hanging full on the dark sky, showering its illusion of water over the parched land. The night forest, repainted in stark black and white, rippled to the drumbeat. My head throbbed painfully to the rhythm, insistent and familiar as an unwanted memory. I wondered if I would ever be free of it.

The moon rose higher as the people formed a double column, men right, women left. I looked down at my dark blouse as I took a place among the white-clad women. They ignored me, their faces rapt, gazing past me. The lines swayed forward onto a wider path.

"*Dameci Ouedo Oh! Kelemanyan Oh!*"

"*Nan point jou ma songe loi moin Aybobo!*"

We wove through silver light and black shadow, deeper into the forest, the bass drum a tidal surge in my blood. The pounding no longer rang painfully in my head. My tight resistance had melted away, heartbeat meshing with the rhythm, feet falling in with it as I swayed with the other women. The chant was a stream flowing through the night. A moonlit river coursing over rocks and around trees. The muffled roar of the ocean rising and falling.

Figures in white glimmered, flowing along the dark path, the two lines criss-crossing, man/woman, man/woman, undulating as one serpentine body with one all-encompassing heartbeat.

The lines reformed, a ripple passing along as torches flared. The drum quickened, driving harder. The chant crescendoed. A tall figure in crimson headdress came slowly down the human passage.

Leon Caviness wore long white robes, embroidered in black and red with elaborate designs. He gripped a shell-encrusted gourd with a wooden handle — the *asson*, symbol of the *Houngan*'s power. Bony face a blank mask, eyes fixed, he swayed to the chant, robes pouring like moonlight around him. Somehow he wasn't Leon Caviness at all, but a spirit-carving with broad incised forehead and sharply cut cheeks.

"*Papa Legba ouvri barriere pour moins!*"

Two women at the head of the passage lifted aside their interwoven palm fronds, and he moved past them into an open, tree-fringed circle. Behind him, men and women with baskets of food, bottles, pitchers. A man carried a white rooster.

I was dazed by the drum, the chanting, the shimmering bars of moonlight through leaves. Mesmerized faces flowed past me down the passage. A tall, slender young woman in a white headdress moved by, lovely face empty and dreaming, dark eyes fixed on the distance.

"Adrienne!" I stepped forward.

She didn't hear me. The slow cadence of her footsteps, her graceful swaying, didn't falter. A hand gripped my arm and pulled me back into line. I hadn't seen Laura. The double line closed together, carrying me along.

The procession flowed into the clearing, around the perimeter lined with torches. I ended up beside jagged black boulders holding back the steeply overhanging forest.

The chanting was a roar now, filling the tree-ringed circle, merging with the drumbeat shaking the earth. I was panting, sweating, the heat sucking my strength. In the moonlight and shadow, faces blurred into one rapt expression. The drummer's muscular arms flailed above his impassive face.

A shrill, inhuman shriek. The chanting and drum died in ringing silence.

The tall, red-crowned figure in white robes stepped slowly out onto the dark stamped earth of the clearing. He paused before a rock pool at the base of the boulders. The pool was dry, only a trickle of water seeping over stone. Parched earth sucked it up before it could reach the runoff ravine on the other side of the clearing. The *Houngan* raised his palms over the dry stream, glided smoothly past it to the center of the circle. He raised his arms again, holding the *asson* high.

A drawn-out wail. A cry of pain. The keening of a predatory bird. No language, every language. His voice swelled and ebbed, and the deep bass drum fell in with its cadence. Shivers ran down my spine.

The celebrants echoed his cry. Another call from the Houngan pierced the shifting mosaic of black shadows and white moonlight. Other drums joined in, quickening. Again and again the wailing calls and the echoing chorus split the night. They became a song, a story to the drumbeat. The tall, white-shrouded figure began to sway with the rhythm, pulling a small bag from his robes and holding it out, arms weaving snakelike.

He danced to the rhythm, turning, crouching, leaping as the chorus echoed his song. A pattern appeared on the dark earth at his dancing feet, traced by the white powder from his bag. The people leaned inward, transfixed by the swirling robes, the whirling figure, as the drums drove him faster and he arched and spun and the design grew beneath him. His dark, masklike face gleamed with sweat, his eyes fixed and blind.

Finally he sprang back. The voices and small drums died away, only the murmur of the big drum pumping its deep heartbeat.

The Houngan lowered his arms. The celebrants sank to the ground, regarding the pattern traced in white at his feet, a convolution of interwoven lines and curves, spiral-topped spikes, short dashes. Seemingly random, but perfectly symmetrical.

White robes flowed like water as the Houngan turned slowly at the hub of the circle. He opened his mouth. The leaping, keening figure had hardly seemed human, and I braced myself to bear that unearthly, shattering cry once more.

It was a shock to hear Leon Caviness's deep, melodious voice. "We come, as one, to seek the *Loa*, the spirit of the source of waters. She is among us. Here is her sign." He gestured. Faces followed the sweep of shimmering fabric above the moonlit *veve* pattern.

"We cannot compel the loa. We can only heed her voice, follow what we can of her dance. But we cannot hear if we do not listen."

He circled slowly to face each celebrant. When he swung my way, he stared straight at me. "You will not hear if you listen to only one voice, to the sound of your own tongue. The loa use many tongues."

He spread his arms, voice ringing out. "We, the people, are a great tree, nourished by the past, sprung from the seed of those who have gone before us and are taken back into the earth. The tree, like an ancient mahogany, has many limbs, but they all spring from one source, one strong trunk sending its roots deep into the earth. It will not fall before the wind, nor wither in the heat like dry grass."

He circled to the slow pulse of the drum. "We must seek strength together, send down true roots for the sustenance of the earth, and we will be nourished. The loa will renew the source, the vital water to refresh our spirits.

"We must give, too. We must listen and give her our spirit-song. When the trees wither and the ground cracks in drought, it is not for us to blame the loa. We are thirsty and we answer the call of the sacred drums, showing our need. The loa is part of us. She sickens with our ills, grieves with our sorrows, falls dry when the barrenness of our lives withers our spirits. We are the drought. Our spirits are dry and brittle. We must ask, have we listened? We offer now what gifts we have."

He walked away from the pattern on the ground.

The celebrants rose, chanting as they moved around the circle toward the broad rock bowl, sweeping me along. One by one, each person received grains of rice or a piece of bread or fruit to lay beside the dry pool, or a bottle to sprinkle over the rock. They returned to their places, careful to avoid the traced *veve*.

Someone handed me a flat little cake, and I set it beside the other offerings. Women in long white dresses picked up pitchers and poured water into the rock bowl. The drum quickened to a driving beat as the pool stilled, reflecting the moon.

The murmur of voices fell away into tense expectancy.

The deep bass note reverberated through the night, pumping without pause. The tall figure in the robes of the Houngan stepped again to the white pattern on the earth. He stood, head bowed over it. The drum pounded. He raised his head and thrust his arms high, calling out in that piercing voice of pain. One hand gripped a long, moon-glittered knife.

Everyone leaned closer, the night holding its breath. A man approached the robed figure. He stepped to the beat, carrying the white rooster, stroking it to the rhythm of the drum. It lay quietly in the man's arms.

The Houngan whirled and grasped the bird by its head. It awakened from its stupor then, flapping frantic wings and shrieking. The knife slashed down.

Drums crashed into a frenzy. Voices cried out. Blood gushed, blotting out part of the white pattern. The crowd surged forward, obliterating the *veve* as they followed the Houngan. He bore the decapitated bird high in his hands toward the spring. Blood dripped over his white robes.

"Tete l'eau! Tete l'eau!" The mob pushed around him to the pounding drumbeat, shouting over and over, *"Tete l'eau! Tete l'eau!"*

He held the body over the rock pool and poured blood from the twitching creature into the water. My heart flailed with the racing drumbeat, the night pulsing with heat. Only the crimson turban of the Houngan floated above the surging crowd, drums and voices an exultant roar. *"Tete l'eau! Tete l'eau!"*

They swarmed over the stamped dirt, pushing the white-robed priest, his crimsoned hands held above them, splashing drops. Dark figures in white stamped and cried out, teeth flashing. Strained faces gleamed with sweat, ecstatic in the moonlight, arms flinging, legs pumping, dancing to the drumbeat under the moon's faint, distant smile.

Behind Caviness and the dancers, to one side of the spring, a small knot of celebrants had pulled away from the others. They crouched secretively over something near the rocks. A few men, looking nervous, and a thin woman in a red dress gleaming in torchlight. The woman stood, shooting a furtive glance toward the Houngan, then raised a dark-smeared hand to greedily lick it. Laura. She closed her eyes and lifted her palms in a summoning movement.

The boulder I leaned against was suddenly heaving beneath me, rippling, giving way in a sickening plummet.

---

*black stone opens on darkness and sucks me inside. A blind stirring inside me, alien presence groping, stretching within my skin. Shifting and rustling of scales, and the serpent uncoils, flexing its power, undulating my form transformed to its vessel. A hot, sexual surge burns through me as I dance the serpent's sway. Hissing whisper from my lips, "Yesss!" and a guttural laugh it's Laura's voice in my throat the loa's red-black song flames flickering hissing swaying to the drums.

Sacrificial blood courses down her arms, my arms, over our crimson hands. I'm swimming in shimmering moonlight, swimming in blood.

Beneath me, rippling with light and shadow, John's drowned face. His corpse-eyes slowly open and he smiles a ghastly rictus emerald eyes glinting it's my own face leering up at me, shadowy knowledge in my eyes. My own hands reaching to pull me into the abyss.

Dying, dead, my body an empty husk spinning away behind, I swim up the cascade of silvery light and gaze into the face of the moon. Its watery orb thickens, solidifies into a gleaming gold mask, horns piercing the night, mouth dripping blood.

Mask of the bete noir. Gloating over me, bending closer. Clawed hands raise to lift the mask reveal the face of death*

The beast's hands grabbed me. Clutched me by the shoulders and shook me. I screamed.

The hands pulled me to my feet. My eyes snapped open. Leon Caviness was bending over me, robes smeared with blood, eyes deep pools of shadow in a face bleached by moonlight to a staring skull. I couldn't move. My skin crawled with the touch of his hands sticky on my arms.

His deep voice called out, *"Faitre, Maitre, L'Afrique Guinin ce'protection. Nous Ap Maide, ce d'lo qui poti mortel, protection, Maitre d'lo pour-toute petites li!"*

I blinked, swaying. All the faces were turned my way. The drums had fallen silent, the circle hushed.

A scream ripped through the shadows.

The crowd fell back. Laura writhed on the ground in her red dress. She uttered a stream of hoarse babble, arching her body until it looked like it would break, then springing straight to her feet. Glimpse of a white design on the ground where she'd furtively crouched apart from the ceremony. Twisted lines and shapes, smaller than Caviness's *veve*. Different.

The pattern flared out of the dimness, searing my nerves with a jolt of genetic memory as something deep inside me writhed and hissed.

The people near the new pattern gave it startled looks and moved hastily away. Clearly this wasn't part of the planned ceremony. Laura yelled in a guttural voice. She twisted, whirled. There were dark smears of blood on her mouth.

She arched her body, writhing and nearly falling. Somehow she stayed on her feet as her body was driven kicking, leaping, stamping over the dirt to wipe out the unsanctioned *veve*. She kept screaming the hoarse gibberish. She tore at her dress until it hung from her shoulders in rags to reveal her bare breasts. She fell onto the ground, hands splayed against the dirt, eyes bulging in her strained face as her pelvis thrust upward and the dress fell away from her spread thighs.

Caviness shot me a furious look and broke through the frozen crowd to Laura's side. He took a deep breath, then spoke in a low voice. She sagged and closed her eyes, lying stunned, chest heaving.

He knelt and raised her to her feet. She stood blinking, dazed. He gestured curtly with his head and women hurried over, wrapping what looked like a tablecloth around her, helping her through the crowd.

Agitated murmurs lapped through the celebrants, and they moved away from me. Eyes rolled. A man made a warding-off sign in my direction. Caviness gestured at the silenced drummers, and a beat started up, slow and soothing.

The women had guided Laura to the black boulders near the dry spring. She sat gazing glassily, red-stained lips smiling the secret smile of the moon.

A breeze stirred the leaves overhanging the circle. The celebrants slowly reformed two lines and filed from the clearing, casting looks over their shoulders. The women raised Laura to her feet and guided her away.

Caviness strode over, looming above me, eyes glittering like bits of obsidian in the moonlight. "Now you've summoned it, Susan Dunne, you're summoned. You must dance to its tune." Turning in a swirl of bloodstained robes, he stalked off down the dark path.

TWENTY-NINE

Sunset burned the coppery heat haze. I cursed Harry's finicky new deadbolt open, pushing into the cottage to dump my packages and the rolled-up Tattler I'd just bought from a spiky-braided little girl by the roadside.

"Susan. About time you called in." Captain Wilkes's rumbling bass through the archives pay phone earlier that day. "Have you read the newspaper yet?"

I hadn't. I'd stayed on digging through documents until they'd finally ejected me at closing, but hadn't been able to trace Caviness's chant that kept pulsing insistently to my heartbeat. Granny would know the face of the *bete noir*. I'd tried to find Lisabet to ask where the herb woman had vanished to, but *Le Lambi's* had a *Closed* sign tacked at the top of the rickety stairs.

I pushed my groceries aside, snapping open the *Tattler*. It was splashed all over the front page, with garish color photos. Pat's wreck, a grim sheeted shape carried up the ravaged hillside. John in a swimsuit, grinning on the Treasure Island dock. One of me, in front of my vandalized cottage, mouth open in a ridiculous expression of dismay. And Vic, in a grease-stained T-shirt, gripping a crow-bar and scowling.

The headline leered, *"Who's Hiding Deadly Secrets?"*

I sat slowly, scanning Shelli's extravaganza. She'd wrung it for every drop – sunken treasure, drug deals, police secrecy, pagan orgies in the rainforest, bitter battles over land-use, and *"...Susan Dunne, the intrepid young archeologist who recently arrived to study petroglyphs. She's spent more time investigating the 'accidental' drowning of her brother and a secret cult active, oddly enough, near the same cove where John Dunne died a year ago."*

She'd tiptoed around Leon Caviness, but stopped just short of accusing Vic of murder. *"Only Susan Dunne's persistence has finally persuaded the police to reopen their investigation of Victor Manden."*

"Christ!" I threw the paper to the floor.

Wilkes had been fuming on the phone. Apparently Vic had read the paper and stormed into the police station, demanding to see the captain. "First time I've been interrogated by a suspect. We've got a lot of questions about Mr. Manden, he could be dangerous. And Leon tells me you've been diving with him again! For God's sake can't you use your head and stick to archeology?" A sigh. "Why do I feel more like Dear Abbey than an investigating officer?"

Taking the groceries into the kitchen nook, I noticed a bulky manila envelope and a postcard on the floor, beneath an old mail slot. I set the unmarked package on the table, flipping over the postcard of cartoon mermaids and drunken sailors:

> *"Hey, Babe, where you been keeping it? Come down to the Watch Deck tonight for some Carnivale reggae. Got a hot news flash for you. Frank."*

I tore open the manila packet. A blue velvet jeweler's box slid onto the table, along with a note.

> *"Good morning, Susan! There's an old Mesquite Indian custom — if you save a man's life you're more or less stuck with him. Vic.*
> *"P.S. You look terrific in seawater and emeralds."*

Inside the box, a beautiful clear green gem shimmered on white satin, light sparkling through its facets. The emerald was square-cut, mounted with elegant simplicity on gold prongs, and suspended from a slender chain. I caught a quick breath, mesmerized by the cool green fire in the stone.

I snapped the box shut, smacked it onto the table, paced across the room. It must have been expensive. He'd obviously left it here before he'd seen Shelli's newspaper article and confronted Wilkes.

I closed my eyes, gut churning. I could taste his lips and skin, feel his hands on me, his heat inside me.

I paced some more. I'd send the pendant back tomorrow. I tried to sit and write a long-postponed letter to my family. I threw the pen down. It was long past dinnertime, but I wasn't hungry. The walls closed in, breathing out heat, pulsing to a sluggish rhythm like the moist viscera of some monstrous beast. I picked up Frank's postcard and tapped it against my teeth.

Snapping off the shower, I stood eyes closed, dripping. I toweled myself dry, pulled from the back of the closet the bold sundress Adrienne had sent me in response to a dream. Whose dream? My hands moving in a strange slow-motion rhythm, drumbeat pulsing in my ears, I wrapped the sun-yellow sarong with the big green leaves around me. Following a hazy, foreordained dance, I stepped into strapped sandals, painted my eyelids and lips with color, brushed and piled my sunstreaked hair into a high cascade of ringlets.

I turned to pluck up my purse, skirt swirling against bare legs, color flashing in the mirror to bring me up short.

A stranger stared out of the mirror, tawny skin entwined with leaves and vines. Coral-painted lips parted, startled-looking and provocative beneath the tumbled locks of pale hair. Face flushed, eyes wide and electric green.

John's eyes.

I fled into the night, kicked the Honda to life, roared in a spurt of gravel out the drive. Hot wind whipped my arms and legs, dark forest swarming past in the swerves of the headlight. I took the curves fast, leaning into them.

Dropping down the plunge into town, I wove through the crazy tangle of Carnivale Village, a shadowy maze of painted plywood vendor booths that had sprung up around the central park. Tonight only a few dim figures slipped through blue-white lamplight and angled shadows. Black and white monochrome transformed the ribald murals into bizarre conjurings.

Black Queen on a giant playing card, pointing a commanding finger. Leering devil with horns and pitchfork, gripping his thick, phallus-tipped tail. A woman running, eyes bulging, long hair transformed to serpents and sea monsters.

My headlights flickered the figures into movement as I shot past, speeding toward the throb of music, voices, and lights around the harbor drive. The waterfront tavern's parking lot was packed solid. Reggae pounded out into the street, strings of colored Christmas bulbs dancing in a hot breeze.

Pushing my way up thronged wooden steps, I plunged into a mass of sweaty bodies gyrating to the deafening bass and drums. *"I say it be a Hard Card! You always pull a Hard Card!"* A bluish smoke haze swirled dimly to the vain thresh of ceiling fans, mirrored balls flickering colored sparks. Grinning faces loomed out of the dimness, gusting alcohol and marijuana fumes. "*She always give you Hard Card....*"

Craning around the packed tavern, I thought I spotted Frank Savetti's partner Mary among the crowded tables. I was pushing my way in that direction when my arm was grabbed from behind.

A piercing whistle. "Whooo-ee! Too hot to handle!"

Frank grinned, dark gaze dancing from my toes to my face. He shouted, "Here, start with this." He thrust a tall glass into my hand, ice cubes rattling.

Throat parched with the heat and smoke, I took a big swallow and choked on straight gin.

Frank laughed, gulped from the glass, and grabbed my arm. "Come on, let's dance." He dragged me into the mob.

The beat intensified, band revving without pause into another song, electric guitar and singer wailing over the heavy bass. Bumping bodies closed around me, my head throbbing to the drums, liquor burning down my throat. Frank's white grin bobbed in and out of the smoke haze. The bass beat shook the floor. Sweat glistened on a dark face, slicked colors swimming. Hands raised clapping overhead, feet stamping. Frank edged closer, pelvis grinding against mine. The singer's voice shrilled into a scream as the dancers whirled a final frenzy. The drums crashed and died into ringing silence.

—•—

"All right! The great Caribbean Orgasm!"

Frank pulled me out of the crush, thrusting his glass into my hand. "Gotta keep charged up. Jesus, you can move it, Dunne!"

I smacked his hand from my breast and sipped thirstily. The ice cubes were melting, and the gin didn't taste so strong now. I pushed his groping hands away again. "Frank, you said you had some news for me."

"Don't you ever quit? You're driving me nuts, you know that." He gave me a drunken leer.

I grabbed his arm and pulled him through the crowd as the band started up again and more dancers swarmed onto the floor. The smoke thinned a little near open windows onto the quay and dark bay beyond. "Tell me."

He shrugged. "Just wanted to let you know. That bastard Manden went to the cops, told them some story he'd cooked up about me and John. Covering his ass. Told them *we'd* been running coke with his boat!"

He gave me an indignant look. "Christ! You know John, he didn't mind sampling, but he wouldn't get mixed up in that kind of shit. And why Manden had to drag me into it...." He swore at length. "Cops hauled me in for questioning today, realized fast enough it was all a crock. Man, what an asshole!"

I set the glass on the windowsill. "Frank, I don't get it. Why would he —?"

"Hey, enough of this shit! Come on, hot stuff, they're playing our song." He dragged me back to the dance floor. *"Traffic tight, Day and night, Traffic tight."* He pulled me into a spin, thrusting his pelvis against mine. "Tell you, Dunne, I'm in love! All right, okay, so I'm in lust."

"So I'm thrilled. Knock it off." I tried to break free of his arms, but it was like grappling an octopus.

He laughed, gin fumes gusting as he pulled me closer, grinding against me. I pushed him back, but he kept grabbing, tugging as I tried to pull free. I turned, and came up short.

Vic stood rooted in the entranceway, people milling past him toward the blast of another Carnivale song. He stared at me and the oblivious, clinging Frank. Mouth pressing into a contemptuous line, he turned away.

"Vic!" I had to explain that idiotic newspaper article. "Vic, wait!"

He'd disappeared into the press of bodies near the bar. I shoved Frank off and fought my way toward the bar. The singer screamed, *"All you woman play you wrong."*

I spotted Vic's broad shoulders at the crowded bar. A bosomy, auburn-haired waitress hovered with her tray at his elbow, smiling. She shrugged and turned away.

I touched his arm. "Vic."

He spun around, then swung back to the bar. "Go back to Frank. I'm waiting for someone."

"Can we talk?"

He glared. "You and Shelli didn't get enough blood yet, siccing the cops on me? I thought we had a truce, Susan."

"Vic, listen —"

"So now you're all over Savetti. Christ." He gave me a scathing look. "Showing your family colors." He headed for the doorway.

"Wait." I tried to catch his arm. "Let me explain. You owe me at least that."

"I owe you —?" His jaw clamped, a muscle jumping. He caught my wrist and held up my arm. The bruises and scrapes looked worse in the fluorescent light from the bar. His gaze snapped to my face, and for a moment we were back on his boat, his face naked, streaked with my blood.

He dropped my arm and turned brusquely away.

"You bastard, Manden! Don't run off!" An angry shout from behind me.

Vic turned as Frank broke through the crowd into the open space by the door. He had an empty bottle by the neck, swinging it in front of him. He didn't look so drunk now.

Vic gave him a scornful look and headed for the stairway. "Go away and play, Frank."

Frank grabbed his arm. "Think you can call the cops on me and just blow it off, you fucker?" He swung the bottle at Vic's head. Vic whipped around and ducked, moving into a crouched stance.

The crowd was falling back, flowing in surreal slow motion. Music throbbed at a muffled distance, drums pulsing. The two men faced off. Frank broke the bottle against a chair, and glass shards sprayed, glittering over the floor. He made a pass with the jagged stump. Vic dodged, eyes on Frank. He breathed deeply and evenly, a faint smile behind the beard.

Frank lunged with the sharp glass, whipping his arm up at Vic's face.

Time leaped into fast-forward. Vic was spinning on one leg. The other leg kicked high. The broken bottle flew into the air and crashed against a wall. In the same blur of movement, Frank was up against the wall, held by his shirt collar as Vic's hand drew back to drive into his face. His arm shook, tensed to strike.

Behind me, the bartender swore loudly.

Pent-up violence quivered in the air, in Vic's taut stance. Bass and drums shivered the floor. Vic shook himself, shoved Frank against the wall, and stalked off down the steps.

Frank slid down to the floor, dazed. I jumped over his legs, squeezing through the crowd toward the stairs.

I spotted him outside, under the colored lights. He'd been halted by a big native man. Vic shook his head and strode off between parked cars.

"Vic, wait!" He was gone.

The native looked up as I hurried down the steps. "Sue!"

"James!" I halted in surprise.

He tilted his head. "You here wi' Vic den? What de score?"

I blew out a breath. "I can't keep track any more."

He frowned. "Vic, he read dat *Tattler* today, he lak a devil down to de karate club." He worked one massive shoulder. "Give me good fall, but he don' get off cheap." He flashed a white grin. "So I say me'n you go Carnivale, Vic. Lively up! Now he pushin' off all rile up again. What you stirrin' here, gal?"

The gin churned, queasy in my gut. "Guess you had to be there...." I closed my eyes, slowly shaking my head.

"You jus' all confuse." His huge hand closed around my arm and guided me across the parking lot to the quay. I sank onto a piling, staring at the dark mirrored surface of the bay dancing colored lights.

James threw a pebble to scatter the reflections. "You got spirit trouble. You mix it wi' dat old Granny, dem power rock. Member dat cat what too curious?"

I laid my head in my hands. "It's coming back to me."

"Now you lissen up. Dat Vic, he one good man. I knows him since he come here. I knows 'bout you brother John, he pressin' Vic to work dat cove. Bad Jumbie dere. Vic don' lissen what I tell him. You don' lissen. But I say, you bes' hear de truth 'bout you brother."

I raised my face, blinking. "You knew John?"

"Vic, he take to John like dey brother. No time, John he makin' bold, do as he please. Talkin' up treasure, big story. Dey go partner, but Vic he put in all de money, all de work searchin' out dem old record. John say he waitin' on some cash he gon' give Vic, but he never do."

"But...." I frowned. "John said Vic was screwing him over."

"Huh!" He spat. "John jus takin' a free ride. An all de time him an dat Frank Savetti, dey usin' Vic, usin' he boat, dey run cocaine to crew on cruise ship. Dey makin' big money an jus laugh. I work de water, I knows. Ol Alf, he work dem cruise boat, he sees it. Frank and John, dey know Vic bin jail, p'lice likely put blame to he. Vic he find out first an he steamin.' John damn lucky Vic jus break off wi' him, don' tell de cops. But I sees it bust Vic up bad."

James flung a pebble far over the water. "You bringin' him moh grief, gal. An grief foh self wi' bad spirits. You got to open you eyes."

Waves hissed against the quay, faint reggae drifting out to us. Patterns of colored light dissolved and reformed and dissolved with the pebbles James tossed.

He was telling the truth. Maybe I'd known it all along, and I'd only refused to see. My grief for John swelled heavier inside me, bitter now with the taste of bile. The Link had only seduced me into believing my own rosy vision of my brother. Was Vic right, we were all islands? Was Laura right, embracing equally the dark and the light? It was too late for John to find a balance in that. All there'd been at the end was darkness.

And the *bete noir*. The killer. Who was he?

Not Victor Manden. On some level, I *had* known that from the start. But now it was too late to tell him, he'd never trust me.

James had run out of pebbles. Interwoven rings of ripples smoothed away over the dark-mirrored surface. He leaned down to touch my arm. "Dat Vic, he de true man foh you, Sue."

I laughed hysterically.

Thirty

Seagulls flew up squawking and scolding as I ran along the harbor drive, lungs burning with exhaust fumes of morning traffic. Sunlight stabbed off the bay. More wings threshed as I jumped the cables binding rusty cargo boats to the quay. I tripped, recovered, and pushed it up a notch, driving myself until my chest ached.

Past the primary colors of the Carnivale Village murals. Down a narrow dirt trail, wooden fishing skiffs pulled onto a trash-littered strip of sand. Shirtless men slapped the barrels of steel drums, ringing rhythms. A chain-link fence sealed off the marina and Bay View Hotel, drawing the line between tourist paradise and native jungle-town.

"Thought I better fill you in on what Manden told us yesterday." Captain Wilkes, tapping a report on his desk earlier.

I'd told him I'd seen Vic the night before, and the conversation had gone downhill fast. He'd been suspicious of James's story about John and Frank setting Vic up, though he'd written down the name of the witness.

"Probably just trying to shift the blame." He'd irritably tossed down the pencil. "You're playing with fire, playing little miss detective here. Even if this story does check out, it doesn't clear him. So leave it to us, you convinced me something's cooking at Ship Bay. Be happy."

"You've got the wrong suspect."

"We'll see. Manden's name keeps popping up too often. So does yours."

I pushed for a last spurt of speed back to the ferry landing, thrusting Wilkes's speculative eyes behind me. Catching my breath, I wiped the sweat from my face. A pelican plummeted in an ungainly splash by the quay, ripples spiraling outward like the island truths I'd arrogantly demanded. *"Cat what too curious."*

The stone prison glowered over me as I crossed the street. Behind one narrow barred window, a pale gleam of eyes. I headed for my bike in the police lot. Traffic choked the harbor drive, grinding to a standstill as I scanned the lot, trying to remember where I'd left the Honda.

Horns honked impatiently. I glanced over, saw a familiar, battered gray Jeep in the far lane. Vic was pulling off his visor, tossing it on the seat beside him and wiping his forehead with the back of his arm. He reached for the stick as the traffic started moving again.

"Vic!" I shouted over the rumble of motors.

He saw me, grabbed his sunglasses, and stuck them on, wrenching the Jeep into gear. The cars ahead of him were picking up speed. Vic pushed closely after them.

"Damn you, wait!" I sprinted over the sidewalk and dashed in front of an oncoming car. Flare of sunlight off its windshield. Squeal of brakes and a shout. I darted through the next lane in front of a car and a van. Ran hard along the far lane of cars, passing two. A last lunge, and I grabbed the Jeep's sidebar just as it accelerated.

My momentum threw me against the side. Vic's startled face swung around, light glinting off the mirrored shades. He stomped on the brakes. I tumbled over the sidebar onto the seat beside him.

"Are you out of your mind!" he bellowed. Behind us, horns blared.

I was sprawled upside-down on the seat, legs dangling over the bar. Kicking, I pulled them in and struggled upright.

He started to reach a hand, then yanked it back and slammed the stick into gear. Horns blasted louder. A car passed, driver shaking his fist and swearing.

Vic drove on, muttering. We passed a block of storefronts. He pulled into a parking strip and reached across me to open the low door. "Try getting out like a normal person."

I shut the door and faced him. "Not until you listen. Two minutes. Then I promise I'll leave you alone."

His face was blank behind the dark glasses, but I could feel the rage lapping off him. "Chumming with the cops again? You and Wilkes have another little surprise cooked up for me?"

"Will you take off those damned glasses?"

He swore and threw them down on the dash.

I was losing the momentum of my adrenaline rush through traffic. I touched his arm. "Please. I was trying to explain last night."

He pulled his arm away. "How stupid do you think I am? You and your spoiled little brother. What the hell more do you want from me?"

"I'm sorry. I was fooled, too."

"Christ! So now *you're* getting jerked around?" He jumped out and strode around the Jeep. Wrenching open the passenger door, he took my arm and pulled me onto the pavement. "Go peddle it somewhere else. Try the tavern again, you were a big hit in that dress."

I flushed angrily.

"What's wrong with Frank? You two were getting along like a house afire."

"Look, all I want is —"

"What? This?" He took my shoulders and yanked me close, turning to pin me against the Jeep and pressing his mouth hard on mine.

I wrenched sideways to break free, but he only held me tighter, teeth grinding against mine. He was hot and sweaty, bearing heavily down on me as the traffic roared past.

I pulled my face away. "Stop it!" I got a fist loose to punch him.

He stepped back, thrusting me against the Jeep. "One day you'll get more than you bargained for, Susan Dunne." He strode off down the quay.

"Damn you!" I ran after him, grabbing his arm. "Don't run off on me again! Just hear me out. You owe me that."

He swung around. "So I'm supposed to let you use me the way John did? Just because you let me fuck you? You're just like him, a cheap little sneak."

"You *bastard!*" Outraged, I slapped at his face. He blocked me. I smacked and pounded at his arms. "You accused me of judging you without knowing! Now you're doing it to me!"

He scowled, catching my wrists and holding them apart as I strained. "So maybe it's my turn."

"Great! How long do you want this bullshit to go on?" I fought against his hold, spitting mad. "Will it make up for everything the world's dumped on poor Vic Manden if *you* act like a jerk, too?"

He dropped my wrists, stepping back with a jolt. He turned to face the bay, sunlight glittering razor-sharp over milky blue. "Shit."

He turned back to me. "Okay." Voice strangely soft. "You're right, I'm acting like a goddamn jerk. Again." He took a deep breath. "I'd like to hear what you were going to say, Susan."

"The newspaper article, that was only Shelli running wild. I just got through telling Wilkes about Frank and John. Last night James told me the truth, what they did to you. Jesus. I never thought...."

I swallowed. "I was blind. I thought I knew John, from the inside out. I only saw what I wanted. He was so wild, maybe he'd be careless about people's feelings sometimes, but I didn't think he *could* be that mean. You were friends! And he set you up, betrayed you, all to make a cheap buck. It makes me sick." Hands clenched, I hurried to get it out and get away. "Ever since he was a kid, he was just too damn charming, everybody always let things slide. He never had to grow up."

I stared at the salt-blurred bay, fists pressing hard against my thighs. "Now he'll never have a chance to grow up."

I drew in a shaky breath. "I'm sorry, Vic. You deserve better. I dragged you right into this mess again." I couldn't look at him. Blinded, I turned to go, bumping into a bench on the quay.

"Susan, wait." He was beside me. "Here." He pressed a kerchief into my hand and eased me onto the bench.

Beside me, he touched my head lightly, rested his hand on my shoulder. I scrubbed my face and sat back, blowing out a breath.

He picked up my hand, turning it over to run a finger along the scab forming on the ragged slash. "It's healing fast."

I looked up. He searched my face, that visceral connection crackling between us. He reached out to tuck a loose strand behind my ear.

"Want to try one more truce? We could take the Whaler out for a picnic to a pretty little cay I know, get away from this damn rock." He waved toward town, traffic past the prison, dark mountain looming over the heat haze and smog.

"Just like that?"

"You coming?" He jumped up, tugging me to my feet, heading back to the Jeep.

"I left my bike in the police lot."

"Meet me at my place, then." He climbed in, flashed a grin. "And watch it crossing the street this time. I'd rather not be scraping you off the road for the day's entertainment."

I climbed into the boat with the hieroglyphs that meant "safe harbor," looking for a place to change into my swimsuit. The main salon was roomier than I'd expected, comfortably lived-in, cushions and shades in tones of blue and rust, with a lot of oiled wood.

A shelf overflowed with books, a paperback sprawling spine-up on the couch. One wall held a stereo system and racks of tape cartridges, everything from Bach to Bob Marley. I stood before a framed photo, drinking in its vibrant color. The viewpoint was high on a hill, morning sun breaking over the photographer's shoulder to light rounded terraces flowing emerald green down another steep hill across a narrow valley. Above the rice paddies a tiny pagoda perched on the slope. The floor of the valley was lost in a mist of pearly fog swirling apart at one point to reveal an elusive gleam of water.

In the lower corner, his initials. *V.M.*

I turned from the haunting scene, following a spiral stairway down to a dim passage. The first doorway was open onto the stateroom, a wide bunk with rumpled sheets and snarled blanket, the clothes he'd been wearing at the tavern flung helter skelter over the rug. I glanced at the dresser and froze. Crimson glistened, pooling over the dark wood beneath a dive knife stabbed upright into the dresser.

Pulse drumming in my ears, I moved slowly toward the dresser and the images I'd seen before.

Bright red Jumbie beads, a jagged chunk of black stone, a fluted seashell, scattered coins. He'd stabbed the dive knife deeply into the wood, embedded beside pieces of a ripped photo. My fingers arranged the pieces, reassembling.

My own face gazed up at me, strangely dreamlike, wet hair smoothed back, arm raised as if reaching for something. Behind me, deep blue water and the distant rock mass of French Cap. The emerald and gold necklace gleamed, eyes reflecting the color of the gems.

"Fresh start?" Vic raised his champagne glass.

I tore my gaze from the clear turquoise shimmer of the cove, sun dancing submerged patterns over the bottom. Ripped puzzle pieces, images wavering through light and shadow. I touched my glass to his and sipped.

Vic punched his cushion and leaned back on the beach blanket, resting his glass on his chest as he looked out over the bay. Filtered light through the lacy mimosa leaves overhanging us played on his skin, picking out the glint of copper in the curly thatch over his pectorals. His chest rose and fell deeply, a relaxed smile behind his beard.

I looked out over the half-moon beach, the gemlike little cove nearly enclosed by a rocky arm of the isolated cay. "It's good to remember there are places like this in the neighborhood." Just putting a stretch of water between me and the dark mass of the island had lifted a weight off me.

"I like to think I'm the only one who comes here. You're the first person I've brought." He rolled over on his side, supporting his head on one arm, gaze traveling leisurely from my feet to my face.

He smiled and I smiled back, almost as if we could replay that first day at the beach. He reached over to run a finger along the top of my hand. The light touch sent a shiver down my spine.

I sat up, hugging my knees.

"You've got to find out, you know."

"Find out what?"

"About us. Whether you want to run from or to." His eyes were the color of the bottomless blue holes that lured divers too deep.

He sat up and started to touch my arm, then paused. "They came!" He jumped to his feet, pulling me up.

"Who?"

"My friends." He pointed at the cove. A dark shape surged and broke the surface. Shiny gray-blue back. Curved dorsal fin. It slid under again, followed by the slap of a flat crescent tail.

"A dolphin!" I ran down to the water's edge.

"I was hoping they'd show. I was following them the day I found the hidden entrance to the cove here."

"Will he come back?" I waded into the silky water.

Two arched backs broke the surface a few feet out. Another followed. One more. A sleek shape glided closer. The long, gleaming body flew out of the water, arched, and crashed down, tail slapping to spray me. He circled back and bobbed his head, grinning, uttering high squeaks.

"Do you think I could touch him?"

Vic nodded at the dolphin eyeing us with an impossibly friendly look. "Go ahead and try."

I talked to the creature, making soothing noises as I slid into the water and floated toward him. He bobbed his head, moving slightly away. I held out a hand and paddled forward. "Come on, I won't hurt you."

He seemed to grin wider and squealed, as if laughing at my absurd reassurance. He edged back, waiting. Teasing me?

I laughed and eased toward him. He turned his head, watching. The dark, liquid eye gleamed with awareness. He chirped and bobbed his head.

The alien gaze held mine, inviting recognition. I remembered John's dream to be reborn in the sea. Holding my breath, I reached out for the smooth, glistening animal. The dolphin let me touch him. A strangeness stirred inside me. *Joy welling, rippling up and outward, boundless as the sea....*

The dolphin exploded in a high-pitched squeal, leaping into the air, splashing under. The others were headed out toward the cut, and he surged up and after them. A last glimpse of a gleaming fin, sleek fleeting grace.

I swam back to the shallows, the link with the dolphin alive in me. Scooping up a handful of water, I tossed it to the sun, dazzles spattering down. I laughed, spinning in a circle of kaleidoscope colors – blue sky, silver waves, green leaves, gold sand. Whipping my arm, I shot a spray at Vic.

He smiled, eyes bright with the sunlight. "You know, the way John felt about dolphins, I was thinking about bringing him here. Before...."

"I'm sorry."

"Don't be. Not today. I'm trying to tell you, Susan, I damned near loved him like a brother. Maybe that's why when I first saw you, I...." He shook his head. "That's not it, it was the other way round. I think it was him reminding me of you, *before* we met." He lifted his palms. "I read some more of that John Donne. *'Twice or thrice did I love thee, before I knew thy face or name.'*"

"Vic, you can't —"

"I can."

His kiss tasted of salt sea and sweet wine. Warm waves rolled over us. His arms came around me and I was pressing against him, our wet skin molten in the intense sunlight.

He eased me back, flashed a fierce grin, suddenly tossed me over his shoulder and charged up the sandy slope.

"You *are* a dangerous lunatic!" I pummeled his back.

He dropped to one knee and dumped me onto the blanket. "No escape now. You're at my mercy."

Blinding sunlight strobed off the sea, the sand, the shiny leaves, shattering through us. The light flung shards like the spray of the dolphin's dive, its touch reverberating in my blood and bones. Vic and I rode the sun-shot waves, plunging deeper.

The link shivered through me, stronger than blood. No breaking free? I didn't care.

Thirty-One

Le *Lambi's* pulsed with radio reggae, candlelight, and shadows, clock ticking down to midnight's *J'ouvert* street-dance. Vic's emerald pendant glittering over the bright "leafy dress" he'd asked me to wear, his eyes cranking up the kilowatts, and James's white teeth gleaming, we didn't need a lamp to light our corner.

James flashed his grin from Vic to me. Drunk on a brew more potent than the Elephant Beer, I beamed back.

Lisabet set down heaping plates of rice and peas, coconut-fried fish, curried chicken with candied yams. The young Haitian glared at James, who was ignoring her. Smacking his plate in front of him, she tugged at the tight red dress accenting her lush curves and big dark eyes. She huffed off. A smile twitched his lips.

"Don't you go breaking her heart, James." I raised my bottle.

"Dat gal, she comin' roun fine."

Vic laughed and touched his bottle to ours. "To Carnivale." He smiled, holding my gaze.

"Eat up now! Look like you two gon' need you strength."

Somewhere along the tipsy blur of the evening, James succumbed to Lisabet's sultry pout and lured her over to our table. He talked her into joining us for a walk to Carnivale Village, where the rival steel bands were gathering on big flatbed carts to be pushed through the streets.

The cobbled lanes seethed with faces blurring in lamplight and shadow beneath shuttered windows. Children, wound up to screaming pitch, chased tag through the crowd, shaking big painted seed-pods and dancing circles around their parents. Young people in sequined, beaded, and feathered Carnivale regalia hurried toward the park, a few ragged Dreads prowling like tomcats through the celebrants. A fitful breeze stirred trash in the gutters, ruffling the feathered hairdo of a Rude with dayglo-striped cheeks. The air was hot, dry and dusty from the drought, a dark fever gripping the town.

We joined the mob surging down Main Street toward the throbbing drums, bodies closing in, all moving to one rhythm. Smell of sweat, perfume, marijuana. Clapping, singing, the crowd jostled, someone stomping on my foot.

A splash of red fabric rippled through a streetlamp's pooled light. Surrounding it, a pack of Rudes in tight pants, gold chains and slit-to-the-navel shirts, black leather unthinkable in the sweltering night. The red dress danced out from among them. Laura dipped and swayed among the men. One reached out and pulled her close, thrusting his pelvis against hers for a few beats. She spun to the next, taking his arm, laughing.

"It's Laura. I have to talk to her." I pulled away from Vic, edging through the crowd.

She stopped dancing and stood hands on hips, streetlights glimmering in eyes and teeth. The Rudes gathered at her back, watching me expectantly.

"Laura, why don't you come celebrate *J'ouvert* with us?"

A short, shrill laugh. "My friends, too?"

I stepped closer. "Use your head."

A shrill laugh. "Use my *head*! It's Carnivale!" She reached to her neckful of beads, chains, and feathers, whipping a strand loose. With a quick lunge, she looped it over my head. Lamplight gleamed on red Jumbie seeds. She twisted, tightening the noose around my neck, yanking me close. "Go home, you clueless bitch," she sputtered in my ear. "Just get out of here!"

She leaned closer, whispering in a desperate rush, "Susie, it's coming down! The Bocor. Don't trust his tricks, he won't share his power, he'll get you like he got John! It's all fucked. John was so stupid, thought I could lie to the Bocor, cover for him. He knows everything. He'll kill us both if you don't leave this goddamn island!"

She stepped back, gasping as she looked over my shoulder. "Him! Susie, don't —"

Vic moved up beside me, scowling at Laura.

Shadows chased over her face. She shot me a pleading look. She glanced at the Rudes, spat at Vic's feet, and whirled away.

The men stood eyeing Vic and me, weighing the fun to be had with us versus Laura. Vic nudged me behind him. I could feel him tense, winding up. The Rudes turned on some silent signal, following Laura.

James stepped up beside me. "Dat gal you frien? She lookin' foh trouble."

I pulled the necklace over my head. "What can I do?"

"Nothing. She'd get off on seeing them hurt you." Vic took the beads and threw them in a trash can.

Lisabet was clinging in agitation to a light pole. She flew into James's arms, shuddering.

His chest swelled. "Bes I take she home." He guided her down the lane. "Member dat cat now, Sue. You listen on Vic, he take good care of you."

Vic drew me closer, urging me into the flow down Main Street. "Smart man, James."

"You two seem to be enjoying yourselves."

"Lisabet appreciates a manly man."

I pulled free. "I'm worried about Laura."

He squeezed my shoulder. "Those Rudes were just strutting their stuff. Laura's lapping it up. Come on, maybe we'll spot her in the dancing." We followed the pull of the crowd, the quickening beat of the steel drums.

The tide of faces swept us along to Carnivale Village, past the plywood liquor and food booths, through sharp black shadows and washes of blue-white lamplight. The drums rang louder. Sweating bodies crushed in. Heat pulsed with the beat, voices chanting, *"Traffic tight. Day and night. Traffic tight...."*

A flatbed cart loomed over us, flashing colored lights. Musicians pranced in tight pants and colorful fringed vests, bare dark chests shining with sweat, arms flailing the metal barrels ringing and echoing off walls. The crowd crammed in tighter, dancing.

I got separated from Vic as the mob pushed the cart down a cobbled street. Lamplight splashed colors from the heaving mass, teeth flashing in the shadows. Heat pounded, heavy with sweat, rum, marijuana. I lost touch with my feet as I was lifted along in the flow of bodies. Everyone was singing now, bumping and grinding against whatever body pressed closest. I was crushed, panting in the claustrophobic heat.

"Susie!" A faint voice called.

Clawing my way up shoulders to look around, I saw no sign of Vic. But the swirl of a short red dress caught my eye, Laura struggling with one of the Rudes at the mouth of a dark alley.

"Hey!" I fought the human tide, forcing my way through. An unseen curb tripped me, then I was plowing along the packed sidewalk toward the alley. I broke free to its entrance. No sign of Laura.

"Susie, help!" She popped into the light at the end of the dark alley. She waved frantically, was yanked around the corner.

I started running down the alley.

"Wait!" Vic, breathing hard, caught me and pulled me back.

"I just saw Laura, she was calling for help." I tugged against his grip.

"Are you crazy? You go running down there, you could run into anything."

"She's in trouble!" I tore free, ran blindly into the shadowed passage. I tripped on broken cobblestones, ricocheted off garbage cans, and fell over someone's outstretched legs, landing on my hands and knees.

"Take it easy!" Vic hauled me up. "It's too late, they're gone by now. She's just screwing with your head, anyway."

Steering me toward the street, he stumbled. "What's this?" He peered down at the sprawled legs I'd tripped over. "Some drunk, passed out. Hey, guy!" He raised his voice. "Wake up!"

I squinted through the dimness. The figure slumped among the garbage cans wasn't moving.

Vic was kneeling beside the man, shaking him. "Jesus!"

"Is he hurt?"

He swore, pulling out keys with a jingle. Flare of a penlight, narrow beam flashing over the tumbled garbage cans, graffiti on the brick wall. Long dreadlocks trailed, the man's head lolling sideways. Bright red was splashed down his chest, a knife imbedded in his heart.

I cried out, rammed a fist against my mouth, and stumbled back.

The penlight snapped off. "Christ!" Bumping noises, clattering cans as he stood, staggered against me. "Son of a bitch." He was holding out his hands, staring down at them.

"Is he dead?"

"You got it."

"Are you sure?"

"I've seen a few casualties." Voice curt. "Got a handkerchief?"

I groped numbly in my purse, handed it to him.

He wiped his hands, threw it violently down. "God *damn* it!"

I shuddered. "Better call the police."

"Yep." He shook his head slowly back and forth, swearing in a monotone.

I touched his shoulder. "Vic, they can hardly pin this on you. We'd better go tell them, Laura could be in trouble, too."

"Another goddamn setup!" He snapped his head up, staring down the alley where she'd disappeared. "She lured us in here."

I gawked at his shadowed face. "That's crazy." Then I realized what I'd seen. "Give me that light."

He turned, took my arm. "Come on. Let's call the cops. Get it over with."

"No. Wait. I need that light."

"He's dead, Susan. There's nothing we can do."

I pried the penlight from his fingers and stepped over to the slumped figure. He was a very dark native, shirtless, wearing ragged shorts, matted dreadlocks hanging over his shoulders. The knife was buried to the hilt in his chest, the handle a curved goat horn, blood pooled thickly over his belly. His head hung sideways, eyes gone glassy, face frozen in a terrible mask of shock and fear.

I swerved the beam hastily aside. Whatever he'd seen, it was still here in this dark alley. I could feel it. The *bete noir*. Watching me now with eyes like ice.

I raised the shaking beam to his face again. Blank eyes reflected the light, and for a sickening second they seemed to move. The light jumped. It picked out the scar dragging the man's lip into a sneer.

I backed hastily away, snapping off the light. "His name is Ngembe Kono."

Thirty-Two

Bleary-eyed Captain Wilkes, hunched in a wrinkled jacket, gave me a brusque nod and glared at Vic. He turned his back on us and stalked across the alley to crouch by the spotlighted body.

A graying woman rose from examining it. "Not more than a few hours. Odd blade, with that goat-horn handle." She shrugged. "See you in the lab."

Wilkes flung an arm toward the knot of onlookers, bellowing to one of his men, "And get rid of the ghouls!"

He scowled at me. "Busy as a bee, Miss Dunne. This better be good." He jabbed a finger at Vic. "I hope *you* have a better alibi than last time you found a body."

A policeman hurried over. "Cap'n." He handed Wilkes a scrap of paper.

Wilkes gave an irritated exclamation and held it in the light of his flash. It looked like a silvered gum wrapper. He squinted at it, shot me an odd look.

"Captain, have you heard anything about Laura?" I stepped closer. "I think she's in danger with those Rudes."

A swatting-off gesture. "Look, I've already got a man on it. Leon reported her missing a couple days ago."

"Missing? After his ceremony?"

"She'll turn up." He shrugged. "Got in a snit when Leon finally took the car away, ran off to play with her Rude boys." He fingered the silvery scrap of paper. "What I want now are some answers from you two about this gum-wrapper."

"We didn't disturb the body." Vic bit off the words, stony-faced.

"Captain, we've told you everything we know." I rubbed my arms. "We'd like to go."
"Not so fast."
"Are we being arrested?" Vic's voice was taut, edgy.
Wilkes scowled. "Don't tempt me. Right now all I want is an explanation for this." He waved the gum wrapper, crinkled silver catching the light.
Exasperated, I burst out, "Explain what? Maybe he liked to chew gum."
"Take it easy." Vic took my arm. He was grinning for some reason. "All right, Captain. What's important about the wrapper?"
Wilkes pursed his lips and thrust it at him, snapping on his flash. The yellow circle of light picked out printing laboriously squeezed onto the paper side in awkward capitals. Names.
John Dunne. I caught a sharp breath, squinting at the list. After John's, two names I didn't recognize. I leaned closer to read the rest.
Dwayne Simmons.
Laura Frankel?
Susan Dunne.

Choked, growling sounds. Hot, sweaty thrashing, and an arm flung over my throat, strangling me.
"Vic!" I clawed at his arm, gasping for breath.
"Uhn!" He flung back from me in the tangled sheets. Beneath us, the boat rocked gently, reflected morning sun casting watery ripples over the bunk. A breeze through the open porthole scattered the last wisps of sleep.
"Damn." He scrubbed at his face. "Not again." He stroked fingers down my face, over my throat. "Did I hurt you?"
"No." I swallowed. "Bad dreams?"
"Thought I was done with that shit." He looked down at his hands. "Guess I'm not the only one. Middle of the night, you were tossing around, muttering something about the stones, death eyes watching you." His gaze lifted to mine. "Not just Kono's?"
I shook my head.
His eyes had gone through one of their sea changes, deep indigo in the subdued light. He reached out and it was my own hand reaching touching somewhere in the middle. His pain lancing, a longing that sliced to the bone. A tiny reflection of myself glimmered in his dark, flaring pupil.

He flinched away.

"Vic. Stay with me."

He caught a ragged breath and groped for my hand, weaving his fingers through mine. He kissed my throat.

"I love you, Vic." The words came out of the blue.

He smiled, then winced and rolled back from me. "Maybe you *should* be running."

My finger slowly traced the livid scar down his back and side.

His hand snapped up to catch my wrist. "Don't ask."

"I have to."

"The scar's so convenient. Label it."

"I don't want to do that."

"I know." His stiff shrug. "It's such a tired old story."

"But you have to live in it."

"And so do you, now? Have to know what you've got by the tail? Am I really a wacko, one of those fucked-up vets, just accidentally push my button, and Bam!" He gripped my wrist tighter.

"Am I not supposed to wonder?" I took a deep breath. "I'm not putting a label on you, I don't see how words like sane or normal could even apply to what went on in that war. Maybe I couldn't understand it, but I'd like to try."

"Why? Bottom line is, we're all of us alone inside our skulls. Damned good thing. Otherwise we couldn't stand it."

What about the Link? "What happened to you over there?"

"It's not what happened *to* me. Don't you get it? It's what I made myself into so I could get through it."

I stared into his unnervingly clear blue eyes. Suddenly I wasn't sure I wanted to know.

His grip tightened painfully on my wrist. "It's not glamorous like some stupid movie, it's just plain ugly. You *can't* know if you haven't been there, seen it all comes down to a big fat zero in the end. Dead or alive, it's all the same, you're just meat. Killing meat."

I looked down at his fingers locked around my wrist. "But you made a choice. You didn't stay that way."

"Maybe."

My gaze jittered back to his. "Why did they put you in the Psych ward?"

"What?" His eyes narrowed. He released my wrist, sitting up. "Didn't Wilkes straighten you out?"

"What do you mean?"

"God damn it! That Carver bitch, digging her dirt!" He shook his head. "Look, Susan, I cleared it up with Wilkes, that bullshit about my military record. They only put me in the Psych ward when I got wounded that second time because they ran out of room in the hospital. I was no crazier than anyone else in that hellhole."

"I'm sorry." I ran my hand over the tensed muscles in his shoulder.

"Goddamn cops. They try to throw me in jail again, I'll –"

"Wait." I gave him a shake. "Wilkes was just posturing." He'd questioned us separately at the station before finally letting us go. "They can't pin this on you."

"Save stirring up the Dreads, rocking the boat with Africa Unite."

"Even Wilkes admits there's something going on, it's way past putting me off or using you as a scapegoat." I rubbed my eyes. "I'll talk to Phillip Holte, see if he's come up with anything."

"Why Holte?" He frowned.

"He wants to help me establish a preserve for the petroglyphs. We can't do anything until this Ship Bay mess is cleared up."

"Caviness wants a preserve, too. So why is he the bad guy?"

"It's more than that! John was trying to tell me in that letter."

"You'll never stop, will you, until it all adds up?"

"It's important. It's my work. And...."

He touched my face. "All right. Let me help." He rose from the bunk, plucked up the folder I'd left on the dresser, and dumped the petroglyph photos onto the sheets. "Never got a good look at them."

Poking through them, he picked up a closeup of the carved spiral eyes. "This is what you saw? In the nightmare."

"And John's eyes." It came out a hoarse whisper.

"Got into my nightmares, too, the way I found him." He shot me a look. "The cops tell you?"

I cleared my throat. "Not much."

"I figured he'd pulled the anchor over on himself, couldn't get free. His arms were all scraped up from fighting it. And his mouthpiece...." He took a deep breath. "When he ran out of air, he should have just lost consciousness, faded out. But he still had a little air left in his tank. He'd spit out his mouthpiece. And his face was twisted up like he was screaming, furious. Like he suddenly saw he wasn't going to make it, and he was screaming, 'Fuck you, Death.'"

It wasn't just death John had raged at. It was the *bete noir*. And it was still crouched out there, clutching its secrets. The stone's secrets. I stared at the petroglyph photos, the mute faces, leaping figures, fierce bird and goat masks. "They're guarding something. The secret of the cove."

"Maybe there is no secret."

"There has to be. What about the *Phoenix*, Vic? What do you think John went back for?"

"He was sure the treasure was there."

"You don't think so?"

"Not any more. Maybe somebody got to it before us."

"But you think there *was* a treasure? Someone stole those documents from the archives?"

"Maybe John."

I frowned.

"All I know is Miss Martin accused me of stealing that Parker Manuscript, she wasn't even sure what was in it. I never saw it. I wondered at the time if somebody had gone through before me, wiping out references to Ship Bay and the *Phoenix*. Wasn't much left. And then some of what I did find disappeared later. Afterwards, I thought maybe John had taken the papers, figuring he'd use them to prove authenticity if he found something on the wreck."

I sighed. "What *did* you find in the archives?"

"Slim pickings." He looked at my face, made a resigned gesture. "I put together a scenario. Got hold of some shipping manifests from the African end, plus a memorial from a friend of Captain Hawkins of the *Phoenix*. Looks like the slaves Hawkins was bringing over were mostly from one tribe, a chieftain and warriors who'd been captured in a skirmish between tribes and sold to the traders. But the manifest also listed some 'small wooden caskets, bound with leather and padlocked,' loaded at the last minute as the captain's personal property."

"The tribal treasure everyone was talking about?"

He rubbed his beard. "Maybe the chief's tribe tried to ransom him with the treasure. Then Hawkins double-crossed them and sailed with the treasure *and* the slaves. The ship did leave early, on an unfavorable tide."

He nudged the petroglyph prints. "Maybe the captain outsmarted himself. Those Africans were a lot more sophisticated than the Europeans thought, even if they weren't high tech. Slave trade wasn't any brave expedition of Great White Hunters into the land of the savages. Most of the slaves were sold to the traders at the coast by the Africans themselves."

"Captives of raids between tribes?"

He nodded. "Those Africans were fighters." Despite himself, he was warming to the tale. "From this end, I found records of slaves here on the island being tortured after attempted uprisings. Seems like they were expecting help from back home. Maybe the Africans

I cleared my throat. "Adrienne, she told me —"

"That's not all. Leon is my father." With a choking sound, she jumped to her feet and strode from the room.

She returned with a battered shoe box. Her face had gone smoothly blank, eyes distant. "Tell me what you think." She handed me the box and stood gazing out a window.

Legal papers inside. On top, wrapped in tissue, another ouanga-bag, tied with a scarlet cord, decorated with feathers and dried blood.

Adrienne's Florida birth certificate listed Pat MacIntyre as the mother, Leon Caviness the father. A carbon copy of a letter from Pat to Caviness, dated not long before her accident, revealed that Adrienne was his child and threatened in vague terms to "expose him" if he continued to oppose her development plan for Ship Bay. An answering note from Caviness to Pat, written in a strong looping script, advised her that she "might as well drop these ludicrous attempts at blackmail," and that she'd "regret this course of action." No response to the news about Adrienne. I shook my head, laid aside some old photos and documents dealing with a Stateside land sale.

Finally, a statement signed three years ago by Frank Savetti and John Dunne. It described how they'd purchased three kilograms of cocaine in Central America and smuggled it to the island aboard a sailboat they were crewing in a yacht race.

Setting the box on a table, I joined Adrienne, staring through the louvres at shifting light and shadow in the leaves.

She released her grip on the slats, absently studying the bluish marks pressed into her palms. "I never really knew her. Or Leon."

"I felt the same way when I found out what John had done."

"I'm sorry, Susan. I had to show you."

"I already knew most of it. But I don't see why Frank and John would have signed that paper. Or why Pat had it."

She sighed and moved to the couch. "Did you see the paper about her land sale in the States? She told me she'd used that money to pay off what she owed on the resort, so she could use it as collateral to get financing for her new development project. But now I see the sale didn't bring in nearly enough." Voice toneless. "She must have backed Frank and John in their drug deal, then used her share of the profits to pay off the debts. We were a little shaky at that time." She spread her hands. "I suppose that paper was Pat's insurance."

"What about the letters between Pat and Leon? Have you talked to him?"

She hesitated. "No." Then, in a rush, "I've been up to Fairview for piano sessions after they wrote those letters. And he's been helping me since the accident, looking for a resort manager. He acts just the same as ever. Maybe he doesn't even care I'm his daughter!" She swallowed, looking away. "Do I know him at all? I don't even know who *I* am now. Why hasn't he said something?"

I took a deep breath. "Adrienne, Leon may have known all along. Maybe he just let Pat think she was fooling him with the adoption story."

Her eyes widened. "But…." Her hands were trembling. "Why?"

I could only shake my head. The man was capable of anything. Had he left that fetish by Pat's bedside? Was his note a threat? Had Pat been my burglar, or had Caviness engineered her "accident?" I recalled with unwelcome vividness our argument at the Great-House, before I happened on the wreck. He'd spoken of Pat in the past tense, saying she was "irrelevant now."

"Susan?"

"You'd better talk to the police. Show Captain Wilkes the fetish, and the letters between Pat and Leon."

She stood abruptly. "You still believe he's your *bete noir*."

"My —" I caught a sharp breath. "Who told you that? Why do you say *bete noir*?"

An odd look flickered over her face. "It's just a term. I could say bogeyman." She lifted her chin on that long neck. "You're wrong about him."

"You just got through telling me you didn't really know him, after all."

"I know that much." Her nostrils flared. "He's been my teacher, my mentor, he's part of my music. He's opened doors I didn't even know were there. Doors you won't let yourself see." She pinned me with her smoldering eyes. "If you accuse him, you accuse me. It's his blood in my veins."

Late morning sun hammered the parking lot, heat shimmering up from cracked concrete and baking the back wall of the police station. Captain Wilkes would have to get used to being interrogated himself. I needed some answers about Leon Caviness, Pat MacIntyre, and the missing Laura. Threading parked cars toward the walkway around the building, I skirted a dumpster and came up short. Caviness's limo was parked in a Reserved slot, near an exit door.

Whoever answered the phone at the Great-House had refused to connect me to Caviness when I'd tried to call about Laura. I could catch him here when he came out.

Behind the dumpster, some flattened cardboard crates leaned against a metal railing, providing a strip of shade where I could watch the limo. I sat on the curb, blotting sweat from my face. I couldn't tell if there was anyone behind the smoked windows of the big car.

Slap of footsteps. A uniformed policeman hurried between dumpster and limo, heading for the door. I waited. The door swung open again in a whoosh of air, and a native woman in a sleeveless dress strolled past my vantage point, heading for the parking lot. The door opened once more.

"...taking care of it. This is just a glitch." Wilkes's low rumble.

"There have been too many glitches." Caviness's deep, melodious voice. Sound of footsteps, and they moved past the concealing crates as I pulled deeper into the shade.

"Don't worry, I'll keep you out of the picture with Kono." Wilkes had paused by the front of the limo, turning my way.

Caviness, facing away from me, said something I couldn't catch.

"I know, blow the whole thing if they tied us together." Wilkes turned his head from side to side, glancing over the deserted pathway. "I think I put the fear of God into her last night, but who knows where she'll stick her pointy little nose next? I'm trying to keep her pacified, told her we're investigating Ship Bay."

"The same way you pacified Shelli Carver?" Caviness had turned to present his profile.

Wilkes swore. "All right. We've got to act fast. How's —"

"Not so fast. What about Susan Dunne? She's becoming more than a nuisance. You've already allowed her meddling to jeopardize everything."

"I could have her picked up, hold her until after Carnivale. Manden, too, keep her company."

"That would look too suspicious. And Manden can be useful on the outside."

"Too bad Kono got pushy," Wilkes rumbled.

"Now listen, Godfrey. We've got to be ready to move the day after the grand parade." He moved toward the limo as Wilkes followed.

I leaned close to the edge of the crates, straining to catch his fading voice.

"I want Miss Dunne out of the way, I don't care if it takes...." The car door opened, Wilkes blocking the rest.

The door slammed, motor starting. I flinched lower behind the crates, pulse pounding. Footsteps slapped past. The limo purred off.

"Shelli." My heart was racing, palms damp. "Are you there?" I gripped the receiver, peering edgily from the phone booth at the police station across the street.

"I can hardly hear you! Why are you whispering?"

I repeated my request.

"You know how busy I am, with the special Carnivale issue? You haven't exactly kept your side of our deal, Susan." Her voice sounded harried and enjoying it. "Okay, okay, hold on a minute, I'll see what I can find." A crash. Scraping. Another shout, "You're gonna owe me big-time!" *Clunk.*

I waited a long time, keeping an eye on the station. The line gave out the ominous squeals and crackles that usually announced a dying connection. Shelli finally returned, breathing heavily.

"I should have my head examined, but so I'm crazy and you better be grateful. I found those names in the obits for last year. Olson in August, VanterPol in October."

"How did they die?"

"Just says 'sudden fever' for each of them. They were both in their twenties."

"Thanks, Shelli." I closed my eyes. The names danced over the scrap of silvered paper under Wilkes's flashlight beam. A death list. "I'm going to put that information I mentioned in the mail to you, you'll get it after Carnivale." I'd written down what I'd overheard between Wilkes and Caviness.

"So big mystery! Come on, tell me now."

"I'll talk to you as soon as I get things clear. Maybe you'd rather have some facts next time."

"So feed me some! What's the scoop with you and Manden? What about that body last night?"

"Stay tuned." Shelli's voice sputtering in my ear, I hung up.

The Honda roared across the crown of the island to the bare East End. Sun baked the exhausted, beaten earth, cracked with the drought. Thorn trees stretched withered branches into the breezeless heat, a scaly gray iguana sprawled on a dead limb, unblinking as I flew past.

Untying the rental dinghy from the marina dock, I started to push off. The sound of a motor swelled through the mangroves, and Phillip Holte chugged around the turn of the narrow channel in his inflatable.

"Phillip!" I scrambled back onto the dock.

The nose of his dinghy nudged the boards, and he climbed out quickly, tying it off. "Susan, I was about to leave you a message."

"Phillip, did you hear —?"

"— about Kono?" He raised an eyebrow. "You're in the thick of it now."

"It's building to a head, Phillip. You should have seen Kono's face, and that knife, in his chest, it had a goat horn handle. Sacrificial death. I just overheard Captain Wilkes talking to Caviness, and —"

"Here now." He took my shoulders, gave me a shake. "Let's take things one at a time, shall we?"

I couldn't get a decent breath, the heat squeezing my lungs.

Sitting against a piling, he pulled out a fat cigar, lighting up and puffing smelly clouds. "Sit close here, the smoke will discourage these damned insects. I'm pressed for time, or I'd invite you back to the boat." He swatted a mosquito as I sank cross-legged onto the dock.

"I don't know where to start." My thoughts kept jittering from one alarm to the next, like a caffeine junkie.

"Try Kono." He shook his head. "Damn shame, I thought we might learn something from him. How on earth did you happen on the body?"

"We were out for J'ouvert. I saw Laura with some Rudes, tried to follow her down an alley. We stumbled over Kono."

"We?" He tapped ash into the water. "You and Victor Manden?"

"Yes."

"Careful, you're losing your armor." He blew out smoke, eyeing me. "I should have been the one, Susan." He leaned closer, lifting a strand of my hair and sliding it through his fingers.

I pulled it free.

"I warned you, I don't give up easily. I've a feeling Manden's rough charms will prove short-lived, and you'll be looking for something... more complex. I won't disappoint you."

I shook my head. "There's no time for this."

His mouth tightened angrily. He made a movement to rise, but checked it, clearing his throat and waving the cigar. "I assume you've somehow absolved Mr. Manden from blame in your brother's death?"

"It wasn't Vic. I'm sure now, it's Caviness."

I told him about James's story, the papers Adrienne had found, the conversation I'd just overheard between Wilkes and Caviness. Phillip sat contemplating the swampy little harbor, craggy features half-obscured by the clouds of pungent smoke.

I swatted a hungry mosquito. "There goes any hope of help from the police. Laura's in danger. That list —"

"Don't let's jump to conclusions. I don't like the sound of that list of names, but what you overheard could have more than one interpretation. You and Laura are too visible, especially after that absurd newspaper article, to be simply disposed of. It's much more likely Wilkes would arrest you on some pretext to keep you out of the way until their plans can be carried through. It would be interesting to find Laura before the police do, I imagine she could fill in some gaps."

"If she's still alive!" My voice shook. "I shouldn't have meddled, she warned me not to. So many people are getting hurt. I wish I'd never heard of this goddamned island!"

"Too late for that now." Phillip studied the glowing tip of his cigar, shot me a penetrating look. "Need I remind you? 'No man is an island.'"

I sighed. "I guess I was involved before I ever came here."

"I'm afraid we must go on now, whatever uncomfortable truths we find." He spread his hands. "I warned you it might not be pretty." He stood. "Now I must be off."

"Where now?"

"I've found out a few things myself. My contacts indicate Mr. Caviness does appear to be expecting an important shipment. Drugs, from regions south."

"What? How did you find that out?"

"Judicious use of bribes. And collecting on some favors." A thin smile. "I do have contacts in the British islands. Surprisingly enough, after all the uproar about Ship Bay, it seems doubtful that's the pickup point. Apparently he's using his cult members as runners, some from the Brotherhood. Supposedly fishing offshore, they could check certain reefs and cays for the drops. His art dealings would provide the perfect cover for shipping north. There is a strong hint of official involvement, which must be where Wilkes comes into the picture."

He flicked the cigar butt into the murky water. "I think we've enough to go on to interest higher authorities. If, as you say, Caviness isn't planning his move until after Carnivale, I have time to sail back to the British islands to speak to officials there. They'll know what channels to go through Stateside, over the heads of the local police. You ought to come with me, Susan."

I climbed to my feet, shaking my head.

"You're trusting Victor Manden far too readily. There are still too many questions."

"If I've learned anything here, it's that not all questions can be answered."

"Of course." Voice brusque. "But there is such a thing as evidence to be weighed."

"The evidence points to Caviness." What *had* he meant by saying Vic could be useful on the outside?

"Listen to reason. Come with me."

I shook my head. "No, you were right, I was overreacting. Besides, Wilkes wanted me to be available on the Kono case. If I disappeared, it might spook them and they'd call off their deal."

"I ought to take you along by brute force!"

I moved back a pace.

"No, no." He lifted his hands. "That's not *my* method. But I'd feel better if you'd stay away from the unpredictable Mr. Manden for now. I hope to be back tomorrow. That's parade day, isn't it? At any rate, I'll send someone here with a message for you. Why not stay overnight with your friend Adrienne? You might even pick up more information via her connection with Caviness."

He took my hand, astute gray eyes searching my face. He turned abruptly, climbing into the inflatable and starting the motor. "Do take care, Susan. We'll settle this soon."

The twists and turns of the mangrove swamp swallowed the motor's buzz, ripples dying away on opaque green water. Heat flattened the channel, leaves hanging limp over spidery roots. Whispering, just beyond my grasp. Some hint, some clue I just wasn't getting. I stared into the shadowed maze of limbs, questions swarming with the mosquitoes.

Thirty-Four

Safe Harbor rocked smoothly to the muted patter of Vic's shower beyond the stateroom wall. I pushed the petroglyph photos to the side of the bunk and sank into the swinging cradle of the sea. The shower's hissing was distant rain, a breath of cool moisture over the thirsty land.

I was rising out of my exhausted body, slowly at first then spinning faster, bursting up and out of the oppressive tropic heat. I flew high among the clouds, blue curve of the globe rolling below. Home's magnet pulled me down over my green Northwest islands. Fir and cedar towered, damp moss beneath my feet, cold gray-green waves slapping the rocky shore and brisk rain-scrubbed air cleansing with each breath.

Expanding, drinking it in, I dropped to my knees to savor the solid cool stones under my palms.

The wind howled, whipping into a storm, pulling me back toward the tropics. I gripped the rock, clinging. But it was melting in my clutch, metamorphosing to a fierce carved face. The stone heaved with subterranean shiftings, rock creatures stirring, swelling up into the air. Chanting a secret song, they danced around me to the furious beat of my heart.

Closing in, they forced me to my knees at the rim of the sacred pool etched with its mysterious designs. I stared into the dark-shimmered water. A dreaming, drowned face floated in the mirrored depths, pale hair fluttering like seaweed.

"No!" Anger sizzled through me, and I plunged my arms into the water, grabbed that face and ripped it out into the air, pulled the empty mask over my own face as the trailing husk of skin closed around my own body.

Looking out through the death mask, I whirled, pounded the dark stone the killing place with my fist. The earth split open. Light spilled into the crypt, beams glittering through an enormous shadowy cathedral of stone pillars and darting black-winged demons. At its heart burned a pyre. Out of the flames, spreading wings like billowing sails, rose the Phoenix.

I sat bolt upright, pulse racing. "The petroglyphs! They're trying to tell me —" I blinked and frowned.

"What?" Vic stood dripping in the doorway, towel around his hips.

"There's something I've been missing." I scrabbled for the glyph prints scattered over the blanket.

"You're obsessed with this. Let it go for now." He took the prints and tossed them onto his dresser.

I jumped off the bunk, stood staring at the photos splayed across the raw knife gash scarring the dresser top, images dimly reflected in the mirror. Above them, a shadowed face floating. My own, a stranger's. "Reflections. That's it." I pounced on the photos, shifting them around.

"Here we go." Vic shook his head.

"Look!" I spread certain prints in a line beneath the mirror. "Those marks. Rain dashes, like the ones on Palm Cay. Phillip said the sacred pool was usually high enough to reflect the rain marks, but they weren't hieroglyphs like the other etchings. Maybe he missed something."

He lifted his palms and stepped closer.

I overlapped a couple of the prints. "This is from the Ship Bay rock. I think it's a fertility grouping, like the one on Palm Cay." Dancing figures, male and female. A spirit figure in a horned mask. Beneath them, wavy rain dashes. "Maybe in the original location up on the cliff, there was a reflecting pool beneath these glyphs, too."

"Get some light on it." He flicked a switch.

In the sharp light, the upside-down reflections resolved into clarity. "Those 'rain dashes' do look like hieroglyphs." I grabbed my linguistic notes. "I've extended Phillip's translation system, maybe I can find some matching figures." I frowned, squinting back and forth.

Vic glanced at my notes, pointed to one set of marks.

"Look, these marks fit the system, too. This means 'death' or 'to bury.' And this one is 'to live.'" I traced the sequence over the mirror. "Did I get the order wrong? No, with this other part, it says, 'to die and live here.' But why in that order?"

I poked through the photos, pushed a closeup next to the mirror. "I can't make out this next part, it's lost. But here, this spells out 'winged one,' and this is 'earth womb.' It must have been a fertility invocation."

"Fits with the figures. Look at that male dancer, talk about all the options." Vic sorted prints. "Here." He showed me a photo of the entire grouping. "That long diagonal crack. Looks like the boulder fractured when it fell, and the pieces shifted. That crazy-looking bird was originally above that priest or spirit figure."

"It was part of the fertility scene." I met his reflected gaze. "It makes sense, ties in with the womb symbols. 'The winged one' — that could mean either bird or spirit — 'dies and lives here.' There's something missing here along the fracture, maybe 'inside.' That would make it 'inside this earth womb.'"

"That a knife the priest figure's holding up? Maybe it was a sacrificial altar. 'The winged one dies and lives here, inside this earth womb.' Or a burial place?"

"This womb symbol could also mean a grave, or a cave...." The cavern in my dream.

My jittering finger stabbed at the photo of the carved bird. "The Phoenix. Death and rebirth. It wasn't just the ship John was talking about." I straightened. "Vic, we've got to go back there."

He groaned. "I must be psychic. I knew you were going to say that."

—⁓—

The moon slipped past midnight toward the dark harbor. Vic eased the Whaler away from the dock, whistling softly at the wheel. James lounged against the inflatable dinghy crammed into the back of the boat, blanket-wrapped rifle on his knees.

Boatloads of laughing drunks careened across the harbor in Carnivale celebration. From the lights of Treasure Island, ringing steel-drum music drifted over the bay. The Whaler swung out in a wide curve and picked up speed heading around the Northwest End, weaving through a maze of shallow coral etched in surreal clarity. High cliffs glowed in the moonlight, creased by black shadows. Water foamed cool silver off the bow.

I rehearsed the steps to aim, fire, and reload Vic's pneumatic speargun. The weapon was heavy and solid in my grip, but it wasn't real. No way could I envision myself firing it at a human being. The Alice in Wonderland feeling was back with a vengeance.

Vic's lips were parted in a glittering grin, like his mad challenge to the storm. His chest rose and fell deeply, eyes gleaming in the dark. The closer we got to Ship Bay, the more he came alive.

I shivered.

His hand dropped over mine. "Want to call it off?"

I shook my head. "I just hadn't pictured all this." I gestured at James's rifle, the bulge of the automatic in Vic's jacket pocket.

"Don't sweat it. We're just out on exercise." He started singing, "*Oo Wah Ditty.*" His voice was tight, charged, turning the playful lyrics into something else.

My gut churned. James shot me a grin.

The moon was riding low over the water when we got to the narrow cut where waves crashed and boiled over exposed rock. No sign of shore patrols, but Vic hadn't used his lights. We slowed, waves tossing the Whaler.

James took the wheel as Vic and I slid the inflatable over the side, loading the dive gear into it.

"Okay." Vic gripped his shoulder. "Rendezvous in three hours. If we're not back, get on the radio to Gaylord and he'll round up reinforcements. Try holing up over by Orchid Bay, don't get yourself in trouble with any patrols."

James flashed his teeth and patted his rifle.

"Be careful." I touched his arm.

"Sue, you de one to worry. Dat no good place." He lifted his chin toward the cove, dark cliffs cupping shadowy seas.

Caviness's deep laughter echoed, Granny's voice ringing, *"You run before you drown, too."* But I'd summoned it, and now I was summoned.

"Let's go." Vic's voice was taut, tension humming as he slipped his pistol into a watertight case and tucked it into his wetsuit. He strapped his speargun to his thigh, gestured me brusquely into the inflatable thrashing on the chop.

He climbed in after me. "No talking once we're inside. Sound carries like hell over water."

The sea roared, foaming through the cut. Waves tossed the dinghy sideways, spray flying. Another big wave crashed into us, throwing us closer to the jagged black rocks. The little electric motor buzzed.

We shot into the gap. Bucking and slithering, the dinghy rode a crest, dipped, and spat out onto glassy dark water.

Vic cut the motor. Silence over the cove, no lights up on the cliff tonight, no drums. He picked up a wooden paddle and stroked toward the rock walls. The moon had dropped behind the mountain. His face was a shadowed blur, pale glints of eyes and teeth. Grinning again. My own lips were pulled back over my teeth in a fierce reflex, breathing gone short and shallow, heart racing. Fear. Eagerness.

"One big fat rush. Right?" His voice close to my ear was curt, tinged with a bitter note. "Slow down. Breathe deep." He pulled back, swearing under his breath.

Shame flushed me with prickling heat. Something here was calling him, too, something he didn't want. And I'd put him here. Like John.

We stopped in the deeper shadow beneath the cliffs. He lowered a small anchor, silently helped me with my gear. Leaning close, he whispered, "We can use our lights to find the cleft. Even if there's someone above, they won't be able to see right to the foot of the drop. Wait below for me."

I balked before the opaque black water. I'd never done a night dive before. My heart was pounding, throat gone dry. Waiting beneath the blind surface, the *bete noir*? Wound up too tight, arms shaking with it, I lowered myself into the cool shock of the sea. A hissing breath, and I was sinking into blackness. The dark sea pressed in. I was floating in limbo, unsure even of up and down.

Light flashed overhead, bright sparks exploding as a school of minnows scattered. The narrow beam sliced blackness, dwindling into the empty depths. Vic beckoned.

Yellow fingerlings darted through my beam. Colors flashed out of the disorienting blackness. Waving sea fans. A bright-striped parrotfish. Dark jagged rock and branching orange coral. A sinuous serpentine wriggling. The back of my neck prickled with unseen presences.

Vic's waving light summoned me to the hidden gap in the submerged cliff face. Shining his flash into the narrow passage, he pulled out a spear and prodded. A green eel darted from a crevice, opened and closed its mouth, retreated.

Tight squeeze of black stone. My tank caught, scraping. I pushed through into a still well of darkness. My light flashed spasmodically, caught a stream of bubbles, Vic searching around the petroglyph boulder. I drifted closer. Carved spiral eyes watched. Primitive figures capered around the fierce animal mask of the priest, knife held high.

They'd caught him here, on a night like this, shadow hands dragging him deeper, his fury screaming down the Link.

High-pitched keening behind me. Heart leaping, I spun around. Vic aimed his light at his watch, gesturing me over. We probed around the jumbled boulders, looking for a gap. Nothing wide enough to pass through. I flashed my light over the petroglyph rock again, coiled serpent and bird wings flickering into ghostly life. A flat stone leaned against the base of it. I finned closer, saw the algae coating it was scraped and scuffed along the edges.

Both of us braced and heaving, the flat stone swung out and over, dropped with a muffled thump and a glitter of rising silt. A narrow passage ran back around the side of the petroglyph boulder.

"It's the goddamn rock!" John's voice echoed through the night sea.

Vic's mask, only a flare of reflected light, swung my way. He slipped into the crevice.

I pulled myself through a sharp turn, rock walls closing in. The passage widened, bottom falling away into pitch-black. Light flicked in quick sweeps ahead. A sloped bottom running up. Overhead, a rippling ceiling. Legs stood disembodied on a slanted boulder, sliced off at the waist by the shimmering liquid roof.

Ripples spread across it. Vic's masked face broke through the membrane. He motioned me up. I took his hand, fins groping for footing, and he pulled me up onto a rock floor. I turned to follow the sweep of his flash.

My mouthpiece popped out. "My God!"

―――

Vic's hand slapped over my mouth as the light snapped off. "Quiet!" he hissed in my ear. "Could be an ambush."

The startled glimpse flared its after-image on the dark:

Rock cathedral vault stretching into blackness. Tapered columns of colored stone. Water dripping from a sharp stalactite. Plastic crates, one lid ajar on white puffs of styrofoam packing. Stone walls lined with heaped piles of ivory and yellow sticks, knobby round balls.

I stiffened against Vic's muffling hand as the shapes translated. Stacks of bones and skulls.

We stood in the dark, dripping. Red sparks flared before my blinded eyes.

Finally Vic nudged me. "Okay. On alert." His shielded flash dimly lit up the nearest bone pile.

"There must be hundreds," I whispered. "It can't be the cult —?"

"They're old." Vic pulled off my vest and tank, tugged me over to a niche uncomfortably close to the grisly mound. He stowed the Scuba gear, took his pistol from its case, quickly checked it.

His whisper gusted against my cheek. "Hang onto your speargun. Just don't aim it at me, really packs a punch on land. Wait here." He darted off into the cave.

Brief flashes lit up stalactites and stalagmites in gleaming rose and orange, darkness soaring overhead, a winged shape darting erratically into and out of the light. Steady drip of water, restless rustling overhead. The air was heavy, cold. A taut wire thrummed down my spine, twisting tighter.

The light bobbed back to me. "All clear for now. They're in the middle of something." His voice had eased. "Come here, you've got to see this."

Jerky sweeps of light stabbed the dark. Piles of ancient bones. Packing crates. Sloping rock frozen in lumpy ripples. Stone columns soaring to an unseen roof. Another bat swooped by. A dark pool at our feet rippled with a falling drop, the splash echoing off rock walls.

Vic flashed his light across the pool. Striated limestone, a frozen waterfall in muted colors. Behind it, the roof dropped lower, angled into darkness. Rising from the rock floor, another column, broad, solid, flared at the base into a gnarled mass like tree roots. Above, a tapering trunk and stone branches melting into the jagged ceiling. The sheer mass of it radiated power and age.

Vic snapped off his light. His fingers gripped my arm, warning. In the dark, we listened. No movement but the stirring of leathery wings. My pulse throbbed and rang in my ears.

"Okay." He flicked on the light. "Look here."

The ground was littered with broken pieces of earthenware pottery, fragments of conch shells. I held up a broken handle shaped like a fierce, grinning demon. "Indian?"

He turned it over. "Could be Mayan. Fancy stuff is probably at the bottom of this pool. The Mayans likely did travel and trade in the Caribbean islands. And this grotto...."

I was kneeling, sifting numbly through the broken, etched shards. More puzzle pieces, dumped into my lap.

"The really sacred Mayan 'temples' were inside caves." Vic was whispering, his light flashing past me. "Their universe was held up by a great tree stretching from its roots in the underworld to its branches in the heavens. Had to keep the gods happy with sacrifices, or the tree would wither. The stone pillars were symbols of the world tree."

I could only stare at the artifacts, the stone column, wheels spinning. It was important, but it couldn't penetrate the jittery buzzing in my ears. Mayans? Africans? It wouldn't add up.

I jumped to my feet. "Those bones."

"And the crates."

My light flickered over the mound of yellowed bones. "They're all —" My voice cracked. I licked my dry lips. "The skeletons, they're all pulled apart."

Vic melted out of the shadows. "I've seen that before, in Honduras. Especially with sacrificial deaths, they dismembered bodies, buried the different bones in separate piles."

I moved to another pile. "These are different." The skeletons were draped across each other intact. "And the skulls...." One sat face to face with me, eye sockets deep with shadow.

The wound-up tremor shook my fingers as I gingerly lifted it. The jawbone crumbled, but the cranium held. "The shape of the skull, Vic. It's different from that other group. Africans, got to be. I'd have to take measurements, but it fits with the petroglyphs."

"Susan! Over here." Vic was crouched beside an open crate.

"Drugs?"

"Not even close. And it's not Indian." Lifting a bulky object, he rose.

I swung my beam his way, fell back in a blinding dazzle of gold.

shadow man reaches for me, the bete noir looming, face a glittering gold mask. Sharp demon horns and glinting eyes, mouth gaping open on darkness opening wider to swallow me

He was standing with the gold mask held before his face, raising one stiff arm in a hieratic gesture. I shuddered. *Icy blue eyes staring through the Bocor's mask.*

Graven image, the face of a golden god. Wide, rounded skull and broad forehead tapered to narrow cheeks carved in deep furrows above a pointed chin. The nose ran straight and long, from flaring nostrils to a thin bridge joining the double curve of arched brows. The eyes were almond slits, rimmed by raised etching, blood-red jewels dangling from chains on intricately carved ears. A seamless circle of open lips made a gaping mouth.

A tiny figure emerged grotesquely from the broad forehead, shape of a dwarfed, faceless man crouching, struggling to be conceived by the god. Two curving golden horns sprang from the brow of the mask, stabbing the darkness.

I'd seen this mask before, Vic's eyes staring through it. I dug knuckles into the dull ache pulsing in my forehead. "Put it down, Vic.

These masks were potent power objects. You shouldn't... take it lightly."

"I'm not." He lowered the wood mask, studying the shifting gleam of light on its gold overlay. "It's heavy enough. West African, isn't it? Didn't the king embody the god's power when he wore it?"

I stepped closer to run a trembling fingertip over smooth gold. "Vic, this is what John must have seen," I whispered hoarsely. "The treasure! The sacred symbol of power carried on the *Phoenix*."

Vic was reaching deeper into the crate. He shook a small object free of packing foam and held it up in the flare of my swinging flash.

I dropped beside him, taking the delicately etched silver bird into my hands. I could almost feel it stir, tiny heart fluttering, wings flexing.

"Look at these." Vic replaced the bird and held up two statuettes. One was bronze, elaborately embellished, a male figure with tall hat, jeweled earrings, carved designs like ritual scarifications over its torso, a broad knife in its hand. The other was roughly hewn of pitted wood. Blocky legs and arms, crude face looking upward with an expression of infinite suffering.

My fingers reached of themselves for the wood figure, cradling it, soaking in its age. "This one is really special. For healing."

There was more. Dazed, I pulled out thick gold arm bands, chased and inlaid with rough gemstones. More figurines. Gold and silver bangles and bracelets. A chased gold cup. A silver rattle inlaid with cabochon jewels.

I finally sat back, eyes dazzled with precious gold, whispering, "Vic, this has to be the *Phoenix* cargo."

"John was right after all." He shook his head sharply, as if shaking off the spell of the treasure. "Susan, we should get out of here."

"Wait." I reached deeper into the last box, pulled out a sheaf of paper enclosed in a clear plastic folder. My light flickered over parchment, yellow and cracking with age.

> *On this Day of Our Lord 24 November, 1768, I Bartholomew Parker, second pilot of the vessel Phoenix....*

"My God. This is it."

"*He* has *the Parker Manuscript!*" John's excited words echoed silently in the dark cavern.

> *Whiles the sea rages... the black fiends on deck do howl and dance... erst did rise from their chains in the hold and take the ship... bearing a great token to free their king from bondage... dark gods have promised them a refuge....*

I whispered, "*Never I fear shall she rise from the ashes of this death.*"

Vic's face was unreadable in the dimness. "John must have stumbled onto this. That's what the letter was about."

"You think Caviness and his Dreads beat you to the treasure?"

"One thing's for sure. This stuff was taken off the ship a long time ago. The wood artifacts would have rotted underwater."

"The survivors must have —"

"Wait!" he hissed, gripping my wrist, snapping off the light.

The bats were stirring, dropping down with shrill squeaks. Above, in the darkness, ringing echo of a pebble falling against stone. Muffled voices?

"Christ, they're coming! Goddamn tunnel rats!" He'd gone rigid, grip tightening painfully on my arm.

I listened, straining in the dark, feeling the weight of the speargun strapped to my thigh. Tension shrilled in my ears. No sound of approaching feet or voices. The bats were still swooping restlessly.

"Let's get this stuff secured." Vic snapped on his light, shielded with his fingers, and we hastily restored the crates. He hustled me over to the dive gear. "I'll go scout it. Has to be a way up." He pulled the pistol out of his suit.

"Vic, no!" I grabbed his arm.

"You lay low." He pried my fingers loose, closed them around the speargun. "Stay put, behind here. Get the dive gear ready. This is my signal, I flick the light like this, three times. Anybody else comes down, you're out of here. That's an order. Into the water, head out to rendezvous with James. Got it?"

My shoulders had drawn up tightly. I forced them down, swallowed, nodded.

"I won't be long."

I'd been waiting forever, crouched blindly beside the pile of bones, breathing in the damp mustiness of the crypt. Feeling the bats' swooping passes through the darkness. Pulse pounding in my ears. Stone demons dancing to the rhythm of the drums, summoning the *bete noir* –

Light stabbed the blackness.

My heart lurched, slamming against my ribs. Three flashes. I took a deep, shuddering breath. Vic's hand grasped my arm. He was breathing heavily.

"Okay, move it out." He held up my tank.

"What did you find?"

"There's an altar, with –" He bit it off, shook his head.

"What? I shook his arm. "What?"

"Later. Gotta go." Face a stiff mask in the dimness.

Suited up, I shot one last look at the cavern, shadows flickering across mounded bones and rock pillar. A bat swooped past as I eased into the sea. Its quicksilver ceiling closed over me, sealing the Bocor's treasure into darkness.

Thirty-Five

"Do have Carnivale guest. Out." The boat radio crackled.

"What's that?" Still shivering with the chill of the night dive, I tugged Vic's jacket closer around me. Strobing images of the cavern, the African mask, the burial mounds kept jittering through my exhaustion.

"Be trouble." James gripped his rifle, peering across the early morning glare off the harbor.

"Shit." Vic swung the wheel, and the Whaler tilted in a sharp U-turn toward Treasure Island. We slid in beside the rusted hulk of a half-sunken freighter, motor chugging down into idle. "Gaylord's trouble code. Cops have been to my place."

"Oh. Shit."

"Maybe Wilkes decided to lock us up, after all."

Another shiver stuttered through me. "We'd better run over to the East Side Marina, hook up with Phillip. If he's made the right connections to bypass the police here, we should fill him in on that cavern."

"Not so fast. I want to think about this." He was staring across the bay.

"We need to stop them before they move those artifacts. And pull off whatever else it is Caviness has planned for the cult after Carnivale."

"That gives us at least another day." He bit it off, still watching the sea.

I'd had to pry out of him a terse description of what he'd found scouting a passage up from the cavern. Steep stone steps, worn with age, climbing a natural fissure into a smaller cave above. Rock walls painted with geometric designs over an altar covered with ritual paraphernalia. Glimpse outside to a stamped-earth clearing, and a path that must have led to the party-shack farther along the cliffside. Two Dreads guarding the place with rifles.

There was something he wasn't telling me. I couldn't get through to him. He didn't seem to care that the cavern, if it showed Pre-Columbian Indian/African contact, could mean a major breakthrough.

I rubbed the pulsing ache in my brow, trying to focus through a feverish fuzzy-headedness. "Vic, we have to stop that gang using the cove. Phillip said—"

"Phillip." He swung toward me. "Look, he may be your hero, but I don't even know him. I'm not about to hand this whole thing over just like that."

"Hand it over?"

"Vic still got claim to dat treasure," James cut in. "He lose a lot of cash an time on dat wreck. Lot of grief. He got de say-so here."

"But.... Vic, you don't mean —?"

"Susan, I do have salvage rights to that treasure." A curt gesture. "At least a pretty good case, even if it was moved off the ship."

"But those artifacts are priceless! They should be in a museum."

"So which museum? Holte's Brits get their hands on it, or the Feds, it ends up in London or D.C., sure as hell not here where they have a claim. I want a say in it. You don't want your site handed over to some big cheese with political pull. And I am entitled to *some* compensation, after everything I dumped into it."

I gaped at him, wheels spinning.

"So now I'm a money-grubbing asshole?" A humorless smile twitched his lips. "Look, archeology isn't your genteel academic sport down here. For some people it's a high-risk business, big bucks and guns, you better make sure your ass is covered before you go revealing your finds. I found out the hard way. I want some choices this time." He snorted. "Besides, once all the jurisdictional hassles get sorted out, I'll probably end up with squat anyway."

James propped his rifle in the stern, leaning against the gunwale and folding his massive arms. "You tink on it, Vic, I say we roun' up we own crew, we go back dere foh de gold."

I frowned at him. "So what about those bad Jumbies now?"

He pursed his lips. "Maybe dem spirits tinkin' it better dat treasure stay here on de island, not get stole by dem drug pushers, stole by de politicians."

I sighed, turning back to Vic. "So what about the cult? Caviness is planning something big. What about Laura, and whoever else is next on their list? At least come and talk to Phillip. We don't need to mention the treasure, but we should let him know about the altar, that ceremonial place you saw on the cliff."

James nodded. "She talkin' sense, Vic."

He said brusquely, "All right. I'll talk to your wonderful Dr. Holte." He climbed onto the pilot seat.

Teeth chattering, I clutched the jacket around myself. There was a heavy lump in one pocket, my fingers touching smooth metal. I pulled it out in a dazzle of polished gold.

A miniature lion arched in my hand, stiff legs stalking, tail jutting. The head was turned watchfully sideways, broadened into an anthropomorphised blend of human and feline, ringed by a spiky mane of sun-flames. The figurine was exquisitely crafted, radiating vitality. I stared, helplessly captivated.

Vic turned on his seat, eyeing me and the lion charm. He reached over to close my fingers around it. "Right now this is mine, and I'm giving it to you. Seem to remember the lion's a guardian."

He finally met my eyes. "Susan...." He shook his head and turned back to the wheel. "Let's go."

The sun was still climbing, heat already blasting the East End, leaves hanging defeated over the opaque green channel through the mangrove swamp. Not a breath of breeze stirred the choking air. The mosquitoes were having a field day.

Phillip had already come and gone. "Damn it!" I swatted at a cloud of insects as I ripped open the envelope he'd left me at the marina office. The thick stationery bore the seal of a British bureau.

"Susan, things are looking up. My British connections are contacting U.S. Federal authorities to step in. Meanwhile, my 'spies' on the island have located Laura. She's safely clear of Caviness, if a bit worse for wear, and wants to talk to you. I'll have a reliable man waiting at the crossroads of Contant Drive and Mountain Road to bring you to her, after the Grand Parade. I'll meet you both there, once I've tied up a few loose ends.

"Laura insists you come alone. She's afraid of Victor Manden, and said you weren't to tell him you're coming to meet her. Take care, my dear!

"Your devoted servant, Phillip."

Enclosed in the envelope was a scribbled note from Laura, barely legible.

> "Susie, your Doc H. looks okay. I'll talk. Don't tell that bastard Vic!!"

"End of the line. We'll never get through." Vic stood braced against the cab of the pickup we'd hitched a ride on, peering over the traffic-clogged harbor drive. "Do better walking."

James patted the feathered braids of two giggling little girls in sequined dresses, shook the hand of an older boy, and vaulted to the pavement. "Maybe we find a cab, other side all dis parade commotion."

I climbed down, blotting dusty sweat from my face. The heat had baked off my chill, but I felt feverish and lightheaded as we trudged past bumper-to-bumper cars idling in clouds of exhaust. Sunlight flared off chrome and glass, shimmering heat waves. The bay stretched dead flat, breezeless, glinting metallic beneath a brassy sky. Motors and voices roared through the acrid haze. I panted, rubbing my damp, aching brow.

Vic took my arm. "You need some sleep. Can't take you home, Wilkes might look there. Christ. If Holte had stayed put, you could've rested on his boat. We'll have to get through this mess, cut around the parade route, try to find a taxi over to Carl and Missy's place. I know where the key's stashed, you can crash there for a while."

I nodded, not meeting his eyes. I'd told him only that Phillip was lining up help and would meet me later. Vic seemed to take the delay as a sign to go ahead with James and round up friends to head back to Ship Bay. They were both jazzed over the idea, and I was too exhausted to resist the momentum of that kind of male energy. Vic was taut, edgy. We were caught in the old, wary dance.

The crowd pressed in, carrying us toward the park and Main Street. James, in the lead, detoured around a ten-foot tall "mockojumbie" wobbling on stilts covered with long, ruffled satin pants. "I go check on Gaylord, see what de score wi'dem cops. I start roundin' up a crew, you meet me back to my cousin place." We'd left the Whaler there to avoid police patrols.

He leaned over me. "Now you go sleep. You makin' you self sick, gal." A stern look, and he was striding off through the throng.

"Okay, let's hustle, maybe we can get past before the parade starts up." Vic pulled me into the crowd.

We were fighting a human tide bobbing a flotsam of fancy hats, garish satin and sequined shirts, feathered masks, ribbon-trimmed skirts. Food vendors jostled, calling out prices. Girls and boys dangled bare legs from branches overhead as we neared the park and the municipal lot. Shouting voices, clashing music, rumbling motors, shrill whistles. My head throbbed as I bumped along in the crush, arms and legs gone rubbery. Sun glittered off tinseled floats, colored satin costumes lining up, what looked like an enormous walking Christmas ornament. Costumed tricksters danced and tumbled through the crowd, stealing hats and scaring kids.

I stumbled in a wash of dizziness. With a bitten-off exclamation, Vic caught me, bending over me to stare into my face.

dark cavern and the swoop of leathery wings, dim light and shadow flickering over the gold mask. Icy eyes of the Bocor hand raised clutching a knife hot stab of adrenaline and Vic's gripping the knife, whirling, stalking, charging through the jungle leaves whipping his face panting fear hunting lust the wild rush of violence exploding

Red stars flared as I pushed away from him.

"What? What's that?" His eyes narrowed, pupils shrinking, then flaring. He shook his head sharply. "Don't fuck with my head, Susan!"

I raised a shaky hand to my damp face. The heat was swamping me, I couldn't breathe. "Vic, what's going on with you?"

He closed his eyes and blew out a breath. Reaching out, he stroked damp strands off my forehead. "Sue, I'm sorry. Everything's getting fucked up." He shook his head. "Over here, sit down, you feel feverish. I'll get you something to drink. Take it easy." He guided me to a thin strip of shade beneath an awning, eased me onto a windowsill. He edged through the crowd toward a kiosk.

My head was spinning, sweat pouring down my face and throat parched, but I didn't know if it was physical illness. The earth beneath me was tilting, rocking, cracking open screaming for rain. Everything off-balance.

Like a diver submerged in an alien world, I pulled in deep, careful breaths. I blinked, peering through the jostling crowd. Finally I spotted Vic beside the kiosk, bending his head to talk with a stocky native in a short-sleeved blue shirt. Vic gestured, nodded. The man said something. Vic raised his palms, turning to point my way. They headed toward me. Sunlight flashed over the badge pinned to the man's blue uniform.

The ground spun crazily. I gasped. Another cop joined Vic, coming to get me. A hot bolt of adrenaline launched me into the throng, and I was shoving past sequined shirts, an angry outburst, flock of scattering paper parasols. The crowd swallowed me, surging toward the parade.

I tripped over unseen steps, wincing in the glare, colliding with people rushing down the cobbled street. I staggered, was caught in another wave. Faces melted in and out of dizzy focus, carrying me along, careening off packed bodies.

We spilled onto Main Street, a swelling roar of voices and pounding steel-drums. No sign of Vic, the cops coming after me. I had to get to Phillip, tell him about the cavern. But I couldn't think with the drums pounding to the fierce beat in my head. My ears were ringing. Sweat slicked my face. I was drowning in the heat. The mob swirled me on until I hit an immoveable mass at the intersection on the parade route. People kept shoving from behind. I was crushed between them in the burning sun. I couldn't breathe. Drums hammered, red haze shimmering. I lost my footing, fell against someone. Faces swung around, dark eyes accusing.

Spiral eyes. Carved stone faces. Surrounding me, pressing in with their whispering demands. Voices calling, but I couldn't understand what they were chanting. Shadowy hands grabbed me.

"No!"

I tore free, breaking through. An angry cry, but I was running, out into glaring sunlight and heat. Colors flashed, flames swirling. Demons in red and black, faces glittering masks, sprang at me. Drums beat. Voices screamed.

A shrill whistle behind me. I tripped, groping, running from the demons.

Nightmare creatures closed in, capering, laughing. Colored sparks and jabbing spears. They shrieked, driving me on through a flock of birdlike creatures with jeweled bodies and outstretched gauzy wings. Long, pointed beaks raised to stab. They swarmed around and past, staring with human eyes.

Horns and cymbals crashed, ringing echoes off stone walls. I tore my way through the clinging tentacles of a giant orange octopus with rolling eyes and gaping mouth. More demons surrounded me. The sky tilted overhead. I was falling. Black horned devils, their faces white skulls, tumbled over me. I scrambled to my feet and ran, mocking laughter at my heels. Snapping whips, they hounded me through rippling sheets of fire.

Bars of blinding sunlight and shadow surged in waves of nausea. Colors swam and focused, and there were glistening serpents dancing around me, scales bright-colored sequins, trailing their tails in the dust and swaying hooded crests. They undulated to the drumbeat, weaving patterns around me, sun gleaming over shiny purple and yellow, green and black.

A young boy stood still among the dancing serpents, thin arms pushing a lizard mask up onto his head. He stared at me with no sign of recognition, dark face utterly blank, thick-lashed eyes empty.

"Samuel!"

I groped toward him, but a crimson serpent writhed between us. Mocking laughter rose into an eerie wail as the snake coiled sensuously around me, long tongue flickering gold in the sun. Beneath the scarlet hood, dark eyes glittered. Laura's face, laughing, taunting.

"Laura!" I spun around as an emerald serpent rubbed against my back, laughing. Laura's mocking face beneath its green hood. A black serpent tripped me. Laura's face again, red-stained lips parting in a triumphant smile.

Lights and colors swam. The serpents, Laura, Samuel, were gone.

Giant rock creatures danced up out of the baking earth, moving in on me, chanting the secret song of my dream. They danced closer, shaking the ground. Carved women of dark stone, fertility-goddesses with enormous legs and arms bare as they danced and their grass skirts twirled below proud jutting breasts and swollen bellies. One figure loomed over me, ageless, towering above the rest.

"Granny!" She held the secrets in her giant hands. "Granny, wait. Tell me."

She stepped over me as if I were an insect, her eyes fixed on the horizon. The earth roared and shook, splitting open. I fell into its dark heart.

"Chile, chile. Hush now."

A hand was gently stroking my forehead. A cup pressed to my lips. I swallowed. Pink flowered hat over gray hair, lined dark face bending over me with a look of infinite compassion.

"Granny!" I clutched her arm.

She chuckled. "Gal, I got plenty gran-chile, you de first white one!"

"Oh." I sagged back. It wasn't Granny. "What happened?"

"You look like death, you faintin' like dat, right smack in de parade! Where you friens be?"

I sat up and thirstily finished off the fruit juice. "Thank you. I feel better now." We were sitting on folding chairs in a shaded doorway.

"Chile, you feverin.' My boy, he go foh a car, find some body take you back to you resort."

I managed a smile. "You're very kind. But I'll find a taxi."

"No body findin' no taxi in dis hullabaloo." She waved a lacy pink fan toward the noisy crowd along the parade route down the block.

A middle-aged balding man in a sequin-trimmed shirt appeared beside her, handing over a flat, amber-tinted bottle.

She uncapped it and sniffed approvingly. "My own 'lixir. You take a good dose now, ever two-three hour." She pressed the open bottle into my hands.

"No, really."

"Drink up, now." She tapped the bottle.

I sniffed the pungent liquid, took a cautious swallow. Penetrating burst of aromatic herbs, familiar, and the bracing bite of alcohol. The elixir warmed my throat and cleared my head, like Granny's potion.

"Good. You go now, be takin' care." She smiled and patted my hand, nudged me toward her waiting son.

My eyes stung with tears at the unexpected kindness of these strangers. "Thank you."

The wheezing, multicolored four-door chugged up steep hills, young man in a knitted Rasta cap at the wheel, a middle-aged woman beside him. I reached into my pocket for Phillip's note about the rendezvous, hastily patted my other pocket. It was gone. I must have left it in Vic's jacket, along with the gold lion charm.

"Shit." I gripped the edge of the seat, arms shaking uncontrollably.

"Contant cross-road." The car had pulled over, the driver turning back to me.

"Oh. Yes." I unclamped my stiff fingers. "There's my friend, waiting." I pointed toward a tall, thin native in sunglasses, standing beside a gray Jeep, hoped to hell he was Phillip's contact. "Thank you for the ride."

Dust swirled behind the departing four-door. Trees loomed over the road, leaves drooping, forest dead still in the brutal afternoon heat. The sky had a molten, ominous look, bearing down on the parched earth.

The man in the dark glasses sauntered over to look me up and down. "You de one. I take you dere."

I was lost in the twists and turns. My head pounded its dull ache, ears ringing to the thresh of the wheels as the silent driver took the twisting mountain curves too fast, dust billowing in our wake. We pulled into a narrow dirt road, bumped along under overhanging boughs to a stucco cottage. The man got out, led the way up the walk, opened the door, and waited for me to pass through.

"Laura?" I peered into the shadowed cottage, made out chairs, a bed.

Rustling, a creak of springs. A dim figure shuffled toward me.

"Laura, my god!"

She swayed before me in a filthy, tattered shift of coarse fabric bagging over her gaunt frame, a foul smell gusting off her. Her hair was dull and matted, face smeared with dark streaks, sallow skin sagging over the bones. A tangle of feathered, beaded, and shelled necklaces still hung over her chest, their weight seeming almost more than she could hold up. Her eyes were fixed on me, but they were glassy, dead-looking.

I caught her shoulders, felt the bones beneath her skin. "What happened?"

"Susie." Her blank eyes didn't flicker, voice toneless. Her hand slowly raised a brown glass bottle. "Drink this."

"Laura." I shook her gently. "What's going on?"

Hands grabbed me from behind. I cried out, tried to break free, but the grip only tightened. Another native man had joined the driver, and they bore down on me as I fought. All I could hear was a terrible roaring in my ears.

Then, through it, Laura's flat voice. "Drink."

The bottle was rammed against my lips, my jaws pried open. I thrashed and kicked, but someone punched my gut and I gasped the fluid down, choking on a bitter gust. A rag reeking of ether crammed over my mouth and nose. Black waves swirled, spinning me fast, faster. Roaring laughter of the *bete noir*, gaping dark mouth of the Bocor's mask swallowing me.

Thirty-Six

The shadows wouldn't let go, sweaty hands pulling me back into suffocating darkness. I groaned. I was awake, but the nightmare hadn't gone away. A vague glow of light slowly focused. There was a foul taste in my mouth.

"What?" I croaked, sitting up, sparks dancing.

A door swung open on a painful burst of light. It came from a propane lantern in the next room of a rough-planked shack. A dreadlocked native grabbed my arm and pulled me roughly to my feet, dragging me into the larger room.

Laura sat on a low stool, still in the filthy rags, arms hanging limp at her sides. Staring unblinking at the wall, she seemed completely unaware of her surroundings. A second Dread lounged against the wall beside a rifle, smoking a reefer. It was the party-shack above Ship Bay.

I tugged free of my guard and dropped to my knees in front of Laura. Her hand lay inert in mine. "Laura, talk to me."

She didn't blink. Her eyes were like Samuel's. Zombi eyes, the walking dead.

The smoke and muggy heat swirled, bile rising in my throat. "I need some air." I staggered to my feet and out the open doorway to the deck, the Dread shrugging and following, carelessly toying with a long knife.

I couldn't swallow the foul taste in my throat, but the realization of my own stupidity was even more sickening. I'd danced right into this trap. *"You've summoned it, Susan Dunne, now you're summoned. You must dance to its tune."* I pressed my fists against the maddening, pulsing ache in my head.

The night offered no relief, breezeless heat pressing down, throbbing in the charged air. The sky was featureless black. No stars. No moon. I could barely make out the darker line of the stone cliffs across the bay. Sulphurous light flared overhead, lightning glowing behind a lowering cloud ceiling. A deep rumble followed, rolling on and on.

No, it was the distant beat of a drum, pounding to the throb in my skull. I groped back inside, sat on the floor beside Laura. She hadn't moved.

I squeezed her hand. "Laura, listen. You have to tell me what's going on. It's not too late. We can do something." The words sounded pathetic even to me.

She didn't twitch.

"Is it the Bocor? What's he going to do?"

Her hand pulled from mine as she stood in a stiff lurch. "Bocor. He called you here." Her voice was a raspy monotone, like a scratchy old phonograph record. "You wanted to know. Now you'll see what happens to the goat."

"The goat! What do you mean?"

"The Bocor's sacrifice." The toneless voice droned on, oblivious to my interruption, the blank face empty of any sign of Laura's personality. "He called you here. No one can resist when the Bocor calls. He knows everything. John thought he could fool the Bocor, thought I would lie to the Bocor to protect him, so he could steal the magic treasure. Steal the power. No one can lie to the Bocor. John was a fool, he deserved to die."

"Laura!" I jumped up to grip her shoulders and shake her. "Laura! You helped the Bocor kill him?"

She didn't resist me, didn't meet my eyes. It was like shaking a rag doll.

"We go." One of the Dreads grabbed my arm and pulled me away from Laura.

Like a robot, she turned and led the way from the shack. The Dread yanked me along, out to the dirt yard. The drumbeat from the forest had picked up its pace, louder now.

Diffuse flare of lightning behind dark clouds. Thunder crashed on its heels, deafening. Rain spattered my face.

The hand gripping my arm pulled me along a narrow path in the pitch-black night, unseen branches whipping, rocks tripping, drumbeat swelling. Lightning crackled, thunder shaking the rock cliff. Drum booming, echoing inside. The sky split open in a violent gush of rain. Cool rain, pouring, pounding, finally coming to end the drought as if conjured by the drums.

The trail turned to slippery mud, and I was stumbling, groping through stinging curtains of rain. My head throbbed to the drumbeat, the pulse of the thunder. I couldn't see the Dread dragging me along. It didn't matter, it was the drum I was following. Shadow hands beckoning, the summons of the *bete noir*.

Rain lashed the cliff, cold torrents racing over the rock track and through a narrow cleft. I groped forward. A hand shoved me from behind, and I fell to my knees in thick mud.

Lightning strobed a seething mass of black and white serpents. Arms, waving wildly. Naked mud-smeared bodies dancing, leaping and sliding, grappling together. Ecstatic wet faces. Dripping feathers, fringed leather, beads, strung shells glistening in the rain.

Spotlights flared, stabbing light through the downpour. The drumbeat boomed over the celebrants, shaking the night. A huge native, painted white circles on his chest, jumped onto a rock above the dancers and threw back his head in a piercing call. The mob turned toward me.

Shrill cries, deep baying like hounds scenting the prey. The goat. Faces bore down on me, lips drawn back from glittering teeth. Men and women, young and old, white skin and brown and black. All of them straining for the kill. The big native stabbed a finger, and the mob leaped onto me.

I was grabbed, plucked up and swept into their midst. Drums beat an urgent rhythm, rain hissing. Hands spun me, flung strands of shells and beads around my neck, passed me stumbling and whirling from one to another. Lightning flashed, thunder echoing the drums. Shrill laughter. Slippery bodies pressed mine. The dancers picked me up by arms and legs, swung me, tossed me into the mud at the foot of a tall boulder flickering with monstrous dancing shadows.

The drums rolled into a frenzy and died. The dancers cried out, turning toward the boulder, raising their faces, hushed.

Red flares sputtered through the rain streaming over the boulder. A man's figure stood atop the high rock, feet planted wide, powerful arms and legs covered with painted designs and strings of shells and feathers. A thick gold necklace glinted over his broad chest. Gold bands, sparkling with colored jewels, gleamed on his wrists as his hands lifted to the sky. One stiffened arm slowly lowered in a disturbingly familiar, hieratic gesture. My hackles rose. It wasn't a man staring down at the celebrants.

The god's face gleamed gold, a mask of inhuman power. Shadow eyes glinted above long, carved cheeks, a gaping mouth. The forehead swelled to a bulbous curve, and from it the grotesque figure of a dwarfed man struggled to emerge. Sharp horns sprang from the golden brow, slicing the darkness.

Rain drummed through a tense silence. The mask of the god stared pitilessly. The jeweled hand pointed at me.

One deep drum pulsed a slow heartbeat. Hands gripped my arms from behind and forced me to my knees. Laura moved out from the crowd with her robot gait, holding a white bowl. She held it up toward the masked god, then turned to me, lowering it. A polished human cranium glowed in the dimness.

"No!" I wrenched back from it, ripping one arm free, punching someone. More hands grabbed me. I fought, scratching and kicking. They pressed me down into the mud, pried my jaws open. Laura poured something from the skull-bowl.

I gagged, spat. She kept pouring. A foot kicked me in the gut. I gasped and swallowed. A noxious, rotting taste filled my throat. My stomach heaved. They yanked me to my feet.

High atop the boulder, the gold-masked Bocor flung out his arms. Lightning ripped the sky, thunder crashing.

The drums exploded into a furious beat. From the mob, a shrill scream. A mud-covered woman with long matted hair sprang into the open, leaping through the rain and spotlight beams. She wailed, fell onto the ground and writhed in the mud. The crowd spilled into a circle around her. They were chanting, moving to the drumbeat. The woman screamed again, wriggling, contorting her body impossibly. Her mouth stretched open in a fierce rictus as she fell back onto the ground, arching and thrusting her hips upward, spreading her naked thighs.

A man wearing only painted designs called out, falling inward from the circle. He sprang, fell, jerked upright again, shouting hoarse gibberish. He danced, stomping, fell onto the writhing woman. Raising up, arching back, he thrust his swollen penis toward the rainy sky. He screamed and pounced on the woman, impaling her. They humped violently, slithering through the downpour.

More celebrants broke free of the circle, dancing inward, flung by the drumbeat and the rain like disjointed dolls. They grappled through the torrents in a frantic orgy.

Dizziness swirled, the nauseating potion roiling in my gut. The earth was spinning, wobbling. Two big natives picked me up, dragged me onto the boulder. The gold-masked Bocor was gone. The men lifted me over a dark crevice. They dropped me.

Darkness opened under me. I fell, crashing against wood rails, clutching, losing my grip, careening off rock and landing hard. I groped blindly, trying to stand, but the ground was tilting sideways. The taste of the drugs swirled in my head, weird shapes dancing over blackness.

Light flared. I cried out, shielding my eyes.

I was plucked up and dumped against a rock wall. Torch flames flickered over white designs painted on the cave walls, demons dancing, swelling and receding. A glittering gold mask swept down, filling my vision with its grotesque features and sharp horns. Cold eyes drilled me.

I shrank back against the rock, gut churning.

The gold face was alive, the gaping mouth moving, speaking. "I am the Bocor. Your *bete noir*. You are my creature now."

I tried to shake my head, but it was heavy, inert.

"Oh yes, Susan." Voice weirdly distorted but familiar, insidious, seeping in through my pores. "It's time. I've summoned you, and you must dance to my desires now, dance to death if I will it. The power is mine."

Spiral eyes whirled me into their darkness. I couldn't move. Ice flowed through my veins as the mask swelled, rippling with monstrous life.

Hands dropped onto me. A man's hands, black paint striping the arms. Caviness's hands. No, paler beneath the paint, broad and blunt. *Vic?*

The ice filled my belly, clamped over my heart. The big hands pressed down my face and neck, fingers tightening. I was frozen by the Bocor's ice.

The hands moved lower, tore away my soaked clothes, passed slowly over my breasts, my belly, my thighs. I shuddered, fury screaming somewhere inside, but I couldn't find it, couldn't make my muscles fight.

Ringing laughter. "You'll beg for it, once I've initiated you." He lifted the gold mask aside.

Shock burned away the freezing grip of the potion. I gasped, scrambling back against the rock wall.

Ironic smile on his craggy face, one shaggy brow lifted, steely gray eyes holding mine. "Welcome to paradise, Susan."

"Phillip." I shook my head in disbelief. "Phillip."

"You disappoint me, my dear. You never even wondered?"

"It can't be." Even as I whispered it, an icy clarity crystallized. I was a blind fool. Laura was right, she'd tried to warn me in her own way. Bile rose in my throat.

He laughed. "Look deep into the abyss. Soon you'll join my disciples in the rites. The sacrifice of the goat."

I clung to the solid contours of the stone. "John fought you. I will, too."

He snorted. "He was a pathetic fool to think he could double-cross me, use Laura for protection. But he made a useful goat. You'll see tonight. As an anthropologist, I'm sure you'll appreciate the ritual." His laughter echoed in the rock cleft. "You'll help me finish the job of killing Laura. As my 'shadow men' helped me kill your brother."

"No," I whispered hoarsely, ground spinning beneath me.

"Oh, yes." He leaned closer, voice low, intimate. "I know about your voices and your visions, Susan. I know far more than you can imagine. You've been drawn to me from the beginning."

I had to wake up from this nightmare. I could only shake my head.

"You know it's true." His eyes pinned me, voice soft and rhythmic. "Beneath your simplistic morality you crave what I offer. You want me to touch you, defile you, you want to betray your pathetic ideals, you're drawn to the forbidden fruits of depravity. Laura knew. But I'll take you much farther than incestuous fantasies. You'll strip yourself to the bone with me, copulate with death. You're going to lust for blood."

"No." I edged away, cold dread settling in my belly. "Does it make you feel better, to believe everyone else is as sick as you are?"

His hand flashed out and struck me across the face in a casual snap like swatting a mosquito. "You're such a child." He stepped back, gestured with his head. A big Dread lifted me to my knees and pinned my arms from behind.

Phillip reached down, slowly stroking my stinging face. "'Shadowing more beauty in her airy brow than have the white breasts of the Queen of Love.' You were touched, weren't you, Susan?" He laughed.

He grabbed my hair, jerking my head back, cold gray eyes drilling mine. "We're not playing your game any more, little *Susie*. I make the rules here."

I'd bitten my tongue, swallowed salty blood. "Why are you playing Bocor? A cover for the drugs? Are Caviness and Wilkes in on it?"

"This is no game! My power is real. When my followers worship me in the ceremony, I become the god in the mask."

He slapped my face again, snapping it to the side. "You never give up with your questions, do you, wanting to make it all add up? There was never a drug ring, you fool. I only told you what you expected to hear, and it was child's play to deceive you." He lifted a hand, familiar urbane gesture bizarrely garbed in paint and shells, jewel-encrusted gold bands. "No, I deal in a different addiction. Disorder. Destruction. Blood lust."

His face was swelling in and out of focus. I swallowed, tongue gone thick in my parched throat. "Why?" His potion pulsed through me, and I had to fight to form words. "What can you get out of hurting innocent boys like Samuel?"

He tilted his head. "Samuel?"

"You made him into one of your zombis, didn't you?"

He threw back his head and laughed. "My dear girl, you've gone to such lengths to create your grand conspiracy! I knew you'd provide me endless entertainment. It will be a delight to guide you down the path. Starting tonight."

His face pressed close to mine. I struggled to pull away, but the Dread behind me was holding me tight, fingers bruising my arms. "You're going to dance to my drums, Susan, you're going to scream praises to my power as I send Laura to her death. She's the goat. You hate her, admit it. She loved your brother, yet she gladly betrayed him to me, helped me kill him. She killed Pat MacIntyre for me, too, ran her off the road. She deserves to die. She took your darling brother away, stole his heart from the sister who really *knew* him. You should have been the one enjoying that cock he shared so promiscuously with all the other girls."

Nausea washed through me. "No."

His face loomed over me, swirling with the drug, features melting from Phillip's to the gold mask and back. "Oh, but it's true, Susie. Tell me you hate her. You want to claw her flesh to ribbons and drink her blood."

I managed to shake my head.

"And you hate me even more, hate me so much we're bound forever in an intimacy you've never known with anyone else. Oh, yes. You're only another puppet in the hands of the Bocor, and you hate me for it."

His eyes burned pale gray, dancing reflections of torch flames. "Say it! Scream it all out, everything you've been holding in so long." His hands were on me again, slapping me, digging into my bruised skin. "You want to kill me, don't you? Tear me limb from limb, make me scream in pain for what I did to your beloved brother." His words hammered like the distant drumbeats. "For what I'm going to make you into."

He laughed. "You're going to be my willing slave, Susan. My worshipper, until I tire of you and let you die. Don't think you'll get away. They won't stop me. We're leaving the island tonight, with the treasure. Nothing can save you."

Icy dread clutched me.

"Say it. Tell me you hate me."

His voice, swirling with the flaring torch flames, was driving me mad. I heaved against the Dread's grip, kicking at Phillip's gloating face. "Yes! I hate you!"

"Good." He pulled back, smiling. "Now we can start." Standing, he stripped off his loincloth to display his penis swollen red in the torchlight.

His smile widened as he jerked his chin at the man holding me. I was pulled back, arms still pinned, stretched arched over the man's lap.

I kicked and fought, sickening taste of his potion rising in my gorge, but two more men darted forward to grab my ankles and force my legs apart.

"I'm going to claim you from the inside out, my dear. Soon you'll know what it really is to hate."

The walls were spinning around me, flames lapping, *veve* designs leaping into life. Phillip lunged onto me, slapping, biting, pummeling as I bit my lips and finally cried out in pain.

"Yes." He pushed my legs wider and thrust himself violently inside me.

Pain, fury, nausea blossomed, swamping me as Phillip ground deeper into me, grunting and howling. I wanted to drown, fall into black oblivion, but my vision had sharpened to cruel clarity. Phillip's sweat-streaked face, straining, grinning. Blunt fingers digging into my skin. His furious pumping, on and on, tearing me inside. Stink of his sweat. Acid taste in my throat. The men holding me leering, laughing. Drumbeat pounding down my bones, revulsion flooding.

And then worse, an alien presence stirring inside my breast, the demon swelling, bloated, bludgeoning. Shadow hand ripping at my secrets, twisting my nerves, plucking my strings. *His* hand. It wrenched open a hidden door and a seething flood swept everything I knew as myself before it.

But I *was* this animal squirming in the dirt, kicking, spitting, howling my brute rage.

"Yes!" Holte panted in my ear. "You hate me. Hate everything."

The hatred boils, my claws flexing, digging into his skin, and I'm shrieking with glee as I tear off dripping chunks with my nails, feel his blood gush over me, snap and bite and savage his throat with my teeth as I bolt his raw flesh, rip off his balls and stuff them into his gloating mouth. Flay the skin from his face, strip away muscle and fat to the bloodstreaked skull.

"Yes!" His empty-eyed skull still laughs, mocking my rage.

I throw the skull at the dancing stone demons, but they only circle around me, laughing, faces melting into John's, and Laura's. Caviness. Adrienne. Vic. They're all laughing at me, dancing, dancing to the death drums. They all deserve to die.

I hurl obscenities at them, words knives poison, the killing/dying fury burning my throat, and it's my brother's voice screaming down the Link, screaming through me, his and my rage all the same love and hate and lust.

"Yes! You're mine!" The laughter of the *bete noir* inside me forever. I'm his creature.

Thirty-Seven

Floating high in the night sky, I gazed down with remote interest at rain-pummeled mud, hissing red flares, tiny humans dancing and fucking and writhing over the ground. Drums beating. Atop a boulder, the gold-masked Bocor threw out his jeweled arms in an exultant howl. My own distant figure, naked, mudstreaked, bruised, adorned with strands of shells, red seeds, and a ouanga-bag made from my stolen nightgown, swayed beside him.

The drumbeat died. The celebrants raised their arms to the Bocor. A chant rose from the gaping mouth of the mask, strange gutturals wafting upward, twining, tugging at me.

The darkness swirled, spun me, faster and faster, sucking me downward out of the clouds. With a jolt, I hit ground inside my aching, rain-chilled body. I blinked down at the grinning, panting celebrants. I tried to make my legs run, but I was anchored beside the Bocor, leashed by his will. His potion still churned in my gut, colored stars flaring over the night.

A slow drumbeat joined with the Bocor's chant. Across the stretch of churned mud, women with necklaces of bones and animal skulls stepped forward through the downpour. They led a black goat, its curving horns decorated with limp, drenched flowers and shells. Bells around its neck rang and clashed as the animal struggled.

Behind the goat, a woman walked stiffly, pale skin wet and glowing through the rain-soaked night, head wrapped with bands of dripping flowers, thin arms bound before her with strands of shells, a necklace of bells around her neck. Laura walked slowly, face blank as she passed through a spotlight beam, her bells still and silent. A sputtering red flare reflected in her glassy eyes.

The procession halted before a low rock altar decorated with scattered coins, bottles, human skulls. A rush of muddy water was flowing around it, over the sloped clearing, around the ankles of the celebrants. The drumbeat quickened. My heartbeat kept time. The faces raised to the Bocor were chanting now, calling out for the blood rites, and I was calling with them, voice of the *bete noir* melded with my own.

A sweeping gesture from the Bocor. The women held the struggling black goat and the passive Laura before the altar. The massed voices chanted louder.

Darkness swirled dizzily, sinking me deeper. I was somehow standing behind the altar. The Bocor, beside me, laid one hand on Laura's head, one on the head of the goat. Laura sank slowly to her knees, smiling faintly, chest rising and falling smoothly beneath the bells. The goat bleated and kicked against the hands of the women holding him down, bells clashing, frantic cries swelling the mob's clamor.

The Bocor whispered. Laura turned to gaze into the goat's yellow eyes. The glittering mask raised, jeweled arms sweeping upward.

A pause, as the drumbeat hung suspended and rain pounded the earth. Woman and beast stared into each other's eyes. A fluttering in the substance of the night, something passing between them, almost visible. Stirring of wings.

Laura suddenly stiffened, wrenching free of the women standing with their hands on her shoulders. The goat as abruptly ceased struggling, amber eyes gone fixed and glassy. Laura screamed, a bleat of pain and terror.

The women grabbed Laura, holding her as she kicked and butted at them, eyes rolling wildly. Her shrill screams were swallowed by the renewed throbbing of the drum.

The gold mask turned skyward, rain streaming over its curves. The Bocor's arm raised high, holding a long knife. The mob shrieked, urgent, demanding. All I could see was gleaming steel, glittering wet reflections of the crimson flares, streaming with rain red as blood. A hoarse cry was ripping out of me, I was screaming my demand for the sacrifice.

The goat stirred, raising its head to me. It looked into my eyes, and in its gaze I saw awareness, recognition. A plea for mercy and forgiveness.

The Bocor's hand tightened on the knife hilt.

*my fingers grip the knife, feel its heft, the gleaming power alive in its sharp blade. I am the god, all-powerful, prolonging the delicious suspense. Balancing their souls on my razor's edge. My heart the heart of the Bocor beats deep and hard, the force flushing my limbs my cock tight throbbing swelling the godhood I wield the ultimate power rushing and my arm the arm of doom flashes down.

    Gush of blood sweet death I suck up her soul my triumph gushing hot from my loins glee screaming life pulsing through me*

I gasped, gut churning with the bitter brew. The goat's head tumbled to the altar, blood splashing my arms and chest, baptizing the ouanga-bag he'd hung on me. Laura's face contorted to a bestial mask of terror as the blood sprayed over her and she bellowed, fighting the women as they struggled to hold her down.

The Bocor lifted the goat's head over the upturned gold mask, blood dripping into its gaping mouth. He flung the head over the roaring crowd. They fought and scrambled for it.

I hunched over the altar, retching. The Bocor's poison surged up, spewing over the offerings. I sank to my knees, laying my face against wet stone.

Lightning flared in a clapping roar of thunder. The muddy mob, oblivious, fought over the goat carcass, lapping its blood. Rain lashed in stinging waves, a river swirling around my knees, tossing sticks and leaves. The man in the gold mask turned sharply toward the cliff, gestured curtly. Two natives stepped forward, dragging me behind the altar.

"Wait!" Twisting around in their hold, I caught a last glimpse of Laura, still struggling and bleating in the hands of the women. The Bocor stood over her, knife raising in a glittering sweep.

"No! For God's sake!" The drumbeat and the storm swallowed my voice.

A hand slapped over my mouth. I was dragged into the narrow cave. Flickering torches, dancing *veve* designs, skull grinning from the altar niche, and then a dark passage. Wavering flashlight beams swung over damp stone walls, crude steps hacked into stone.

The men hurried me downward, one holding my legs and the other my shoulders as I fought futilely. A stream of muddy water gushed down the steep cleft, and one of the men slipped, slamming me down, breath knocked out of me. Cold water splashed. One of the flashlights spun off, cracked against rock. The other beam flared over a tense dark face, muscular back, jagged stone ceiling.

The cavern opened around us, echoing with the roar of the flood down the passage. Torchlight flickered, grotesque shadows leaping from the rock columns over layered stone. Overhead, shrill squealing. Bats flitted erratically through the dimness.

Gasping for air, I was dragged past the mounds of skulls and bones. The plastic packing cases were gone, except a single box with the lid ajar. Beside the dark pool of the underwater passage out to the cove, Scuba gear. A husky native guarded it, spear-gun across his knees.

"Bocor say we take she to boat now. He come soon." The man shot an apprehensive look back at the water rushing down through the stairwell cleft.

They pushed me roughly down beside the gear. One of them prodded my bruised ribs with his foot and snorted. "She done makin' fuss." They all headed back toward the passage, muttering.

I sat rocking myself, shaking with chill, staring blankly at the Scuba equipment. Tanks, fins, masks, spears. I watched from far away as my hand slowly reached for one of the spear-guns.

The saltwater pool stirred, ripples moving toward me. A primitive fear crackled through my numbness. Monster rising from the depths. I clutched the spear-gun, fumbling to load the sharp metal rod. A masked face rose from the pool, streaming water. Through the mask, glinting eyes met mine.

The emerging diver made a startled movement, then surged up out of the pool. My hands rammed the spear into the gun.

A shout behind me. Adrenaline launched me to my feet, and I was dodging around the pool. The native guards came running, started for me, stopped short eyeing my spear-gun raised shakily toward them. I glanced back at the pool. The diver was heaving himself out of the water, ripping off his fins and tank, bringing up his own spear-gun to aim. Crouching on the sloped rock, he tore off his mask.

My battered body was numb, beyond reach. But my brain could still reel with one more shock. The Bocor's drums were pounding, ringing in my ears.

Behind the spear, Vic stared at me. Ice blue eyes. Killer's eyes. His lips pulled back from his teeth. He raised the gun at me, aimed, and fired.

I couldn't move. The spear flashed out at me.

Past me. A howl of pain behind me. Reflexes spun me around to see one of the natives staggering back from me, face a mask of shock as he crumpled over the metal rod impaling his chest. A long knife fell from his fingers.

"Susan! Get back!" Vic was scrambling around the rocky lip of the pool.

Alarm, relief, shame buffeted through me, signals clashing, shorting out. I could only stand there staring.

"Susan! Snap out of it!" he shouted, rounding the slippery rock, ramming another spear into his gun.

One of the guards lunged past me to grab a spear-gun, aim it at Vic.

He dodged and slipped on the wet rock, trying to bring up his gun as the native got a fix on him.

My hands had a life of their own. They tightened on the spear-gun I was still clutching, bringing it up, squeezing the trigger. The rod shot out through flickering light and shadow, into the native's thigh. He spun around, screaming, falling to one knee but swinging his spear to bear on me. His face streamed with sweat, the gun wavering, steadying. I stared transfixed at the sharp tip aimed at me.

A whoosh of air. Vic's spear plunged into the man's back. I threw myself to the side as he toppled, his weapon discharging against the rock wall.

"Susan, for Christ sake grab a tank and get out of here!" Vic flung away his empty spear-gun, reaching inside his wetsuit as the last guard leaped over the rocks at him, knife glinting in his hand. Vic tore open a plastic case and drew out a pistol just as the man jumped him, blade flashing. They grappled, rolling over the rocks, and the pistol skittered away into the shadows.

The husky native was on top, then the bottom, as they rolled, Vic gripping the hand with the knife. The guard kicked, heaving onto the top again. My legs launched me at the pile of Scuba gear, and I grabbed up another spear-gun, cramming a rod in.

A shout. Two more men came running from the passage at the back of the cave. The first one, a short, stocky Continental with a black mustache, pulled a knife from his belt and lunged toward me.

My finger clenched on the trigger. Blood sprouted around the shaft of the spear as the man stared in horror at the rod imbedded in his groin. He crumpled, whimpering and clawing the rock. I backed off, acid taste rising in my gorge. The spear-gun clattered onto the rocks.

Hoarse wheezing echoed through the cavern. Vic was still wrestling the husky native among the shadowed rocks. They rolled, crashed into mounded bones. The pile scattered, bones splintering beneath them. The other arrival, a Dread, grabbed the knife from the collapsed Continental and darted toward the struggle.

I scrambled across rocks in the dimness, fingers scrabbling for Vic's pistol where I'd seen it go flying. The Dread was swaying, holding the knife poised. The other native rolled over, exposing Vic's back as they fought. Panting in short gasping bursts, I gave up looking for the gun, dashed to the Scuba gear, blindly grabbed a webbed belt strung with lead weights.

Vic heaved against the man with the knife. They came rolling toward me. I jumped aside into shadow. The Dread ran after them, pulled back his arm with the knife, moving in. Vic was on top now. He pounded the native's arm against a rock. The knife spun away into the water. Vic brought his hand back, jabbed it sharply against the dark throat. The man went limp.

The Dread moved in. Vic dodged a jab of the knife, ducked and rolled into the dimness where the gun had flown. The Dread tore after him, ignoring me.

More scuffling. A metallic clatter, shrill squeal. A bat flew out past my face. Vic backed slowly into the open, breathing heavily, gripping the pistol. The Dread followed, still clutching his knife, gaze fixed on Vic.

He jerked the pistol. "Drop it."

Standing to the side, I saw the Dread's gaze flicker. "Vic, watch out! Behind you!"

He whirled just as a new arrival straightened from the piled Scuba gear, heaving a steel tank at his head. Vic ducked. The heavy tank crashed onto his arm. He cried out, the pistol scattering off across the rocks. His arm dangled at a grotesque angle. The man picked up another tank. Vic, hugging his broken arm to his chest, spun with a harsh grunt, leg kicking high. The man fell back, cracking his head onto the rock floor and lying still. Vic lost his footing on the wet stone and fell against him. A short, sharp bark as he landed on his injured arm. The Dread with the knife moved in again, grinning.

Clutching the weightbelt, I stood watching the Dread close in on Vic. Even the jolts of adrenaline were shorting themselves out, my mind futilely spinning gears. Vic, struggling to pull himself up, shot a look my way, back at the Dread.

The whirling narrowed and spun into a white-hot wire up my spine. *Kill.* There was nothing but that primal command.

My legs launched me forward. I swung the weights. The Dread looked around, startled. With the perfection of choreography, I was flying forward, bracing, flowing into the heavy arc of the weights. The lead caught him squarely on the side of the head. Visceral crunch as the skull gave way. The man toppled. I released the weights, springing back lightly in the culmination of that perfect, killing grace.

Everything had gone still. I stood half-crouched, panting, electric charge pumping through me. Sounds suddenly blossomed: the flood roaring into the cavern, bats rustling overhead, someone's heavy breathing. A man's body lay crumpled at my feet, glassy eyes staring. Lights and shadows blurred and swam.

A groan, scuffling. A hand touched my shoulder. Spinning around, I threw out my hands, claws flexed.

"Jesus, Susan!" Vic, grimacing with pain, cradled his broken arm. "What did they do to you?"

I blinked, looked blankly down at my mud-streaked, bruised skin, the strings of beads and seeds lashed around my naked arms and legs, the gouges and welts, the bloodstained ouanga-bag. I closed my eyes and saw the mob screaming for blood.

"Laura! They're going to kill her!" I spun toward the flooding passage.

His good hand grabbed my arm. "Christ!" He winced. "Susan, wait. It's too late." He blanched as I pulled against his grip.

Pain stabbed through me. His? "Your arm."

"Susan, come on." He touched my face briefly, then cradled his arm again, turning for the pool. "We have to go. Now." His voice was clipped, urgent. "Nothing you can do for Laura. We don't have much time. Got to get out. Here, help me with this gear." He crouched awkwardly beside the Scuba equipment.

I stood looking from him to the shadowed passage up. I shivered. "Laura's the goat," I whispered.

"Susan!" His voice lashed. "Let's go. There'll be more of them, coming down. The ravines are flooding, they'll have to go out this way."

Everything had gone fuzzy again. "Vic. This is the Bocor's cave. It was Phillip all along."

He gave me an odd look. He took a deep breath, said gently, "I know that, Susan. We put it together after the cops snagged me, but we couldn't find you. Caviness and Wilkes were planning to bust the cult, they moved their plans up, took their men in to raid it from the land side. But they radioed us on the boats, they can't get through." He took another deep breath. "The roads are all washed out. You see that water flooding down? You understand? There could be a landslide. We have to get out. Now."

I blinked, slowly nodded.

He was tugging at the Scuba gear, broken arm hanging crookedly. He winced. "Susan! I need some help here."

"Oh. Yes."

"That's good. Help me on with my vest." He bit down hard, face gone greenish beneath the tan, as I helped him ease his injured arm into the vest attached to his tank. "Grab a tank and mask for yourself. Hurry."

I seized on each separate task, following his orders as I dragged over the gear, put his mask on his face, found fins for myself, tested the regulator.

"You go first, Susan. Take the light."

We sank into the dark pool. Reality dimmed, reduced to what the flashlight's narrow beam picked out. The flooded passage. A sharp, angled turn. Vic's pinched face behind his mask. Wavering shadows over John's petroglyph rock. Demons capering in the dark, horned goat-head priest with a knife, spiral eyes watching. The black emptiness of the cove swallowed the light.

Vic kicked ahead, followed a line up to an inflatable dinghy bobbing on waves lashed with rain.

Out of the darkness, a deep voice. "Sue! Bless de lord!"

"James, help me here. Get her out of that vest. Leave the gear. Hurry. We've got to get clear of the cliff."

My mind had gone numb, sealed-off. Big hands were pulling me into the dinghy. Then Vic. A motor buzzed. We were moving across dark waves through driving rain.

A flash of dull yellow lit the night. Thunder crashed and shivered. Then a deeper roar, echoing, rending the air. Tearing the earth. The dark sea heaved, hurled the boat, flung it up and then plummeting down. Cold waves drenched us.

"Look!" James pointed.

Another flash of lightning lit the sky. Behind us, where the cliff had towered over the Bocor's cavern and the sunken petroglyph stone, was only an explosion of rock and churning mud. Trees and boulders flew spinning over the cove. The earth roared again. The cliff broke away, plunging into the sea.

Thirty-Eight

The sun seethed at the horizon, molten red glass poised for its fiery plunge into the tempering sea. Its burning threw a bizarrely cheerful rosy light over Harbor Drive, the flood-damaged buildings and shattered palm trees, heaps of mud bulldozed from alleys and storefronts and sidewalks, piles of sodden refuse, cracked timbers and tiles, drowned rats.

The Jeep rumbled slowly around the curve of the bay, skirting potholes, bumping across stretches of torn pavement. I stared blankly over the glittering bay into the sun's fire. A turn of the road finally swept it behind me, its image still burning on my retinas.

Vic turned his head my way, let out a gusting sigh. He downshifted for the steep climb up the mountain, awkwardly tugging the wheel, left arm encased in plaster from knuckles to biceps.

The mountain roads were a tangle of detours, fallen boulders, deep puddles and washboard ruts, narrow tracks skirting cliff-edge gaps like the bites of hungry monsters. Around a tight turn, a muddy road crew leaned against their truck, filthy tools piled in its bed, raising beer bottles as we chugged past.

The disaster crews had finally given up searching for more bodies in the unstable landslide that had swept away the cult's ceremonial ground, buried the Bocor's cavern and the petroglyph boulder. They hadn't found Laura's body, but I knew that was her grave. They'd found no trace of Phillip, either.

Captain Wilkes in his office, wearily shaking the baggy folds of his face. He pushes a grainy photocopy at me, blunt finger jabbing the circled face among a gathering of old-fashioned suits. "This is the only thing we could dig up, some academic conference thirty years ago. Far as we can tell, the Phillip Holte who was operating here in the islands must have taken over the older professor's identity, changed all the records. God knows why."

I stare at the tiny face in the old photo. Square-cut jaw, thick gray eyebrows, ironic twist to his lips. Phillip. Unchanged.

Wilkes's voice rumbles on, oblivious, "Too bad nobody looked closer at that smeared part of your brother's letter, obvious now it wasn't 'He'll kill me,' but 'H.'ll kill me if he finds out.'" A cough. "Still no sign of Holte's yacht. Must have been offshore, ready for his getaway, whoever was aboard took off. Our patrol only intercepted a couple of his men who got out early through the cove, before the landslide. While Holte was still finishing up his... ceremony." He clears his throat. "No one got out overland. There's no way he could have escaped."

Mocking laughter of the *bete noir*, echoing inside me. Phillip was out there, alive. He'd never die.

The Jeep growled along, taking us around another bend, between leaf-stripped trees and jagged snapped trunks, cottages still half-buried in mud. An elderly native couple paused with their rakes beside piles of leaves, palm fronds, broken branches.

Vic waved as he slowed. "Looks like you're getting there."

The man laughed. "We does it all again nex year!"

A few trees had fallen along the high stone wall of the Fairview Estate, but inside the open gates the driveway and gardens were as well-groomed as ever.

"Susan." Vic turned off the motor. "You don't have to see him, you know."

"I do." I pushed open the door and started up the walk.

Vic caught up, stepping ahead to ring the bell beside the carved mahogany doors, but they swung open before he could touch the switch.

Adrienne stepped out smiling, reached up to kiss his cheek. She turned to me. "Susan!" She embraced me.

I knew I should lift my arms in response. The motions wouldn't connect.

She stepped back, gazing into my face, but I didn't meet her eyes.

"Please, come in." She ushered us into the chessboard-tiled hall, down a passage and out onto the back verandah where a table sparkled with crystal and silver, flowers and wine and hors d'oeuvre.

I took in the elegant array, Phillip's voice echoing, *"Come, try my 'pleasant fruits and princely delicates.' I crave a victim for my experiments."*

Footsteps behind me. "Susan Dunne." The deep, musical voice sent a shudder down my bones. Leon Caviness's dark, deepset eyes studied me. He held out a long-fingered hand. Black spider, plucking the strings. Reluctantly I returned his grip.

He stepped over to Vic, took his hand and clapped him on the shoulder. He smiled at Adrienne. "Would you be so good as to entertain Victor?"

He turned back to me. "Please come with me before the light fades." He took my arm, started down the verandah.

Vic stepped forward, but I shook my head, said, "It's all right."

Adrienne gave me a dazzling smile and gestured Vic to a chair.

Shadows gathered under the leaves as Caviness ushered me down a shelled path past the swimming pool. I followed the pale glow of his tailored white shirt into the gloom of the rain forest. We emerged onto the open, rocky plateau, steep point running out in fissured fault-blocks of black stone, giant stair-steps to the sea. On one side, open ocean hurling waves to crash in white foam against the rocks. On the other, a dark bay mirroring the thin slice of crescent moon. In the fading light I could barely see the spiral eyes of the petroglyph.

Caviness was standing with his back to me, gazing over the bay. "Twilight is a threshhold, a pause when the wall between daylight and darkness weakens and dissolves."

His voice murmured with the breeze stirring the leaves. "We may reel back in horror from that glimpse of the abyss, our world become suddenly alien. Or step for a timeless moment through that doorway into the ineffable. We stand at the cusp of life and death, the fascination of ultimate knowledge always beckoning with the smile of the skull beneath the skin."

His low voice had become a rhythmic chant, woven from the essence of twilight. "The shell of flesh encasing our hearts and souls, housing the *ti bon ange*, softens, yields to the penetration of the spirit realm. The voices of the dead whisper their secrets in our bones. We must listen, though we tremble."

A gusty sigh. The wind? "The *zombi* of the Bocor is also a creature of the twilight world, caught on the brink of the revelations of that great teacher, Death. But he is tragically frozen there, unable to pass beyond mortal life into the wonders of the unknown."

Wind shivered a thread of cool silver over the glassy black surface of the bay. Face of the moon hidden, but I could feel its secret smile.

Caviness swung around to me, invisible robes of the Houngan swirling. "Adrienne was right, I was mistaken about you, about the forces focused through the lens of your presence here. They were costly mistakes. I'm sorry."

I finally found my voice, said brusquely, "*My* mistakes cost everyone."

His bony face hovered above me in the shadows. "You know the *bete noir* is still alive."

My shoulders hunched.

"You can no longer deny your gift."

"Gift?" I spat the word back at him.

"No more games." A sweeping gesture. "You have been like a child turning the pages of a forbidden book, a child who never learned to read. The images you see can be dangerous if you act upon them in ignorance."

I closed my eyes, resisting even the memory of the visions pulsing against my shields. "Obviously."

"Just as clearly you are still in spiritual peril." He grasped my shoulders, calling out as he had at his ceremony to the source of waters, "*Faitre, Maitre, L'Afrique Guinin ce' protection. Nous Ap maide,' ce d'lo qui poti mortel, protection, Maitre d'lo pour-toute petites li.*"

His power swirled around me, but I wouldn't let it touch me. I stiffened, stepping back.

"You must face yourself, Susan Dunne. And the responsibilities of your gift. Stay here and study with me. With Adrienne."

"No."

"You have been baptized in blood, against your will. You don't yet understand that blood can be a sacrament. Just as the spirit gives birth to the flesh, the flesh gives birth to the spirit, to the gods."

Glittering gold mask of the god, tiny human figure emerging grotesquely from its forehead....

"When we drink the blood, pulsing with the life gift of the gods, we become a god incarnate, honoring the spirits alive within us."

"The way Holte honored them?" I lashed. "When he killed Laura as the goat? While I stood beside him and screamed for her blood?"

"Holte succumbed to the temptations of power, the deceptive glamor of violence." He sighed. "As did Laura. That is always a danger, as I'm certain Victor knows. Yet to live fully is always to court peril. You have a choice. To remain half-alive, or to embrace your totality, the darkness and the light. Study with me, and you will begin to understand."

"I can't stay in this place. I have to find my own way."

Silence, as he contemplated the moon rising higher above the bay, rippling its silver trail. Finally he turned back to me. "Your homeland calls you. Perhaps your teacher there has more... affinity with your ways."

"What teacher?" Why had he chosen that word? *Affinity.*

"He's waiting. Hopefully you won't be too stubborn to see him."

Within Caviness's dark eyes I could see the glimmer of sly laughter in the eyes of old Willie Raven. Cool green arms of the cedars beckoning me home.

—◆—

Sunlight glimmered over turquoise water, the perfect golden curve of beach around the tiny cove. Flute notes rang out clear and precise as the demarcation of light and shadow under the tropic sun. Bach. A clean sweep of uncompromising order, untouched by time and decay.

I lowered the flute, sat gazing over the empty cove.

Behind me on the blanket, Vic sat up and touched my shoulder. "They'll come another day."

"Who?" I pulled away from his touch, taking the flute apart, putting the parts in their case.

"I was hoping the dolphins would come, too." Voice gentle.

"They can read us with their sonar. They've done studies, they're drawn to children, to...." I snapped the case shut. "They wouldn't want me touching them."

"Susan, stop it! Haven't you had enough flogging yourself?"

"Doesn't matter, does it? The Bocor's not done with me. You should know that."

He winced. "Don't."

"He won, Vic! Don't you get it? He said he'd make me his creature, and he did. He showed me just how pathetic and disgusting we all are, rotten to the bone. Evil isn't something out there. I'm crawling with it, with him, I *am* the *bete noir*. I look at myself and I want to puke. I can't...." I was panting, couldn't seem to get enough air. "Can't —"

"Can't trust yourself?" He trailed a finger through the sand. "I know, Susan. You just have to go on without it."

"Don't *you* start with the platitudes!" My jaw clamped tight as I stared over the bay.

He lay back on the blanket, cradling his bulky cast. Silence, but for the shush of sea on sand.

"You asked me... before, about that photo on my boat. From 'Nam. The rice paddies, the little temple?" His voice was slow, quiet, merging with the lapping sea. "I didn't want to bring it all out in the daylight again, better just seal it off, but I always kept that picture hanging around. Like some kind of... I don't know. But there's something important in it. Maybe I was reaching for it even then, but I didn't know it."

Warm breeze stirred the mimosa leaves overhead, rippling the tracery of shadow. "The whole thing, that war, it was insane, unreal, more real than anything before or since. A whole different world. Beautiful, strange, like landing on another planet, some jungle fantasy sprouting all around you. Panthers and monkeys, fifteen-foot boas sunning on a trail. You'd break out of dense cover, and there'd be this incredible ruin, temples and crumbled walls dripping with vines, carvings of gods and demons wearing away from centuries of rain. Maybe you're the first person to see them for a hundred years. You're walking along in this dream.

"Then out of the jungle they're firing at you. Your buddy walking point catches a booby-trap and you're covered with his blood, trying to pick up pieces of him and fuck he's dead anyway and you're all just meat. You're the fucking Army's machine firing back at the jungle, making all the moves on adrenaline, never even see goddamn Charlie, he's just screwing with your head, too, and then you get so pissed at all of them, asshole C.O. on down getting you into this mess, you want to start screaming and dive in and tear them all apart with your bare hands, rip out their guts, cut off their ears and hang them on your belt —"

His breathing had gone harsh, labored. "Shit. You wanted to know what 'Nam did to me. Holte showed you. But I didn't want you to know. Didn't want you to have those things inside you couldn't look at.... Christ! I should have stopped you. Made you stop. If I saw Holte, I'd kill him with my bare hands."

"Vic."

He lay staring at the sky, hand fisted, tears streaming, glinting in his beard. His pain knifed through me, my throat aching. All we could do was hold each other, rocking mutely, locked inside our separate selves.

"Don't go."

"I have to."

"But you haven't finished your research." He gestured at my notes tossed on the cottage table.

"Vic, the project is dead. Buried with the petroglyphs and everyone under that landslide." With Laura, and John. I pulled my empty suitcase from under the bed.

"What about the pre-Columbian contact evidence? You *cared*, Susan. You need to write that paper."

"It doesn't matter. It's too late." I strode outside to the clothesline, gripping the folds of a damp shirt.

He followed. "It does matter. Maybe not to you, right now, but it's important. Write it up, get it out there. You've got the photos, the linguistic system, testimony about the landslide. I saw the boulder, too, you know." A snort. "If a reference from me would help."

"Vic." I shook my head, gaze fixed on the laundry. "It's gone. I don't even know if I can work as an archeologist any more. I was so proud of my objectivity. Holte was right, I saw just what I wanted to see."

"So you made some mistakes. Holte only wins if you let him." He turned me toward him. "Susan. Don't do this to yourself. Don't throw the good after the bad. You don't have to stop loving John. Maybe he screwed up, but in the end, he was fighting Holte, trying to break up the cult."

He took a deep breath. "Don't lock yourself away in there. Let me love you, Sue."

I winced away from his face, too naked, blue eyes too clear on mine. "Vic, I'm just sort of propped up with scrap lumber and two-by-fours. Even a little breeze, and the whole thing crashes."

A gusting sigh. "If you can't stay here, I'll go with you."

"No. You have a life here. You fit on the island, everything all Glorious Technicolor, on the edge. I can't live that way. I can't even think here." I blew out a breath. "And I'm not going to mess up your life any more than I have already."

"No man is an island." He caught my arm as I turned sharply away. "You showed me. We're all making ripples messing up everybody else's ripples. I *want* you to mess up my life, okay?"

I couldn't help smiling. I shook my head. "Maybe sometime later. When I figure things out."

"The world isn't like that! It doesn't hold still while you tidy it all up." He leaned closer, intent. "Susan, let me help you. I meant it, that John Donne poetry. We *know* each other, we always have, we're supposed to be together."

"Vic, I don't even know who I am now!"

"I won't let you bury us." He touched my face, turning it toward the sun. "You and I, Susan Dunne, we have a blood bond."

Islands scattered behind the plane, lost pieces of a jigsaw puzzle.

The shapes were all different, some long and thin, some twisted, some rounded, yet all the same in the harsh delineation of sunlight stamping each alone and separate on the sea. What picture would they make, gathered together?

I shook my head. There was no big picture, only shifting bits of color in a kaleidoscope, dazzling the eye, constantly changing. All we could expect was the momentary grace of clarity, glimpse of a design blazing with light.

I turned away from the window and the islands slipping away. They were only sandy shapes of earth, tawny yellows washed by a turquoise sea. Squinting against the brightness spilling into the plane, I reached into my briefcase, took out the petroglyph photos, met the stare of carved spiral eyes. I sighed and stuffed the photos back in the case.

My fingers encountered a lumpy shape wrapped in cloth. I pulled out a faded kerchief, unwrapped it to a leaping sparkle of gold. "Vic!" He must have hidden the charm in my briefcase when he dropped me off at the airport.

The miniature African lion looked pleased with himself, stalking over my palm, broad humanized face turned toward me, ringed with a mane of sun flames. Lion-spirit, the guardian. The little manimal's stance fiercely proclaimed his intention to survive even the wreck of another *Phoenix*.

I slowly stroked the silky-smooth, polished gold, savoring its solid curves. My fingers tightened, holding fast to the charm as I closed my eyes and leaned back into the bath of sunlight.

Islands

The author on a petroglyph trek for *Islands* research.

Sara Stamey – novelist, freelance editor, and creative writing instructor for Western Washington University – has returned to her Pacific Northwest roots after years of wanderlust. Her journeys have included teaching scuba-diving in the Caribbean and Honduran islands, trekking around Greece and South America, operating a nuclear reactor at Hanford, and owning a farm in southern Chile. She stays "grounded" with her native-plant restoration project in her sprawling Squalicum Creek backyard, shared with her husband, cats, and birds.

For more information, see www.SaraStamey.com

Tarragon
Books

Tarragon Books is supported by a grant from a generous patron of the arts who wishes to remain anonymous. Our goal is to bring the work of Pacific Northwest novelists to readers who enjoy lively stories and distinctive voices – with the conviction that "entertaining" and "thought-provoking" need not be mutually exclusive.

Tarragon is the Dragon-herb, our logo adapted from a Viking carving of the winged serpent embodying wisdom and power.